QUITE TAKEN

Both of Alex's chestnut eyebrows rose. "I believe I mentioned the Crime Museum was closed to the public, Alix."

I watched him step onto the landing, then snapped my mouth shut. "Wait a minute, you just said you would take me, and now you're saying you won't?"

He had one foot on the bottom step of the last flight of stairs. The stairwell was too dark to see the expression on his face until he leaned to the side, into the light from a window behind him. He looked just like the Cheshire cat—my jaw dropped at the sight of his grin. The little frisson of fire that had started with our flirtation burst into a full-fledged roaring volcano, threatening to consume me where I stood. I grasped the door frame to steady my suddenly weak knees.

"You asked me to take you, Alix, and I fully intend to honor that request. Unfortunately, it's not possible for me to take you to visit the Crime Museum."

I felt as if every bone in my body had melted to pudding under the influence of that wolfish grin. "But . . . but . . . you said . . . you'd take me. . . ." A light bulb lit up over my head. I stared at him, unable to believe what I was thinking. Surely he hadn't meant . . . he couldn't, he was English, and everyone knew Englishmen were cold and reserved and didn't flirt like that, certainly not suit-wearing detective inspectors. "Uh . . ."

"Close your mouth, Alix," he said softly, and with a graceful tip of his head, he disappeared up the stairs.

Other books by Katie MacAlister:
NOBLE INTENTIONS

Improper English

KATIE MacALISTER

LOVE SPELL   NEW YORK CITY

A LEISURE BOOK®

October 2009

Dorchester Publishing Co., Inc.
200 Madison Avenue
New York, NY 10016

ISBN 10: 0-505-52846-0
ISBN 13: 978-0-505-52846-9

Visit us online at www.dorchesterpub.com.

ACKNOWLEDGMENTS

This book wouldn't be in your hands now without the support and encouragement of the best agent in the world, Michelle Grajkowski, and the most brilliant of all editors, Kate Seaver—thanks for believing in me, ladies. My fabulous critique partner, Vance Briceland, worked his magic by pointing out—with wickedly funny notes—everything that struck him as not quite right. My undying gratitude and profuse thanks go to my husband, family, and friends for their patience and understanding whenever I told them I was busy writing, and therefore couldn't be bothered to do the dishes.

Improper English

Chapter One

Lady Rowena gasped in horror at the sight of Lord Raoul's majestic purple-helmeted warrior of love.

"Lawks a-mercy," she swooned, her eyes widening as the warlord strode forward, his massive rod waving before her. "However will you fit that mighty sword into my tiny, and as yet untrammeled, silken sheath?"

"Thusly," Raoul growled, and throwing himself upon her, he plunged deep, deep, oh so deep into her depths, rending from her that most precious jewel of womanhood, making her scream with pleasure as he drove his lance of love home.

"So, what do you think?"

A pronounced silence met my ears.

"C'mon, Isabella, you said you'd help me with this. What do you think of it so far? You can be honest, it won't hurt my feelings."

"Well . . ."

"It's vivid, isn't it?"

"Well . . ."

"Do you like the imagery? I tried to make it colorful." I reached for the teapot and felt its round little brown belly. It was cold. Rats. I hoisted myself off the floor pillow and padded barefoot over to the cubbyhole that passed for a kitchen.

"Yes, it's colorful . . ."

"And you'll notice I have them in bed in the first chapter. Sex sells, you know, and I've started things off with a bang. Ha! A bang! Get it?" I snorted to myself as I checked the water in the kettle and plugged it in.

"Erm . . ."

"Heh. So what do you think? Do you think it's good?" I marched back and stood in front of the vision lounging on the wicker chaise. Isabella bit her bottom lip and looked vaguely uncomfortable, despite being in possession of the most comfortable piece of furniture in the flat. "Alix . . ."

"Yes?"

"It's dreadful."

I frowned at my critic. Dreadful? *My story?* "Surely it's not that bad?"

Isabella grimaced and waved a rose-tipped, slender hand at me in a vague fashion as if she were swatting an unimportant gnat. "I'm sorry, darling, it is. It's perfectly dreadful. Terrible. Trite, in fact, and almost sickeningly brutal."

"Brutal? It's not brutal, it's erotic! There's a difference."

She shook her head at my protest, her hair a shimmering curtain of silver-blond that aroused the fiercest

2

envy in my brunette-headed heart, and eased herself into a sitting position. She tapped at the stack of manuscript pages sitting on the small wicker end table at her elbow. "This isn't erotic, it's tantamount to rape. There are no emotions involved in either character, no foreplay, no affection, just a man bent on taking what he can."

"Oh." I felt my face fall with my spirits, but immediately began the buoying process. After all, Isabella herself admitted that she didn't read romances and probably wouldn't recognize a good one if it came up and bit her on the backside. Still, it was important I get this right on the first try—I didn't have long to prove myself with it. "You didn't like Lady Rowena? Or the dashing Lord Raoul? What's not to like about Raoul?"

"Neither. No, I tell a lie, I liked Rowena. And I suppose Raoul shows promise." She waved her hand again and gave a little shrug as I hooked my foot around a three-legged stool and pulled it over, carefully lowering myself onto it. I'd had experience with that stool during the ten days I'd been living in the flat, and now approached it with the respect it was due. More than once I had been unwary, only to have it buck me off, resulting in gruesome rug burns from the horribly scratchy polyester burnt-orange carpet.

"Honestly, Alix, it's not the characters, it's the writing."

I sat up straighter and snatched the plate of lemon biscuits from where she was about to snag one. Now this was hitting a little too close to home! "What's wrong with the writing?"

"Well . . . it's a bit purple."

"Purple!"

3

"Yes, purple. Exaggerated. No one calls a cock a purple-helmeted warrior of love."

I blushed a little. "Well, I don't call it . . . it . . . *you know,* either."

"What?"

"You know. What you called it. The c-word."

"Cock?"

"Yeah."

"What do you call it?"

"I use creative euphemisms instead," I said with great dignity and allowed her to have just one lemon biscuit. They were my favorites and very expensive, but she was my landlady and she had volunteered to give me her opinion on my work in progress. Sacrifices were sometimes inevitable. "I am, after all, striving to be a writer. I am expected to be a bit on the exuberant side, verbally speaking."

Isabella pursed her lips and tapped an elegant finger to their rosy fullness. Seeing her perfect mouth in her perfect face, topping her perfect body, made me suck in my bottom lip and gnaw off the few tendrils of chapped skin that graced it, all the while making a mental note to check out whether or not the National Health Insurance plan for visiting Americans covered plastic surgery.

"Euphemisms like *lance of love* and anything with a helmet are passé, Alix. I suggest you try something a little less flowery."

"Flowery, huh?" She nodded. I thought about it. "How about if I change that first line to read *Lady Rowena gasped in horror at the sight of Lord Raoul's throbbing manhood . . .*"

"No," Isabella said firmly, shaking her head at me, her pageboy swinging emphatically. "No throbbing. Nothing

4

should throb, it sounds like it's infected. Find another phrase."

"Mmm . . . gear and tackle?"

She raised a perfectly shaped pale eyebrow. "I should think not."

"Um . . . donkey rig?"

"No."

"Nature's scythe?"

"Really, Alix, you're not being serious."

"How about tarse? Tarse is good. I like tarse. Tarse sounds manly and firm, and not in the least bit infected."

"No-o-o," she drawled after considering for a moment. "It's too blunt. If you'd take my advice—"

"Pintle?"

"What?"

"Too archaic?"

"Definitely."

"How about poleax?"

She shuddered delicately. "Too violent. Why must you beat around the bush? If you won't call it a cock, simply use the word *member.*"

"Member," I scoffed. "Member! How prosaic. Member."

She glanced at the thin gold watch on her delicate wrist. I abandoned my protests and hurried on, deciding it was better to fight the big battles. If it's one thing I've learned, it's not to sweat the little stuff. "Well, all right, for the sake of moving on, I'll go with member. Now, about the next scene—"

"You know, darling, honestly, I think you're just a bit over your head with this project. You said yourself that you've never written anything, and to plunge in with a romance seems a bit . . ."

5

"Daring?"

She sighed. "Ambitious. Alix, I think you should reconsider your plan. Surely your mother would understand if you decided it was too much for you to do in three months. Why don't you just enjoy your holiday rather than trying to write the entire time? You could travel about, visit Europe, see the rest of England—" She stopped when I made a rude face.

"I don't imagine you learned too much about my mother from the draft she sent for this flat, but I can tell you that our agreement is iron-clad, with no changes allowed: She pays for this very expensive flat for two months, and I write a book. It's as simple as that. If I don't succeed . . ." My mouth went dry at the thought of the alternative. "Well, I'd rather not think of that. Assuming I do finish the book, I'll be sitting in clover. Mom's agreed I can spend a year rent-free in the apartment over her garage, allowing me to establish myself as a writer. After that, my future is negotiable."

A languid hand reached for the red lacquer fan sitting next to the tea tray. I avoided the questions in her eyes, and went to check on the water.

"In case you're wondering, I threw away those tea bags and I'm making tea the way you like it, although I have to admit, it never fails to amaze me how you English drink hot tea in the middle of summer." I swished out the teapot with hot water and added fresh tea. "You'd think everyone would drink iced tea when it gets this hot out."

Isabella examined her perfectly painted rose-colored toenails. "Tea should be hot, not iced," she said pedantically, then allowed a smile to curl her lips as I carried the tea to the small table next to her. "And coffee should be white, not black."

I shuddered as I kicked the floor pillow next to the table. "You're not going to get me into that argument again. You forget I'm from Seattle—if it's not strong enough to strip paint, it's not real coffee."

"You say that with pride."

A smart-ass retort rose immediately to my lips, but it withered when I met the look of concern in her eyes. I hadn't told her much about my life, but Isabella seemed to have an uncanny knack of seeing through the usual screens. I gave her a rueful smile instead, and plopped down on the pillow. "Seattleites take their coffee very seriously."

"What will you do if you don't finish your book?"

I considered what to tell her while I played mother and poured tea, adding milk to hers and lemon to mine. I'd only known Isabella for a little more than a week, having met her the day I took over the sublet on the flat. She was polite but rather distant then, warming a little each day until the previous day when I admitted my purpose for being in London. Although our contact was limited to a few hours each afternoon, our friendship had grown into something very comfortable. I trusted her where I trusted very few people.

"If I can't cut it as a writer, I will . . ." I paused, staring into the tea, hoping for inspiration, hoping for a life-altering event, hoping for hope. ". . . I will be an indentured servant with no future. None. Ever."

Her eyelids dropped over her brilliant blue eyes. Outside, a siren Dopplered against the building and in through the three open windows as a panda car swerved in and out of the busy afternoon traffic, around two corners of Beale Square, finally heading off for God-knows-where. We sipped our tea in companionable silence, the fragrant smell of Earl Grey mingling with the tang of fresh lemon and the faintly acid bite from the bouquet of flowers I'd bought at the corner shop. I stopped avoiding the inevitable and glanced at Isabella.

"I must be going," she said with what sounded like genuine regret, and set her cup down next to the few pages of my book. A slight line appeared between her eyebrows for a moment as she eyed the papers; then her brow smoothed as she rose gracefully from the chaise and ran her hand down the tunic of her hand-dyed primrose silk hostess pajamas that I coveted almost as much as I had coveted everything else she had worn. "There is such a thing as trying too hard, darling. Perhaps if you were to forget everything you've read about writing a book, your prose might be less . . ."

I stared at the hostess pajamas for a moment, calculating how much they must have cost, finally determining that they were probably more expensive than my entire stay in England. "What?" I scrambled up from the pillow and walked the ten feet over to the door. "Purple?" I tried on a little pout for size.

She smiled suddenly, tiny laugh lines appearing around her cerulean eyes. She patted my hand reassuringly as I smiled back. "Ghastly."

My smile slipped a little, but I managed to murmur my appreciation for her advice.

"Do you know what you need?" she asked, her head tipping to one side as she ran her gaze over me. I straightened up from my habitual slouch, and wished I had on something more elegant than the plain Indian sundress I'd picked up at a tiny shop in the tube station. I also toyed with the idea of wishing I wasn't quite so Amazonian and more in the line of Isabella's sylph-like figure, but shrugged that thought away. Wishing wouldn't make me shorter, skinnier, or more graceful.

"What do I need?" I asked as soon as she completed her survey of my rumpled dress, bare legs, and unpainted toenails.

Her smile deepened, a dimple peeking out from one side of her mouth. "A man."

"Ha!" Surprised, I hooted with laughter. "Sure, you got one in your pocket? I'll take him!"

One perfect blond eyebrow rose quizzically.

"You thought I was going to say I don't want one, didn't you? You can think again, sister. I've been looking for a man my whole life."

"I see."

"I've had some, too—I don't want you thinking I haven't, because I have."

"I never imagined you hadn't."

"It's just that they've all been creeps. I'm a bit of a creep magnet, you see. If there's a flaky guy around who thinks it's sexy to rub Cheetos all over your erogenous zones, I fall for him."

"That sounds rather uncomfortable."

"The Cheeto-rubbing or the creeps? Doesn't matter, they are both uncomfortable, so if you have some guy just hanging around looking for a babe, I'm your girl."

"I'm not sure he is hanging around looking for a babe . . ."

"Course, he's got to be fun. I don't like those stodgy types, like lawyers and what-have-you. And I don't have time for a real romance, you understand, just a quickie or two."

Isabella frowned. "I'm sure my friend would want more from a relationship than just casual sex."

"Oh. Damn. Well, then, you'd probably better not fix me up with him. I don't have the time or strength to go through the whole serious-relationship thing with a guy. Do you know of anyone who does want casual sex?"

She smiled a distant, rather cold smile. "I'm sure you could find any number of such men at the Drake's Bum."

I made a face. I'd been to the Drake's Bum—it was a local pub that had been modernized within an inch of its life. Now it was a trendy hangout, populated with people there to see and be seen; not my type of crowd at all. "I was kind of hoping for a guy who had been creep-vetted already."

"I'm afraid I can't help you there. I seldom count creeps amongst the men of my acquaintance." She tried to sidle past me.

I turned to block her progress and took a moment to wax philosophical. "You know, Isabella, I've always said that men are like a bag of potato chips. They may look scrumptious and tasty, but once you've had them, all you're left with is an empty bag."

She paused, frowning slightly. "I don't quite see the analogy."

I waved a dismissive hand. "It doesn't matter. The point is that unless you know of a non-creep who wants a fling, I'm not interested in this guy of yours."

She eased past me. "If you change your mind, let me know. The man I have in mind is a perfect match for you. I thought so the day you arrived, but I wanted to know you a little longer before I suggested him."

A matchmaking landlady—just what I needed to complete my happiness. "Thanks, but no thanks."

She nodded and stepped out the door. I watched her start up the stairs to the floor above, which she divided with another tenant, and leaned back against the doorjamb to scratch an itch between my shoulder blades. A perfect man. Ha! In the whole of my twenty-nine years I'd yet to see such a thing. Perfect for someone else, no doubt, but not me. I wasn't going down that slippery slide into hell again. No sir, not me. Once burned, twice shy. Fool me once, shame on you; fool me twice, shame on me. A bird in the hand is worth two in the . . . oh, dear.

"Um . . . Isabella?"

"Yes?" she called down without pausing in her ascent.

"You said this guy is a *perfect* match?"

"Perfect for you, yes."

She rounded the landing and disappeared up the last flight of stairs.

"How perfect?" I yelled after her, good manners flying out the window even as I told myself I wasn't in the slightest bit interested.

"Perfect." Even her voice was elegant, all rounded vowels and languid English richness.

I walked to the banister and peered up the stairwell. "Is this *perfect* man a friend of yours?"

"In a manner of speaking." Her voice drifted downward, growing fainter. I heard the chimes that brush her door tinkle softly as she went into her flat. "He's my lover."

Chapter Two

"Oh, that my sainted Lord Raoul would find me here in this evil place!" The Lady Rowena's creamy, bounteous bosom heaved as she wailed to the silent cell she had been imprisoned in, wringing her hands and rending her clothing without regard to modesty or economy. *"Oh but that I could at this dark moment kiss his firmly chiseled lips! Oh that I could hold him in my arms, stroking the tousled curls back from his broad and manly brow! Oh that I could seat myself upon his manly pillar of alabaster and ride him as he's never been ridden before! Oh! Oh!"*

"Be honest now, is that something you'd like to read more of?"

"Well . . . it's very explicit, isn't it? I mean, what with his pillars and her bosom and all."

I leaned forward onto my knees and wriggled my right

ankle to bring feeling back into my foot. I'd been squatting next to the library cart so long my feet were going numb. "All romances have sex in them in the U.S. You did say you read romances, right?"

The librarian ducked her head in a shy gesture and pushed the cart down the stack. I followed on my knees.

"Other than his pillar and her boobs, what did you think? Is this a book you would buy?"

The woman looked around nervously, then leaned her head close to mine and whispered, "I think you should take the smut out of it. Romance isn't about sex, you know. It's about two people committing themselves to each other."

She smiled a tense little smile and nodded as she wheeled the book cart away. I looked at the manuscript in my hand. *No sex?*

I considered the no-sex angle while I marched home to my lovely little flat, the same lovely little flat in which I had laughed long and hard the day before, chortling merrily over Isabella's offer of her latest boy toy. Oh yes, I laughed when Isabella called down to me that this perfect man—the man she thought was meant for me—was her lover. I laughed and rolled my eyes as I wandered back into my tiny little flat to ask the room, "Yeah, right, like I just fell off the stupid wagon?" The sad reality is that after I got through laughing, I started seriously considering what Isabella had said.

I suppose a few words are needed to explain why an offer of Isabella's *homme de l'heure* would strike a chord of interest in someone who'd spent the last ten years of her life bouncing from creep to creep, with a few intermittent losers tossed in just to break up the monotony.

My mother's best friend from school married a rich

Brit, and they had a daughter, Stephanie. Steph was off to Australia for the summer, leaving her flat in an old house on a relatively quiet square in need of a subletter. After six long weeks of negotiation, Mom and I made a deal, with her agreeing to pay for the flat while I tried my wings as a writer.

There was much more riding on the situation than just an arrangement between Mom and me, though; there was a little matter of my entire life, my future, my hopes and dreams and . . . well, I'll be honest, I've never been much of a success at life, something my mother brings to my attention frequently. I'd been married once, to a workaholic Microsoft yuppie who divorced me after telling me I was bad luck. I've had eighteen jobs in the last ten years, doing everything from scraping up gum at a movie theater, to staring blindly at microfilmed checks at a bank, to walking dogs for people who were too busy to walk their own dogs. I've had a slightly fewer number of boyfriends in those same ten years, hooking up with some guys who could easily outcreep Charles Manson.

Although it may seem that my one and only goal is being successful at writing a book—and the motivation for success is strong, since failure means I'd have to give up my life to stay in a hick town in a desert in eastern Washington taking care of my paternal grandmother's bodily needs—more important than *that* is my need to prove to my mother once and for all that I can succeed at something. Anything. Just once, I'd like to come out on top and have her witness my triumph.

The need for parental approval—it's a massive, unwieldy weight to bear.

When I first arrived at the house in London, Isabella greeted me politely, gave me the keys to the doors, showed me my new home for the next two months, and briefly explained who the other tenants were.

"The ground floor has two families and their children," she said in a plummy English accent that sent little goose bumps of delight up and down my spine. England! I was really in England!

She frowned for a moment at an oversized gold floor pillow and adjusted it infinitesimally to the left. "The families are related—sisters—and both spend their summers in Provence. Their flats are let to visiting scholars. This should be fixed."

I looked where she was pointing at one of the side windows which didn't quite close all the way. "It's not a problem, I doubt that anyone would scale three floors to crawl into the flat."

"Mmm." She moved on to straighten an ugly Van Gogh print. "The first floor is shared by Dr. Bollocks— he teaches at London University—and the Muttsnuts." She pursed her lips and shook her head briefly at the mention of the last name. "They're newlyweds. We hardly ever see them."

Dr. Bollocks? Muttsnuts? Quaint English names—you gotta love 'em!

"The second floor has two women, Miss Bent and Miss Fingers, and Mr. Aspertame. Philippe is from the Bahamas."

I watched as she fussed briefly with a hideous yellow-cracked vase full of wilting daisies, and wondered when she was going to leave so I could quietly collapse on the small daybed that lurked in the corner. "Fingers. Aspertame. Bahamas. Fascinating."

Isabella pushed back the beads that hid the entrance to the cubbyhole of a kitchen while I sent a brief glance of pronounced longing toward the bed, but as she showed no signs of leaving, I stiffened my knees against the jet lag that was threatening to make them buckle, and tried to pay attention to what she was saying.

"You'll be careful with this gas ring?"

I nodded my agreement. Honestly, I was willing to forgo ever using the bloody thing if she'd just leave me alone.

"The third floor consists of this flat, and across from you are two university students, Mr. Skive and Miss Goolies. They're very quiet, so you need have no worry about late-night parties, loud music, or any other violations of the house rules. You did say you were looking for a quiet flat?"

I maneuvered all the muscles necessary into a smile, but I was sure the result was less than pretty. Isabella's startlingly blue eyes quickly slipped away as I confirmed that I was indeed seeking quiet to work on a personal project.

"Mr. Block and I share the upper floor," she said smoothly as she opened a battered wardrobe and wrinkled her nose at the musty smell. "You should air this out before you hang your clothes in it."

"Thank you," I said firmly as I sidled toward the door. "I'm sure everything will be perfect, and I'll fit right in."

"Mmm." She looked rather disbelieving as she glided past me and out the opened door. I kept the tepid smile on my face for the count of ten, then closed the door softly, took a proprietorial look around the small flat, and headed straight for the bed.

By the time ten days had elapsed I had met most of my neighbors and felt happy in my new digs, happy enough to smile at Isabella's ridiculous offer before trotting out to do a little research for my book. It was a Regency romance, and I wanted to be sure to have all of the twiddly bits right—descriptions of Rotten Row, Kensington Park, White's, and other such landmarks. I spent an agreeable hour getting a reader's card at the British Museum's new library, returning home in a most satisfied state of mind. Satisfied, that is, until I came face to face with my nemesis.

Isabella's house wasn't really what we West Coast Americans think of as a house—it was part of a long line of connected buildings that ran the length of one side of the square. Made of white stone, each house had nearly identical black metal railings, white stone steps, and white net curtains at all of the front windows. Our house had a rich mahogany-colored door that I swore came straight from the depths of hell. That door hated me— or rather, the lock did. I'd seen it work for other tenants, so I knew it wasn't defective, but let me approach it with my arms full of shopping, and it would turn its face away as if it couldn't bear to allow me across the threshold.

"So, you're in *that* sort of a mood today," I muttered as I jiggled the key in the lock, twisting it back and forth in an attempt to engage the mechanism. "Well, my steely friend, I have news for you—I have a little something here guaranteed to make you see the error of your ways!"

I set down a stack of paperbacks I'd picked up at a mystery bookshop, my bag of groceries, and a small spiky plant I'd bought off a street vendor. "Aha!" I cried, flourishing the small metal awl I had found in a jar with a bunch of Stephanie's ceramics tools, and subsequently had placed in my purse for just such a moment. "Vengeance is mine, you little bastard!"

I set to work poking the awl into the lock and muttering imprecations under my breath. "We'll just see how you like to be gutted," I said with a particularly vicious jab at its inner workings. "Won't open up to me, will you? Ha! No lock can keep me out, I'm . . ." I struggled with the tool and leaned my weight into it. The metal in the lock squealed against my prodding. "I'm . . ." A slight metallic snap sounded. Sensing victory, I gnawed on my lower lip and jabbed the awl in at a different angle. "I'm . . ."

"Breaking and entering is, I believe, the term you're looking for."

"Bugger and blast," I swore, and whirled around with the awl still clenched in my hand. The man standing on the steps leading up to the house wasn't familiar, so I assumed he was there to visit one of the residents. I stared for a minute into the loveliest pair of green eyes I've ever seen on a man, and let my gaze trail upwards, over a forehead with a few faint frown lines etched in it, up higher to gorgeous chestnut hair with just a hint of curl hanging over his forehead, then back down over his nice cheekbones, long nose, lips that were thinned with annoyance, and a gently blunted chin. I made a concerted effort to pull myself together and tried not to think about what his lips would look like if they weren't mashed together in a thin line.

"Um . . . the lock doesn't work."

He looked again at the awl in my hand, and one dark chestnut-colored eyebrow rose in question. I felt a little blush moving upwards from my neck. "I have a key, it doesn't work, so I thought I'd try this and see if I couldn't—"

"—persuade the lock to open. Yes, I heard you." He looked me up and down in an arrogant manner and shifted a leather satchel from his right hand to his left. From his pants pocket he pulled out a key ring and without so much as a by-your-leave, shouldered me aside and fitted a key. The bloody door opened without a peep.

"It hates me," I muttered as I gave it a good glare, then stooped to pick up my belongings.

"One moment, if you please," said the green-eyed locksmith, holding up a restraining hand. He stood rigidly, clutching his satchel and keys, a faint sheen of perspiration beading on his forehead. It had to be at least eighty, and this joker was decked out in a black and charcoal suit, looking like a hot, mildly pissed lawyer. He reached behind him and pulled the door shut.

"Hey! You can just open that again." I reached into my bag of groceries and pulled out a loaf of French bread, waving it in what I hoped was a suitably threatening manner. His eyes narrowed as I took a step closer, ignoring the whiff of spicy cologne that curled around me in an intoxicating manner. "You open that door up again, or I'll bop you on the head with my bread, and I just bet you wouldn't like a head full of crumbs! They might get on your suit!"

His eyes widened in surprise. "Are you threatening me, madam?" he asked in a low, rich voice that reminded me of Alan Rickman, the dishy English actor.

"You got that right. I live here, buster. See, I have a key!" I showed him the key clenched in my palm, along with the straps of the shopping bag, the awl, and the three paperbacks. I hefted my fresh-baked weapon a bit higher. The man was a good four inches taller than me, but even though he was on the step above me, I figured that if push came to shove, I could beat him about the head and shoulders with my bread until he opened the door.

He didn't look intimidated by the threat of being impaled by a loaf of French bread, but he didn't look happy about it either. His eyebrows came together in a frown as he gave me the once-over. It was apparent from the look of distaste that flickered across his face that he wasn't impressed with what he saw.

"You're no prize either, you know." He blinked in surprise as I poked him in the chest with the bread. That was a lie, but I wasn't going to stand there and be examined like I was a piece of moldy cheese.

"I beg your pardon?"

"That look you gave me—it wasn't very flattering. I just wanted you to know that you can speak in that Alan Rickman voice all you want—it's not going to do a thing for me." I nodded and pulled myself back from where I had leaned in to deliver my warning. Somehow that cologne he wore seemed to pull me in closer. I fought a curl of lust that flared briefly to life, and matched his frown.

"I see. Thank you for telling me that. Now perhaps you would care to show me your identification?"

I goggled at him. The nerve of some people! "My what?"

"Your identification. I assume you're American or Canadian?"

"American, not that it's any of your business. Just open the damn door, Bulldog Drummond, and let me get to my flat before my ice cream melts."

"You must have a passport," he insisted.

I looked around in an exaggerated manner. "Gee, I could have sworn I went through passport control at

Heathrow. If you won't open the door, the least you can do is step out of the way so I can kick it down."

He gazed over my head for a moment, sighed, then slipped his hand into his suit jacket and pulled out a leather wallet. He flipped it open. A thumb-sized image of his face, minus frown, stared back at me. I read the words at the top.

"Metropolitan Police."

"That's right."

"Scotland Yard?"

He closed his eyes briefly and nodded. I looked again.

"You're a detective inspector! Cool! Who are you visiting here?"

"No one. I live here, which puts me in the perfect position to know that you, my fair little bread-wielding housebreaker, do not. Now please show me your identification."

"I'm subletting Stephanie Shay's flat," I told him, suddenly noticing that his hands were large, but nicely shaped. I admit to having a thing about men's hands, and the combination of a real live Scotland Yard 'tec, his hormone-stirring cologne, and those hands was making me a bit woozy. "You can ask Isabella. You're not one of the people who lives on the ground floor?"

"No, I live on the fourth floor."

It was my turn to blink in surprise. "You live above me?"

"Evidently." He frowned once more for good measure, then picked up my spiky plant and gave it a curious look. "Are you accustomed to carrying illegal drugs around with you?"

"Huh?"

He held out the plant. My fingers overlapped his as I

21

tried to take it, but he wouldn't let go of it. I tugged harder.

"You're aware that this is a marijuana plant, aren't you?"

I stared at my cute little spiky plant. It looked so innocent! "I . . . no! I bought it off a guy outside the tube station. He had a whole row of them—he said it was . . . oh."

He cocked an eyebrow at me, but released the plant. The sensation of his fingers sliding out from under mine made me babble. "The guy selling it said it was a homeopathic herb used to bring enlightenment and peace, and was harmless." I felt my face flame up as I admitted to my naivety, but said nothing more when he unlocked the door and held it open for me. I gave him a quick, crooked smile, the door a muffled promise of retribution, and swept into the tiny hall.

"I *will* ask Isabella about you," he warned as I started up the stairs.

I shrugged as best I could with my arms loaded, and heard his footsteps follow me up the uncarpeted stairs. "It's no skin off my nose; she'll tell you the same thing I did."

I looked over my shoulder as I turned on the landing and was delighted to see that his eyes had been solidly fixed on my derriere. "Well, well, so there is flesh and blood beneath that suit."

His emerald gaze shot up to mine. I cocked my head at him. "Gee, I can't remember the last time I made a man blush."

He seemed to grow more rigid, if that was possible, his jaw tightening until the muscles there jumped with tension. Obviously, Mr. Detective didn't get a whole lot of yucks during his day. Poor guy, here he was sweltering away under a hot suit and I was teasing him.

"Hey, it's all right," I said with a reassuring smile, giving the hand clutching the banister a friendly little squeeze. "If it will make you feel any better, you can walk in front of me and I'll ogle your ass."

His eyes bugged out a little at that, and he looked like he couldn't decide whether he wanted to yell at me or laugh. I turned my smile up a notch and poked him in the ribs. "It was a joke, Sherlock. You're supposed to laugh. You know, ha ha ha?"

One corner of his mouth twitched, then the other, and then lo and behold, Mother Mary and all the saints, he smiled. I took a step back and clutched the bread to my chest. "Oh, be still my heart! I shall have to avert my eyes lest such a devastating smile brings me to my knees and strips me of what sensibilities I possess," I said in my best Regency heroine voice, and grinned when he laughed a rusty-sounding little laugh.

"Don't use that laugh much, do you? I bet it's all of those dead bodies and master criminals you investigate, right?" I started back up the stairs, adding a little hip action just to see if he was watching. He was.

"You're doing that on purpose," he accused me.

I tossed a flip smile over my shoulder. "You take your pleasures where you can," I said archly, and rounded the next flight, pausing so he could come alongside me. "Hey, can you get me into that Black Museum I heard about? I'd love to see all of that Jack the Ripper stuff, and the death masks, and the Dr. Crippen memorabilia."

Detective Grumpy gave me a weary look and shook his head. "The Crime Museum is not open to the public."

"I know, that's why I want you to get me in."

"Miss . . . Mrs. . . . what *is* your name?"

"Alix."

"Yes, and your name?"

"Alix. What's yours?"

I stopped in mid-flight when he grabbed my elbow. "Why are you asking me if you already know it?"

"What? What are you talking about?"

The frown was back. "I asked you what your name was."

"And I told you—it's Alix. Short for Alexandra, if you hadn't guessed."

The frown deepened for a minute, then smoothed out, and a smile flirted with the corners of his mouth again.

"You better watch out for that, it'll become a habit soon." I marched up the rest of the stairs and stood fumbling for my keys in front of my door.

"My name is Alex as well," he said in a monotone voice as he plucked the plant and bread from my hands so I could unlock the door. He held the door open for me and watched as I unceremoniously dumped the carrier bag, books, and my purse on the distressed table next to the entrance. I took the proffered bread and added it to the stack.

"You're kidding! You probably thought I was an idiot just then." I grimaced, wondering what was behind that emerald gaze. It was amazing how much heat it suddenly seemed to carry. "Imagine that, we've both got the same name. Well, Bob's your uncle!"

One eyebrow went up infinitesimally.

"What?" I asked.

"Bob's your uncle?"

"I didn't say it right? I heard someone use it on the telly. I thought it meant *there you are.*"

One side of his mouth twitched. "It does."

"Then why did you give me that funny look?"

He reached toward my cheek and tucked a strand of hair that had come out of my ponytail behind my ear. A rush of blood swept up my chest, tightening my nipples and making my breath catch low in my throat.

"It sounds a little ridiculous when Americans say it."

"Oh." It occurred to me that I had just been insulted. I ignored my nipples' pleas to throw themselves on him, thinning my lips and frowning at him instead. "Bollocks! That's a stonking great lie! You're trying to cheese me off, aren't you? What a load of cobblers! That's total pants! Why, I can speak—"

He held up his hand in defeat and a real, honest-to-goodness smile danced across his face. "I concede the point. Bob's your uncle it is."

I smiled back at him for a few moments, watching his eyes darken as the smile faded from his lips. I had an almost overwhelming urge to taste him, just run the tip of my tongue on that spot where his jaw met his neck. I ignored the sensible voice in my head when it pointed out that I had just met him and he wouldn't be interested in the likes of me, and humored the other voice, the fun voice, the voice urging a little flirtation just to see where it would get me. I leaned in toward him and breathed in his scent. It was cologne and man and . . . something else I couldn't quite put my finger on. "Have you been there, Alex?"

A muscle jumped in his jaw, but he didn't step back. He didn't grab me and lay his lips on me either, but we can't have everything. "Have I been where?"

I leaned a little closer and gave him my best sleepy bedroom eyes. "The Black Museum."

I could see the pulse beating strongly in his neck. His Adam's apple bobbed up above the knot in his tie. "Yes, I have."

"Take me?" I whispered.

His pupils flared in those lovely green eyes. "What?"

I tipped my head slightly and blew a little line of breath at his ear. "I lied to you, Alex. That Alan Rickman voice does do something to me. Will you take me to the Black Museum?"

"Do you always seduce someone when you want a favor?"

I grinned when he took a step closer. I could feel his breath fanning around my face, mingling with the spicy cologne I swore was made up of pure pheromones. "Not always. Only when threats of assault with bread don't work."

"I see," he said in that sexy voice, turning his head slightly.

I tilted my head and opened my mouth just enough to steam his lips. "So will you?"

"Take you?" His lips brushed mine as he spoke, feather light and very warm. I gave a little gasp and wondered what happened to all of the air in the room. "Yes, Alix, I suspect I will take you."

I let my lips curve a smile against his, enjoying the frisson of heat which that contact started in my belly. I hadn't felt anything like this before—not even when I was dating my ex-husband. "Good," I breathed. "When?"

"Soon. I'd like to know you a little better first, but . . . soon."

"Good," I repeated, wishing I had the nerve to just wrap my arms around him and plant my lips on him, but

I am nothing if not circumspect. I clutched my hands behind my back instead.

He made a little hum of agreement and slowly stepped backwards until he was outside the doorway.

"Let me know when you want to go," I said with a rueful smile, a little worried about the sense of loss I felt with his withdrawal. I'd just met the man, for heaven's sake; surely even my starved libido couldn't set its cap at the first gorgeous Englishman it clapped eyes on. "My schedule is pretty easy, and all I need is a day or so warning in advance."

His lips weren't smiling, but his eyes were. Ve-e-ery interesting. He nodded his head and turned to take the stairs up to the top floor.

"My sister is going to be terribly jealous, you know," I called after him.

"Is she?" He stopped and gazed at me over his shoulder, an inscrutable look on his face.

"Yep. She's a really big mystery fan, and she's always wanted to see the Black Museum. She'll be spittin' kittens when I tell her you're going to take me there."

Both chestnut eyebrows rose. "I believe I mentioned the Crime Museum was closed to the public, Alix."

I watched him step onto the landing, then snapped my mouth shut. "Wait a minute, you just said you would take me, and now you're saying you won't?"

He had one foot on the bottom step of the last flight of stairs. The stairwell was too dark to see the expression on his face until he leaned to the side, into the light from a window behind him. He looked just like the Cheshire cat—my jaw dropped at the sight of his grin. The little frisson of fire that had started with our flirtation burst into a full-fledged roaring volcano, threatening to consume me where I stood. I grasped the door frame to steady my suddenly weak knees.

"You asked me to take you, Alix, and I fully intend to honor that request. Unfortunately, it's not possible for me to take you to visit the Crime Museum."

I felt as if every bone in my body had melted to pudding under the influence of that wolfish grin. "But . . . but . . . you said . . . you'd take me. . . ." A light bulb lit up over my head. I stared at him, unable to believe what I was thinking. Surely he hadn't meant . . . he couldn't, he was English, and everyone knew Englishmen were cold and reserved and didn't flirt like that, certainly not suit-wearing detective inspectors. "Uh . . ."

"Close your mouth, Alix," he said softly, and with a graceful tip of his head, he disappeared up the stairs.

"Well, stone the crows," I said to no one, looking after him at the dark passageway. "I'll be . . . hoooo!"

I closed the door quietly behind me and leaned against it, reviewing what he had said, what I'd said, wishing I hadn't been such an idiot, then allowing myself to bask for a moment in the warm promise that was heavy in his voice. I had just gotten to the point where I was imagining him stark naked on the chaise when I remembered what I had said to Isabella about her perfect man. Although Fourth Floor Alex was my type, I was sure he wouldn't be interested in the sort of relationship I wanted. He didn't look like the quickie type. Besides, there were other drawbacks.

I mentally ticked off all of his bad points as I picked up the bag of groceries, my books, and the bread. He clearly had little to no sense of humor, was arrogant, prickly, serious-minded, wore a wool suit even in the middle of summer, and probably wouldn't know fun if it came up and dropped its drawers in front of him.

I looked down at the books and groceries, then frowned and added another sin to the list. "That little rat! He took my pot plant!"

Chapter Three

The Lady Rowena was on her knees in supplication before her lord, tears streaming down her ivory cheeks, over her chin, down her neck, up over the neckline of her gown, splattering and streaking the thin muslin of her gown, making that fabric nigh on translucent, baring her breasts and her pert little pink nipples to Raoul's heated gaze. She hiccupped, then dabbed at her running nose with the hem of her gown. "Oh, please, my dearest darlingest beloved! You cannot abandon me and marry the bastard daughter of a duke!"

Lord Raoul turned his back to the sight of the damp woman and looked out upon the velvety green lawns at Firthstone. He was saddened he had to give up the bit o' fun that was Rowena, but after all, she didn't have nearly the dowry that Pruenella, the natural daughter of the Duke of Colinwood, had, and dammit! one didn't pay for the cow when one had the milk for free!

"Why should I not marry her?" he asked carelessly.
Rowena looked at him as if he'd lost his senses. "Er
. . . well . . . for one thing, she's a bastard, Raoul. Not
legitimate. Her parents weren't wed. You do understand
that concept, don't you?"

"So, what do you think? Is it too harsh? Do you think Lady Rowena would speak in such an insolent manner to her beloved Lord Raoul? Is he too unsympathetic?"

Kamil the grocer had that look peculiar to deer caught in the headlights of a speeding truck, but he gamely rallied a smile and smoothed a hand over the stack of evening tabloids next to the cash register. "I'm sorry, I can't help you. You talk to someone else, a woman maybe, someone who reads books. I can't help you. You want to buy something else, maybe?"

I scooted over so a customer could plop down his packet of shrimp-flavored crisps and a six-pack of shandies in the tiny clear space on the counter. It wasn't much of a space, about a foot across, the rest of the counter being taken up with racks of candy, newspapers, snack foods, postcards, and miscellaneous odds and bobs. Kamil's store was one of a dying breed, a tiny oasis of fascinating British and Pakistani foodstuffs crammed together so tightly on the shelves, it was impossible to extract an item without a positive cascade of tins, packets, and jars falling upon the unwary shopper. I peered through the stacks of items on the counter to wave a friendly goodbye to Kamil, and gathering up my manuscript pages and groceries, headed out the door toward home.

I like walking around London. It has a nice feel to it for one of the world's major cities—neighborhoods have a distinct feel to them, some warm and homey, others hip and exciting, and still others dusty and dry with history. I lived within walking distance of the British Museum in a very pleasant area that had several green squares, aggressive squirrels who panhandled anyone incautious enough to bring food to the square, and lots of dark, mysterious little shops filled with intriguing antiques, books, and artifacts guaranteed to delight even the most sophisticated of hearts.

Heat shimmered up through the thin soles of my sandals as I strolled down the pavement, swinging my bag of groceries and breathing in deeply.

"Ah, the smell of diesel on a warm summer's eve," I said happily to an elderly lady who stood at the zebra crossing with an armload of shopping.

"It's terrible, innit?" she nodded, shuffling forward at the traffic break. "You'd think with the price of petrol these days, fewer people would drive, but it seems like more and more are." She sniffed and gave me a curt nod, then marched off toward a block of flats.

I turned and started down the street toward Beale Square, content to listen to the sounds of life around me—music drifting out from open windows and shop doors, the dull roar and whine of traffic as it started and stopped up and down the street, and the wonderful ebb and flow of conversation. It's amazing how many variations there are on an English accent, everything from the guttural and harsh Cockney and its variants, to rounded words of the western counties, the occasional swoop and sway of an Irish accent, the warm burr of the Scots, and the plummy, silky smooth BBC-type accent that sounds just too, too teddibly top drawer. I loved them all, even the ones I couldn't for the life of me understand, and secretly lay in bed at night and worked on perfecting my own English accent.

I hummed a bit of "Moondance" to myself as I strolled along, wondering what Mr. Dishy Detective Inspector Alex would be doing that evening while I was up visiting his neighbor. Isabella had invited me to meet her friend, *the* friend, her perfect lover friend who was even more perfect for me. I had agreed to meet him only after I spent two days thinking nonstop about the man upstairs, telling myself with more than a hint of desperation that maybe Isabella was wrong, and Mr. Perfect would be interested in a little summer fling. Mr. Alex certainly wasn't—I had seen neither hide nor hair of him since he ran off with my cute little spiky (alleged pot) plant.

"This fascination with him is not a good thing, Alix," I had told myself sternly the day before when I caught myself staring out the window and picturing Alex lying starkers in the patch of sun that warmed the chaise. "Keep your mind on business. Work, work, work, that's what you need."

I grimaced at my own words—I'd had experience with workaholics and had no desire to become one of those obsessed perfectionists. Life was too short and too uncertain to do nothing but work, especially when there were green-eyed Englishmen reposing seductively on the chaise, offering up their sleek, muscled bodies to be kissed and caressed and licked and nibbled . . .

"Sweet Fanny Adams, I'm doing it again! Right, that's it, I clearly need help." I scribbled a brief note, marched upstairs, and wedged the paper between Isabella's door and the frame. I will admit to glaring briefly at the door opposite hers, but went back downstairs feeling much better, convinced that if I met this perfect man of Isabella's, the less than perfect Plant Thief would be washed from my mind.

It didn't strike me until the next day when I was dressing for Isabella's dinner that the two men might be one and the same. I stood naked, balancing on one foot while the other hovered in the air as I paused in the act of pulling on a pair of underwear, blinking at nothing as the thought swam around in my mind. Alex? My perfect man?

I finished donning the appropriate underthings while I mused over the pertinent facts, but could find no validity in the idea. All Isabella had said was that the guy was perfect for me, and Detective Inspector Starched Shorts was anything but that. Besides, if she had meant him, she would have surely said so, since he was so handy for introductions. As for him being her lover . . . I pushed away a vague sense of unhappiness over that idea and shrugged at my image in the mirror on the wardrobe door.

"So they're doin' the nasty—big fat hairy deal. Means nothing to me, nothing at all, and you can just stop shaking your head at me, because that's my story and I'm sticking to it!"

I gave my reflection a good glare just to let it know it wasn't going to goad me into admitting anything, and sat down to apply rarely used cosmetics. I couldn't remember the last time I wore makeup. Probably one of the few times Matt dragged me out to a corporate dinner.

"This one's for you," I said, saluting the mental image of my ex-husband with a five-year-old container of mascara. It was a bit stiff and clumpy, and I managed to get mascara damn near everywhere, including the bridge of my nose and my left earlobe, but at long last I had several coats on, enough to turn my brown lashes the same shade of inky black they wore in the 1960s. It was really, really black, and not a little sticky-feeling. I peered at the small hand mirror I was using and decided it looked better than it felt. I tried to remember if I was supposed to put blush above, on, or under the cheekbones for maximum effect, and decided a bit everywhere would give me a healthy glow. A small dusting of gold glittery powder turned into an unexpected avalanche when the container spilled down my cleavage, but I got most of it out without too much trouble. A dashing bit of crimson lipstick, a splash of my favorite perfume, and the face staring back at me from the tiny mirror was ready to dazzle the pants off of my prospective perfect man.

It was just too bad that Alex wouldn't be there to view my triumph. I was conscious of a deflated sort of feeling around my midsection when I thought of how disappointing the evening would be without him.

"Stop it," I told myself sternly as I pulled on the nicest of my dresses. "Stop it right now. This is the perfect man we're talking about here—let's not screw this up with foolishness over a guy who thinks you're an idiot."

I was about to pull my hair back, but I decided it was sexier hanging down my back, so I fwoofed a little gel in the front to keep it out of my eyes, and blow-dried it into submission. The final step was to debate the pantyhose issue—I hate wearing the things, I really do, but there are times when bare legs just look too informal. Since my dress ended a few inches above my knees, there was a lot of leg showing. I eyed them critically. The fact that I had gone European and hadn't shaved them in a while decided me—I dug out my sole pair of pantyhose and pulled them on, praying I wouldn't run them before the night was over.

Hated pantyhose on, I grabbed the bottle of wine I'd bought from Kamil and prepared to march upstairs, determined to enjoy myself despite the fact that the Wonder of Scotland Yard would not be present. I wouldn't think of him, I told myself as I checked my face one last time. I wouldn't dwell on his fascinating green eyes that changed color so quickly, I wouldn't remember that knee-melting cologne he wore, I wouldn't recall his sexy voice, and I wouldn't allow myself to feel even one atom of desire for him. He was history as far as I was concerned, and the immediate attraction I had felt was nothing more than a sign I really should consider finding someone to scratch that particular itch, someone who wouldn't *mean* anything to me, someone who knew how to have fun, and who wasn't interested in anything serious. I was, after all, prepared for just such an eventuality. When my sister Cait asked if I was bringing any raincoats with me on the trip, I had pointed out that it was July, and unlikely to rain an amount where I'd be needing a raincoat. She had laughed and handed me a box of condoms, saying, "It's time to get over Cheeto Boy. Here's some raincoats. Put them to good use."

Curiosity got the better of me, so I dug around in the bottom of my travel bag until I found a somewhat squashed box of condoms. I chortled to myself at the image of me casually inquiring of a sexual partner if he preferred the strawberry, banana, or "Kiss of Mint" flavored raincoat. I tossed the condoms on the table next to the chaise, and snickered my way up the stairs to Isabella's. I was feeling pretty good, and for once, in complete control. My cute red swishy dress swished sexily when I moved. I felt very seductive. I didn't even look over at Alex's door when I knocked on Isabella's—Alex was totally gone from my mind, finished, finito.

"Nevermore," I said firmly as the door opened.

"Quoth the raven?" Alex asked.

I goggled for a moment. He was even more drool-worthy than I remembered.

"Sorry, I must have the wrong . . ." I looked across the landing. I wasn't mistaken, I *was* at Isabella's door. "Oh, you've been invited too?"

Stupid, stupid, stupid! He's standing right there in her flat, of course he's invited!

He stepped back so I could enter. I felt my uterus stutter once or twice as the Alex Scent of Manly Man hit me, but I successfully fought the urge to rip off his clothes and wrestle him to the ground. "Don't you wear anything else but suits?"

"Seldom."

"Alexandra! I'm so glad to see you. Do come in."

Isabella stood in a small room by a solid glass dining table, lighting tall white tapers. She was dressed in a flowing white and silver dress, and looked like a vestal virgin.

It struck me as I walked past Alex that his presence here meant he *was* the man Isabella had intended for me. I was curiously elated and depressed by that thought, but had no time to say anything before Alex grabbed my arm and hauled me up close to his side. Good Lord, he was going to kiss me! Right there in front of Isabella! Should I meet him halfway, or should I play it cool and pretend I didn't know he was going to kiss me? My mind ran around in frantic circles like a deranged hamster on a wheel, and just as Alex leaned in close to me, I decided that while modesty had its benefits, so did brazenness. I drooped against him and offered up my lips.

"You need to adjust your dress," he hissed, his mouth an inch or so from my ear.

"I—*what*?" I turned slightly so I could frown at him. Our noses brushed. His eyes glittered emerald as I stared at him, unable to think of anything beyond how attractive he was. He seemed to be likewise affected, but managed at last to speak.

"Your dress. You need to adjust it."

I dragged my gaze off him and looked down at myself. Sure, the area between my boobs was awfully gold and glittery from the powder spill, but there was none on the dress.

"What are you talking about?" I asked him in a breathy voice.

He made a sound of annoyance, grabbed my shoulders, turned me around, and tugged at the back of my dress.

"It was tucked up in your . . . erm . . ."

Oh, good Lord! I spun around, mortified. A smile flirted with his lips. He leaned in to whisper, "I didn't think a face could turn that color of red. It matches your dress," just before Isabella came over to us, holding out both of her hands.

"You look charming. That color suits you, although Alexander must have said something quite risqué to make you blush like that. You have met, have you not? He said he had seen you having trouble with the front door."

"Yes, we've met," I choked, damning the owners and all the shareholders of the pantyhose company all the while I wondered what he had told her about me. I hoped

38

she didn't know I'd been threatening to do the door bodily harm.

"Good. Now come and let me introduce you to Carol."

I looked at her in surprise. Carol? Who was this Carol? I thought she was just having an intimate dinner for Mr. "I see London, I see France" and me.

"Carol?"

"Carol. The man I told you about." She patted my hand and gave me a brilliant smile. "Alexander must have said something quite unforgivable if he's rattled you this badly. You do remember that you are here to meet the man I think is perfect for you?"

"I—" I looked back to where Alex was stalking behind us, a familiar frown affixed to his face. "Well, yes, but I thought . . . that is, I assumed . . ."

Isabella glanced at me out of the corner of her eye as she steered me toward a candlelit sitting room. "You thought I meant Alex? Lord, no! He's the last man I'd pair you up with."

Well, hell, was it that obvious?

"This is Carol Coventry, Alix. Carol, this is my summer tenant Alexandra Treebark. Alix is here to do research for a book she's writing."

I stared at Isabella, aghast at her cruel joke. *Treebark?* I was about to correct her when she grabbed Alex's arm and insisted he look at a new print she had framed. I watched them leave the room, then turned back to the man who had stood to shake my hand.

"My name is Karl," he said with a wry smile and offered his hand. "Karl Daventry. You have to excuse Isabella, she has a terrible memory for names. I assume you must be an Alicia or Allison if she's calling you Alix."

I shook his hand and smiled. He really was quite

pleasant-looking—a bit taller than me, dark hair and eyes, long English face, and a cute little skull-and-crossbones earring. He was nice, but . . . I couldn't help but think he wasn't perfect. Or maybe he *was* perfect, but perfect in that white-bread, bland, unexciting sort of way. Even his earring was the perfect balance of hip and different, and yet not silly-looking or offensive.

"Actually, my name is Alix, although my last name is Freemar, not Treebark. That's a little odd about Isabella's name hangup. Does she do that to everyone?" I couldn't help but wonder about Dr. Bollocks and the Muttsnuts newlyweds.

He smiled. It was a nice smile with nice teeth. Perfect teeth, in fact. I waited for a wave of emotion to roll over me at the sight of his perfect smile—love, lust, happiness, excitement, pleasure—any emotion would do. I waited while he speculated as to the cause of Isabella's little memory problem, then I waited some more while he told me about the joys and sorrows of being a dentist (it explained his perfect teeth).

I was still waiting for Karl to generate some sort of emotion within me, something—*anything*—when Alex and Isabella returned. The hair on the back of my neck stood on end when I glanced over at them; Isabella was laughing up at Alex, her arm tucked around his, her head of silver-blond hair contrasting beautifully against the stark black of his suit. He was smiling back at her in a way that made me want to rip his traitorous lips right off his face and do a spot of Riverdancing on them. In clogs.

The evening went downhill after that. My eyelashes underwent a hideous mutation into giant clumps of sticky black tar that clung with a fervor I hadn't expected from eyelashes to the skin just above my eyes. It made blinking a dangerous experience.

"Erm . . . you've got something there," Alex said softly to me, gesturing toward my face. We were all sitting at Isabella's glass dining room table, enjoying her scampi fettuccine, my wine, and fresh basil-garlic rolls that were so good they made me want to weep with joy. Isabella's table was all in white and silver, matching her ensemble perfectly. I couldn't help but wonder if she had chargers, candles, napkins, and accoutrements to match all of her evening wear.

I stopped counting the candles on the table and looked to my right, where Alex was sitting at the foot of the table. "I've got lots, buster, but don't be thinking you're going to be trying it on for size, because you're not. At least, not now. Well, maybe a little later, but I haven't made up my mind yet. Not completely."

His face was a study in puzzlement, with surprise, confusion, and finally a tiny flicker of annoyance all taking a turn in the spotlight. He narrowed his eyes and lowered his voice as he stared pointedly at my left cheek. "You have a black smut on your cheek."

I crossed my eyes trying to look down at my cheek, but couldn't see anything. "Oh. Thank you. Just forget I mentioned trying anything on for size."

I reached up to see if I could feel it and encountered a blob. It was a dung-beetle-size ball of mascara with several eyelashes stabbed through it. "Great," I muttered, the blob of mascara on my fingers. "Now my eyes are going to be bald."

"You're very outspoken," Alex said sotto voce in a tone that indicated it was not a compliment. "Are all Americans like you?"

41

I shrugged and looked covertly around the table but didn't see anywhere I could dispose of the blob. I'd be damned if I ruined one of Isabella's nice linen napkins with it, but I really couldn't sit with it in my hand all night. "It depends. I come from a family of outspoken women. We believe in calling a spade a spade. Why, does that bother you? Don't tell me you are one of those guys who gets into playing head games with people—the kind who is into power trips?" I peered at him suspiciously. "You're not one of those weirdos who goes in for bondage and domination, are you? 'Cause if you are, I'll tell you right here and now, there's no way in hell I'll put a dog collar on."

His eyes widened and he started to shake his head.

"And don't expect me to wear stiletto heels and call myself Mistress Cruella, either, because this girl doesn't go in for that."

"I never said—"

I pointed my blobby finger and shook the black ball of mascara at him, half hoping it would go flying off of its own accord. It didn't, of course. They should glue the tiles on the space shuttle with old mascara. "And if you're into being dressed up in diapers and being spanked, well, just don't come running to me to get your jollies! Well, OK, maybe the spanking, but no diapers! I draw the line at diapers!"

A dull color tinted his cheeks a faint pink. I watched, fascinated, feeling a bit wicked and very powerful with this skill at making him blush, before I realized that no one else was speaking. I looked over at Isabella and found her and Karl looking at Alex with speculation. I peeked at Alex out of the corner of my eye. He was glaring at me, his fingers twitching like he wanted to get them around my throat.

"Strangling someone is a felony," I murmured at him when Isabella turned back to Karl. "You'd go to jail for the rest of your life."

"It might be worth it," he growled, and looked away.

I was about to poke him when I realized the black blob of mascara and eyelashes was still holding steadfast to my finger. My opportunity to dispose of it came a few moments later. Under the cover of laughter from Isabella and Karl over an amusing anecdote, I wiped it on the side of my plate, hoping it would blend in with the arugula. It didn't. It clung to the rim of the plate, proudly sporting its growths like a great, hairy black gonad. I stared at it in horror, but I didn't know what else to do with the damned thing. I looked around the table frantically, but there were no tissues or anything else I wanted to ruin with the beastly thing. My palms went all sweaty when I glanced at Isabella—she was speaking with Karl, but I knew that the minute she looked over at me, she'd see the horrible malignant growth sitting there on my plate. I swear I could see its feelers waving around in the warm air generated by all of the candles. I watched it carefully, horrified that it might start moving of its own accord.

"Alex?" Karl asked.

"I've never seen it before in my life!" I shrieked, startled. Three pairs of eyes turned to look at me. I laid my fork across the hideous thing, but the eyelashes it held hostage poked through the tines.

Isabella looked a bit taken aback, but Karl looked downright worried. I didn't look at Alex. I had a feeling

Katie MacAlister

he had seen me with the thing, and would think the worst of me.

"Sorry. Daydreaming. You wanted to know something, Karl?"

He glanced over to Alex. "Actually, I was asking Alex what he thought of the Wolves and Dons game."

"Oh, hockey." I glanced down at my plate. Had the fork moved a little bit?

"Football, not hockey, Alix," Karl said with a smile.

With the attention off me, I picked up my fork and tried to think of an excuse to take my plate with me to the bathroom so I could dispose of The Entity.

"It's a bit confusing with so many Alexes here," Karl laughed, raising his eyebrows at Alex. I looked at Alex as well, expecting to see him respond to the comment, but he was staring at the atrocity on my plate with the look of horrified fascination one wears when passing a particularly bloody accident.

"Is something the matter, Alexander?"

I whipped my head around so fast that I almost knocked a candle over with my hair. Isabella was leaning slightly to the side to peer through the forest of flames to see what it was that had generated such a look of horror on Alex's face.

"It's nothing, Isabella," he replied, pulling a handkerchief from an inner pocket.

While the talk turned to local sights that I shouldn't miss in my quest to visit all of the tourist attractions within the greater London area, Alex's hand disappeared under the table. I felt it nudge my knee. I groped for the handkerchief, sent him a look of ardent gratitude that promised him the moon and the sun if he only cared to take me up on it, and with cautious glances all around the table, wrestled the thing off my plate.

I had only to dispose of the handkerchief, since I was fairly certain Alex wouldn't want it back. I noticed a painting across the room and leaned forward to wave toward it. "Is that a Monet print, Isabella?"

A slight frown wrinkled her brow as she turned to look. "Monet? No, I did that myself. It's a watercolor of wildflowers in Scotland."

I stuffed the handkerchief down the front of my dress while everyone was looking at the picture, then flipped my hair back over my shoulder and would have given a sigh of relief had Alex not chosen that moment to go insane. He threw his napkin over my head and started beating my skull.

"What the hell do you think you're doing!" I yelled, and struck out with my fists. I connected with someone a couple of times, presumably Alex, since the response was a deep, masculine grunt of pain.

As the napkin was pulled off my head, I jumped from my chair and grabbed Alex by his lapels, shaking him while yelling that he was an idiot. He held me off with one hand, cradling his right eye with the other. As soon as I let go of him, he sank back into his chair, groping blindly for his napkin. I picked it up off the floor and threw it at his head.

"You rat! How dare you treat me like that? Well, I've got witnesses to your assault, and don't think I won't use them!"

I spun around on my heel and would have made a highly dramatic exit except Mr. Mad as a Hatter ruined it.

"Your hair was on fire," he said in a distracted tone. I

looked back. Isabella was standing at his right side, pressing a wet napkin to his eye and making tutting noise at him. Karl was on his other side, offering to see if the couple of blows I had landed had damaged his teeth. I reached to the back of my head to swing my hair around and show him it was just fine, but what my hand pulled forward was an alien thing made up of ragged, charred, *stinking* strands of hair. Most of it wasn't even there to be pulled forward.

"My hair," I whimpered. I may not be vain about many things, but I do have nice waist-length hair. It's not an exciting color, but it's thick and it has a lot of body . . . or it did, before the raging inferno took most of it.

"You're going to have a black eye," Isabella told Alex, and pressed his hand over his eye to hold the compress in place while she came to examine my hair. She tsked over it. "You'll have to have it cut. There's not much of it left past chin level."

"I never cut my hair. It hasn't been cut in anything but a trim in over five years," I said, my lower lip definitely quivering. I felt like bawling, I honestly did. There is just so much humiliation a girl can take before she starts wailing.

"I know a very good stylist," she said, patting my arm in encouragement. "I'll ring him up tomorrow and tell him it's an emergency."

I stared at the motley strand of hair that was the sole survivor below my ear on the right side of my head. "Isabella?"

"Yes?"

"Thank you for dinner. I've had a lovely time, if you can forget the embarrassment of walking around with my dress tucked up into the waistband of my pantyhose, the huge black blob of mascara that has probably melted through Alex's hankie and is even now coating my breasts, and of course, setting fire to my head. I would like to go home now."

"Of course you would," she said soothingly. "I'm sure Karl would be happy to walk you downstairs."

"Certainly," he said, standing up from where he was trying unsuccessfully to get Alex to open his mouth.

"It's not necessary," Alex said with a little grunt as he stood and set the wet napkin down next to his plate. "I think I'll go as well. I'll make sure Alix gets to her flat safely." He glared at me out of an eye that was starting to swell. I winced. Isabella was right—he was going to have one hell of a mouse.

"I can walk down a flight of stairs by myself," I said with dignity, and turned toward the door. Alex grabbed my arm, muttering something about Isabella needing to increase her insurance on the house while I was staying.

He said nothing else as we went down the flight of stairs, and stood equally silent while I fumbled to unlock my flat.

"I'm sorry about hitting you," I said as I opened the door. "I thought you had lost your senses or something."

"I'm not accustomed to losing my senses at a dinner party," he said, gingerly feeling first his eye, then the area below his cheekbone. He looked pitiful—wounded, and needful, and sexy as hell. I told myself that since I had caused the problem, it was my responsibility to fix it, so I grabbed his hand and dragged him inside the flat and closed the door.

"Sit," I told him, and nodded toward the chaise as I started for the tiny kitchen. "No, wait, lie down. It'll help take the swelling down."

He stood in the middle of the room for a minute, then gave a little sigh of resignation and sat down on the wicker chaise. It creaked ominously as he lay back on it, careful to keep his shoes off the cushions. I poked around in the tiny freezer compartment of the refrigerator and ousted a pint of ice cream.

"I'll be there in a sec, I just have to look for something to put this in . . . oh, well, I guess a plastic bag is as good as anything else." I scooped the ice cream into the bag with a muttered "waste of perfectly good toffee crunch," sealed the bag, and went over to see how the wounded warrior was doing.

He was lying down with his eyes closed. I plopped the makeshift ice pack onto his injury. He jumped, swore, and tried to sit up.

"Stop being such a baby," I said, holding him down, and replaced the bag of ice cream on his eye. I sat down on the edge of the chaise, pried his hand away from his face, and gently felt his cheek. It was a bit swollen, and looked like it was going to bruise.

"You look horrible," I said, shifting the bag of ice cream to see if it was helping to reduce the swelling at all. The flesh beneath his eye had taken on a dark, mottled red color that indicated it was going to be very colorful in a day or so.

"You don't look much better," he replied, cracking his good eye open to examine my head. I reached back for my hair, grimaced at the few strands long enough to be pulled forward, and went to find the scissors. Popeye watched me with a faint frown showing on half of his forehead.

"You're going to cut your own hair?" he eventually asked.

"Nope," I said, returning to the chaise and sitting down on the floor next to him. "You're going to do it for me."

He sat up, lowering the bag of ice cream from his face, a faint shimmer of panic in his eyes. "I don't think so."

I pushed the scissors into his hand and turned my back to him. "Don't look so scared, I just want you to even it up. I can't stand having a few straggly long ends and the rest charred stumps. Just cut it off so it's all one length."

"But—"

"I'd do it for you," I said slowly, watching him over my shoulder. He gave me a long, unreadable look, then nodded for me to turn my head. His hands were tentative at first, fingers almost unwilling to touch me, but he snipped diligently away with only minor murmurs of distress.

"Thanks," I said when he was finished, turning halfway around to take the scissors from him. I ruffled my hand through my hair and encountered his fingers as he pulled a cut strand of hair from where it was dangling from my shoulder. Heat flashed through my fingers as if someone had splashed me with a bucket of hot water, tiny little flames licking their way down from where my hand was touching his, up and over my chest like a flush, pooling lower, deep within me.

"Wow," I breathed, mesmerized as his pupils dilated slightly, his eyes turning almost black. His fingers rubbed against mine, slowly stroking them from knuckle to fingertip. "All that from just fingers."

He didn't say anything, but a shuttered look fell over his eyes. He glanced toward the door. "I should be leaving."

"No, what you should be doing is lying back and let-

ting this ice cream take the swelling down on your eye."
He's not for me, he's not for me, the little voice chanted
in my head. I told the voice to get stuffed, and reached
down to push him back onto the cushions. He resisted
for a minute, his eyes wary; then he allowed his body to
sag backwards.

"Here, put this back on your eye. It won't stay cold
for long, but it's all I have." I handed him the ice cream
and gathered up the scissors and my comb.

Neither one of us said anything for a few minutes,
other than me asking if he'd like coffee, and him accepting. I pulled out my precious container of pre-
ground Starbucks, plugged the kettle in, and assembled
a couple of mugs, milk, and my secret stash of chocolate
orange truffles on a tray.

"How do you like England?" He finally broke the silence.

"I love it," I answered, wishing I had an exotic pastry
or two to compensate for Alex having missed what I'm
sure was a fabulous dessert at Isabella's. "I haven't been
anywhere but London, but I plan on doing a few touristy
day trips in a bit."

"To where?"

I poured water into the French press and added it to
the tray. "Oh, here and there. Windsor Castle, Bath,
Cambridge, the Lake District—those sorts of places."

"Ah. The Lake District is nice. Isabella said you're
writing a book?"

I hauled the tray out and set it on the end table, then
dragged both around from behind Alex's head to a position alongside the chaise where he could easily reach
them. As I pulled the table into place, a magazine slipped
off the edge, exposing the box of condoms Cait had given

me. I had a brief moment of sheer panic as a picture rose in my mind of me trying to explain away grape- and banana-flavored condoms, but I quickly snatched them off the table and slipped them beneath the cushions under his head. "No, don't sit up yet, keep the bag on your eye. I was just plumping up the pillow. White or black?"

"White, please."

I poured cream in a cup, then pushed down on the coffee press. "I am writing a book—a romance. I don't suppose you read them?"

His eye opened briefly, then closed again. "No. I don't read for pleasure."

I leaned over him and lifted the bag of ice cream to cover his eye better. He must have felt the movement, because he suddenly opened his eyes.

And got a good look down my dress to where my boobs glittered in all of their golden glory.

"Sorry," he said in an embarrassed voice, slamming his eyes closed. He grimaced at the resulting pain when his swollen eye protested the cavalier action, and allowed me to replace the bag over it.

"It's OK, they're just boobs. I'm sure you've seen them before."

His good eye cracked open. I smiled and straightened up. "Well, maybe not these particular ones, but others of their ilk. Why don't you read for pleasure? I thought you being a Scotland Yard detective and all, you'd be an avid mystery reader."

His eyelid lazily drifted down again. I went out to the cubbyhole kitchen to dampen a clean dishcloth.

"I'm in the Obscene Publications and Internet Unit."

I stopped wringing out the cloth and cast a worried glance over to the bookcase beside the door, squinting at it and wondering if he could make out the title of the Victorian erotica book I had bought at a used bookstore a couple of days before. For research, of course. Purely for research, nothing more.

Alex's voice continued on in a weary monotone. "I have nothing to do with murders or solving crimes unless they are related to Internet pornography, and I don't read novels because I don't have the time to."

"Internet pornography?" I asked coming back to the chaise.

"Yes," he said without opening his eye. I folded the cloth and laid it on his cheek, accepting his murmured thanks without comment.

"You mean like those online sex sites and stuff? The ones with the women bumping and grinding to web cams?"

"Some. Our department focuses mainly on the pedophile sites."

"Oh." I nudged his hip with my knee. He scooted over a bit, his good eye open to watch me sit down beside him. "That's a good job to have. I mean—it's not good that it exists, but it's good that you're doing it. I bet you take a lot of satisfaction in getting those slime balls sent to jail."

He pinned me with an emerald-eyed gaze. "It's very satisfying, yes."

I couldn't help myself. I reached out to smooth the faint lines between his eyebrows. His eye warily watched my hand withdraw, almost as if he expected a blow. I folded my hands together in my lap to keep from touching him. "Even my husband Matt, who was the biggest workaholic in the continental United States, took time out occasionally to play, although his idea of having fun was sweating on a racquetball court. What do you do for fun if you don't read?"

"Your husband?"

I nodded, tightening my grip on my hands. That look of puzzlement he was wearing was just so damn adorable!

"Isabella said you were interested in meeting available men. I assumed that's why you wanted to meet Karl—"

"Ex-husband," I interrupted him, smiling at my own foolish thoughts. His interest in my marital state didn't mean anything—no matter what he claimed, he *was* a detective, and everybody knows detectives detect when they come across something that doesn't add up. "So what do you do?"

"For fun?"

"Yep."

He closed his eye again. "I don't indulge in frivolous pastimes."

"Well, that lets out running around the neighborhood clad in nothing but a pair of frilly knickers and a fright wig, but there must be something you do for entertainment."

"No."

I resisted the urge to peel his eyelid back; his jaw was set so firmly it's a wonder he got that one word out.

"What do you do when you're at home? What do you watch on TV?"

"I don't have one."

"And you don't read for pleasure? *Anything?*"

"No."

"Oh. How about music? You must like some sort of music."

The eye opened. "I don't listen to music, I don't have

any hobbies, and I don't care to be interrogated about this any further."

Well, that put me in my place.

"Sorry," I said, and rose to clean up all of the bits of my hair he had cut off. *Prickly, prickly, prickly—that was his early warning system coming into effect,* my inner voice warned. *Don't think about getting too close to this one—just when you think he's eating out of your hand, he'll snap your arm off.*

"What did you think of Karl?"

I frowned at the wicker wastebasket as I tossed my hair into it, then turned back to assess his expression. His voice had a slightly apologetic tone to it, and was a good deal warmer than the previous sentence he'd spoken. "Why do you ask?"

"You were there to meet him, weren't you? Isabella said she'd asked you there for that purpose. I merely wondered what you thought."

I took a few cautious steps toward Alex. Why on earth had he taken his yummy Rickman voice and turned it into a sterile, emotionless parody? "Karl? I think he's not in the remotest sense of the word perfect."

His good eye opened and watched me as I again seated myself carefully next to him and reached out to flip the dishcloth over to the cool side. "That's all? He's not perfect?"

I nodded, letting my fingers gently graze the bruised area, then replacing the cloth, lightly tracing a path down his jawline. His cheeks were a little bristly, but the rough texture of his beard stubble wasn't unpleasant. In fact, it made me a bit goose bumpy. "You're not perfect either, in case you were wondering."

"I wasn't," he said softly as I followed the line of his

jaw to his chin. More bristles, but better than that, his lips were directly above. Alex shifted slightly and pulled the bag of ice cream off his eye, dropping it onto his chest. I took the half-closed lids and darkening eyes to indicate interest, so I brushed my fingers over his lips. They were warm, so very warm, and parted just slightly so I could feel his breath steam softly on my fingertips. I traced the seductive curve of his bottom lip, outlined the soft lines of his upper lip, and with my stomach tensing and my breath caught in my throat, let my finger sweep across the long length of his sensitive mouth.

"You aren't what?" I asked, forgetting what it was we were talking about.

Halfway across his lips he opened his mouth slightly, allowing my finger to slip inside. My stomach twisted into a tight little coil as he sucked my finger in deeper, his tongue a little rough, but hot and wet and wonderful, and doing things I never thought could start little fires all over my body, but damned if it didn't! The coil inside me tightened even further when he gently bit the pad of my finger, making me shiver with desire, building a pressure inside me that cried out to be satisfied. His lovely green eyes went completely black as I leaned forward, intent on replacing my finger with my mouth. His right hand swept me forward suddenly, pulling me down across his chest, our lips a hairbreadth apart.

"Alix," he said in that sexy, almost hoarse voice that pushed the pressure inside me even higher. I breathed in his scent and felt myself melt against him as his hand brushed down my back, over my hip, and started up my ribcage. I stopped breathing altogether when he paused at the underside of my breast.

"Yes?" I let my breasts rub against his chest, feeling

55

my nipples tighten and swell, watching his eyes fill with hunger, knowing that my own reflected my longing. I flicked my tongue and tasted the edge of his mouth just as his hand moved upward and cupped my left breast, palming it and squeezing ever so slightly. Passion so hot it felt icy cold washed over me, down my chest, down further toward the core of me, sending the pressure inside spiraling out of control. I slid my hands up his arms, over his shoulders, and around the back of his head just as I pressed closer to taste all of his mouth. His lips parted as mine just touched his.

"Dammit!" I jerked back, looking down at myself, over to his chest, then up to his eyes. He looked slightly red, and very annoyed.

"I apologize. I should not have taken advantage of you like—"

"The ice cream's melted," I said, heedless of both manners and the thrill his thickened voice sent racing through me. I looked down to my chest. The upper slopes of my boobs and the bodice of my lovely red dress were tan and white with gooey ice cream. "There must be a hole in the bag. It's all over you, too. I hope that wasn't an expensive suit."

He closed both eyes. "It *was*. Very expensive."

"Shit."

"My sentiments exactly."

Chapter Four

Lady Rowena gazed across the crowded ballroom, her heart fluttering madly just as a dove would should it be confined in a rounded, breast-shaped cage. She gasped in horror and clutched her throat as she watched Sir Thomas Cholmondley-Featherstonehough, Bart., stride toward her beloved Raoul. The latter was standing negligently within a circle of young bucks, carelessly sipping from a flute of champagne, his dark eyes flashing around the room, his exquisitely handsome face showing disdain, boredom, and a soupçon of hauteur that belied his noble lineage. Rowena fluttered her dainty lace hanky at him as he turned her way, but his eyes passed unseeing over her.

"Sirrah, you have dishonored a lady. For that you will die upon the morrow," Sir Thomas bellowed as he came to a stop before Raoul, throwing his glove at the duke.

Lord Raoul's ebony brows rose in mock surprise. "You

57

annoy me, Cholmondley-Featherstonehough, you really do. Begone, puppy."

"You refuse to give me satisfaction?"

Lady Rowena pushed forward between two matrons, the better to witness the scene. She was thrilled to death that dear, sweet Thomas—her childhood friend—had taken her seduction by the manly-thighed Raoul as a slight against her honor, but truthfully she didn't want him hurt. Not seriously, anyway. Perhaps just a romantic dueling scar or two, although there was no doubt Raoul would be the victor should Thomas successfully call him out.

"I refuse."

"Coward!"

Raoul took one long step forward and picked the baronet up by his neckcloth. "No man calls me that and lives to tell about it!"

"Then accept the challenge, damn you!" croaked Sir Thomas. Rowena gasped again, clutching her lace handkerchief to her mouth. Would he? Could he? Would her dashing Lord Raoul risk his life on her account?

Raoul tossed Sir Thomas across the room with a flick of his manly wrists. "I've dishonored no lady. Begone! You bore me."

"You've taken Lady Rowena—"

"Rowena is no lady!" Raoul growled, and without a glance at her, he turned on his heel and strode from the room. Rowena tried very, very hard to faint.

"Ow!"

"*Peste!* If you'd just sit still, that wouldn't happen."

I rubbed my ear, looking with dismay at the spot of blood on my fingers.

"It's just a tiny little nick, nothing to fuss over."

I rubbed my ear again and glared in the mirror at Manuel. "I had to get the next chapter out of my bag. You want to find out what happens to Rowena, don't you?"

"Oh, certainly, certainly. But you can read and sit still, yes?"

"Fine. What do you think of it so far?"

Manuel paused in combing my wet hair and tipped his head to the side while he considered my reflection in the mirror. He pursed his lips. He tugged on his earlobe. He made a rude body noise, flagged his hands in the air while muttering an apology, and then said, "It's too slow, too boring. Bland, you know, tame, just like your hair when you came in here—that awful blunt cut! Not you, darling, just not you. What you need is something exciting and adventurous. I think you should have a mysterious Spaniard, you know, something gothic, like *Rebecca*—that's all the rage now! Now, *that* was a movie, and the clothes! Oh, God, the clothes were to die for!"

"Gothic? You think I should add mystery to my book?" I looked down at the manuscript pages in my hands, wondering whether he thought I should add excitement and adventure to my life, my hair, or my story. Probably all three. "I suppose I could add a touch of mystery, if you think it will pick the story up."

"Oh, yes! Yes! Definitely. Sit back, would you? No, head up, darling. Yes, a bit of mystery, that always makes a story just sing, don't you think? A mysterious Spanish lover—now, that's just a grand idea. Something exotic and unexpected, you know, always brings interest to an audience. I always try to bring the exotic and unexpected to my shows. Bully, bring me that mousse, will you? No, not that one, the industrial-strength one. No, no! Oh, hell, I'll get it, you'll never find it as long as you're wearing those ridiculous purple glasses." Manuel patted me on the shoulder. "You just sit tight, chica, and I'll be back in two tickety-boos."

"Alex was right," I grumbled as the famed Manuel Sorby-Ruiz waggled off to get the industrial-strength mousse.

"What was he right about?"

I glanced over to where Isabella was sitting in the chair next to mine, flipping through a fashion magazine. "He said that some things sound silly when Americans say them. I think *tickety-boo* is one of them. Honestly, Isabella, where did you find this guy? He's the embodiment of a stereotypical gay hairdresser—all flamboyant *your hair should be a reflection of your inner goddess, not of the outer whore*-type comments. And to add insult to injury, he's from Pittsburgh or somewhere god-awful like that! He's just *not* what I would expect in a chic London salon."

Isabella waved at the framed awards on the wall above the mirror facing me. *The World's Greatest Hair Artist* blared out from one of them. I leaned in closer.

"He's been named International Hairdresser of the Year three times," she murmured, studying the magazine.

I left the hairdresser accolades and sidled over to a framed magazine article. " 'Revered by his peers, Manuel Sorby-Ruiz pioneered well-known cuts such as the White Russian, the Elf, and the Imogene Coca,' " I read out loud. "Huh. It says his motivating factor is to create 'ordinary hair for ordinary people.' "

I considered that sentiment for a minute as I resumed

my seat and glared in the mirror at my wet head. With my hair skinned back I looked like a petulant seal. "I think that's a bit insulting, really, saying he wants to make ordinary people look even more ordinary."

"He's very much in demand," Isabella said, unconcerned, leisurely flipping a page.

"I'm sure he is, and I'm sure he's very good, and I can't thank you enough for getting me an appointment this morning, but truthfully, I'm not used to having my hair cut by"—I glanced at Manuel's wall of fame and picked out a good line—" 'a god amongst hairdressers.' "

Isabella glanced up and smiled at my reflection. "He does have an ego, but I assure you it's well deserved. Stop worrying and enjoy the experience. You'll look wonderful when he's done."

"After paying ninety pounds for a simple cut and blow-dry, I'd better look bloody fabulous," I retorted, but I did so quietly because Manuel returned chattering non-stop, followed by a flunky toting several bottles of hair products and an armload of fluffy yellow towels.

Two hours and a head full of Manuel Sorby-Ruiz-brand mousse later, I was walking through Covent Garden swinging my hair from side to side. Although I mourned the loss of my hair, I had to admit I liked the feeling as it swished on my bare neck. Perhaps this change would be good after all. Perhaps it was a sign my life was taking a turn for the better.

"It's kicky!" I said, watching my hair in every window I passed. "I never thought I'd have kicky hair. Although it's a bit gunky kicky right now, it'll be truly kicky later, after I wash all of the steel-girder-strength mousse out of it."

Isabella, who had been looking on indulgently while I

studied my hair from every possible angle, cast a horrified glance at my head. "Manuel said your hair was too thick to maintain that style without mousse."

She nudged the bag of hair products he had pressed upon me as I left (to the tune of some £30, I found out later when I looked at the charge slip), adding, "It won't look the same if you try it without following his instructions."

"I have a neck," I said in wonder as I toyed with the few tendrils he had snipped to softly frame my face. "Will you look at that? I have a neck! You know, Isabella, this may not be the tragedy I first thought it was; this may end up being a good thing. I mean, look at me! My hair is actually cute now. It's so short. And it's shorter in the back than the front! That's so sexy! I actually look sexy! I've never looked sexy before. Hey, if I stand like this, and you were a man, would you fall to your knees before me?"

Isabella made a little face at my dramatic pose, grabbed my arm, and steered me toward the Lamb and Flag. "Come along, we won't be able to get a table if you stand about admiring yourself much longer."

I allowed her to hustle me down Rose Street to the ivy-covered pub and up a dark flight of stairs to a charming little restaurant. We squeezed into one of the last tables, ordered gin and tonics (Isabella's with a twist of lemon, mine with half a lime—I have a little weakness for limes), decided on lunch, then sat back to enjoy the people-watching.

"That couple over there are tourists," Isabella said quietly, nodding toward a man and woman in their mid thirties who were seated in the middle of the room.

I swiveled around to look at them. They weren't wearing anything that immediately stood up and shouted tourist. "How do you know that?"

A tiny smile touched her lips. "Watch them. They're so busy looking around at the pub and everyone in it, they are hardly speaking to each other."

I stopped gawking at everyone and everything in the pub and turned back to Isabella with a wry, "Sorry."

She smiled an honest smile. "Don't apologize, you're not quite that bad."

"It's just that there's so much to see," I tried to explain. "I've never been anywhere except Disneyland, and this is so . . . *exotic* to me! I mean, I'm halfway around the world from home! In another country! I can't quite wrap my mind around the distance issue."

Isabella shrugged and took a sip of her gin and tonic. "Distance is all relative. What you think of as being halfway around the world is really just a phone call or e-mail away from your family and friends."

I flinched a bit at that. I was supposed to have set up an Internet account as soon as I got settled, but hesitated to do so because it would mean my mother had instant access to me. Although she had telephoned after I first arrived, she told me she wasn't going to waste good money calling when she could contact me for free via e-mail. I wasn't about to tell Isabella about my embarrassing relationship with my mother, however. I was twenty-nine years old, not sixteen. I had been married, divorced, lived by myself, and had jobs. I just hadn't done any of it with success.

I dragged my mind from contemplation of the mess that was my life, and did an experimental little head bob to feel the soft sweep of hair at the top of my neck. Manuel had trimmed it jaw length in the front, a bit higher in the back, and took out some of the bulk by snipping it into a few soft layers. It was curly, cute, and totally unlike any other hairstyle I'd ever had.

"He was worth the ninety pounds," I replied to Isabella's knowing smile, and tackled my roast beef with gusto. "I can't wait to show it to Alex."

The words were out of my mouth before I even realized it. I stared at Isabella in surprise and horror. "That is—I just want to show him that everything ended up all right. After last night, I mean."

A flush crept up my face as Isabella set her fork down carefully. "Oh?"

There was something possessive about that "Oh," something that made the little hairs on the back of my neck stand up. Surely she couldn't be having an affair with more than one man? If she was doin' the nasty with Mr. Perfect Karl, she couldn't be playing squishy-squishy with Alex, too. Or could she?

"Um . . . Isabella . . ."

She leaned over and touched my arm, her eyes glittering with emotion. "Alexander means a great deal to me, Alix. He is a very close, very dear friend."

Right. No further warning was needed. That was the clearest *hands off* I'd ever had leveled at me. Now it was obvious why she wanted to pair me up with Karl—she wanted to dump him for Detective Inspector Hunk.

"When I said 'last night,' I meant last night when my hair caught on fire," I clarified, nodding my head for emphasis. "Not last night when we got ice cream all over each other."

I clapped a hand over my mouth while she toyed with the slight bit of lemon skin in her drink.

"It sounds like you had a much more adventuresome

evening than I had imagined. I take it you and Alexander—"

"No, of course not!" I wanted to smack my forehead over my stupidity. I may be many things, but I have a rule against dallying with men who are involved elsewhere, and yet that was what I was about to do last evening when the ice cream saved me.

I looked at Isabella, speechless, wondering if my guilt was written on my face for all to see. "How can you think I would . . . you know . . . with Alex? The thing with the ice cream isn't what you think. It was the only cold thing I had, so I put it on his eye. It melted," I finished lamely, positive by the look in her cool blue-eyed gaze that she suspected the worst.

"Ice cream does that," she agreed easily.

"Yes, well, you don't have to worry, nothing happened except I ruined his suit with the ice cream." I wasn't about to tell her I got it on my dress as well, because then I'd have to explain just what I was doing on top of him when the ice cream spread.

A faint line of puzzlement creased her brow. "Why would I worry?"

Why indeed? I looked at Isabella's chic silk suit that matched her eyes, and knew I posed no threat to her. Mind you, Alex hadn't seemed to be repulsed by me the past evening—in fact, he seemed rather to approve of the whole general layout that was me. I grew a bit warm remembering the form his approval had taken, and promptly damned myself for sitting in front of his significant other as I thought about all of the things I wanted to do to him.

"Are you all right? You've turned red. Are you *blushing* about something?"

Amusement sparkled in her eyes, proving to me that she *had* suspected the worst, and clearly felt confident of her own hold on Alex. Still, I felt a little distraction would be timely. "I'm fine, just a bit warm. Where do you think the best place is for me to buy a boom box?"

"A what?"

"A CD player. Stephanie either doesn't have one, or if she did, she took it with her. I'm dying for a little music."

While Isabella rattled off a number of shop names, I worked on thinking non-Alex thoughts. I needed to count my traveler's checks again to see how much money I had left after the morning's trip to Manuel. I had offered to pay Alex to replace his suit, until he told he how much it had cost. He wouldn't even accept money to have it cleaned; he just mopped up the worst with the damp dishcloth, scowled something fierce at me, and left.

"Alexandra, you haven't heard a word I said."

I looked up from where I was squashing my mushy peas into an even mushier state. "I was. You said I should always go to Marks and Spencers for underwear, and Tottenham Court Road for electronics."

"You looked like you were a million miles away. You weren't thinking about—"

I interrupted ruthlessly. "Just doing a mental count of my money, and wondering if I'll have enough to last the rest of my stay."

Isabella's gaze dropped. "I'm sorry, Alix, I had no idea you were short. I'll be happy to pay for lunch."

I waved her offer away. "No, I'm not that tight, it's just that I've been a bit extravagant these past couple of weeks, and I need to stick to a budget to make my money last the summer."

Curiosity mingled with reticence in her eyes, but human nature won out. She leaned forward and dropped her voice. "Forgive me, Alix, this is unthinkably rude of me to ask, but why did you decide to come to London if you are so short on money?"

I smiled. I didn't mind if she knew I was dirt poor. "You know about the agreement I made with my mother."

She nodded.

"Mom is what she calls *comfortable,* but what everyone else in the world thinks of as affluent, if not downright rich. She's got more money than she knows what to do with, courtesy of her last husband, but I grew up during the lean years, and things . . . well, things have never seemed to go right for me. I didn't make it all the way through college, I had a crappy divorce lawyer who ended up costing me more than the settlement I received after three years of marriage, and all of my jobs just haven't seemed to work out. So when my mother offered me the chance to stay in Stephanie's flat, I jumped at it even though I'm pretty much broke. I figured I didn't need a lot of money to write, just the odd meal. After all, I can eat anywhere, but to be in London! That's a life experience!"

She smiled. "And ninety-pound haircuts are not in your budget?"

I grinned in return. "Exactly. But it's not as desperate as you think—I've got a few bucks left, and I don't mind eating a lot of meals of baked beans, especially if it lets me splurge now and again and have roast beef in a restaurant that is older than the United States."

We wrangled over the check for a few minutes, then went out to browse through a few of the shops in the

Market. The buskers were out, playing a variety of music from twelve-string guitar to a jazz trio, as well as a number of other street performers. Isabella said they were present all year long because it was the only area in London for street entertainers to legally ply their trades. In summer the buskers are as thick as flies in Covent Garden. We watched two guys do a comedy magic act, a woman who walked a tightrope strung from the columns outside of St. Paul's Church, and an incredibly agile old man who worked himself out of a straitjacket.

"There's a cyber café," Isabella pointed out helpfully at one point. I had noticed it before she did, but avoided commenting on it since there was really no one I wanted to e-mail, least of all my mother. I felt an odd sense of possessiveness about my stay in London, and didn't want to share it with anyone back home.

"Thanks, I'll remember it's here if I need it," I said hurriedly, squinting against the afternoon sun. "O-o-ooh, look, Crabtree and Evelyn! I love Crabtree and Evelyn!"

I dragged Isabella off to the store, and two lovely hours were spent shopping (mostly on her part), window-shopping (both of us), and gawking (solely attributable to me). After we parted, I took the tube to Tottenham Court Road, picked a likely looking electronics shop, and emerged with a brand-X CD boom box in hand. By the time I hauled home all of my shopping and the boom box, my cute kicky hair was wilted, I was undeniably sweaty, and my sleeveless gauze dress was clinging to me in a most unbecoming manner.

"If you know what's good for you, you'll open," I told the door to the house as I stood before it. It just smirked at me, waves of heat rolling off its dark surface, causing a trickle of sweat down my back while I jiggled the key in the lock. It refused to open. I shifted my purchases and tried it again, muttering under my breath, "You stroppy little bugger! Open! *OPEN!*"

It took five minutes of solid cursing, twisting the key, and ultimately kicking at the door before I made it in, and that's only because Miss Fingers on the first floor took pity on me while she was fetching her mail.

"Door's a bit shirty," she said, holding it open while I collected everything I had set down.

"Shirty?" I added that one to my collection of English slang. "Oh, yes, it's definitely shirty. Very, very shirty. I haven't seen a door that shirty in . . . oh, I don't know how long. Shirtiest damn door around."

Miss Fingers watched me wrestle all of my packages and bags through the door, and offered to help me up- stairs. I accepted gratefully and shoved the boom box into her waiting arms.

"It's a bit hot out today," I said pleasantly as we started up the stairs, trying to remember what Isabella had said about Miss Fingers and her flatmate. "Is it always this hot in July?"

"Not often, no. You're the one who's taken over Shay's flat."

"Yes, until the middle of September. I'm Alix."

She shifted the boom box and stuck out her hand. "Ray Binder. I thought it was Alice. Isabella said so. Alex like the bloke in number eight?"

I tucked a bag under my chin and freed up a hand to shake hers. "It's Alexandra, really, but no one calls me that but my mother when she's annoyed, and I spell the shortened version with an I not an E, but yes, it's more or less the same. I've been told Isabella has a bit of a problem with names. She told me you were Miss Fingers."

Ray barked a short laugh that echoed up the stairwell as we marched upwards. "Been called worse. Fingers. Have to remember that one for Bert."

We rounded the landing between the second and third floors and started up the last flight of stairs. "Perhaps we could have dinner together one night. There's a lovely Italian restaurant I found a couple of blocks away—you probably know it. They do the best chicken Caesar salad I've ever had—"

"Stella's," she interrupted me, and stood by my door as I unlocked it. "Couldn't go without Bert."

"Bert?" I dumped my bags on the little table next to the door and turned back to take the CD player from her, but she held it tight. She gave me a long, steady look.

"Bert's my partner. Just so you know."

"Your partner?" I reached for the box she held and then paused. She had a short pony tail with cropped hair on top, was dressed in a T-shirt and scrungy pair of khaki shorts, and wore socks with her leather sandals. "Oh, your *partner*. No, that's fine, I wasn't trying to pick you up or anything, I just thought it would be nice to get to know the people in the building. Besides, I'm not—I don't—that is, I'm into men—"

"It's frowned on here," she said, shoving the box into my arms.

"It is?" I felt my jaw sag at this bit of startling news. Heterosexuality was frowned on here? Was it in the lease?

"Loud music." She nodded toward the CD player. "Disturbs everyone. No loud music after ten p.m."

"Oh, the music! No problem, I'll keep it down low.

Thanks for your help, and let me know about dinner one night. You and Bert and me."

She flashed a blinding smile, nodded, gave a little wave, and trotted back down the stairs.

After a quick shower in the minuscule bathroom that shared a wall with the cubbyhole kitchen, I spread out all of the hair products and tried to pick one that looked like it wouldn't harden to the consistency of shellac. I did my best to follow Manuel's hastily spoken instructions for duplicating my kicky 'do, pulled on another of the cool Indian gauze dresses from the shop in the tube station, and ran back downstairs to pick up my mail. Generally most of my mail consisted of Stephanie's mail that I forward to her parents; this day was no different, with one letter for me, a handful of what looked like junk mail for Stephanie, and something from British Telecom addressed to Philippe Aspertaille, Flat 3.

"Mr. Aspertame, I just bet," I said, and went to plug in the new boom box. I rummaged through the few CDs I had brought with me and tried to think what I was in the mood for.

"When in Rome," I sighed, and popped in the Austin Powers soundtrack. I waited for my favorite song to start, and almost jumped out of my skin when the music blasted out at a decibel level I didn't think was possible from a cheap knock-off CD player. I leaped for the volume control, well aware that with the heat, everyone's windows were open to catch a draft, and no doubt the music was being heard all over the neighborhood. I turned the knob to the left, but the song still blared at a deafening volume.

"Damn, damn, damn," I swore, and turned the knob to the right. The volume dropped slightly, but I was sure it was still loud enough to be heard throughout the house. I tipped the player face down on two pillows, and deciding it was bearable, grabbed Philippe's letter, bossa-ing my nova down to the floor below.

Right foot back, close left foot to right. Left foot forward, close right foot to left. Remember to bend at the knees and add a touch of hip action.

I danced my way downstairs, the sound of the Soul Bossa Nova drifting after me. I tapped at Philippe's door, improvised a turn, and let my happy feet go wild while I waited for him to answer.

I had just worked up a nice rhythm when Philippe appeared in the doorway wearing a thin white cotton shirt and matching pants. I bossa nova-ed a step to him, handed him the letter, and on the backswing explained it was delivered to my box by mistake.

He looked at the letter, frowned at it for a minute, then tossed it onto a chair and stepped out toward me. I was just dancing my way back to the stairs when he grabbed my hand and spun me around. As I stepped back in surprise, he stepped toward me. Suddenly it struck me what he was doing.

"You bossa nova!" I said with delight, holding out my hands to him as I gave thanks the CD was set up to repeat the song.

"Doesn't everyone?" he asked with a charming smile. I grinned back and we cut loose, dancing all over the landing. Philippe was a bit taller than me, had a lovely head of soft black curls, and skin the color of a double tall latte. He was from the Bahamas, Isabella had told me, and had an accent that could melt butter. He was also very, very thin, probably weighing a good thirty pounds less than me.

A rush of warm air swirled around us as the door behind me opened. I looked over my shoulder and saw Ray Binder glaring at us with her hands on her hips. Behind her was a tall woman dressed in linen pants and a green raw silk tunic.

"Sorry, the volume control doesn't seem to work very well," I called out to them as Philippe pushed me through a twirl.

"What's all this?"

"They're dancing, Bert," Ray answered the tall woman, frowning a little at the sight of us.

"We haven't danced in an age, Ray."

The two women watched us for a moment, looked at each other, and with a shy little smile, Ray pulled Bert out to join the fun.

"Don't you know how to bossa nova?" I asked them when they did a sort of polka step around Philippe and me. "It's easy. One step forward, pull in your other foot, do the same back, then repeat it in the other direction. Watch!"

Philippe threw himself into the demonstration, bringing an elegance and sophistication to the dance that seemed to pass me by.

Ray and Bert were just catching on when a young couple on their way down the stairs joined us. The woman, a short redhead, squealed when she saw us. "O-o-oh, Basil, look! Dancing! Right here on the stairs! How romantic!"

"My apologies," I said as Philippe twirled me past them. "The volume knob seems to be broken on my new CD player."

"Looks like fun. Shall we, love?" The squealer's companion, a friendly-looking guy with a brown goatee and a little gold nose ring, grabbed her, and they joined in, laughing and trying to match our steps. It was getting crowded on the landing, but we were all having such a good time no one really cared. I switched partners and danced for a bit with Ray while Bert tripped the light fantastic with a glowing Philippe.

"What—" Isabella suddenly appeared at the top of the stairs, followed by Detective Inspector Steamy Lips. Her eyebrows were raised in surprise, but other than that she showed no sign that the sight of her tenants having a mini rave on the landing was anything out of the ordinary.

"Sorry. Little volume problem with my CD player. I'll get it fixed as soon as possible."

I was dancing with Basil at that point, but he dumped me when Isabella set her bag down and stepped forward, her lips curving into a smile of delight.

I grinned at Alex's cool gaze, and danced over to him holding out my hands. If Isabella wasn't going to dance with him, I sure as hell would. "Hi, Alex, your black eye looks better. What do you think of my hair? It's kicky, huh? Come on, dance with me."

He shook his head and tried to step around me to the stairs going up to the next floor. "Your hair looks lovely, but I will pass on your invitation. I don't dance."

"Neither do I, not very well anyway, but anyone can bossa nova." I grabbed his hands and dragged him toward the corner where there was a free spot. "It's easy! Come on, how many chances do you have to bossa nova on the stairs? Live a little, Alex! I promise you it won't kill you."

He frowned at the others, laughing and dancing and having a good time.

"I don't—"

"But now you do," I said, squeezing his hands and explaining quickly how the dance worked.

His scowl got blacker as I let go of his hands to dance a little circle around his unmoving body; then he gave a martyred sigh, tossed his satchel on the steps, and grabbing me by the hips, swept into a perfect bossa nova.

It was heaven, sheer heaven. Alex was a marvelous dancer. For a man who professed to not dance, he was grace personified, moving with me in a manner that Philippe hadn't, moving as if he were part of the music, the rhythm flowing from him until it swept over me. It was very sensual and definitely started my motor running, but I took a quick look at Isabella and demanded that my motor turn itself off. Motors seldom listen to threats, however, a fact that might have caused difficulty once Alex pulled me so close we were almost rubbing on each other, but his action served as an effective dampening device once I realized that he was flirting with me. In front of Isabella!

He danced with me for the duration of the song, never once cracking a smile, but I swear I saw a little flicker of enjoyment in his emerald eyes. I alternated between anger that he was such a cad he'd act in this manner in front of his girlfriend, and a familiar sense of failure. It seems like I always end up at the wrong place at the wrong time. As the song ended, I took a step back from him, praying the bout of self-pity welling up inside wouldn't make me cry in front of everyone.

"See?" I said as I took another step back, trying to force a light note into my voice. "You survived the ordeal."

His eyes narrowed. "It wasn't an ordeal, Alix. Why do you do that?"

"Do what?" I asked, scooting around him and dashing up the stairs.

He shot a look over to where Isabella was dancing with Philippe, then grabbed his satchel and started up the stairs after me. Damn it! Didn't he see she was watching him? "Put yourself down in that manner."

I shrugged, anger swamping the self-pity. So he wanted to play games. The old "make Isabella jealous with Alix" game, eh? Been there, done that, won't do it again.

"Self-preservation. I'm aware of my flaws. I just bring them up before anyone else can," I snapped, wishing with one breath he'd just leave me alone, and hoping with the other he would tear off our clothes and make mad, passionate love to me. Right there on the landing.

Alex grabbed my arm as I started toward my flat. "Why do you think I would insult you like that?"

His spicy cologne coiled around me, sinking effortlessly into my pores, kindling fires deep within me, but it was the slight look of hurt in his eyes that was my undoing. That and the memory of Isabella's cool, possessive smile during lunch when she spoke about him.

"You bastard," I snarled, and shoved him backwards. He staggered back, surprised by my attack, but started toward me with a look that should have dropped me where I stood. I spun around and stormed toward my open door.

"What the hell's the matter with you?" he bellowed.

"What's the matter with *me?*" I yelled back, loud enough so Isabella, coming up the stairs behind him, would hear. "I have no intention of being the third side of a triangle, Detective Hot Pants. Now if you'll excuse me, I've got to find a hammer so I can beat some sense into this stupid CD player!"

I closed the door with more force than was strictly necessary, and jerked the CD player's plug out of the wall.

"I won't cry, I won't cry, I won't cry," I chanted to myself as I went to the tiny kitchen sink to run cold water. I had just stuck my head under when someone knocked on my door.

"Doesn't know how to take a no," I growled to myself as I stomped over to the door. I flung it open, snapping, "What?" before I could see who stood there.

It was Isabella. Her bright blue gaze rested for a moment on the water dripping down from the back of my head, then moved to take in the accompanying wetness on my cheeks. She reached out one elegant finger and touched the trail of a tear.

I stepped back as if she had burned me.

"I thought you might like to know that Alexander and I are no longer lovers."

I blinked at her, not understanding. Not lovers? "Since when? Ten seconds ago? Not good enough for me."

She smiled faintly. "Our affair has been over for more than two years."

"Oh." I blinked again, suddenly realizing what she was saying. Joy welled up inside me, making me want to sing and shout and dance a victory dance. "Oh! You mean, there's hope for Alex and me?"

Her smiled faded as she sadly shook her head. "I'm sorry, but I don't think so, no."

The wellspring of joy shriveled and dried up into a hard, painful knob in my stomach. "Oh, right, because I

called him a bastard. You don't think he would understand why I said it? That I thought he was trying to get
a bit of nooky on the side?"

She shook her head again. "It's not that. Alexander
has never been a man to seek shallow relationships. I'm
afraid if that is all you are looking for, he won't wish to
become involved, no matter how much he might otherwise desire it."

"Gee, thanks for not holding back on me, Isabella," I
managed to get out despite the pain at her words. I
would have said more, something to hurt her as she had
hurt me, but deep down inside I knew I didn't have a leg
to stand on. Shallow, cheap, easy—I'd heard all of those
words before, but I had hoped to be past all that. It
looked like my usual run of luck was following me here,
too. I swallowed hard and rallied a smile.

She smiled back, opened her mouth to say something,
then closed it again and just gave my arm a squeeze instead. "I didn't intend on hurting your feelings, Alix, but
I like you and Alexander too well to see you unhappy
with each other."

I nodded. There was nothing else to say.

"I enjoyed the dancing. Thank you for the music."

I nodded again, watching her walk up the stairs to the
floor above, unable to speak around the lump in my
throat. I turned back to survey the sanctuary of my flat,
but found there wasn't a whole lot to be seen through
tears.

Chapter Five

Rowena waited in an adjoining room for the opinion of the mysterious Spanish surgeon, Sabatino. The veil had been torn from her heart, and she saw, for the first time since the phantom had made its unholy appearance in the ruins of the abbey, its true emotions. She loved Thomas! But how could that be—she loved Raoul as well!

At length the surgeon came out of Thomas's chamber. She inquired as to the state of his wound.

"You are, perhaps, a relative of the gentleman?" the dusky-eyed Spaniard asked her.

The question vexed her. In her embarrassment, she repeated her inquiry into Thomas's health.

"Perhaps madam is the gentleman's sister?" asked the surgeon, disregarding her question much in the manner she had his.

She blushed and wrung her lace handkerchief between her hands. The ebony-haired surgeon leaned closer and ask in a sultry whisper, "Perhaps you are his wife?"

Rowena stepped back, and snapped, "Attend to my question. How does your patient do?"

The surgeon bowed. "That is a very difficult question to be resolved, but alas, it is in my office to discharge ill news—for it is surely ill news that he will die."

"Die!" Rowena exclaimed in a faint voice, then seemed to gather her wits. "Die!" she shrieked, rending her handkerchief into minuscule little shreds. "Die! Die! Oh, not die!"

"So, what do you think so far?"

The gray-haired man sitting next to me on the park bench scratched his head and thought for a moment. He was one of those people of indeterminate age, so buffeted by life he looked at least eighty, although I knew from his voice he must be a good deal younger. "I think that chap's in for it."

"No, not about whether Thomas is going to die, what do you think about the mystery. Does it add a certain something to the story? Does it pique your interest? Does it make you want to hear more?"

He scratched at the dirty checkered shirt that covered his narrow chest. I eased away a hair, starting to feel kind of itchy myself from watching him scratch. He cleared his throat, spat off to the right, reached down to make a slight adjustment to Big Jim and the Twins, then sucked his teeth and said, "No, it don't."

"Oh." I looked back down at the manuscript in my hand and scratched at a spot on the back of my neck. "Well, if you read romances, do you think you'd like this one?"

He rested his left foot on his right knee, took off a

ratty tennis shoe, and started to peel off a holey sock. I backed down the bench a bit farther and scratched at a spot on my back. Damn him and his creepy crawlies!

"Mebbe." He started picking at his toes. I scratched at a spot near my temple and stood.

"Oh, well, OK. Thanks for your time. Here's your pound."

He paused in his foot examination long enough to catch the coin I flipped him. I backed off hastily, promising myself a long shower the second I got home, but just as I was about to scratch myself out of the square, he called out.

"You need more shagging!"

I stopped and turned to look at him. "Me personally? I'm with you there."

He looked me up and down and winked. I grinned back.

"Not you, your book."

"Oh, the story. Do you know, someone told me they thought it had too much, and that romance wasn't about sex, so I took a bunch out."

He pulled out a pocketknife and started paring his toenails. "They was wrong, then, wasn't they? You add in a bit of rumpy pumpy, that's what you do, just like proper books has."

"OK. Sure. More pumping rumps. Thanks for the advice. I'll think about it."

I hurried away from the bench and out the gate. I itched all over, but I thought about what he said. More sex. Well, he had a point there—sex does sell. I had read somewhere that in the world of romance books, sex was good, readers ate up graphic, no-holds-barred sex. But

Isabella thought my first sex scene was too brutal and unrealistic, which meant . . .

"It's research time!" I said happily to a couple who were snogging while waiting for the light to change to the happy little green man.

"Eh? What?" One of the snoggees asked me.

"Never mind, you're doing just fine," I reassured them, and headed home, going through my mental list of men I'd met since arriving two weeks before, men who might be willing to help me with a little *research*. Alex, of course, headed up the short list, but according to Isabella, he wouldn't be interested in helping me with anything, let alone a practical demonstration of my love scenes. So that left Karl.

I jumped into the shower and tried to picture Karl naked. The thought of him sprawled out on my bed made me feel vaguely queasy. I turned up the hot water and let it pound away the thoughts of Clammy Karl, then allowed my mind to dally with the mental image of Alex minus garments, lying all sleek and elegant, his emerald eyes hot with desire. Immediately I started sweating. I turned the hot water off altogether and lectured myself about my foolish thoughts.

"OK, so I've got the hots for one particular guy, not just any guy. Fine. Now what the hell do I do about it? It's not like I can just go up there and say, 'hey, Alex, you wanna get it on?' If he's only interested in serious, possibly permanent relationships, he's not going to want to break in a few of Cait's raincoats in the name of fun."

I thought about our near kiss the other night and heaved a sad sigh. It was just a shame he wasn't interested in helping me research a love scene. It was a damned shame. It was more than a damned shame, it was positively heartrendingly tragic. . . . I frowned at a pair of cotton shorts I was in the act of pulling on. How did I *know* he wouldn't like a little fling? Isabella said he wouldn't, but what did she know? She wasn't here when he was sucking my finger! Maybe she was projecting her own possessive feelings about him. Why did I assume she knew what Alex was thinking?

"Give me one good reason why I should listen to her!" I demanded of my flat.

Nothing answered me back. That's the problem with living alone without even a plant to talk to, you feel like a nutter when you talk to inanimate objects like chaises and books.

"I feel like an idiot talking to nothing. I really need to get a plant or a goldfish or something," I said, then paused as I reached for my shoes.

"I *had* a plant," I informed the sandals. They looked surprised at that information. "But someone took it. Why, I think I'll just go get my plant back from Mr. Friendly Policeman."

My right shoe thought it was an excellent plan, but the left shoe pointed out that the last time I saw Alex I had not only sworn at him, I had also struck him in the chest.

"You're right," I told the shoe. "You're abso-bloody-lutely right. I owe him an apology, don't I? So maybe I should whip up a dinner for two as an apology? A romantic dinner that could also serve to see if he's interested in furthering Anglo-American relations with a bit of *how's your father?*"

It sounded good to me, and an examination of the sole cookbook in Stephanie's bookcase provided me with a chicken and olives dish that looked possible to make in the tiny kitchen, so I sat down to write Alex an invitation to dinner. I started off to stick the note in his door, but decided halfway up the stairs that my apology demanded a grand gesture. I ran down to a flower shop a few blocks away and asked for a small bouquet.

"What kind of arrangement would you like?" the woman in the shop asked.

"Something manly," I said, looking at a pretty offering in purple and blues.

"Manly?"

I smiled at the note of uncertainty in her voice. "If you were a man, what sort of flowers would convey an apology to you?"

"Oh." She gave me a sympathetic smile. "Roses are always nice. Very romantic, too."

We agreed that white was more masculine than red, so I had her wrap up a dozen white roses, and took them home. I left them in front of Alex's door with my invitation to dinner tucked inside, and then went back downstairs to look over my story.

Two hours later I trotted off to a local cyber café with my manuscript on disk. When Isabella had asked earlier during lunch if I had an agent, it occurred to me that I was now living in a veritable hotbed of agents, and it would be idiotic to ignore such a fabulous resource right at my doorstep. A couple of hours spent online resulted in a list of London-based agents; a little more time in front of a photocopier, and I had five copies of the first three chapters of my epic tome in my hot little hands. I started calling agents the minute I got back to my flat.

"North Mills Literary Agency."

"Hi, my name is Alix Freemar, and I've got a story I think would really sell."

"Send us a query letter and an SAE," a bored, adenoidal voice said, and then hung up.

"Well! Screw North Mills," I muttered to myself and crossed out their name. I picked up the phone and tried the next number.

"Madelyn Gregory Associates."

It can't be said that I don't learn from my mistakes.

"Hi! I was wondering what the procedure is to submit a book to an agent."

"Genre?" The person on the other end of the phone didn't sound too interested, but at least she didn't tell me to send in a query letter and hang up on me.

"Genre? Oh, it's a historical romance."

"Margaret Hendricks is taking romance and women's fiction clients. You may address your query to her."

"Oh. You mean query as in a query letter?"

"Yes." The voice was getting a bit snippier now. Don't people have any patience these days?

"Isn't there some way that I can just meet with Ms. Hendricks and tell her about my story? I'm here in London, staying for a few months while I research the book." Yes, yes, I was stretching for Brownie points, but it couldn't hurt to point out just how dedicated a writer I was. "I'm from Seattle."

"Mrs. Hendricks only meets with clients by appointment."

"But—"

"Be sure to include an SAE if you want a response. Goodbye." Click.

"Fine," I snarled at the phone, and pushed up the sleeves of my thin cotton blouse. "You wanna play hardball, I'll play hardball."

An hour later I was the proud possessor of two appointments—the first for that afternoon (never let it be said that moss grows under my feet) the second three weeks away. I was a bit surprised I managed an appointment for that very day, but I wasn't about to question my luck. Instead, I perused my wardrobe to find an outfit that shouted AUTHOR, but alas, I didn't have a tweed jacket with leather patches at the elbow, so I settled for a pair of ivory linen pants, a garnet-colored blouse, and to show I was of an artistic bent, a colorful scarf knotted around my waist as a belt.

I even splurged on a taxi, since I didn't want to arrive at the Tully Literary Agency and Editorial Service sweaty from walking the half mile from the nearest tube stop. I was early as usual, and ended up sitting in the waiting area watching a dark-haired woman type industriously for a half hour before I was ushered in to the office of Maureen Tully, Literary Agent.

"Alexandra Freemar?"

"Hi," I said, covertly wiping the palm of my right hand on my thigh. There's nothing quite so off-putting as a damp, humid handshake.

The small, light-haired woman behind a huge desk rose and came around the side to shake my hand. She was short, coming up to my armpit, and had eyes an odd, washed-out shade of blue. Her stature was the only thing about her that was unimpressive, however—she waved me into a wooden chair and started pelting me with rapid-fire questions in a forceful and no-nonsense voice.

"How long have you been writing?"

"Me? Oh, well, that's kind of hard to say. I started writing stories as a kid—"

"Is your story complete?"

I blinked at the interruption. "Um . . . not quite."

She tightened her lips and returned to the plush chair behind the behemoth desk, looking a lot like a kid sitting in her daddy's office—until she pinned me back with the steely force in those pale eyes. "How much do you have done?"

"Oh . . . um . . . it's at about ninety pages, but I have—"

"What's the storyline?"

I fought the urge to tell her to give me a frigging chance to speak. "It's about a woman and the two men she's in love—"

"It would never sell," Maureen said, lighting up a cigarette and quickly batting the blue smoke away. "What other stories do you have?"

I coughed a delicate little cough into my shoulder. Smoke brings out my asthma, and I could already feel my bronchial tubes swelling up and slamming shut. "That's it, I don't have any—"

She leaned forward and peered at the envelope on my lap. "Do you have sample chapters with you?"

I coughed again. She waved at the smoke but didn't bother to open a window.

"Yes, I have three," I said quickly, determined to get a whole sentence out before my eyes started streaming and I began to wheeze like an elderly pug.

She held out her hand. "Good, let me see them."

I handed them over and took a moment to cough into my shoulder again. The room was thick with stale smoke, and I could feel it soaking into my clothes as I watched her read the first couple of pages, reaching blindly for a red pen as she read. I made a mental note to haul the clothes I was wearing to the cleaners as soon as I got home, and gave myself up to watching the expression on the agent's face as she perused my literary masterpiece. My delight soon turned to horror as she slashed and hacked her way through the rest of the first chapter. With a final grunt, she made a notation, then set the pages down and leaned back to give me narrow-eyed consideration.

"It's not bad," she said at last, surprising me out of my stupor. I immediately stopped vindictively picturing what her lungs must look like and brightened at the praise. "It shows promise, but needs work, quite a bit of work. Many authors are afraid of revision—are you one of them, or can you take an edit and turn your book into a best-seller?"

I clutched the empty envelope to keep from doing a victory dance right there. It wasn't bad! It had promise! It could be a best-seller! "Oh, I am happy to revise. I know it's not perfect, and I'm more than willing to make whatever changes you think are—"

"Good." She stubbed out her cigarette and riffled through an open drawer. "Sign all three pages. The top copy is yours."

"Um . . ." I looked at the papers she shoved across the desk at me. "What's this?"

"Standard contract," she said, and rustled around in another drawer, then pulled out a receipt book. "You pay the edit fee in advance. Three hundred pounds."

I dropped the contract and stared at her. I had a horrible suspicion my mouth hung open at her words. "Three hundred pounds? Edit fee? I don't understand, I thought agents take their fees out of the money the book makes."

She lit another cigarette and nodded. "That's right. Fifteen percent. That doesn't include the editing fee.

Your book needs editing—you'd pay more if you went to an editing service. I make my editing expertise available to my clients, so they save money. It takes up a good deal of my time, but I believe in supporting my clients, not using them as a mean to an ends."

I was ashamed of my parsimonious ways and my plebeian suspicions. "Sure, I can understand that, I just wasn't expecting . . ."

She gave me a gimlet-eyed look and took a long drag on her cancer stick, but didn't say anything when my voice trailed away helplessly.

I glanced at the contract. I tried to think of everything I had read about finding an agent. I thought about the stories I'd heard about how hard it was to find an agent. What was I doing acting squeamish about paying to have my work edited, if it meant I'd have an agent going to bat for me? It wasn't as if I was paying for nothing, after all—I would be getting something in return.

"OK, so, if I pay you the three hundred pounds, you'll edit my book and then try to sell it?"

"I *will* sell it," she promised, stabbing at the air with her red pen. "My success rate is very high, even with unknown authors." She leaned forward in her chair again. I uncrossed my legs and shifted uncomfortably in my chair, hoping she wouldn't notice I'd moved back when she waved the cigarette toward me. "I like you, so I'll be honest with you. I don't take on many new clients, I'm too busy with the ones I have. But your voice struck a chord with me instantly, and I pride myself on my snap judgments. I'll sign you, edit your book, and sell it for you, but I expect you to have confidence in me and the job I do."

I hesitated for a few seconds—£300 was a lot of

money, and ate significantly into my budget. I gnawed on my lip as I debated waiting until I saw the second agent three weeks hence, and then gave myself a mental shake. I was being an idiot! I was throwing away my big chance to have an agent! *To hell with caution,* my sister Cait always said; *success comes to those who take the bull by the balls.* I snatched the pen out of Maureen's fingers and signed all three contracts.

"I've got the confidence in you if you have it in me," I said, reaching for the travel neck pouch hidden under my blouse. She smiled and sat back, watching me, a strange light in her pale blue eyes.

"Are traveler's checks OK?"

I couldn't wait to tell someone, anyone, about my good fortune, and as luck would have it, when I toddled back home the first person I told wasn't Isabella, or Alex, or even Ray or Philippe. As I was unlocking my door, I could hear the phone ringing inside. I thought it might be Alex, too shy to accept my offer of dinner face to face, so I flung myself across the room, grabbing the phone as I went down on one knee, acquiring a doozy of a rug burn in the process.

" 'Lo," I said, sitting on the floor and rubbing the injury gingerly.

"Alix? I'm glad you answered, I was about to hang up. This is Karl."

I looked at my leg critically. Knees aren't the prettiest of spots to begin with, but mine had definitely taken a turn for the worse with the rug burn, and it stung like the dickens.

"Hi, Karl. What can I do for you?"

"It's more along the lines of what I can do for you. I

was wondering if you'd like to go to Windsor on Saturday. We could make a day of it, if you'd like, and see Hampton Court as well. I think you'll find I'm a rather good tour guide—I read history before I decided to become a dentist."

O-o-oh, touristy things! Karl may leave me feeling a bit cold sexually speaking, but I wasn't one to turn down a chance to go sightseeing, especially with a man who had an interest in history. I accepted with alacrity, assured him I was over the trauma of losing several inches of hair, and managed to steer the conversation in the direction I wanted.

"How is your writing going?" he asked politely. I knew he probably wasn't really interested—he certainly hadn't expressed any interest in it during the ill-fated dinner—but I was bubbling over with glee about my agent coup and couldn't resist sharing my news.

"It's going very well, thank you. As a matter of fact," I said, "I just signed with an agent today."

"An agent? You must be very pleased."

I tried to tone the smug factor in my voice down to a tolerable level. "Oh, it's just an agent, you know, not a big deal at all. I still have to finish the book. She has high hopes for it, though."

"I'm sure you'll do fine. Shall we say nine, then?"

We agreed on the place and time, and I hung up feeling very happy. Everything was falling into place for me at last! England was turning out to be the promised land: I had an agent who was going to whip my story into shape, I had a tour guide who promised me he knew all of the fabulous historical spots around the town of Windsor, and I had formulated an intricate plan for the seduction of Alex. An agent, sightseeing, and sex—what more could a girl want?

I was still mulling over my good fortune when I answered a knock at my door.

"Alex!" I said with delight when I saw who was standing there. My welcoming smile quickly evaporated under the grim green-eyed stare he leveled at me. He thrust a familiar-looking bouquet of roses into my hands. I stared at them stupidly, then looked up when he spoke.

"I'm not in the habit of accepting flowers," he said frostily. I glanced down at his feet to see if the ice cubes dripping off each word were piled up there. "I am unable to accept your invitation to dinner as well. Thank you. Good night."

He turned around to leave when my brain finally kicked into gear.

"Alex, wait!" I grabbed his arm and held on as he tried to walk away. He looked down at my hand like it was something offensive. "If you can't make it tomorrow night, we can do it Sunday. Or another night, I'm easy."

His gaze touched mine for just a second, but the fury in it was enough to send me reeling backwards a few steps.

"You know, you're not being very polite," I said as he walked toward the stairs.

"On the contrary, I believe I'm being quite polite." He didn't even turn around when he said it, he just kept going up the stairs.

"Oh, really? Where I come from it's not considered nice to turn down someone's apology."

He stopped at that, and half turned toward me, a pale shadow blending in to the dark of the landing behind him. I couldn't help but wonder how he could stand to wear a suit in this warm weather.

"The flowers." I waved them at his silent figure. "They were my way of apologizing for calling you a bastard. I thought you were going at it with Isabella, you see. I didn't know you weren't."

He turned a fraction more toward me. "Going at it with Isabella?"

I took a little step toward him, certain that if I moved too quickly he'd dart away like a startled deer. "Yeah, I thought you two were . . . uh . . . intimately acquainted."

He didn't move a muscle, didn't even blink. I took another step forward and slowly held out the flowers. "That's why I said what I did—I thought you were flirting with me right under Isabella's nose. So would you please accept the flowers? And my apology for what I said?"

He turned to face me briefly, then suddenly shook his head and started back up the stairs. "I accept your apology, but not the flowers."

Damn the man! Why was he making it so bloody hard? He obviously had his knickers in a twist over the whole stupid event. Fine, if he wanted to have his ego massaged, I'd massage it.

"It's just flowers, Alex, not a proposal of marriage!" I yelled as I marched up the stairs after him. He stopped in mid flight and frowned down at me. I continued to move up toward him.

"I don't like flowers." If his words were any more frigid, I could keep a side of beef in the stairwell.

"God, you are the single most obstinate man I've ever met," I said loudly, shaking the roses at him. Several petals fell, but we both ignored that to glare at each other. "Take the damn things, will you? I feel like an idiot chasing you down, begging you to take them. They're yours, I bought them for you!"

"I don't want them," he snapped and started back up the stairs. I grabbed the tail of his suit coat and held on.

"You're taking them, you pigheaded boob!" I shook the flowers at him again and tried to shove them into his hands. Petals scattered like snowflakes. "Put them in water, sprinkle them in your bed, make a stew out of them, I really don't care what the hell you do with them, but you're taking them!"

Even though the staircase was dark, I could see his eyes glittering with green fire. In for a penny, in for a pound, I thought to myself. "And while you're at it, I want my cute little spiky plant back."

His frown acquired monumental status. "What?"

"The plant you stole from me last week!"

"That cute little spiky plant, as you mistakenly insist on calling it, is a controlled substance."

"*Alleged* controlled substance!" I whacked him on his arm with the roses as he took a step down toward me. More petals fell. "It didn't have a tag on it saying it was marijuana, so until you can come up with some sort of proof that that is what it is, you can just give it back!"

He descended two more steps until he was toe to toe with me on the landing. "What makes you think I still have it?"

It was distracting to have him standing so close I could feel his warmth. There was a very faint beading of perspiration on his forehead, and a couple of damp, hot-looking tendrils of hair curling over the outer edges of his ears. I gave in to temptation and laid my hand on his chest. He glanced down, startled.

"Don't you get hot wearing suits all the time?"

He looked into my eyes, his gaze scorching what remained of my wits. His Adam's apple bobbed up and down above the knot in his tie as he grabbed the roses.

"I accept the flowers." My fingers wouldn't unlock when his hand slid over mine. His voice was husky and rough, but not nearly as seductive as the feeling of his breath fanning out across my face. A need for him slammed into me with such force I swayed with the impact, my fingers tightening around the stems of the roses. As we stood and faced each other, the only sound to be heard was the flutter of white petals as they drifted softly to the landing.

That and the noise of my heart pounding wildly as it tried to burst out of my chest.

"Alix . . ."

It was only one word, but it felt like a caress against my skin. My breath caught as I stared dumbly into his eyes, unable and unwilling to gaze at anything else. I just wanted to look at him for a lifetime or two, to map the fascinating black starbursts leading out from his pupils, to watch the color in his irises change from startling emerald to a shadowed green that made my breath come fast and shallow.

"I'm sorry," I whispered, goose bumps rising on my bare arms as he slid his hand up my fingers to my wrist, then higher.

"Sorry?" He was pulling me toward him, or maybe it was just the magnetism between the two of us that brought our bodies together until we were pressed against one another.

"For yelling at you. I didn't mean—"

My hand was caught between us, still holding on to the roses when his mouth settled on mine. Instantly I was in an inferno of heat that surrounded me, consumed me, starting a burning deep within me and rushing outwards until it surely must be melting Alex as well. I didn't think the fire could burn any hotter, but the minute I opened my mouth to his gently questing tongue, I went up in a fireball of desire, want, lust, need—I couldn't begin to separate the emotions, they were all fused together into one white-hot, blinding blast of sensuality. His tongue slid alongside, around, and under mine in a sinuous motion that made my knees weak, and probably would have felled me if his arms hadn't been wrapped around me. I clung to his shoulders, mindless of the flowers crushed between us, of our very public location, of the fact that I had dug my fingernails into the cloth of his suit to keep myself upright, mindless to everything but the aching, driving need to merge myself with him.

His mouth shifted, parted from mine, leaving me empty and bereft. A sob escaped from the back of my throat as agony cut through me as real as any pain I've felt. I grabbed at his hair and tugged his head down to mine, frantic to taste him again, desperate to burn bright with his fire. Our teeth clinked as we frantically nibbled and licked each other, our mouths joined together in a way that seemed more intimate than any sex I've ever had. His tongue danced around mine again, enticing it, seducing it, luring it into the warmth of his mouth. One of his hands slid down my back, cupping my behind, pulling me tighter against his groin. I arched up against him and suckled his tongue, taking his breathless groan of pleasure into my center, giddy with the knowledge that he felt the same rush of pleasure that threatened to overwhelm me.

With exquisite slowness, he slid his mouth a little distance away from my burning lips, resting his forehead against mine as we separated long enough to catch our breath, our bodies still melded together. He removed the hand tangled in my hair and traced his fingers past my ear, down my cheek, to my mouth, rubbing gently on my lower lip.

I opened my eyes and tipped my head back so I could see him.

"You're crying." The concern in his eyes almost undid me.

"Yes." It was an effort to get that one word out; speech seemed so meaningless, so unnecessary when I was with Alex. He kissed my eyes, kissed the trail of tears down to my jaw. I knew that if I didn't get a hold of myself and quickly, I was going to end up one big puddle of goo on his shoes. I would embarrass him with my brazenness, repulse him with the desire I felt so strongly it made me shake. Isabella had warned me not to go too quickly with him, and here I was throwing myself at him. I ignored the soft whisper of his kisses on my cheeks, and dug my nails into my palms to regain control.

"Alex?" My voice sounded hoarse and thick, like I had a cold.

"Mmmm?" He had reached the spot behind my left ear where my jaw connected to my head, tearing a low, throaty whimper from me. I closed my eyes and briefly gave myself up to the wonderful feeling of his hair as it slid like silk over my mouth. The need to kiss him again was building again, threatening to shred the little control

I had left. I desperately fought the need his touch ignited, knowing that if I didn't, I would be completely lost. With more strength than I'd ever found before, I dragged my fists to his chest and pushed myself backwards, ignoring the searing pain that followed our physical separation.

He raised his head and looked at me, our noses almost touching, his eyes black with passion.

I swallowed and tried to wake up my numb mind before it gave up the ghost. A faint flutter against my arm warned me the roses were falling as he stepped back. I caught them and held them out to him. All that was left was a bunch of stalks and a couple of stray petals clinging drunkenly to several naked rose hips, but he took them nonetheless. I swallowed again and tried to think of something to say, something that would tell him just what that kiss had meant to me, something that would let him know it transcended the purely physical for me, that I felt as if our souls had entwined, merged, blended into one being.

I tried to think of the words, but my mouth—my brainless, tactless, idiot, *bane-of-my-existence* mouth— had other ideas.

"Alex, can I have my pot plant back, please?"

Chapter Six

"Open. Yield to me."

The deep growl warmed Lady Rowena as no other voice ever had. She parted her cherry-kissed lips, moaning gently as Raoul's tongue surged into her mouth like an enthusiastic spelunker in a particularly moist cave, drawing from her the passion that he kindled deep, deep within her core of womanhood. Every part of Rowena's being vibrated with pleasure in response to the forceful love play of Raoul, leaving her feeling like a smoldering ember of love, craving his touch, needing his incandescent fire to set her soul ablaze, desperate to taste him just one more time.

"Alix?"

"What?" The memory of Alex's fiery kisses dissolved as I blinked at Bert, sitting across from me. She blinked back owlishly through an oversized pair of glasses.

"You stopped. Is there more? I'm enjoying it tremendously."

"Romantic," scoffed Ray as she handed me a glass of wine before walking back to the kitchen.

"Terribly," Bert said with a smile. I grinned back, happy to have found someone who was a dedicated reader of romantic novels, pleased that Ray had interrupted me earlier in the day, when I was hard at work on my story, to invite me down later for drinks and nibblies. Once I had accepted, she inquired why the flat was papered in manuscript pages.

"It's the way I plot," I had told her. "I'm writing a book, and I've got all this stuff to keep track of. I read somewhere that a famous author spreads out all of her notes and picks them up randomly, then assembles a story from them. I'm at a bit of a sticking point on my story, so I thought I would give that a try."

"Does it work?" she asked.

I looked down at the handful of pages I had picked up before answering the door. "Well—I'm not sure yet. Do you read romances, by any chance?"

Her eyebrows pulled together in a solid line. "Never."

"Ah," I said, mentally striking her off my list of potential readers.

"Bert does," she added thoughtfully, then reiterated what time they would expect me, and jogged off down the stairs.

Three hours later I was seated on a green and gold couch, sipping chardonnay and eating brie while discussing popular romance authors with Bert. I pegged her as being in her mid to late forties, and knew from a prior comment that she was a secretary to a high-powered solicitor. She was also a good five inches taller than Ray, had lovely honey-brown hair that framed her heart-shaped face perfectly, and glowed with a warm, sunny nature that stood out starkly against Ray's gruff, abrupt manner. I liked them both very much, but was ready to name Bert as my best friend when she asked if she could read some of my book.

"I just happened to bring the latest chapter with me," I said without the least little bit of guilt, and spent the next half hour telling the two women the storyline, then reading the chapter aloud. It's just too bad that the images the words generated brought to mind the unpleasant scene of the evening before.

"Yes, there's more," I told Bert when she prompted me to finish reading the chapter. I glanced down at the paper in my hands, a sour taste in my mouth as I remembered the scenes written hours before I had made the trip upstairs to see Alex, before I had experienced the giddiness caused by his kisses . . . and more. I looked at the words on the page, but my mind refused to resolve them into meaning; they were only black marks on a white page, nothing more. Just black marks—appropriate for someone who consistently ruined every good thing in her life.

"Yours will be a life of bleakness and loneliness," my mother had once prophesized, then proceeded to tell me I had a lead touch. I was beginning to think she might be right.

"May I hear more of it? Alix? Is something the matter?"

Dammit, I wasn't going to cry in front of Bert and Ray, and I wasn't going to wallow in self-pity anymore either. I was a strong person, I could handle a little thing like a romance crushed before it even got off the ground. I could handle this disaster—Lord knows I'd handled plenty like it before. I was woman, hear me roar.

Everything was all right until I glanced up and saw the concern in Bert's eyes. Ray came and stood behind her, one pale hand resting on the warm tan of Bert's shoulder, her own gray eyes mirroring the concern in Bert's hazel ones. Both women were dressed in shirts and shorts, but where Ray wore a pair of baggy, beat-up khaki shorts and a stained yellow T-shirt, Bert wore a cream and white striped blouse belted into a pair of linen navy shorts. I envied their freedom, their happiness, their obvious satisfaction with life. Self-pity welled up inside me, rocketing off my misery meter.

"No, nothing's the matter," I lied, and with a little sob set down my manuscript. "I'm sorry, I think you're about to be exposed to a shameless scene now. If it embarrasses you too much, I'll be happy to leave."

Bert leaned across the ottoman that stood between us and handed me a box of tissues. I gave in to the inevitable and had a good cry. I was really getting into it, wailing and sobbing into a succession of tissues, more than a little worried because I didn't seem to be able to stop myself, when a timer went off behind me.

"Three minutes," Ray said from the kitchen, and walked around to hand me my wine glass.

"Three minutes?" I asked, blowing my nose and mopping up the rest of the waterworks.

"We have a rule," Bert explained, scooting over to sit next to me, putting an arm around me in a little hug. "When we get depressed, we let ourselves have three minutes of solid cry time. After that, we're ready to talk about whatever is causing the problem. You don't have to tell us what's bothering you, of course, but if you'd like to, we'll be happy to listen."

"Bound to be a man," Ray said darkly, perching herself next to me on the arm of the couch.

Bert made a little shooing motion with her hand and gave my shoulder another squeeze. "It doesn't have to be a man, Ray. Probably Alix is just a bit homesick."

"No," I sniffled, going through another handful of tissues in an attempt to stop my nose from running. "She's right, it is a man."

"Black," Ray nodded, and went to check on the bacon-wrapped shrimp she'd stuck in the oven. I stared at her in horror and wondered if my sins were written on my forehead.

"Alex Black in number eight?" Bert asked me.

I nodded dumbly and, wiping my nose, asked Ray how she knew.

"Saw you dancing," she said cryptically.

"Oh, yes, that's true," Bert said, giving my arm a slight squeeze before moving the platter of cheese and crackers. "I'd forgotten that, but you're absolutely right, Ray. Just so you know," she said, handing me a little plate and a napkin, "both Ray and I were married before we met each other, so don't feel like you can't mention certain subjects to us."

I looked at the two women. Ray was sucking on a finger she had burned pulling out the shrimp, a short, stocky, disheveled, and unkempt woman whose abrasive exterior no doubt hid a proverbial heart of gold. Bert was a study in contrast: Tall and elegant, she had a soft voice, warm smile, and she smelled like she worked in a flowery glen. She was the mother I had always wished I had.

"What on earth brought you together?" I asked before I could stop myself, then blushed when I realized how unkind the question sounded. "I'm sorry, that was rude of me—you don't have to answer. It's just that I'm always curious how people find each other when there are so many pitfalls and so many . . . well, *losers* out there."

Ray snorted and went back into the kitchen for tzatziki and pita bread. Bert smiled and offered me the shrimp. "Our husbands worked for the same company," she said, nibbling a piece of brie. "We knew each other for years, and knew we were meant to be together, but I wanted to wait until my children were grown before I left my husband."

"That's so considerate of you, putting your children's happiness before your own," I said, awed that she had that much moxy. And determination. I wondered if I would sacrifice my life that way for my children.

To my surprise, she shook her head at my comment. "I'm not proud of what I did. If I had it to do over, I would have left Max and moved in with Ray as soon as possible. I know now that it would have been better to bring the children up in a loving home, rather than perpetuating an unhappy marriage. It would have done far less damage to them to have their mother known to be a lesbian than to suffer through ten years of verbal and emotional abuse by their father."

"But surely you were thinking only of their good—"

"Life isn't fair," Ray said, setting down the bowl of tzatziki. Bert nodded.

"I believe that we are blessed with finding our true soul mate but once in our lives," she said, giving Ray a private little smile. "To risk losing that person because of minor inconveniences, or because you anticipate trouble where there is none, is foolishness. Life is too short and too uncertain to let that one person who is meant for you slip away without doing everything you can to be with him or her, don't you think?"

I shrugged. I knew exactly what she was hinting at, but I didn't think it applied to my situation. "I'm afraid you're asking the wrong person when it comes to happily ever afters. My track record is one of failures: a failed marriage, failed relationships with men, failed relationships with my family, failed jobs . . . the list is pretty much endless. And even if what you are oh-so-subtly hinting about Alex is right, it wouldn't matter. I failed there, too."

"Don't have to tell us if you don't want to," Ray said as she plopped down on an oatmeal-colored chair. "But Bert's a smart woman. She'll pick through the rubbish for you."

"And Ray's an excellent listener," Bert added with an encouraging smile.

I stared glumly at the tzatziki and wondered how much they wanted to hear. How much did I want to tell them? That whole evening with Alex had been such a disaster—with one shining, brilliant exception. Almost.

Alex had been utterly shocked when the words that came out of my mouth following The Kiss concerned my cute little spiky plant.

He needn't have looked at me like I had an extra head, though, for I was just as surprised at what I said as he was. More than that, I was embarrassed, since it made me sound like an utter airhead, a cheap little ditz who used her body to get what she wanted.

"Alex, can I have my pot plant back, please?" I had moronically asked.

Alex's eyes narrowed as my words sank in, and with only a tightening of his jaw to show what he thought of them, he let go of me and spun around to walk up the stairs. I slowly followed after him, mentally kicking myself and asking what the hell I thought I was doing. Alex said nothing. I wasn't sure if he was so angry with me he couldn't be bothered to say anything further, or if he was struggling to keep control and needed a little distance after that powerhouse of a kiss.

He stood waiting by his opened door, a tall, dark shadow in the gloomy upper landing. I knew what I had to do. I didn't want to, but I owed it to him. When I was about a foot away, I sucked in my gut, squared my shoulders, raised my chin, and tried not to flinch when I met his eyes.

"Alex, I'm sorry, what I said came out all wrong. I don't really care about the plant."

He didn't move a muscle, just stood holding the door to his flat open, his eyes lifeless and flat. An excruciating minute of silence passed before he spoke. "Then why did you say it?"

I looked away for a moment. What I could see of his flat wasn't comforting—it was done in stark black and white. I glanced back to the stone statue of a man who was standing before me. His jaw was tight, the knuckles on his fisted hand showing white, and he was very, very still, watching me like a predator watches its prey. This was one angry Alex.

I looked back up into his eyes. When you strip all of the pretence away, what you're left with can leave you vulnerable. Not a comfortable feeling. I hoped I hadn't misjudged him. "I'm not sure why I said something so asinine. I think perhaps you scared me."

He became more still, if such a thing were possible. I wasn't sure he was even breathing when he asked, "How did I scare you?"

"That kiss, Alex." I smiled and leaned toward him to trail a finger across the lush curve of his lower lip. "Nobody's ever kissed me like that before. I've never kissed anyone like that, either. In fact, I didn't know it was possible to feel all those wonderful, marvelous, earth-shatteringly fabulous things just by swapping a little spit."

One chestnut eyebrow rose as he reached out and grabbed my arm, pulling me toward him. I let my lips curl a little more. Suddenly he wasn't a stone statue anymore, suddenly he was very much a man, a man who looked like he wanted the very same thing I wanted.

"Swapping spit?" he growled, and pulled me up against his chest. I let him. I'm a sucker for an alpha male. "Was that all it was to you?"

His eyes weren't flat any longer, now they were hot with a promise I fervently prayed he intended on keeping.

"No, it was much more than just a kiss," I smiled against his mouth. "It was—"

It's a good thing he didn't let me finish that sentence, because I had no intention of telling him just how important he had become to me, and how much I suddenly realized I wished I were a different person, one who could have a life with him. Luckily, I was saved from baring my soul by the sound of voices on the stairs. Alex pushed me into his flat, closed the door, and pressed me up against the wall in a kiss that was hot enough to scorch paint off a barn.

I held out against the lure of his mouth for as long as

I could—about three seconds—then gave in to his wordless demand and parted my lips enough for him to sink inside. If I thought he had me burning with desire before, now he sparked a wildfire, starting deep in my belly and spreading out to warm every inch of my skin. Coolness from the wall I was pressed against seeped in through the thin cotton of my sleeveless dress, coating my back like ice from Siberia compared to the heat generated by the man covering my front.

"Please," I begged when he pulled back just long enough to take his hands out of my hair, running them down the length of my arms before sweeping around to cup my breasts. I groaned at the marvelous way his hands fit.

"Please what?" he asked, grunting his approval when I slid my hands up his chest and over his shoulders, pushing his coat off. He shook his arms free of the jacket, then grabbed me by my hips and pulled me up tight for another mouth-plundering. I instructed the S.S. *Tongue* to lower its cannons and prepare to be boarded. Surrender was never so sweet.

Alex pressed harder against me, holding me steady when my hips instinctively tried to cradle his hardness. He groaned into my mouth, sending ripples of pure delight spiraling outwards. Pleasing him became far more important than seeking my own pleasure; I wanted to hear his moan of desire again, I wanted to see his eyes darken to inky blackness with passion, I wanted to watch him when he lost control and gave himself up to bliss. I tugged at the back of his shirt and freed it enough to slip both hands inside. My fingers stroked and sculpted along the strong planes of his back, caressing the muscles along his ribcage around his sides to his front. Two tugs and his shirt was pulled free. I spread my fingers out and slipped them under it to comb through the hair on his chest.

"Oh, God," he murmured, pulling his mouth from mine for a moment. "I shouldn't—"

It was my turn to cut him off. I used my free hand to grab his hair and pulled his mouth back to where I wanted it, then decided to do a little spelunking of my own. I let my tongue go to work on the roof of his mouth while I tried to bare his chest. His tie proved a minor obstacle in the process, but a little tugging and some one-handed help from him soon resulted in both the tie and the shirt being discarded. My plans to do a little chestal exploration went asunder when he tried to slip his hand down the bodice of my sundress. It was too tight and too awkward an angle for him to do anything more than tease the tops of my breasts.

"It fastens in the back," I whispered when he muttered in frustration, and let my hands wander over his wonderful chest while I nibbled my way over to his ear. He shuddered for a moment, his hands pausing on the buttons of my dress when I sucked on his earlobe, but the feeling of air on my lower back soon told me he hadn't been immobile long. He pulled the dress down to my waist, then tugged again. It fell to the floor with a swoosh. The only thing I had on underneath was my underwear. Alex stepped back and stared.

"Christ," he swore, not in the least offensively because of the reverence in his voice. It made me go hot and cold at the same time. His gaze flickered over the length of me, then settled possessively on my breasts. My nipples pebbled as if he were touching them. "Christ, Alix, this isn't a good idea."

"You're absolutely right," I said, kicking off my shoes and lunging for him. I bit his chin, nibbled on his lips, and let my hands go wild on his back. "It's a better idea if you're naked, too."

After a second of hesitation, he ran his hands up my sides, then cupped the weight of my breasts against his palms. I couldn't help groaning and rubbing myself against all of his various hard bits. Fingernails bared, I gently scratched them down his back, feeling his quickening breath as I moved away just enough to tease his belly.

"Buckle," I said breathlessly as he started kissing a path down my neck to my collarbone. His buckle was undone in no time.

"Be . . . be . . . belt." Good Lord, were my legs supposed to turn to jelly? Alex slipped one arm around to hold me up while the other went visiting with his mouth to the Wonderful Land of Breasts. I pushed his belt aside and reached for his zipper.

"Zipper," I hissed as he took a nipple in his mouth. I pressed my hand hard against him as I pulled his fly open. He bucked in response and moaned against my breast, gently tugging on my nipple with his teeth. My legs gave up the fight.

"Pants," I gasped, and shoved them down over his hips.

"Trousers," he corrected, lifting his head from my chest long enough to shake off his pants and his shoes. I remembered that *pants* in Britain meant underwear, and nodded wisely as he turned his attention back to me.

"Pants!" I said triumphantly, snaking my hands along his hips, under the waistband of his underwear, then pulled them down as well.

"Christ," he groaned again as he kicked them off. I stared down at what I had uncovered. I blinked at his nether parts. I stepped to the side to get a better look from a different angle. I leaned in to get a closer view. Alex moaned and twitched when I wrapped my hand around the Big Kahuna. He felt hot and hard and velvety smooth all at the same time. I straightened, letting my fingers trail up the long length of him as I looked him in the eye. The musky, wonderful smell of aroused male merged with his spicy cologne and almost did me in on the spot.

"That's a very impressive undercarriage you have there, mister. You must have to beat the women off with a stick."

He closed his eyes briefly, then opened them quickly when I rubbed up against him.

"Oh, God, no, Alix, don't—oh, Christ, don't touch me there. Just give me a minute—"

I relaxed my hold on his jewels and kissed a trail along his jawline. "You seem to be having trouble breathing, Alex. If you relax a little, I'm sure all that twitching will stop."

My fingernails raked gently along his tightened balls. He grabbed me suddenly and all but tossed me onto a pristine white couch.

"Don't count on it," he growled, and came down on top of me. I squirmed beneath him, trying to get my hands free, but he had pinned them between us. I gently bit the tongue stroking the roof of my mouth, and pushed back slightly on his chest.

Alex lifted his head and looked down at me, confusion written upon his handsome face.

"Raincoat!" I gasped.

"What?"

"Condom!"

He closed his eyes briefly, breathed heavily on my shoulder, then nodded and rolled off me, padding quietly across the room. I let my eyelids drift shut as a breeze blew over my body from a nearby window. Even though it was warm air, it felt cool on my overheated skin. Just as I was imagining it was Alex's wicked fingers caressing me with a feather-like touch, he was back, hovering over me, kissing and licking my neck. He settled down on top of me, but something else was wrong.

I squirmed again.

"What now?"

"My underwear," I explained, and tried to wiggle out of them without using my hands. It was a futile effort, but had the benefit of rubbing me all over him. "I've still got my underwear on."

A slow, sensual smile curved his lips. He lifted himself slightly, his hands lightly caressing down my breasts toward my stomach. My back arched without my consent, pushing my breasts into his hands. He paused for a moment, then, kissing each one in turn, said, "Allow me to do the honors."

His hands stroked over the curve of my hips as he shifted slightly to one side, then they slid around underneath me and cupped my behind.

"Oh, Lord, I'm going to die," I moaned as he hooked his thumbs around the tops of my underwear and slowly peeled them off. His breath was hot on my belly, kissing it, lathering it with his tongue, nipping little love bites that made me want to scream with frustration.

"Alex, please, if you have a single bone of mercy in your body, stop toying with me and do it! *Now!*"

He kissed both hip bones, then slid his hands along my thighs. I pulled one leg up so he could remove my underwear.

"Slowly, sweetheart," he said, tossing my undies aside. I caught him around the waist with both legs and locked my ankles on his behind, pulling him to me. "Slowly. We'll do this very slowly. There's no reason to hurry."

"Oh, yes, there is," I said, wrapping both hands in his hair and moving him down onto me. He was a couple of inches taller, several inches wider, and who knows how many pounds heavier, but we fit together like two pieces of a puzzle. "If you don't make love to me this very second, I'll die and you'll be left to explain why you have a naked, dead, *unsatisfied* American on your couch."

His arousal poked against my pubic bone as I arched up to kiss him. Who could imagine that something so mundane and functional as a tongue could start such raging fires? I sucked his tongue into my mouth and took his groan of pleasure deep into me.

"Alex!" Was that whimper mine? It had to be mine, his mouth was engaged in exploring the area behind my ear, an activity that made me shiver with delight. I tugged his hips and pulled my knees up higher on his back. I could feel him poking at my entrance, felt the tip of him slip along the wetness there, and wanted desperately for him to fill me.

I shifted and felt the thick head lodge just inside my opening. "Alex, if you're not deep inside me in the next two seconds, I'm going to scream."

He chuckled a rusty chuckle and grabbed my hips to keep me from thrusting up toward him. "We have all night, sweetheart. This is an important step for both of us; I want to make sure it's right."

I writhed and twisted beneath him. I've heard that men think with that all-important part of the male anatomy, but I've never heard of one thinking for itself, and yet I could swear that's what Alex's was doing. It was tormenting me, sliding along the length of me, teasing me by pushing ever so slightly into the place I wanted it more than I wanted anything else in the entire universe, and that included breathing and world peace.

I clawed his back and thrust my hips up toward my goal. "Damn you, it's right! It's right, I promise you it's right! *Just do it!*"

He chuckled again and pushed into me slightly, allowing maybe an inch of him to sit just inside me. My body gave willingly, accommodating his size, clinging to the little part of him that had entered. I arched back, closing my eyes with the wonder of the feeling of him, so hot, so strong, so perfectly formed just for me. Tears leaked out the sides of my eyes as I waited for him to surge into me, to possess me fully, to join with me in body and soul.

"Open your eyes, Alix."

Slowly my eyelids lifted to find him poised over me, his eyes glittering a dark, dark green.

"I want to watch the passion fill your eyes when I take you."

He pressed in just a bit. Another inch. I moaned and raked my nails up his back as I bit at his shoulder. "I need you, Alex, I need you right now. Please, don't tease me like this—just do it this once and I promise I'll do anything you want. Oral sex, kinky stuff, anything you want, I don't mind, just please do it now!"

The agonizing sense of loss was the first sign that something had gone wrong. He pulled out of me completely, but not to thrust back in as I had hoped. Instead, he rose up on one arm and narrowed his eyes at me.

"What did you say?"

My mind whirled around in a lust-crazed whirlpool of confusion. What did I say? How was I supposed to know what I said? Why had he left the warm sanctuary my body was offering? I whimpered in frustration.

"What? What I said? I said I needed you, Alex. I want you—please don't tease me this way. I can't take much more!"

His eyes narrowed farther as he pushed back, unlocking my legs around his hips, shifting to the side until he was lying next to me on the couch. "Did you say what I think you said? Did you offer sexual favors if I give you what you want now?"

I looked into the depths of his lovely green eyes, swallowing back the physical pain that came with our separation. Something was wrong, something was obviously wrong, but I'd be damned if I knew what it was. What had I said to him? I concentrated on his words, and tried to figure out what I had done to mess up the best thing that had ever come into my life.

"Sexual favors? Isn't what we're doing sexual favors? I don't understand, Alex. Are you angry with me? What did I say that made you mad?"

He wrapped one big hand around my upper arm. "Did you mean what you said?"

I couldn't stop the tears now, but they were tears of frustration, not joy. "I don't understand why you're so angry. All I did was promise to give you what you wanted, what every guy wants. It's OK, really, I don't mind a little oral sex, and as long as you don't get too kinky on me—"

He sat up suddenly, swinging his legs off the couch,

giving me his back. He ran a hand through his hair, then down his jaw. "Jesus Christ, Alix, what sort of man do you think I am that I would be willing to barter for sex? I thought you understood I am not interested in a quick tumble. I thought you were interested in starting a relationship, a real relationship, not just a bit of torrid sex to pass an hour or two."

Damn it! Why didn't I listen to Isabella? She had been right all along, and now I'd gone and ruined everything by throwing myself at Alex and showing him just how easy I was. I stared at him, speechless with horror at what I'd done, suddenly embarrassed and ashamed of being naked in front of him.

"I'm sorry, Alex," I said carefully, looking at the hard muscles of his back. How could a man who spent his days using a computer have so many muscles? "Isabella told me you wouldn't be interested in anything but a serious relationship, but I thought—I thought perhaps you felt the same thing I felt for you. I was hoping we could just enjoy each other's company while I'm here."

Alex cupped my chin in his hand and wiped a tear with this thumb. He didn't need to say a word—I could read the rejection in his eyes.

"It's OK," I said quickly, slipping out from behind him and hurrying into my dress.

"Alix, I do feel the same attraction you do, but I'm not interested in casual sex—"

"No, really, no explanation is necessary. I'll just grab my shoes and go. It was a bad idea all around."

He caught one of my hands and tried to stop me. "Alix, please allow me to—"

I pulled free, slapped a brittle smile on my face, and snatched up my shoes. "Not necessary. We're on two different wavelengths, you and I. Hell, when it comes right down to it, we're from different worlds. You belong to the Isabellas of the world—classy and chic, and not at all given to throwing themselves at men they've just met. You don't have to worry that I'll bother you again; if nothing else, I do learn from my mistakes."

I threw the last words at him as I slipped out the door, closing it quietly behind me.

"Christ, woman, will you listen to me for a bloody minute?" Alex's words reverberated around the landing, counterpointed nicely by the sound of his door being thrown open. I glanced back as I ran down the stairs, holding the front of my dress against me since I hadn't been able to button it up.

I raced off the last step and grabbed my key from where I kept it above the lintel. Footsteps thundered behind me. His bare feet came into view for a minute; then he swore when he realized he was wearing nothing but a scrap of latex. "God damn it, Alix, I'm not done talking to you!"

"Goodbye, Alex. It was nice knowing you. I hope someday you find a woman who deserves you."

He swore again and started down the steps, but I skipped inside my door and made sure he heard me close it. I half hoped he'd pound on the door, demanding that I let him in so he could apologize to me and ravish me on Stephanie's daybed, but no sound penetrated the door.

The evening ended as so many have in the past—in tears and a good old-fashioned pity party. Without a doubt, I felt like the biggest loser on the planet, friendless, alone, and with the morals of an alley cat. I couldn't believe I'd thrown myself at Alex like that. What had I been thinking? I knew, *I knew* he wouldn't be interested in a meaningless little fling, and yet, let me get within ten feet of the man and I forget everything except the lure of his seductive self. The really tragic thing was that he was completely different from anyone else I'd ever lusted after, and I doubted if anyone would ever come up to the standard he had set.

A couple of hours after I crawled into my cold, lonely bed, I admitted that he was probably the nicest man I'd ever met, and if circumstances were different, I could quite happily spend the rest of my life with him. But they weren't, and I couldn't, so I moped about the rotten tricks life had handed me until I was sick of my own company. That's one reason why I had accepted the invitation the next day to visit with Bert and Ray—the other reason being that I was desperate for company, and couldn't face the thought of having Isabella's cool, knowing, former-Alex-lover eyes on me.

As I sat before the two women, I shook away the memories of the night before and looked up at their expectant faces.

"More wine?" Bert asked.

I had half a glass of chardonnay left. I downed it in one gulp and held my glass out for more.

"There's not that much to tell," I fibbed, and let the warmth of the libation spread throughout me, numbing all the sore parts of my heart and easing the sense of shame slightly. "Last night Alex kissed me."

"Oho!" Ray said, rubbing her hands and leaning forward to pour me more wine. I dutifully took a few sips, breathing in its heady, sharp scent. It reminded me of something pleasant, something to do with Alex, something naughty . . .

"His balls!"

"Whose balls?"

I blushed at the look Bert was shooting my way and drained my glass, hoping either that I'd pass out from overindulgence of alcohol or it would wipe my memory clean of my ungoverned mouth. "Sorry, I didn't mean to be rude. It's just that the wine reminded me of something . . ." I let the words trail away. It was bad enough, I would only make it worse.

Ray sniffed her wineglass. "Don't know what Black has been doing with his goolies, but I've never known any to smell like this."

I accepted her offer of a refill, and felt it necessary to explain. "They don't smell like this, not exactly, it's just that the sharpness of the banquet reminds me of his noogies. Somewhat. Oh, hell, I'm looped already, I don't know what I'm saying. Just ignore me."

I grabbed a hunk of pita bread and dunked it into the tzatziki. Bert laughed as Ray grunted in approval of my enthusiastic praise of the food.

"Truly, Alix, you don't have to say any more if you don't wish to. We have no intention of prying into your private life. I just thought that since your family and friends were so far away, you might feel like confiding in someone neutral."

Tears welled up in my eyes at her kindness. Really, she was so sweet—both of them were. They had taken me into their home, listened to my story, fed me, tried to bolster my spirits with wine and a friendly shoulder to cry on, and all I did was natter on about Alex's balls, as if they cared about them in the least.

"No, no, I'd be happy to tell you what happened," I sniffled, and grabbing the box of tissues and a bacon-wrapped shrimp, proceeded to tell them everything about my disastrous experience with Alex. There may have been some slight skewing of the basic events, but I was pretty sure I had covered all of the major points by the time we had killed two more bottles of wine, eaten all of the tzatziki, shrimp, and brie, and gone through countless tissues. I went through the tissues, that is— Bert and Ray seemed to be made of sterner stuff.

By the time I finished my sorry tale, I was lying on the floor with my feet resting on the seat of a chair (Ray swore it would stop my "everlasting grizzling" and she was right; it's impossible to grizzle for any length of time when you're lying on the floor with your feet in a chair), Bert was curled up on the couch, and Ray was pacing in circles around us, making periodic grunts of outrage or agreement as the situation warranted.

"So that's it, that's what happened," I said, finishing my tale of woe and sitting up so I could dab at my damp eyes. "You can see now why there is no future for Alex and me. We're just not comparable."

"Communicable," Ray said sternly as she held out her hand. I took it and let her hoist me to my none-too-steady feet. "You're pissed."

I frowned at her. "I am not! I'm not mad at all, it's just the way my life always seems to go."

"The word is *compatible*," Bert corrected. "And you're both a bit squiffy. Pissed means drunk, Alix."

I nodded and grabbed onto the chair when the room gave a slight twirl to the left. "Oh, that's right, I knew that. Pants and pissed. Rumping pumps. Got it all up here." I tapped the side of my head and gave Bert a knowing wink. She blinked owlishly back at me.

"The hell you're not comparable!" Ray suddenly

shouted, swaying gently before me as she poked her finger into my chest. "That rotter has no right treating you like that! Seducing you on the stairs, then dragging you off to his love nest, stripping you naked, then shoving you out the door before you've had a chance to get your jollies. Typical man thinking only of himself. It just isn't right!"

I looked at Bert and grinned. "That's the most words I've ever heard Ray say."

Bert sighed, tried to frown, then giggled instead. "Oh, dear, I think I'm a bit squiffy as well."

Ray stalked over to her and put her hands on her hips. "Why shouldn't you be? That blighter upstairs has taken advantage of this innocent young girl, a young thing come recently to our fair isle, and tossed her out like yesterday's used paper. We've got to do something about it, Bertrice. Fair makes my blood boil, it does!"

I sank bonelessly into the chair that suddenly materialized behind me and waved a languid hand. "I'm afraid, dear, sweet Ray, there is nothing you can do. The man simply doesn't want me, not even when I bared all of my many and glorious charms for him."

"Maybe he's gay," suggested Bert with a polite little burp. I shook my head and had to clutch the arm of the chair to keep from sliding out of it when the room lurched again.

"Nope. Not possible. My gaydar didn't go off, and besides, a man who kisses women like he kissed me is not uninterested." I had a hard time getting that last word out. It took me a couple of tries, but at last I succeeded and continued on, ignoring the snickers from the peanut gallery. "Besides, the stallion was waiting at the door, if you catch my drift. I don't know what the problem was, exactly. I think he told me, but I've forgotten."

"Not getting away with it," Ray stormed, and marched over to the door, stopping only to take a long swig out of an empty wine bottle. She belched, waved for us to follow her, and stalked out the door.

I looked at Bert. She looked at me, sighed, and rose in one graceful motion. It took me three tries to get my feet under me properly, but at last I was mobile, and I made it up the two flights of stairs by clutching the back of Bert's blouse and holding on for dear life. By the time we reached the top of the stairs, Ray was pounding on Alex's door and bellowing for him to come out and face her like a man.

"What the hell is going on out here?"

"Oops," I said, peering around Bert's back. "I think she woke him up. See what I mean about the stallion being ready at the door? And it's a lovely stallion, too, isn't it? I like men who sleep naked, don't you?"

Alex, standing at his door stark naked, his hair tousled, obviously just arisen from his bed, must have felt the weight of three pairs of eyes dwelling on his rampant nether bits, because he suddenly looked down at himself, swore, and slammed the door shut in Ray's face.

I released my hold on Bert's blouse, slumped back against the wall, and let myself slide down to the floor.

"You see?" I asked. "He hates me. One sight of me and he takes his stallion back into the stable before I could even pet it. I ask you, is that the sign of a man who wants to get into my pants?"

"Never mind," Bert said at the same time as Ray started pounding again on Alex's door. She got two pounds in and was just delivering the third when he whipped the door open again.

Even dragged out of what was probably a sound sleep, the man had quick reflexes. He grabbed Ray's fist just before it hit his chest, and looked all of us over. I was on the floor weeping softly to myself over the sad state of affairs, Ray was struggling to retrieve her hand, and Bert was swaying slightly and patting the top of my head while murmuring soft little platitudes.

"Would one of you care to tell me just what the hell you think you're doing?" he asked.

I looked him up and down. "I liked you better without the bathrobe," I said, sniffling.

"Christ, you're pissed," he said, narrowing those lovely green eyes at us. "You're all pissed, aren't you? Go back down to your beds and sleep it off."

"Not till I've said a few things to you, Black," Ray said, and pushed past him into his flat.

"Atta girl, Ray," I bellowed after her. "Give 'im hell, Harry!"

"Harry who?" Bert asked.

"Dunno," I said, waving the question away. "It's an espresso I heard. Why don't you ask Alex? He probably knows. He's a smart man even if he doesn't want me to ride his stallion."

Bert nodded and turned to ask Alex, but before she could, he muttered an imprecation about women placed on the earth to drive him mad, grabbed Bert and pushed her into his flat, then marched out to loom over me in an intimidating manner.

"Hi," I said, trying for a minxish smile.

"Would you like to explain why you and your friends are knocking me up at two in the morning?"

I giggled at the image of him being knocked up, and stroked the top of one of his bare feet. "You have nice feet, Alex. You don't have six toes or warts or any weird things people can get on their feet. I don't, as a rule, like feet, but I like your feet. They're handsome, manly sort of feet."

He sighed again, then grabbed me under each armpit and hauled me up until I was standing.

"Carry me!" I demanded, throwing my arms around his neck and letting my legs go boneless. He swore again, put an arm under my knees, hoisted me up, and carried me into his flat in the best manner of romance heroes everywhere.

Bert was rustling around in his kitchen, singing a little song to herself about tea, while Ray was pacing back and forth in front of his couch.

"Alex," I whispered into his ear. He stopped before a white chair and turned his head until we were nose to nose. I smiled as I admired his mesmerizing green eyes. "I think you're in trouble with Ray."

"Bloody hell, look at him!" Ray turned and caught sight of Alex holding me in his arms. "He's at it again. This time in front of us. Man's got no decency, trying to shag poor Alix right there in front of us."

Bert turned to look while Alex tried to set me down in the chair. I decided he was more comfortable, especially since I discovered I could slip a hand in through the opening of his bathrobe and stroke his chest.

"Alix, stop that," he growled as I closed my eyes and hummed my happiness over finding such a warm, lovely chest beneath that bathrobe. "Here's the chair. Let go of me and I'll put you in it."

"You see?" Ray stormed, stalking over to Bert and waving her hands around wildly. "He's giving her orders! Just like a man, always giving orders, always telling us what to do. And he's got his hands all over her!"

"It doesn't look like he's shagging her, Ray. He looks like he's trying to set her down in the chair."

"Thank God there's one sober member of this goon squad," Alex grumbled as he tried to peel me off him without dropping me.

"You smell wonderful," I said, nuzzling his neck and giving him a few nibbles. "You smell sleepy and male and delicious. I like that. I like you. I like you a whole lot. Let's go to bed."

"Alix, please," he started to say, but stopped when Ray stomped over to him and poked a finger in the part of his chest that I wasn't covering.

"Look at him! Just look at him! He's all over her! The randy little sod!"

"You're a bad, bad man," I pointed out as I teased my tongue around his ear. "Randying all over me like that when you don't even like me."

"Ought to be ashamed of yourself!" Ray said, and poked him in the chest again.

"Ashamed," I agreed, nibbling gently along the outside of his ear.

A little tremor shook him; then his chest expanded as he took a deep breath. "Christ Almighty—"

"Taking the Lord's name in vain won't help you, either! If my father were alive, he'd horsewhip you for what you've done to that poor girl!"

Alex hitched me up a bit higher. "I haven't done anything to her!"

"That's just it," Ray snapped, and turned on her heel to pace over to the window. "You should have."

Tears pricked again at the memory of the tragic past evening. "Yes," I sniffled wetly, and gave him a forlorn little kiss on his jaw. "You should have, but instead you rejected me."

"Alix . . ." He looked from Ray to Bert and back to me. "You're all out of control, and none of you are making any sense. This is hardly the time to discuss what happened last night. If you still want to talk about it in the morning, I will be happy to explain it to you, but right now I'd like to go back to bed."

"So would I," I said, snuggling up against him. "Do you prefer grape or banana flavored raincoats?"

"It's two in the morning," he added, shaking his adorable head at me.

"I know. They made me come up here. Ray's mad at you, you know."

"You're damned right I'm mad!" Ray nodded, then accepted the cup of tea Bert handed her. "No biscuits?"

"I'm sorry, I hadn't planned on entertaining this morning," Alex said acidly, giving me another hitch up his chest, the better to glare at me. "You are the most undisciplined, unsettling woman I've ever met. You have absolutely no inhibitions, do you?"

"I'm not the one who answers my door starkers," I pointed out.

He took a deep breath. "Alix, you have to leave now. You're not yourself."

"Everyone rejects me," I mumbled into his neck, dwelling on that fact. It suddenly seemed important, and very, very sad. Alex was my last hope, and now he, too, wanted nothing to do with me.

"Christ—"

"Is there a horsewhip around here?" Ray asked, peering around with an avid look in her eye.

"Now, Ray, he hasn't done anything to deserve physical violence," Bert said. "Although if that mournful tone in Alix's voice doesn't tear at his heartstrings, it should. Imagine rejecting such a sweet, lovely girl."

I sniffled my agreement.

"I didn't reject her—"

"You didn't boff her either, and that's a rejection in my book!" Ray said over her shoulder as she poked around in the couple of kitchen cupboards above the two tiny counters. "There must be biscuits here. Everyone has biscuits. What sort of man doesn't have biscuits?"

"Maybe he's not interested in her." Bert curled up on the white couch after setting two more mugs of tea on the end table.

I put one hand on Alex's chin and turned his face until we were nose to nose again.

"Are you interested in me?"

He closed his eyes briefly, then opened them and frowned. "Alix, I am not going to discuss this with you now. I'm going to take you downstairs to your flat, and then you are going to sleep. We can talk about this—"

A hot tingle in my eye region heralded the formation of more tears.

"—later when you're . . . ah, Alix, don't cry."

"Too late." Two fat tears rolled down my cheeks.

Alex swore again, then turned around and carried me over to the door.

"Open it."

Another tear tracked down my cheek as I grasped the doorknob and turned it.

"Good night, ladies."

"What? What do you mean, good night?" Ray asked, her head in one of his cupboards.

"I mean just that. Good night. I want to talk to Alix,

and obviously I can't do that with you here, so you will please leave now."

Bert tipped her head to one side as she considered Alex, then nodded and called to Ray as she stood. "He's right, Ray. This is between the two of them, and we should leave them alone."

"Thank you," Alex said gruffly. Bert smiled and tugged a resistant Ray past him and through the door.

"But I haven't had my biscuit yet," the latter said plaintively, still clutching her cup of tea.

"You can have a biscuit at home. Leave them to themselves, Ray."

"Hrmph." Ray stopped three steps down the stairs and turned back to Alex. "You'd just better not hurt her again or I'll find a horsewhip and—"

"I haven't done anything to hurt her," Alex protested.

"Yes, you did," I said softly to his neck, waving my fingers at Bert and Ray.

Alex dropped my legs but kept an arm around my waist as he closed the door behind us.

"I didn't mean to hurt you."

I answered the siren call of his bare collarbone, tracing the length of it with a finger. "You have a nice collarbone, too, Alex. I know you didn't mean to hurt me. It's not your fault, really, no matter what Ray says. She's just a little sizzled, you know."

One warm hand cupped the side of my face and tipped my head back until I was looking straight into his green eyes. "I think you're a bit sizzled yourself, Alix. I'm sorry you were hurt last night, but—"

I put two fingers across his lips. The lovely warm fuzzy feeling that had held me in its grip had started to evaporate, and it struck me that Alex had been sorely treated this evening.

"I think I'm the one to give you an apology, what with us descending upon you and waking you up, and seeing you naked, and Ray demanding a horsewhip and biscuits. I'm sorry about that, Alex. Somehow she seemed to get the idea that you were at fault last night."

"It doesn't matter."

I shook my head. "Yes, it does matter. You have every right to be furious with me. I owe you for the trouble I've put you through after trying to seduce you and waking you up like this."

"Alix?"

"Hmm?"

The look in his eyes warmed me to my toes. He opened his mouth to speak, then closed it and shook his head. "Never mind. I'll take you downstairs now."

He kept his arm around my waist, allowing me to relax against him as he walked me down the stairs. I was conscious of a terrible sense of injustice regarding Alex, and wondered what I could do to make it up to him, to try and show him how sorry I was for annoying him.

The image of a castle came to mind, pennants flying in the wind. Who wouldn't like a visit to a castle? That was the perfect solution to my problem. "Windsor Castle!"

"What?"

"Windsor Castle. It's a castle in . . . uh . . . Windsor, I think. That's what I'll do," I said, trying to make him to understand that it was the answer to everything. "You can come with us tomorrow to Windsor Castle. You'll like it, it's historic. After Windsor, we're going to look at the maze at Hampton Court. You'll like that, too, it's perfect for a detective. You can use your skills to find a way out of the maze."

Alex was shaking his head, but I ignored that as I reached up to the lintel for the key. "No, really, Alex, it's perfect, just perfect. I'm sure Karl won't mind if you come along, and it will relieve my mind greatly."

"I have work to do this weekend, and I have no intention of being the third party on your date—"

"Oh, it's not a date," I said, smiling at him. "It's just Karl, and you'll have a wonderful time. We'll look at Windsor and we'll look at the castle, and we'll have races in the maze, and I'll feel much, much better after messing up your evening. Doesn't that sound great? It's Saturday tomorrow, so you won't have to work or anything, but you have to be ready early because Karl's picking me up at the street promptly at nine."

"Alex, I can't go. I've no interest in Windsor Castle, or Hampton Court for that matter."

I stopped trying to unlock the door to my flat as the horrible truth struck me as I stood there full of glorious plans for spending the day with Alex. He didn't want to spend it with me. He truly didn't want to have anything to do with me, and that business about the stallion waiting at the door was all a sham. My shoulders sagged as I leaned my forehead on the panel of the door. It was nice and cool. "Oh."

Two hands clamped down on my shoulders. "Alix—"

The last little bit of my heart fractured under that husky, sexy voice. "No, it's OK. I thought we might . . . forget it. It was a stupid idea, you're right to not want to come. We'll forget the whole thing."

I fumbled with the lock, unable to see it through the tears. It struck me that I was doing an awful lot of crying since I had come to England, but there didn't seem to be much I could do about it. Maybe it was something in the water.

"No, I won't forget it." The hands on my shoulders tightened and turned me around until I was facing him. One long finger wiped away my tears.

"I'm sorry, I'm not usually such a watering pot." It seemed like I was doing an awful lot of apologizing lately.

He leaned his head down and kissed me very gently. "If it means that much to you, I'll ride to Windsor with you."

I looked into those green eyes, those deep, mysterious, green eyes that seemed to hold all of the wonder and joy of the world locked within them, just waiting for me to discover them. A little flicker of hope flared in my chest. "Do you mean that? Truly? You changed your mind?"

"*You* changed my mind," he corrected me, and breathed another kiss on my lips. I moaned softly and swayed into him, relishing the feeling of his strong arms sliding around behind me, pulling me closer to him, closer to the source of all the fires he built up within me.

"Alex," I murmured, and drank in his kiss. It was hot and sultry and held so much sweetness it almost brought me to my knees.

"Alex," I said again, unable to catch my breath. "Do you want to—"

"Yes," he said, pulling my hips forward to rub his groin. He did want to. "But not now, not with so much unsettled between us." He bent down and kissed away the objection I was about to make. "We'll talk about it later, sweetheart."

With a quick flick of his wrist he had my door unlocked and held open for me. I walked past him, flipping on the lights, then stopped and turned back to face him. "Am I?"

One chestnut eyebrow rose a quarter inch. "Are you what?"

"Your sweetheart."

I held myself still while he gazed at me with those unfathomable eyes, then sighed my relief when he wrapped one hand in my hair and held me while he ravaged my mouth with a kiss that not only took my breath away, but melted my knees and puddled my insides. When he released me I was panting for air, while he smiled a smug smile of complete male satisfaction.

"Good night, Alix."

"Holy cow!" I gasped, clinging to the door to keep from collapsing from the effect of that kiss.

His smile deepened in its smugness. I closed the door and slid to the floor, fanning myself and wondering what the hell I'd done.

Chapter Seven

"You are mine, woman," Lord Raoul growled, pulling Rowena to his manly chest and ripping her golden gown asunder. "All of you, you're all mine! From your tawny crown, to your rose-tipped breasticles, to your ten delicious little toes. Mine, mine, mine!"

"Oh, Raoooooul!" Rowena swooned.

"Breasticles? What is a breasticle?"

I heaved a sigh and would have rolled my eyes, but the way they felt, I wasn't entirely sure they wouldn't roll right out of my head and across the ugly carpet, picking up lint and who knew what else. Come to think of it, my eyes already felt a bit linty. "It's a silly word, Mom. It's Raoul's way of showing he's playing with her. A love word, you know, the silly kind of talk lovers have with one another." At least I think she knew—I didn't want to inquire too closely into my mother's love life. There were just some things that were better left unknown.

"I don't like it. It doesn't make sense. What does this agent you found think about breasticles? Does she have anything to say about it? Is it even in the dictionary? If it's not in the dictionary, no publisher will publish it. You have to stick with words that are in the dictionary, Alix."

"Mom, you know that it's only six-eighteen in the morning here, don't you?" I spoke softly, hoping the pounding in my head would lessen if I didn't move anything but my lips.

"Of course I do, that's why I waited until now to call you, and I have to say that I don't appreciate that snippy tone. This is an expensive phone call, and I don't expect you to waste my time with silliness like breasticles and such. Why do you sound so odd? Are you sick?"

I pressed two knuckles to my temple and wondered about those ancient cultures that believed drilling holes in the skull would let out the evil spirits. At the moment I would have paid good money to have someone drill a few escape holes in my head. "No, I'm fine, just tired."

"Good. How far are you on the manuscript now?"

"Almost finished." I yawned, trying to stifle it but not succeeding. Gingerly I touched my tongue. It felt like it had been dipped in wax. Furry wax. "I'm going to take in the part I have done to my agent and have her start editing it."

"I wish you had mentioned that to me, before you spent your money," my mother fretted. I curled my toes into the mattress and wondered how I was ever going to tell her that I'd cashed in my plane ticket to pay for the editing. "I would like to have checked out this agent before you paid her. You said she has a real office, not just a rented room?"

"She has a real office, Mom, with her name on the door plate and everything. If that's all you wanted, I really have to go."

"Go?" The sharp tone in my mother's voice sounded like it always did—like fingernails on a chalk board. I flinched and held the phone away from my ear. "Where can you possibly have to *go* at six in the morning? You're not consorting with inappropriate people, are you?"

"No, Mother," I sighed.

"I hope you're not foolish enough to waste your precious time chasing after men when you should be writing."

I mouthed the words I knew would be coming next just as she spoke them. "I didn't spend all of my hard-earned money just so you can waste your time."

I stretched and braved twitching back the curtain just enough to let in a bit of air. Unfortunately, sunlight came with it. Drat the stuff. I closed my eyes and prayed for instantaneous death. "I'm not looking for a boyfriend, Mom. I'm writing. Don't worry, I'll have this book done and marketable by the time I come home."

I had to. The future that faced me if I didn't was too grisly to contemplate.

"I hope so."

"Mom, I really have to go now . . . and that's go to the bathroom, not go out, so if there's nothing else, I'll say 'bye."

It took another five minutes of listening to my mother alternate between warnings to save my money and not go anywhere alone, and her predictions of doom and gloom connected with my agent, book, future, and pretty much life as I knew it. Finally I told her I was about to wet the bed, and managed to hang up without annoying her too much.

"Twenty-nine years old and I'm still afraid to tell my mother off," I grumbled to myself as I staggered barefoot to the tiny bathroom. The grumbling continued over the course of the next few hours while I took a couple of paracetamol for my killer headache, showered, dressed, took another paracetamol, tidied up the kitchen, avoided looking directly at any food substances, then, after consulting the paracetamol package and deciding I didn't really need my kidneys as much as I needed to be able to blink without flinching, downed a couple more of the painkillers. That was followed by a half hour's worth of yoga, most of which was spent in the Flattened Roadkill position—that's lying prone on the floor while breathing very, very carefully (moan as you inhale, groan as you exhale).

By the time nine o'clock rolled around, I was feeling less like a Klingon having a bad day and more like someone who was going to spend the day touring around a castle with two handsome men in attendance. I grabbed my purse and notebook, turned around twice before the little mirror to make sure my chic retro 1950's black-and-white polka dot chiffon dress wasn't tucked up in my underwear, and toddled off to meet Karl.

"Lovely morning, isn't it?" I called to Ray as I trotted downstairs, adjusting a straw hat I had picked up the day before from a shop around the corner. "I'm going to see Windsor Castle. Shall I remember you to the queen?"

"Urgh."

The sound was halfway between a cat retching up a hairball and a death rattle.

"Ray, you OK there? Are you having some problem with your key, or are you trying to listen through the door? Wood usually isn't conducive to passing sounds."

Silence greeted my chirpy attempt at humor. I stopped my descent down the stairs and took another look. "Ray?"

"Mwah."

"Ah," I said, and hopped back up a handful of stairs. Ray was plastered to the door, waving a hand ineffectually toward the latch as she clutched a small carton of milk to her chest. "I know that sound, I was making it earlier. Before the paracetamol, that is. Ray, honey, I'll help you open the door if you can peel yourself off it. There we go, now if you'll just hand me your key. . . . Lord, you look terrible!"

Ray was dressed in a khaki T-shirt and matching shorts, which would have been all right except her complexion matched the ensemble. I hesitated to peer under the big, black sunglasses she wore, but that gruesome curiosity that makes people look at traffic accidents forced me to peek.

"O-o-oh, not good. Let's get you inside. I hope Bert's not in the same condition. Key?"

"Nnnng."

Poor Ray. I scratched gently at the door, and turned her over to Bert when she answered.

"I was wondering where she had gone," Bert said with a sympathetic smile. "Thank you, Alix. That's a charming dress—is it new?"

I gave a little twirl and struck a pose. "It's my retro fifties dress. It's kicky, huh? I'm going to Windsor Castle with Karl, a friend of Isabella's, the one she thought was perfect for me."

"Very nice," she said, bundling Ray over to a chair. "I'm sure you'll have a wonderful time."

I turned to start back down the stairs when Bert called out to me. "Oh, Alix, did . . . ah . . . everything go all right last night?"

"Last night? Oh, you mean with Alex? Everything is just peachy. He's going with us to Windsor."

Bert pried the carton of milk from Ray's stiff fingers and glanced at me where I stood in the doorway. "With you? He's going with you and Karl?"

"Yup, it should be fun. Karl has a degree in history, so I'm sure he knows a lot about everything we'll see." I waved them both a cheery goodbye and trotted down the stairs and out the door.

A familiar leather satchel was sitting on the front steps. An even more familiar man was standing nearby, leaning on the railing and looking annoyed.

"Alex!"

He turned and gave me a stiff nod of the head in greeting. "Good morning."

I grinned and skipped down the couple of steps to where he was standing. "My, so formal, and after you were so very"—my grin hitched up to a leer as I waggled my eyebrows at him—"*informal* last night. What do you have in your bag? Lunch? Champagne? Something naughty?"

His cheeks turned a dusky red. "I would prefer to forget about last night, as would, I assume, you, Bertrice, and Ray."

I felt a little blush of my own creep up at the look he was bending upon me. "I *did* apologize, Alex, and if it makes you feel any better, I had a hell of a hangover this morning, so you needn't be quite so snippy about the whole thing. It's a lovely day, and for once you're not dressed in a suit—I like the linen look on you, by the way, you should wear it more often—and we're going to have a marvelous time, so why don't you lose that Eeyore gloom and show me what you have in your bag. Sandwiches? Fried chicken? Bread and cheese?"

He frowned. "My laptop."

"Huh?" My determined smile lost significant wattage. "You're bringing your laptop with you? To Windsor? How come?"

"I have work to do."

"But you can't! It's Saturday! We're going to a castle! You can't compute in a castle, it's against all the laws of nature!"

"Nonetheless, I have reports that I must have completed by Monday morning. I tried to warn you last night I would be unable to spend the day in a frivolous manner, but you were very insistent that I come with you." He glared at me as if it were *my* fault he was going with us.

I glared back. "I wasn't insistent! I told you it was OK if you didn't come, that I understood if you didn't want to spend the day with me—incidentally breaking my heart a second time, I might add, not that I'll be foolish enough to ever give you the chance to do it again, Detective Inspector Tight Ass—but *you* changed your mind. You agreed to come with us!"

Alex waved away the last part of my sentence, narrowing his eyes and jutting his chin out at me. "Broke your heart? I haven't broken your heart! You don't have a heart to break, all you have is . . ." He waved a hand toward my groin.

"Oh!" I steamed, turning my back on the street in order to face him nose to nose. "Don't you dare imply I have no heart! I know I have one, because you broke it when you threw me out of your flat." I thought for a few seconds. "Twice! You threw me out twice! You're the one with no heart! And what's worse, you don't even have . . ." I waved at his crotch, doing a pretty good imitation of the disdainful look he had just given me.

"I bloody well do too have a . . ." he bellowed, waving at his fly. "And it must be a damned good one, since you were begging for it just two nights past!"

My mouth dropped open over the audacity of the man. "Begging for it? *Begging for it?*"

He crossed his arms over his chest. "Begging for it. I seem to recall you promising me all sorts of things if I would give you what you wanted."

He had a point, but I wasn't going to admit it. "Well, you wanted it, too, Mr. Greet People Naked at the Door with Your Lance Fewtered!"

That caught him by surprise. "My what?"

"Lance fewtered. Don't you read any medieval books? You ought to read a little Roberta Gellis. You'd like her—she writes about all sorts of obstinate, pigheaded alpha males that I just bet you'd relate to."

"I have no intention of reading anything with—"

"Of course, those men had sex with people, they didn't just lead women on and then dump them the minute things got a bit steamy."

"I have never led a woman on in my life—"

"You know what they call a woman who does that? A bimbo. Guess what? That makes you a mimbo!"

"Alix—"

"It's not like I wrestled you to the ground and tore your clothes off, you know. You were right there with me, panting and heaving and nibbling and kissing, and doing all of those things that indicated the stallion was not only at the door, he was ready for a long, hard gallop!"

"Alix—"

"Don't you dare make *me* sound like a trollop! You were quick enough taking my dress off, and *you're* the one who made sure he rubbed himself all over me when you peeled my underwear down, slowly, inch by inch!"

"ALIX!" he roared.

"What?" I roared back, hands on my hips, my face thrust into his.

"Your boyfriend is here."

"He's not my boyfriend! You are!" I punched him dead in the chest, then winced when I realized what I had just said. I closed my eyes for a second, took a deep breath, then looked over my shoulder. "Oh, hi, Karl. You remember Alex, don't you? I invited him to come with us today. Hope you don't mind. Isn't it a lovely day, though?"

Karl pursed his lips and looked thoughtful.

The drive to Windsor was, for the most part, a pleasant one. Karl did indeed know his history, and he pointed out all sorts of landmarks in London, as well as en route to the cute town of Windsor, home of the famous castle. I have to give him credit, Karl recovered quickly from the embarrassing scene on the front steps—which is more than I could say for Alex.

"You have to forgive Alex," I said a short while after we set off. "He's in a pissy mood today. He's feeling guilty because he's broken my heart—twice now—and doesn't want to admit it."

"Stop putting words in my mouth," Alex growled from

the back seat of Karl's Honda. The faint tickety-tickety sound of laptop keys being pressed confirmed my suspicion that he was back there working.

"One of the interesting locations you'll see shortly is Runnymede," Karl said, ignoring Alex's bickering. "Just on the left ahead. You know about Runnymede, don't you, Alix? That's where King John signed the Magna Carta in 1215."

"The Magna Carta. Fascinating," I said, glancing out the window to a grassy parkland that looked no different from any other grassy parkland, then turning back to glare at Alex. "And I'm not putting words in your mouth, I'm simply explaining to Karl why you're being such a pain in the patootie. He's anal," I confided to Karl. "Have you ever heard of a man who insists on working seven days a week?"

"Mmm. You know, of course, that the Magna Carta was used as a basis for your Constitution. In fact, the American Bar Association commemorated it by erecting a monument here in 1957."

"I am not anal, I simply have an important report due on Monday. My work is such that I must be available to act at any time. Perhaps you Americans are unfamiliar with such a thing as a dedicated work ethic, but I assure you I am not."

"Oh, let's start flinging nationalistic slurs about, shall we? Then try this on for size, Mr. No Sex Please, We're British. I was married to a workaholic who spent damn near every single moment of the day working on 'important' projects, and I can tell you from experience the only reason people like you spend all day, every day working is because there is nothing else to fill your lives."

"There is also an RAF War Memorial on the hillside,

as well as the John F. Kennedy Memorial."

A silence heavy with unspoken anger wafted forward from the back seat, finally followed by a low, "I'm here. What more do you want from me?"

"Many people are unaware of the fact, but the actual ground the Kennedy Memorial stands upon was given to the United States by the queen in 1965."

"A dubious honor," I snapped at Alex, turning toward the front and staring out the window at the passing scenery.

"Do you think so? I thought it was a rather generous gesture."

I stared at Karl. "What? What's a generous gesture?"

His gaze flickered to the rearview mirror. No doubt he was noting Alex's childish behavior. I shrugged. I certainly wasn't going to make any more excuses for the man's rudeness in going on a sightseeing tour and ignoring all the sights.

"It doesn't matter, Alix. Now, just ahead is—"

I turned back to glare at Alex one last time. He ignored me, his fingers flying over the black keys of his laptop as he frowned at the screen. "What a pain you're being! You're going to miss all of the good historical stuff if you keep your nose buried in that laptop all day."

"—Eton, famed for Eton College, where generations of noblemen, royalty, and politicians have been educated. If you are writing about gentlemen who were well educated in the early nineteenth century, you'll want to look at Eton. Many of the upper class were sent here."

Alex didn't look up at me, not even a glance my way to acknowledge that I was speaking to him, but his jaw made a tight little movement that made me think he was grinding his teeth. I smiled and returned my attention to the area we were passing through.

"This is very pretty," I said to Karl as we zoomed past a quaint little town. "I can't wait to get to Windsor and see the historic sites. I love history, you know, and since I plan on writing lots of historical romances, this trip is the ideal research opportunity for me, so be sure to point out all of the important stuff. I don't want to miss one single thing, no matter how many party-poopers are along with us."

"I am not a party-pooper," came clearly from the back seat. I ignored him just as he had ignored me.

"So, Karl, can you tell me anything about this area? It looks old. Anything of interest around here?"

Karl shot me a quick, steely look, then returned his gaze to the road. "Erm . . . no. We're almost to Windsor. I'll just find a car park, and we can walk to the castle first, if you like, then explore the town."

"Sounds fabulous," I agreed, leaning toward the window until I had Alex in the side mirror. He was glaring at the back of my head. "Doesn't it sound fabulous, Alex?"

He turned his glare back to his laptop. "I'm sure you'll have a pleasant time. I will wait for you at the Fort and Firkin."

I craned my head around to look at him. "The what?"

"It's a pub," he said without looking up.

"Here we are in historic Windsor. Alix, to your left there you'll see St. George's Gate and the southeast face of the castle. We'll park there, see the castle, then stroll down through the town afterwards."

I spent a moment in awed appreciation of the sight Karl was pointing to. The gate was a tall, two-story squared-off archway that was dwarfed on the right by two huge round towers, and further on by a block of square towers. Each of them had a face of tightly set stones, arrow slits, and beautifully arched windows. I was in heaven. "Wow, that's so fantastic! It looks just like a real castle!"

Karl chuckled as he whipped into a parking stall. "It should. Windsor Castle has been standing for nine hundred years."

The sight of the castle drove from my mind all thoughts of Alex's frustrating refusal to join us—until he muttered something about meeting us later and started to stalk out of the car park with his satchel slung over one shoulder.

"Hey! Wait just one minute there, mister. Where are you going?"

Alex ignored my bellow and continued walking. I glanced over at the castle entrance. There was a line of people waiting to get in. "You get in line, Karl, and I'll go snag Detective Spoilsport. Won't take me a minute."

"Alix, if he doesn't want to come with us—"

I waved away his objection and started off after Alex. A little ahead of him, coming toward us in a solid chunk of humanity, was a group of about twenty tourists following a woman in a snazzy blue blazer with the name of a tour company embroidered over her left breast.

"Drat the man and his long legs," I huffed as I trotted after him, then turned around and yelled back to Karl, "Of course he wants to come with us, he's just being difficult. Men get like that all the time. You buy the tickets, and we'll be right there." I turned back and resumed my trot. "Alex, dammit, stop pouting!"

Twenty yards ahead of me he stopped, his shoulders

slumping briefly as I ran up to him. The tour guide halted next to a black metal fence a few yards away and hallooed up her stragglers. I ignored them as I prepared to grovel.

"Come on, I know you're in a bad mood, but just look at that!" I waved my hand behind us at the magnificent sight that towered over everything. Several of the tourists started taking pictures while they waited for the rest of the group to gather. "Look, Alex, it's Windsor Castle! It's nine hundred years old! It's positively *oozing* with history! You can't miss that!"

He whirled around to face me, his mouth open to issue a refusal. I put a hand on his arm and gave a little squeeze, trying to stop the words before they were spoken, ignoring as best I could the tremendous jolt of pleasure that shot through me at the feel of his bicep beneath the thin material. "Alex, please don't go off in a sulk. You'll have time to work later, I promise. It would be a shame to miss Windsor."

His gaze held mine, his eyes so brilliant they looked like onyx set in emeralds, but his face was all angular planes, his jaw held tightly. I knew then with absolute certainty he was going to refuse to come with me.

"Please," I whispered, leaning closer in hopes he would see how much I wanted to spend time with him. "It won't be the same if you're not there."

He glanced over to where several of the nearest tourists were watching us interestedly. The muscles under my hand tensed as he tried to tug his arm away, but I held tight. "You're making a scene, Alix. Although that doesn't seem to bother you at all, I'm not used to public displays."

I refused to let him sidetrack me with inconsequential

issues. I took a step closer until my breasts brushed the soft green of his shirt. "Please, Alex."

"Karl is very knowledgeable. You'll enjoy your visit to Windsor with him." His gaze never left my face. I threw every bit of emotion I had into my eyes, hoping he could read the sincerity in them.

"Yes, he is knowledgeable," I agreed. "He's also very smart, and a nice man, and I like him, but, Alex—he's not you. I want . . ." My breath caught as I realized that despite my earlier claim, I was making myself vulnerable again, giving him another chance to break my heart. I couldn't help it, though, I had to say it. I just wished there wasn't an audience of tourists watching. "I want *you.*"

"Vhat did she say?" a soft Germanic voice asked.

"She said she wants him."

"Who wants what?" A third, English, voice asked. I kept my eyes on Alex, refusing to be distracted, refusing to let him slip away from me.

"That woman wants that man," the second tourist, also a woman with a German accent, informed her companions.

Out of the corner of my eye, I saw a middle-aged woman with faded blond hair raise a camera and snap a picture of Alex and me. I hoped his peripheral vision wasn't as good as mine.

"Ah. Lovers they must be," the first woman said.

Alex's jaw clenched again at the words. I tugged him away from the tourists, back toward the entrance to Windsor Castle, but he halted after about twenty feet, spinning me around to face him. I held out a hand to forestall his objection.

"I meant what I said, Alex. I'm sorry if you think I'm

147

making a scene, but I thought you would like to know how I feel. I thought it was important. I just want you to know how much I want to be with you."

His eyes had darkened, the thin black waves of color radiating out from his pupils seemingly absorbing the surrounding green. "Do you know what you're saying? Do you understand what it is you're really asking of me?"

I didn't, not truly. I didn't know anything other than that I wanted to be with him desperately, but I knew, in some dim corner of my mind, that if I let him go now, I'd never get him back. My fingers tightened on the thin cotton of his shirt sleeve. Just touching him made me feel better, made me feel more complete. "Yes, I do. To both questions. I understand."

Alex shook his head as his eyes went darker, sending my heart plummeting to my sandals. He was going to turn me down again. I didn't think I could take it, not three times, not with the man I wanted so much I could feel him in my blood.

"I don't think you do understand."

My breath stopped, my heart stopped, the *world* stopped while I stared into his eyes, braced for the *coup de grace*. He leaned forward until I could feel his breath fan out over my face.

"But you will."

He traced my lower lip with his thumb as I stood there blinking in the morning sunlight, staring at him, staring into his eyes and hoping to God I hadn't misheard him.

"Alex, I—"

He smiled then, a real smile, not the polite parody he'd worn as a mask earlier. This was a true smile, one that made his eyes sparkle and two faint dimples appear in his cheeks.

148

"Ah, look there, is that not pleasant? The man is kissing the woman who wants him. It's good, yes?"

The cameras clicked as I allowed Alex to make a spectacle of us in public.

We trekked all over the parts of Windsor Castle open to tourists—with the exception of Queen Mary's Dollhouse, which the men refused to visit—seeing more history than I could possibly take in. There were moats filled with gorgeously landscaped gardens rather than stale, stagnant water; gargoyles and statues on the beautiful St. George's Chapel; a huge Round Tower that wasn't really very round; and a rather austere quadrangle that bordered the Royal Apartments. It was a huge site with an upper, middle, and lower ward that seemed miles apart as we walked under the broiling July sun. By the time we finished the tour, we were all dragging, and went to the pub that Alex had recommended for lunch and a couple of rounds of liquid refreshment.

We toured briefly through the town of Windsor itself, but by then there were so many tourists about, it made walking the cobblestone streets (authentic, but uncomfortable in heels) unpleasant.

"It's a darn shame," I grumbled to Alex as I clutched him while balancing on one foot in order to shake a pebble from my sandal, "when I'm in one of the oldest civilized spots in England, a place so soaked in history that everyone around the world knows its name, a town that for nine hundred years has been the residence of the reigning monarch, and what do I see?" I waved my hand at the street ahead of us. "A McDonald's, a Starbucks, and a Pizza Hut all on one street."

"Global village," Karl said as he passed by us on his

way to the river where we were going to watch the swan upping.

"I don't believe that's quite what the term is meant to imply, but I agree with the sentiment."

Alex waited until I put my sandal back on, then slid his arm around my waist as if he had been doing it for years.

"Smooth move," I said softly to him, enjoying greatly his little possessive display.

"I thought it was," he replied, with only a slight twitching of his mouth.

I may be naïve at times, but I am not completely clueless; it was evident that something of importance had passed between us earlier when we were emoting for the tourists. I had asked him for something and he had given it, changing the entire nature of our relationship, but . . . well, I guess I *am* completely clueless, because I wasn't quite sure what the terms were that I had offered and he accepted. I didn't waste my time worrying over it, however. Experience has taught me well that the fates always saw to it that, sooner or later, the rules were explained. I just hoped they got around to it before I had to leave Alex and go home to face a life without him.

Chapter Eight

"I know not what to do, my lord—my mother, the Lady Ermintrude, has forbidden me contact with you in order to force me into marriage with the loathsome and ancient Sir Wenceslaus Lecher-ffokes, the man who has wedded and buried seven wives. Should my mother catch you here now, in my bedchamber, while I am in a state of undress and you are exhibiting your manly form to much advantage by having donned nothing more than a pair of skin-tight buckskins and a billowing soft linen shirt that is unbuttoned and displaying such hirsute sights as to make my maiden's cheeks blush, why, she would not hesitate to call her lover, Captain Montague, he who is the Queen's champion and expert par extraordinaire with both swords and pistols, in order to challenge you to a duel over my honor, and oh, my lord, after you survived that last duel over just that, I could not bear for you to suffer the same again."

"Rowena! What are you doing here? I thought this was your mother's room!" Lord Thomas cried, holding aloft those masculine columns of banded steel that were his arms in order to keep Rowena from launching herself onto his handsome and virile person.

Rowena gasped and paused in the act of throwing herself in his arms, cut to the quick, nay the very marrow of her bones by Lord Thomas's rejection of her. Her heart shattered and dissolved into tiny, infinitesimally small fragments that would never, ever be whole again. She clutched her hands to her bosom, breathless and on the verge of a swoon as the razor-sharp agony cut through her very soul when she realized that Lord Thomas had been toying with her, leading her on, making cruel sport of her all the while he had no intention of fulfilling the many, many wicked promises made by his treacherous, if finely chiseled and manly to the extreme, lips.

"Oh, perfidious traitor!" Rowena cried. "Oh, soulless wretch who would cruelly tease and torment an innocent and comely maid such as myself! Oh, that I should never again have to cast my eyes upon your rampant stallion waiting at the door!"

"The depth of your subtlety overwhelms me," Alex piped up from the back seat.

"What?" I asked, turning around to glare at him. Who did he think he was, criticizing my lovely story?

"Hmmm?"

"Don't you cock that delicious eyebrow at me, mister. You know what."

The frown wrinkling his brow smoothed out as he tapped away industriously at his keyboard. "I have no idea what you're talking about. I am innocent of all things."

I snorted in disbelief. "Oh, be quiet and do your work so we can enjoy Hampton Court. What did you think of it, Karl?"

"Oh, me? What did I think? Is that what you asked? What I think?"

I nodded even though I knew he wouldn't see it, Karl's eyes being firmly fixed to the road ahead, his lips (nowhere near as finely chiseled and manly as Alex's) turned down at the corners.

"To tell you the truth, Alix, I don't read that sort of book, so I'm not the best person qualified to give you an opinion on it."

I waved away that paltry excuse. "It doesn't matter if you read romances. What I want to know is whether or not the prose is vivid enough, if it brings a picture to your mind, if you can really *see* the characters. Anyone can give their opinion on whether or not they think the writing is good."

"Ah. Well . . ." Karl's forehead wrinkled in thought. "Ah . . . oh, look, here we are at Hampton Court already."

"How providential."

"What's that supposed to mean?" I asked, turning around in my seat to glare at Alex.

"I'm sorry, I can't talk to you now, I'm working," he said, his fingers dancing over his laptop's keyboard.

"Hrmph." I turned back to Karl and caught the vestiges of a smile passing between the two of them. Men. They're so childish. "Karl, I want to know what you think, and I want to know now. I'm not getting out of this car until you tell me."

He chanced a quick glance at me and sighed. "Give me a moment to find a parking spot."

I could have sworn I heard a soft "Delaying won't do you any good," from the back seat, but when I looked, Alex was still busily typing away.

Five minutes later I pinned Karl to the wall, metaphorically speaking. "So?"

He took my right hand in both of his. I watched his lips move as he spoke, and wondered why Karl could hold my hand, stroking the top with one hand, and rubbing my fingers with the other, without stirring the slightest bit of feeling other than the desire to tell him to stop waffling and get on with what he was going to say, whereas the slightest brush against Alex's hand sent waves of heat billowing over me. He had actually given me goose bumps once or twice at Windsor when we were walking and inadvertently touched.

"—so my thought would be that you might want to add in a bit more description."

"Huh?" I recalled my mind to where it was supposed to be. "You think I need more description? Details, you mean?"

"Take that scene you just read to us. You describe the gentleman's billowing shirt, but nothing about where the two people are standing, whether it was hot or cold, what their surroundings were like, how they were feeling—say whether they had a toothache, for example. People in that time had terrible dental hygiene, and many of them lost most, if not all, of their teeth by the time they were into their early thirties, so constant toothache would not be out of the question."

"Oh." Toothaches? He wanted me to give Rowena bad teeth? No romance heroine ever had bad teeth! Or body odor, for that matter, it just wasn't heroine-like. "Description. OK, I can see what you're saying. Maybe talk about the environment a bit more? Like if it's raining or something?"

"Exactly," Karl said with obvious relief. "And now, Hampton Court awaits, my lady. If you will avaunt this way, I shall be delighted to escort you to the royal apartments."

I looked back to where Alex was tucking his laptop away in the leather satchel. "How come *you* never talk like that to me?"

His raised eyebrow spoke volumes.

Where Windsor Castle was magnificent and awesome in its size and strength, Hampton Court was seductive and elegant. We joined the queue and took the tour through the many rooms available to the public, including a visit to the Tudor Kitchen that inspired me to think about writing a medieval romance. In the Georgian Rooms there was a demonstration of Georgian dancing, which was a bit early for my book, but fascinating nonetheless. By the time we'd spent three hours tootling through the palace, we were dragging. There was one more thing I *had* to see, however.

"Come along, gentlemen," I said, heading off in the direction a sign pointed. "We have to see the maze. No lagging, now! We'll have a maze race."

I stopped and looked back to where the two men were plodding along slowly.

"Alix, it's sweltering out, and we've walked at least twelve miles today, so why don't we leave the maze for another time?"

I frowned. "The maze is famous, Karl! Famous! Everyone visits the maze. I didn't come halfway around the world not to visit the famous maze! So get those loins girded, and let's get cracking!"

Alex veered to the left. "There's a restaurant over there in the old tiltyard—why don't Karl and I wait for you there while you see the maze?'

I felt like stamping my foot, but decided it would look too petulant. "You don't understand. The fun in seeing the maze is seeing it *with* someone. I read about it in a London tourist paper—you're supposed to make a bet with each other to see who can make it through the maze first. I can't race myself, so one of you is going to have to come with me."

Alex looked at Karl. Karl looked back at Alex. "You wanted her, you can take her through the bloody thing," Karl said.

I stood, frowning, while Alex looked me over. He looked hot and grumpy, but that was no excuse for what he said next. "I've changed my mind. She's all yours."

"Alex!"

"No, no, I wouldn't dream of usurping your place," Karl said, backing away and holding out his palms as if Alex was going to dump me on him. "According to Alix, you're the one who peeled her knickers off, so she's yours by right."

"Hey!" I made the meanest eyes possible at Karl. He ignored me.

Alex rubbed his chin thoughtfully as he cast a longing glance at the restaurant tucked away behind a tall hedge. "I haven't actually claimed her as such, so technically, she's open to all comers."

"ALEX!" I shrieked, garnering attention from nearby tourists. I lowered my voice to a hiss and walloped him

on the arm. "You have too claimed me—not that I'm a possession to be claimed, mind you, but you have none-theless, even if we discount that night when all of the underwear peeling was going on, so there's no techni-cality about it!"

Alex grinned at me, an act that stopped me right in the middle of my rant.

"You're attracting attention again, Alix."

I narrowed my eyes at him. "I'm going to make you pay for this, Alexander Black, just you see if I don't."

He laughed—he actually threw his head back and laughed at my threat—but at least he took me by the hand and started off toward the maze while Karl made a beeline for the restaurant. I waited until Alex's laughter had run down, then asked him what he wanted to wager in our maze bet.

"It's traditional that the winner stand the loser a round of drinks at a pub."

An idea occurred to me as he spoke. I examined it for a moment, decided it was feasible, it was good, it was meant to be, and pulled him to a stop outside the gate at the maze.

"That's a bet for wusses," I said, trying to keep the gleam of anticipation from my eyes. *To catch your vic-tim, first you must bait the trap.* "Why don't we make a real bet? Something that matters?"

"What did you have in mind?"

Step into the parlor, my little fly. "Well," I drawled, glancing at the opening to the maze. I had always been very good at paper mazes, and the maze at Hampton Court was nothing more than a three-dimensional ver-sion. It was almost a done deal that I would beat him through it. "I thought we could each have our own wager, a boon to be given by the loser. For instance, if you wanted me to buy you a round of drinks if you win, why then, that would be my boon to you. If I win, however"—my eyelids half closed seductively—"you would grant me a different boon."

His eyes glittered at me. *Go ahead, my sweet, you know that curiosity is driving you wild. Ask.*

"And what boon would you ask of me should you beat me through the maze?"

Ah, my darling, the possibilities I have in mind for us. . . . I put a finger to my lips in apparent thought, then donned my best cat-into-the-cream smile. "If I win, you will spend the night with me."

His eyebrows shot up.

"All night."

His eyes turned dark.

"Naked. In my bed. Doing whatever I want you to do."

A slow smile curled his luscious lips. "Very well," he nodded, "I agree to your boon."

I blinked at him, startled by the ease with which he agreed. I figured I'd have to force him into accepting my terms. "Oh. Well . . . that's good. Shall we go? First person to the center wins, or first person to the center and out wins?"

He put a hand on my arm to keep me from entering the maze.

"Just a moment—you haven't asked what I want from you if I win."

I leered. "Does it involve well-oiled, naked flesh?"

The smile reached his eyes. "No. It doesn't."

I pretended to pout. "Your loss. So what boon do you want from me if you win, not that it's likely you'll win, mind you, 'cause I'm really good at mazes?"

He pulled a strand of my hair from where it had plastered itself to my hot forehead. "I believe I will reserve the right to declare what I will ask as a boon until I win."

I frowned. "That's not fair. I told you mine, you have to tell me yours."

The two faint dimples appeared in his cheeks. "Afraid you'll lose?"

"No, of course not. I just told you I was good."

"Then you have nothing to worry about, do you?"

He had me there, blast his delectable hide, but I didn't have to like it. I stuck my hand out and he gravely shook on the wager; then we decided that the first person to the center and out of the maze would win. I stood for a moment before the maze opening, my eyes closed, my senses attuned to my surroundings, hoping for a bit of psychic guidance. It was hot even in the shadows cast by the tall hedges of the maze, and the sheer numbers of tourists trekking through the gardens and maze made it impossible to catch any scent of flowers or plants, but I did my best to commune with Mother Nature.

I hit the maze running at full speed, dodging around clumps of people as they stood laughing and calling to one another. I made a couple of wrong turns at the beginning, but by the time I worked my way through to the center, I was confident that I made up for my errors with my speed. Even if Alex got all of the turns right—which would be impossible—I was still faster than he. I dashed toward the exit, whipping around corners and bumping into one or two people, trailing apologies behind me as I planned just exactly what I would do to Alex when I had him in my bed.

He was waiting for me at the exit.

"You . . . what? . . . hey, you . . . cheated . . ." I panted, grasping a nearby bench to keep from collapsing in the heat. He looked a bit hotter than he had before, but he wasn't even breathing hard. "You . . . didn't go . . . in . . ."

"Shall I describe the heart of the maze for you?" he asked, another one of his Cheshire-cat smiles gracing his lips.

"Yes," I snarled. He did, including the description of two elderly tourists into whom I had almost run. Twice. Dammit, he *had* been to the center and back before me.

"All right," I pouted, visions of a lovely, smut-filled evening evaporating in the warm amber of the afternoon sun. "Fine. You win. What'ya want from me?"

He held out his hand. I thought about refusing to take it, but I liked holding his hand too much. I held on to my pout, however, as he tugged me toward the nearby restaurant. "I want you to go to dinner with me."

I peered at him, every nerve screaming a suspicious warning. "Just dinner? With you? Where?"

He smiled. "I want you to come with me to dinner at a friend's house. Probably tomorrow night, if I can arrange it, otherwise sometime next week."

"What friend? Is this a weirdo friend, someone I won't like? Does she eat repulsive things like grubs and such? Because I can tell you right here and now, I don't do grubs."

He chuckled his sexy chuckle, the one that makes my innards go all quivery. "I can assure you there will be no grubs. My friend is a man, an author, quite a well-known one in his field. I thought you would like to meet him."

I stopped dead in my tracks, pulling on Alex's hand to get him to turn around. An author? He was going to introduce me to a real author? I was flabbergasted.

"Alex, that's—I don't know what to say. That's very sweet of you. *Very* sweet. I'd love to meet a real writer, especially if he's a friend of yours."

Our gazes met and caught. A familiar flicker of heat started deep within me, making me take a step closer to him. Of its own volition, my hand moved up his bicep to his shoulder as his arms slid around behind me. The heat of the sun was lukewarm compared to his mouth, his lips branding mine with his passion and desire. Just as I opened my mouth beneath his to taste him, a high-pitched titter shattered the moment of intimacy.

"I've never before met a woman who gets such pleasure out of public scenes." Alex shook his head a moment later, after he had pried me off his chest. I shot a glare full of annoyance at the group of girls who stood snickering at us, then turned back to Alex with a grin.

"You're learning, sweetie, you're learning. I have high hopes for your complete and utter downfall into the status of a mere human being."

One sleek chestnut eyebrow rose in question.

"*Very* high hopes," I grinned.

"How did you get through the maze so quickly?" I asked Alex an hour later, when we had returned to Karl's car and were on our way back to Beale Square.

Alex punched a few keys on his laptop, then spun it around to face me. I read the web page that was displayed.

"You rotter! You did cheat! That's not fair—you knew the key to get through the maze!"

He grinned as Karl gave a hoot of laughter. I glared at both of them.

"You didn't say anything about not preparing for the

visit. I like to know what I'm going to see before I get there."

"Anal," I told Karl. He nodded.

"Alix—"

I ignored the warning growl and chatted happily with Karl the rest of the way home. The day had turned out better than I had expected, with Alex and me reaching an understanding (of some sort—I still wasn't exactly sure what it was), and the promise of a meeting with a real author to look forward to. And then there was that night.

I had plans to challenge Alex's win, demanding that he pay me the boon I deserved by being the first non-cheating person through the maze. Once we arrived home, I thanked Karl profusely for taking us out, and made him promise he'd save an upcoming Saturday night so I could repay him by cooking my famous killer lasagna for him. As I trotted up the front steps and past Alex, who was politely holding the stroppy door open for me, I smiled my most enticing smile and tipped my head to the side.

"Could I interest you in dinner tonight, hmm? Just the two of us? I have a delicious-looking recipe for chicken and olives that I'm dying to try out."

Alex was shaking his head even before I finished speaking. "I can't, Alix. I have to finish the report by tomorrow morning. As it is, I will have to work all night on it because I spent the day with you."

I stomped up the stairs until I reached my door, glaring at my purse as I fumbled for my keys, and then lied through my teeth. "It's just dinner. I wasn't planning on seducing you, you know. Even workaholics like you have to eat sometime."

Alex stood so close behind me I could feel his heat.

"I wish I could, but this is an important report. Without it, we can't proceed further on charges against a man running a pornographic Internet studio out of his house."

"Well, I certainly don't get into porn," I said as I opened the door to my flat, stepping aside to avoid the wave of heat from inside, "but I don't see that a delay of an hour or two while I tempt you with olives and chicken is going to hurt anyone."

"It's not that at all—"

I tossed my bag, notebook, and hat onto the side table and turned to face him. "After all, what is porn? It's just a little sex that other people are paying to watch. I agree it's tacky and tasteless, but who is it really hurting?"

He put both hands on my shoulders and leaned forward to kiss my nose. "This particular man uses children."

Children? My stomach roiled at the thought. I blinked at Alex for a moment, then slid my hands behind his neck and kissed a spot just next to one corner of his mouth. "Ick. That's different. You need to get that guy closed down and in jail as soon as possible."

He nodded, and feathered a line of kisses along my jaw.

"OK, I'll excuse you for the evening, but as soon as you're done with this report—"

"I'll knock you up," he finished.

I stared at him, wondering if he knew just what that phrase meant to Americans, then decided he did when the corners of his mouth curled up. He leaned forward for what I knew was going to be a kiss that would turn my legs to jelly. I slipped backwards, out of his arms, placing a finger on his lips as I did so.

"I think not. I want to give you an inducement to finish early."

He kissed my finger, then picked up his satchel and headed up the stairs. I went into my hot little oven of a flat and melted, but it wasn't due to the heat of the day—it was the promise in Alex's eyes that left me feeling singed around the edges.

It was difficult to write after that. Guilt over trying to pry Alex away from his job battled with blatant lust when I thought of all the things I had planned for him, but the guilt won out (it usually does), so I didn't call upstairs the half-dozen times I wanted to.

"He's busy catching pedophiles and child molesters, and all you can think of is how you want to jump his bones," I lectured myself as I fired up my computer and loaded the latest version of my work in progress. "Poor little children abused and scarred for life, all depending on Alex to save them, and your sole thought is to wonder how many positions of the kama sutra you can talk him into."

Erotic visions of Alex naked, with my legs wrapped around his waist as we perfected Kirtibandha (the Knot of Fame) danced through my mind, but I am not one to be swayed by thoughts of a little pleasure when there's work to be done.

"Nose to the grindstone," I told myself, and decided, after some thought, that poor Raoul and Rowena deserved a full-fledged love scene in which to demonstrate just how perfect for each other they were. Several hours later, I was deep in the middle of it when I was distracted by a quiet knock at the door. I padded barefoot over to the door, a surge of hope swelling that it was Alex there to seduce me, but knowing it couldn't be.

I am so often wrong about things.

"Am I disturbing you?" Alex asked with a wicked smile, his eyes dark and full of secrets as he leaned against the door frame holding a bottle of wine in one hand.

I grabbed his free arm and pulled him in, stepping into his arms as easily as if I had done it a million times before. "You always disturb me," I said against his lips, and set my soul a-flying as I kissed him with every ounce of longing I had.

He kissed me right back, which is the beauty of kissing, really. It's not the mere act of pushing your lips up against someone else's lips, it's the sharing, the give-and-take, the wonderful sense of oneness that a truly inspiring kiss generates, and Alex was nothing if not inspired. He started my blood boiling, warming the fires sleeping within me, filling me with languor and excitement at the same time.

"I think we'd better slow down a little," he said once I peeled myself off his lips. I nodded, gasping a little for air, too overwhelmed by his passion to do or say anything that required coherence.

"I've come prepared," he added, turning his wicked smile up a couple of notches. He held up the bottle of wine. "Libation."

"Oh," I said, still a bit befuddled by his kiss. "Wine. Nice."

"And I brought this." A small white and blue plastic package dangled from his fingers. "I thought it looked like it might rain."

"You are truly a wicked man," I smiled. "Which is no

165

doubt why I like you so much, but you needn't have brought your raincoat—I have several myself. I'm sure we can find something that suits you."

I made a valiant attempt to throttle back the leer playing about my lips while Alex opened the wine and I turned up my love-scene-writing music (Burt Bacharach and Dusty Springfield—puts me in the mood every time). My attempt at cool sophistication wasn't successful, but it's hardly my fault. Every time I got a hold of myself, I'd glance over to Alex and see his gaze smoldering at me.

"I feel like I should be saying I will slip into something more comfortable," I giggled, striking a seductive pose by the chaise. "But this truly is the most comfortable thing I have."

Alex set the wine and two glasses down in front of the chaise and snaked an arm around me, pulling me tight to his chest. "I've always found T-shirts to be very sexy, especially when they have Mickey Mouse emblazoned across the front."

Little nibbles around the neckline of my oversized T-shirt followed his words. I sighed and tilted my head to give him better access to all of those spots that loved to be nuzzled. A groan rasped from deep in my throat as he kissed a hot, wet path down my neck to my collarbone.

"Alex," I gasped, clinging to the strength of his arms lest my legs give way from under me. "You're melting me. You make me ache for you. This isn't fair—I want you to ache for me, too."

Abruptly he sat down on the chaise, pulling me down so I sprawled across his lap, still clutching his shoulders. "I do ache for you," he replied, one hand sliding up my thigh as he nipped my bared shoulder. "You're always in my thoughts; no matter what I'm doing, I'm distracted by visions of you lying in my arms like this, warm and sweet and so tempting."

"Did you finish your report?" I asked breathlessly as his hand moved up over my hip. "Can you stay the night?"

"Yes," he answered, bending me backwards against the chaise cushion. Both of his hands slid along my sides and higher, pushing my T-shirt up before them. He bent over me, kissing one breast. "And yes." He kissed the other one. I lifted my arms as he pulled the T-shirt over my head, then I arched beneath his roaming hands.

"Oh, yes," I agreed fervently, mindless as to what it was I had asked him, content to clutch his shoulders as he nibbled around my front side, never touching my nipples, making my breasts swell and long for the heat of his mouth.

"You've haunted my dreams," Alex whispered against the underside of my breasts. Long fingers made lazy circles around them, drawing ever closer to the taut peaks. I wanted to shriek at him to stop toying with me, but oh, it was such sweet torture.

"The silky feel of your skin fills my mind," he murmured, kissing a path around my chest. "The way your curves fit my hands perfectly drives me mad . . ." Both hands slid down my ribs and over the flare of my hips, then underneath to cup my behind. His fingers rubbing the satin of my underwear against my heated flesh was enough to make my toes curl. ". . . the taste of you flavors every breath I take." His mouth and teeth and tongue nibbled their way across my belly, setting my skin afire wherever his lips touched me. It was too much, too much for me, too much pleasure and pain and need and desire, all rolled together into an indescribable maelstrom of emotions that brought tears to my eyes. I grabbed his hair and tugged until his lips were above mine.

Eyes as dark as a forest at midnight held me in their gaze, wanting me, desiring me, making me feel as if I held the future in the two palms that framed his face. "Alex, there is a time and place for foreplay, but right now isn't it. Maybe later, but right now I'm going to go out of my head if I don't have you inside me. Please. *Now!*"

A lovely deep chuckle rumbled out of his chest. "Are you saying you don't want me to do this?"

His hands trailed down my hips and legs, pulling my underwear off and tossing it God knows where. I didn't care, my attention was on the warmth of his hand when it returned to the inside of my thigh, sliding up slowly, going straight to where my need was the greatest. His fingers curled into me, gently probing and seeking until his thumb brushed up against the very center of my desire, making me jump with the waves of pleasure that followed his touch. One finger dipped into me as he leaned forward to reclaim my mouth, leisurely tasting me, teasing my tongue with a seductive, sensual dance.

"No," I gasped once he pulled his mouth away, writhing against the gentle ministrations of his fingers below as they generated an exquisite pleasure that was almost pain. "You can do that, I guess, if you really want to, but it hardly seems fair since you aren't enjoying . . . oh, God, right there, just do that again, please."

He did it again, and again after that. My back arched of its own accord, thrusting my hips forward into his hand, my breasts hard and begging for his touch. "No, Alex, no more—you've got to stop now. I don't want to do this alone!"

"I'm right here," he breathed, his lips sweet on mine as his fingers continued their erotic dance. My belly tensed in anticipation as thousands of little nerves came to life under his touch. "I won't leave you."

"Alex!" I shrieked, clinging to his shoulders, unable to keep my head from thrashing side to side, my body shaking with the nearness of ecstasy.

"Let yourself go, sweetheart," he said just before he kissed me, his fingers thrusting into me, teasing me until I couldn't stand the strain any longer. He took my shout of pleasure into him, took my shudders of joy and held me tight, safe in his arms, and by doing so, took the one thing I never thought I would give.

He took my heart.

Hot tears leaked out of the sides of my closed eyes, tears of joy, tears of happiness, and tears of sorrow because I knew what would happen. I'd been through it before, but this time I knew it would be worse. When he left me, this time my heart wouldn't recover.

"Do you always cry when you find your pleasure?" his soft voice asked, accompanied by softer lips as they kissed away my tears.

"No," I whispered, opening my eyes at last to look into his. They were dark and misted with passion and need. "Only you make me cry."

His head dipped and he gave me another leisurely, thorough kiss. The fires he started within me burst into immediate flame.

"Is that a compliment or a complaint?"

I combed my hands through the silkiness of his hair

and pulled him back to my mouth. "No one has ever moved me the way you do, Alex. No one has ever made me feel the things you make me feel. You are . . ." I let myself drown within the depths of his emerald eyes. "You are everything I have ever wanted."

He gazed back at me, the smile that quirked his lips fading as I stripped away every defense I had and let him see the real me, the Alix only he had touched, the woman who wanted him and who would never again be the same. Emotion so thick it was almost tangible wrapped around us, encasing us in a warm cocoon, bonding us together with silken threads of desire, yearning, need . . . and love.

Warning bells went off in my head, screaming that his expression was too serious. The emotions I was feeling were too much, too fast, too frightening in their intensity. I had to bring us both down to earth and fast, before he—or I—said something that shouldn't be said yet, maybe never would be said.

I pushed on his chest, sliding to the side so he ended up on his back on the chaise with me lying halfway across his chest as I hastily undid his shirt buttons. "You have too many clothes on," I told him.

"I do," he agreed, tugging his soft linen shirttails from his trousers. I peeled off the garment and spent a moment admiring his chest.

"I really like your chest," I said, wondering if he heard the odd little hitch in my throat. "It's a lovely chest, nicely furred without being grossly hairy, and you've got the cutest little nipples I've ever seen on a man."

"The feeling is mutual," he said, reaching for me, but I scooted down the chaise out of his reach.

"Huh-uh, this time it's my turn to make you crazed

with lust and wanting and everything you just gave me. My, my, my, what do we have here?" I put my hand on his fly and felt his hard length jump beneath my hand.

"Alix—"

"O-o-oh, I like it when you growl like that, it's very sexy. I think we'll just leave this little fellow alone for a few moments while I take care of some other business."

"Little?" The word dripped outrage.

I grinned up his long body as I slipped off his shoes. "Sorry, figure of speech. No slurs intended. Are your feet ticklish?"

"Yes, and I would appreciate it if you didn't touch— *ALIX!*"

"Hee hee hee. Sorry, I won't do that again. Well, maybe just on this foot—"

He cursed and jerked his leg back when I slid my fingers along the underside of his foot as I pulled his sock off. I made a mental note to investigate his ticklish spots later as I reached for his belt. He obliged by lifting his hips when I pulled the rest of his clothes off. His stallion wasn't just ready and waiting at the door, it was champing at the bit, pulling at the traces, and waiting to be sprung. So to speak.

"Wow," I breathed, staring at it. "You know, I've never thought this particular part of a man was at all attractive—functional, yes, but attractive? Not really—but I have to say, Alex"—I reached out and wrapped my fingers around the base—"yours is really, really nice."

"Thank you," he groaned, his hands clutching convulsively at the chaise cushions. "It reassures me to know my genitalia meet your exacting standards."

I touched the very tip of him, spreading the bead of moisture around the sensitive underside of the head. He

171

groaned even louder, his eyes closed as I stroked down the long, hard length of him, teasing him with soft little squeezes of his taut balls. I raked my nails softly on them, then up along the underside of his shaft, wrapping my fingers around him, enjoying both the feel of hot, velvety skin sliding over the steel beneath and the soft little moans Alex was making as he thrust his hips upward, pushing himself through my hands. I didn't stop to try and figure out why I was gaining so much pleasure by merely touching him, I just was, and since the look on his face bordered on blissful, I figured I was making him a happy camper as well.

"Let's see how you like this," I crooned as I leaned forward and licked a circle around one dark brown nipple that poked oh, so insouciantly up from the surrounding soft brown hairs. I gave his balls a friendly little squeeze when I bit down gently on his nipple, then giggled at his shout of surprise. His chest was heaving as he tried to catch his breath, a light sheen of sweat adding to the erotic sight of his body bucking beneath my hands. It was a heady moment, full of the power and the knowledge of generations of women, but Alex was yelling at me to stop before he lost control, so I reluctantly released my grip and instead kissed a line along his jaw.

"Alix," he gasped, his body as taut as a bowstring.

"Yes, my pet?"

"You were right. There is a time for foreplay, and this isn't it."

I gave a little scream as he lunged forward at the last couple of words, grabbing me around the waist and hauling me over the top of him. I squirmed off him, explaining, "Raincoats! I've got special raincoats my sister gave me. Hold on a minute, you'll like this!"

The box of condoms had been moved over to a small wicker end table next to the window. I grabbed them and, shaking the box at Alex, did a few bossa nova steps back to where he lay sprawled on the chaise. "We have cherry and banana and mint and grape—take your pick!"

His gorgeous, lust-muddled eyes narrowed as I placed the condoms on his chest and leaned down to nip his chin. "What are you talking about?"

I smiled brightly and prodded the box toward him. "Raincoats! Flavored condoms! You just tell me what flavor you want, and we'll get you all gussied up and ready to play."

He peered down suspiciously. "Your sister gave these to you?"

"Yep. Cait's a firm believer in everyone having raincoats. These are special ones. You like grape?"

One chestnut eyebrow arched as I plucked the protection from his chest. "I don't believe my preference is the deciding factor, Alix. There's no physical way I can . . . erm . . . appreciate its . . . uh . . . flavor."

I rooted around in the container, blinked a couple of times as I acknowledged the truth in his statement, then found what I was looking for and flourished a tiny gold and purple packet. "Grape! No, it's mine." I pulled my hand back when he tried to grab for it. "I get to put it on you. It's erotic that way. I read that in a magazine."

"Alix, if you do anything else erotic to me, I won't be needing a condom," he warned.

I smiled. "It's OK, I'll be careful. I don't want you grabbing the brass ring before the carousel has stopped. Let's just see if this has any instructions."

"Instructions?"

My smile deepened. "Well, you never know. I might

have to lick something to enhance the grapeness."

Alex groaned and closed his eyes, his hands fisted next to his hips. "Just put the bloody thing on me before I expire."

"OK. Um . . ." I opened the package and pulled out the lavender condom. It smelled grapey, but something the label said made me curious. I consulted the directions, then eyed Alex, trying to measure that part of him with my eyes, wondering where Stephanie would keep a ruler.

"What the devil are you doing?"

I glanced back at where he was frowning at me. "How big are you?"

"What?"

"How big are you? You know, how long?"

Alex stared at me in open-mouthed surprise. "Do I take it you suddenly don't like what you see?"

I gave him a couple of strokes just to reassure him that I was more than happy with his meat and two veg. "On the contrary, I think you're a little on the oofy side, but I'm sure everything will work out just fine."

"Oofy?"

"Big."

"Ah. Then why do you want to know—"

I held the box out to him and pointed to the big red letters emblazoned there. "This says the raincoats are extra-extra long. They call it 'Gladiator-length, for the barbarian in your life.' I was just wondering if you are gladiator material."

"Oh, for Christ's sake, Alix, just—"

"OK, OK." I pushed him back down from where he was trying to get up and turned around to apply the grape condom to the appropriate body part. "No need to get up in arms, I'll put it on you."

He growled low in his chest.

"Um . . . hang on, there seems to be . . . blast, I think it's stuck . . . no, wait, there it goes. I guess it sat in the sun too long, it's kinda sticky, but"—I looked up with a reassuring smile—"really, really grapey. Oh, hell."

Alex sighed, his eyes closed, his face resigned. "It broke?"

I pursed my lips and looked at his purple-covered manly bits. "Um . . . no. Evidently you're not gladiator-length. There's a bit extra left over, but it doesn't matter, I'll just leave it rolled up there." I patted the extra rolled-up bit of condom firmly into place at the base of his penis, and looked up and gave him another smile. "All done. So, you ready to rumble?"

One eye opened and looked at me.

"Oh, come on, Alex, don't look so cranky. I know that was a bit of a bother, but now you're all suited up and we can get down to business."

He growled again, but hauled me over his chest, swinging around until I was underneath him. To tell the truth, I was a bit relieved that the condom interlude had shattered the strangely charged, emotional moment that had overtaken us earlier. If I wasn't sure before, I was now. I was falling in love with Alex, and I was fairly certain he could see the depth of my feelings mirrored in my eyes, but it wasn't something I wanted to talk about. I needed some time to get a grip on my emotions before I faced the issues of love, separation, and the resulting heartbreak.

The breather had done much to lighten Alex's mood as well. He was positively playful as he nibbled and nipped me, teaching me just how sensitive the skin at the back of my knees was, moving quickly to assault my belly with tongue and teeth, kindling the fires of desire until I swore I was going to spontaneously combust. I did my best to drive him into the same inferno that consumed me, raking my nails up and down, nipping and kissing him, making him pant and groan his pleasure at my touch.

"Enough!" I cried, desperate to feel all of him. Curving my hands around his wonderfully smooth behind, I begged, "Alex, stop teasing me, stop tormenting me. I'm going to go up in flames if I don't have you inside of me. Now, Alex, please, now!"

He made a soft, seductive noise deep in his chest that made me wild with need. I wrapped my legs around his and flexed my fingers into his behind as he pushed slowly into me. He was big and hard and hot and fit oh, so perfectly. He sank into me, filling every crevice, burrowing deeper, making room for himself within my core, my center, the part of me that needed him most. All of those marvelous little muscles that lay dormant down there just waiting for this moment suddenly went to work, gripping him, tightening and releasing, flexing around him as he moved even farther into me. I tossed my head back and groaned with the soul-deep satisfaction of joining with him.

"Are you all right, sweetheart? I'm not hurting you?"

"No," I panted, pulling my knees up higher to take him in deeper. If he pushed in just a little more, I was sure he would touch my heart and our bonding would be complete.

"Can you take more?"

"Yes, oh, yes, Alex, more." The inevitable tears started

behind my eyes, tears of utter and complete joy as he filled me to completion, then began rocking his hips in a rhythm so instinctive it beat in my blood, demanding an answering rhythm.

"Open your eyes, love."

My hips thrust up at him as he increased his movements, no longer gentle and tentative, now demanding as he pounded into me, the age-old dance holding us firmly in its thrall, one being, one body, one soul. I opened my eyes.

Green so pure it could outshine the finest emeralds blazed back at me as he thrust into me, his breath as ragged as mine, his back slick with sweat. I bit his shoulder, crying wordless words of wanting, praying I could hold out until he was ready to find nirvana.

"Alex, please, I don't think I can wait . . ." The words died in my throat as his hoarse shout of completion thrummed deep in my blood.

"Now, Alix, now. Come with me now, love."

The acid, coppery taste of his blood was on my tongue as I bit his shoulder again, unable to speak, able only to feel as the wave of rapture broke over us, carrying us higher and higher, until Alex yelled his exultation against my neck as we were transported beyond elation into euphoria.

I drifted lazily back down to earth, conscious of his weight on me but comfortable bearing it, as if I had been made solely for that purpose. I stroked his back, reveling in the rasping of his breath next to my ear, proof that he was as affected as I. Common sense went out the window as I lay there, feeling him still deep within me, tasting him, smelling that wonderful spicy scent that was Alex mingled with the baser, more earthy scent of our lovemaking, knowing in my heart of hearts that parting with this man would mean my destruction. I turned my face away from that knowledge, determined only to hold on to the present and not worry about the future.

Alex stirred, then levered himself up on one elbow and gave me a look of profound masculine satisfaction before he hauled me on top of him as he rolled onto his back.

"Christ," he breathed, his eyes closed, a smile curving those fabulous lips.

"Not quite, but I'd say you're damned close to godhood."

"Mmm." He pulled me closer. We lay like that for some time, my legs entwined with his, our breathing perfectly synchronized. I was halfway asleep when he slid out from under me.

"Come to bed?" I asked, getting up and stretching. I went over to fluff up the pillows on the daybed.

Alex sat on the chaise with his back to me, hunched over and muttering to himself.

"Alex? Are you OK?" I stood clutching a pillow to my chest, worried about this reaction to our lovemaking. I've had guys tell me I wasn't any good at putting out, but I've never actually made one ill as a result. "Alex?"

"What's in those bloody condoms?"

"Huh? The condoms? What do you mean, what's in them?" I dropped the pillow and walked over to face him.

He looked up with a "what now?" expression etched on his handsome face. "The damn thing is stuck. I can't get it off."

"Stuck? No, it's just latex and a little flavoring, it can't be stuck. Move your hands and let me try."

"I know how to get a condom off—the damn thing is stuck to me!"

I put my hands on my hips and glared down at him. "That's impossible. Condoms do not get stuck!"

As it turns out, they do, especially if they've been treated with a flavored coating, and even more so when they sit in the sun, melting the coating and turning it into a pretty powerful adhesive.

I threw away the condoms after that. Alex's bellows of outrage as I ripped the sticky part of the condom from where it had bonded to his pubic hair just weren't at all conducive to romance.

Chapter Nine

Lady Rowena lay in her lover's arms, sated, happy, fulfilled in every womanly way. She turned her head and nuzzled the broad expanse of masculine chest that lay under her cheek.

"Raoul, my beloved, you are not still pouting over that little accident with Doctor Beesom's Eternal Balm of Aphrodite and my best silk stockings, are you? I have apologized over the mishap—who knew the balm would turn into a substance resembling glue if left near the fire too long?—and promise you I will dispose of the bottle as soon as possible."

Lord Raoul grunted and absentmindedly rubbed at the reddened shilling-size bare spot on his groin. "I'll look a damned fool if my short and curlies don't grow back!"

Rowena patted the manly curls that surrounded the unfortunate bare spot, and sighed again. "At least we saved my stocking. Silk is so very expensive these days."

* * *

I glanced up from my manuscript. "That's the end of chapter twenty-eight. I'm almost to the end of the story. What do you think? Is it a best-seller?"

Jacquie, the receptionist at Maureen Tully's office, gave me a look of profound indifference. I didn't know if it was me, my writing, or the fact that she was working on a Sunday. "I don't read that sort of book, Miss Freemar, so I couldn't say."

"Really? Too bad. What sort of books do you read?"

Staccato noise burst from her keyboard, then paused just long enough for her to favor me with another disapproving glance.

"I don't read any books, Miss Freemar. Now if you'll excuse me, I have work to do."

"You mean you work for a literary agency and you don't even read the stuff your boss sells?"

She didn't deign to reply.

"Huh. I would have figured you'd have people hitting you up all over the place to try and get in good with Maureen by sending you stories to read. Well, OK, so you don't read much—you can still tell me if you thought the love scene I just read you was effective. How did it rate on your personal tinglemeter?"

She stopped typing and stared at me. "My what?"

"Your tinglemeter. You know, did it make you feel tingly all over? Was it sexy? Did it make you feel all hot and flushed and wanton? Are you ready to jump the nearest thing in trousers?"

"Miss Freemar!"

"Sorry, didn't mean to step over the line, but I'm desperate for love scene feedback. I just have my own response to go on, you see, since the only people I know in London are either men, lesbian, or not given to smut, so it would mean a lot to me if you could tell me if my love scene turned your crank or not."

Her eyebrows collected into a frown as she turned back to her work with a decided sniff. "I do not answer such personal inquiries by clients."

I sighed and moved over to the chair she had indicated when I arrived, absently poking through the stack of magazines on the table. I flipped through an old copy of *Writer's Life*, stifling an inner sigh. I'd given it my best shot, but I was simply going to have to hand over the almost-completed manuscript to Maureen and hope the love scenes were tingly without being too blatant.

"Eight point five."

"Hmm?" I glanced over to where Jacquie was busily tapping away on her keyboard.

"That's how I would rate the scene. On a scale of ten, it was an eight point five."

A victorious smile crept across my face. "Thank you, that's nice to know." Eight point five, that had to be a good sign! Of course, it wasn't a perfect ten . . . and damn it, it should be! I had written my heart into that love scene, attributing to Rowena everything I had felt with Alex, and our evening had certainly been a ten—if not more. "Um . . . if you don't mind my asking . . . what would have made it a ten?"

Tackidy tickedy tackidy went the keys. After a minute and a half, she spoke.

"If Lord Raoul had tied Rowena to the bed, it would have been a ten." She gave a little shiver and sighed heavily.

"Ah. I believe I see what you mean." Bondage? Bondage would have made that scene perfect? I thought back to the wonderful second act Alex and I had performed in the comfort of Stephanie's daybed, and tried to envision the same events with me tied down. I made a face. It just didn't appeal to me, but if it were *Alex* whose hands were tied to the brass railing of the daybed . . .

"How about if Lord Raoul were tied and Lady Rowena had her way with him? Would that be a ten?"

"No," Jacquie said abruptly, pursing her lips and typing away industriously. I turned back to the table of magazines when she added an afterthought. "That would be a fifteen."

I smiled. We were in agreement at last.

"Good morning, Maureen. It's nice to see you again. I've brought my manuscript as you reques—"

"Morning. Sit. I'll be with you in a moment."

"—ted." I narrowed my eyes and mentally rolled up my sleeves as she talked quickly and without stopping into the phone, telling someone named Cerise that she had to be patient, that patience was almost as important in this business as talent, and that she (Maureen) had promised she would sell her (Cerise's) story, and she (Maureen) would if she (Cerise) would stop calling her every week to find out what was happening.

Polite conversation would obviously be wasted on my busy agent, so I decided to pare down my own comments to the bare minimum. Two could play the telegraphic talk game.

"Synopsis?"

"Huh?" I looked up from where I was folding and refolding one corner of the cover sheet. "Oh, yes, the synopsis. I have it here. I wasn't quite sure what you wanted, so I threw a bit of everyth—"

"I have someone who might be interested in your book," Maureen interrupted, lighting one of the inevitable cigarettes while she held out her hand for my manuscript.

I stared at her, unsure I'd heard her correctly until her open hand started fluttering at me.

"Oh, sorry, here." I put both the manuscript and the synopsis in her hand, backing away quickly so as to keep from breathing in any of the smoke. "I'm a bit confused—you say you have someone who might be interested in my story?"

She nodded and waved away the blue haze of smoke as she leaned back to read my synopsis. "That's what I said. He's a new publisher, looking for something different and cutting edge. Beyond *Bridget Jones*. I told him you were perfect."

"But . . . but . . ."

Her light blue eyes flickered toward me and pinned me back in my chair. "You said you were willing to work, to take chances. Are you backing out now?"

I sat up straight and tried to look cutting edge and different. "No, of course not, I'm just confused how a publisher who hasn't even seen my work can be interest—"

"I know what he likes. He'll like this." She tapped on the manuscript, brushing away a blob of cigarette ash.

"But it's historical. I haven't read it, but I thought *Bridget Jones* and those sorts of books were contempor—"

"Voice."

"—ary. Ah . . . voice?"

She nodded. "It's all in the voice. Bryan is looking for a strong, sassy voice. That's what you have."

I gave her a watery smile. I wasn't sure it was good to be sassy; my mother always used that word as an insult rather than a compliment. "Oh, OK. I'm sure you know best. So, you'll edit what I just brought you and wait until I finish the last few chapters before sending it to this publisher?"

"Three chapters."

The telegraph talk was giving me a headache. "What about them?"

"I'll edit the first three chapters and we'll sell it as a proposal."

My head felt like it was filled with molasses. I just couldn't keep up with her jumps in logic. "I read in a writer's magazine that new authors always had to finish a book before they could find either an agent or a pub—"

"I signed you, didn't I?"

"—lisher." Well, she had a point there. I never would have thought I could find an agent without having a completed manuscript, but I did. And not just an agent, one who also ran an editing service. Surely the odds against that were tremendous. Maybe luck was on my side this time.

"That's true, but publishers—"

"Do you have faith in me?"

That stopped me cold. "Well . . . that is, of course you . . . it's not that I—"

"Do you have faith in me?" Those pale blue eyes were almost frosty in their regard. I swallowed back my objections and nodded.

"Yes, I do."

"Good." She gave me a curt nod and ground out her cigarette. "You do your job and let me do mine. I wouldn't be here working on a Sunday if my clients didn't have faith in me. I'll have the edited three chapters ready for you in two days. Make an appointment with Jacquie to come in then, and I'll discuss them with you."

"OK." I gathered up my things and headed for her door, pausing as I worried over what she had said. "Maureen, I know you know your job and all, but are you sure you can sell my entire book off of just three chapters?"

"You have to have faith," she said, tossing my manuscript onto a towering stack of paper on the left side of her desk. It looked like those other papers were manuscripts as well, since they were all neatly rubber banded. If she had all of those to read and edit, how would she ever find time to get to mine, let alone give it the attention she said was needed?

"Faith," I said, experiencing a decided lack of that particular sentiment. I let Jacquie set up another appointment for me, and wandered out of the dark, cool office into the street feeling a strange combination of hopelessness and bemusement.

"It's her job to worry, let it go," Bert said to me an hour later when I stood on the landing and recounted my experience. She and Ray were going out for the day, she told me, out boating on the Thames with some friends.

"I suppose you're right," I said with a rueful smile. "I just can't help but worry a little, though. It is my whole entire life we're talking about!"

Bert laughed as she adjusted a stylish straw hat and called over her shoulder for Ray to hurry. "You need to stop working so hard, Alix. What are your plans for the day?"

I blushed a little as I recalled asking Alex that very same thing earlier in the morning, when I lay sweaty and exhausted across his heaving chest. "I thought I would go see Westminster Abbey and maybe St. Paul's."

"I'm sure you'll enjoy them," Bert said with a knowing smile. "Will you be going with anyone in particular?"

"Coyness does not become you, Bert." She giggled. I snickered with her. "If you're asking how things are going with Alex"—she nodded and patted my hand as Ray marched out of the flat with her arms full of a red plastic cooler and two bulging cloth carrying bags—"you can rest assured that all is well there. Alex and I have resolved our differences."

"Knew that," Ray said, rolling her eyes as she pushed past a widely grinning Bert to stomp down the stairs. "Your bed squeaks."

"Huh?" I glanced between the two women for a few moments, then looked upstairs. My flat was just above theirs. "Oh, good Lord! Don't tell me you heard us—oh, hell!"

Bert laughed and patted me on the arm one last time as she followed after Ray. "Don't let it bother you, Alix. We were pleased to know that you and Alex turned out to be compatible after all."

"Oh, Lord," I moaned softly to myself, closing my eyes as I made a mental promise to hunt down a bottle of household oil so I could lubricate the daybed's springs.

"Even if the noise from your morning bout of compatibility woke us up," Bert continued.

"Oh, Lord!" I moaned louder. I'd have to move the bed to the other side of the flat.

Bert's voice echoed slightly as it wafted up the stairwell from the floor below. "The first bout, that is. I didn't hear the second one since I was in the shower then, but Ray says it sounded very . . . vigorous."

"Aaaaaaah!" I screamed in embarrassment, covering my face with my hands and wondering how I could ever look either woman in the eye again.

"Have a lovely day," Bert called up as she continued her descent.

"Gah!" I yelled down at her, and trod slowly up the stairs, praying that no one else in the house had heard Alex and me being compatible.

I paused for a moment at my floor, then climbed the next flight. Alex had said he had to go in to work that morning to deliver his report, but he hoped to be home by lunchtime. It was still morning, but I thought I'd see if he had made it back earlier than he expected.

I tapped at his door, but there was no answer.

"Poop," I told it, then decided I'd go move the bed by myself.

"Alexander? Oh, it's you, Alix. How lovely you look this morning. Your dress is just the shade of Alexander's eyes when he's aroused. Do you have a moment? I'd like to ask your opinion about a wall treatment."

I looked down at my sleeveless dress. She was right about the color, damn her! "Morning, Isabella. Sorry if my knocking disturbed you, I was just checking to see if Alex was home yet."

"You didn't disturb me at all, dear." Isabella held her door open and waved me in. I followed obediently as she led me down the little hallway to a huge room that opened at the end. "What do you think of the peach? Is it too pink? Too boudoir?"

I stood in the doorway of the room and blatantly gawked. It was Isabella's bedroom, a study in oatmeal and taupe and teal, but what made me stand and stare like a rube was the bed. It was huge, shaped like a scal-

188

loped clamshell, framed with teal curtains that formed a huge bow above a gilded miniature replica of a boat's prow proudly riding a teal wave.

"That's some bed," I said, wondering if she ever cracked her head on the odd headboard. "I don't think I've ever seen a clamshell bed outside of the movies."

Isabella turned from where she was contemplating two chairs holding a variety of wall-treatment samples. "The bed? Oh, yes, Anton gave that to me. He fancied himself Poseidon. He was Greek."

"Ah. Anton was your . . . husband?"

Isabella tittered a light, twinkling little laugh that I could never achieve if I tried for a hundred years. "I've never been married, Alix. Anton was my lover."

"Oh, of course, how stupid of me. He was your lover. No husband. Sorry." How many lovers had she had? There were Alex and Karl that I knew about . . . not that I wanted to think about Alex with Isabella, especially at that moment when I could still feel the fires that his hands and mouth had started earlier that morning. I eyed her, trying to determine how old she was. She certainly didn't look like the type of woman who had lots and lots of lovers, not with that cool, elegant, silver beauty, but I knew her type. Men dropped at her feet, giving her the pick of the litter while the rest of us made do with her rejects.

"Cheeto-rubbers," I muttered.

"What was that?"

"Nothing. You were saying?"

"You have nothing to apologize for regarding Anton," she smiled, and picked up one of the treatments, running her fingers over a peach and ivory floral brocade wall covering. "He was my favorite lover. He was a very good friend as well, very intelligent. He loved to talk, and appreciated anyone who would listen to his tales of growing up in Greece." A fond smile curved her lips as she glanced around the room. "He left me this house, you know."

I blinked a couple of times, surprised, but touched by the obvious affection in her voice. She must have loved him very much to speak so fondly of him still. I envisioned an elderly rich Greek gentleman, obsessed with Isabella's silvery, untouchable beauty, entranced by her calm air of interest. She had obviously meant a lot to him, too, if he'd remembered her in his will. "No, I didn't know. That was very sweet of him to remember you like that. Has he been gone for many years?"

She waved a hand and held out a treatment board. I took it, not even glancing at the wallpaper and paint samples it held. "Six years. I miss him still."

Tears welled up at the tragic story of lovers parted by death. "Isabella, that's so sad." I set the treatment board down and put a comforting arm around her shoulders. "I can remember how devastated I was when my grandfather died. He was everything to me—the one person who understood me, and didn't expect me to be anything but myself. I know your relationship with Anton wasn't the same, but I'm sure you grieve for his loss just as I grieve for my grandfather."

Isabella cocked her head, her silvery-blond hair swinging gracefully to the side. Bright blue eyes looked steadily at me. "Anton isn't elderly, nor is he dead."

I stepped back, confused. "Oh. I thought . . ."

She shook her head, her shoulders giving a little shrug. "He tired of me eventually, and left me for another mistress. But he was extremely generous in giving me this house—our arrangement called only for a flat."

Mistress? Arrangement? Huh?

"I don't think I understand, Isabella . . ."

She smiled then, a bright smile that had a bit of pity mixed into it. "It's very simple, dear. Before Anton left me this house, I was a mistress."

I nodded. "Yes, you said Anton was your . . . er . . . lover."

Her hair swung as she shook her head. "I wasn't just Anton's lover—I was a professional mistress. I maintained relationships with gentlemen of means who wished to keep an exclusive sexual partner."

My mouth dropped open. She was a mistress? A real mistress, the kind I read about in historical romances. "A Cyprian? You were a lightskirt?"

"I am unfamiliar with those terms, but yes, I believe you're on the right track at last. It was quite a lucrative business. I only accepted employment by very . . . shall we say *discerning* gentlemen?"

I just bet they were! But if she was a professional, that meant . . .

"Alex!"

She took the treatment board from me and handed me another. I glanced at it. The colors were red and yellow. "Ick."

"Alexander moved in after Anton had seen to my financial security. Our relationship was one of pleasure, not business."

The hairs on the back of my neck started to rise at her words. Alex's pleasure with Isabella was something I really didn't want to contemplate.

"If you recall, I told you that relationship was over a few years ago."

191

"Two," I ground out.

"Yes, two years. What do you think of the peach?"

I looked at the sample she held out. "It looks trollopy."

She pursed her lips as she studied it. "I thought it looked warm. I'm redecorating the bedroom—oatmeal and taupe are passé—and I thought something warmer might be nice for a change. Trollopy?"

"Tart-like. Sluttish. Wanton."

One silver eyebrow raised at my words. "Dear, you're not upset because I was forthcoming about my relationship with Alexander, are you?"

"*Former* relationship, and the answer is no, I'm not upset."

"Good. You have no need to be, you know. You've quite captured his heart in a way I never did."

That made me feel a bit better. I let my hackles deruffle. "Oh?"

Her eyes smiled at me. Dammit, she was enjoying toying with me! "Yes, indeed. He would never have spent a day with me when he had work to do. You must present him with quite a dilemma, his desire to be with you warring with his need to fulfill his duties at the Yard."

I hadn't thought of it like that. It made me feel small and petty for teasing Alex and yelling at him about being a workaholic.

"Are you sure about the peach?"

"Hmm?" I looked at the color samples Isabella held out. "Oh, that. Yes, I'm sorry, it looks like something out of one of the tackier French bordellos. Why not go with the Warwick blue and champagne combination? If you'll excuse me, I have to be running. I need to . . . ah . . . leave someone a note."

"Alix?"

I paused at the door to her bedroom and looked back.

"Are you in love with him yet?"

"Isabella, you have a penchant for making my mouth drop open with surprise," I said, having suited action to words. "I never know what you're going to say next."

She smiled a warm smile that made her suddenly look very human. "Oddly enough, I've heard the same thing said about you recently. Are you in love with him?"

"Honestly, I thought you Brits were supposed to be so circumspect and unwilling to bring up personal topics with people you don't know really well." I waved and started down her hallway.

Her lilting tones followed after me. "You should tell him, Alix. He needs to be loved. You're not a cruel woman; don't keep him guessing."

"I'm not going to stand here discussing this with you," I said as I opened her front door, enjoying the silvery tones of her door chimes. They sounded just like her laughter. "And besides, too many things can go wrong once you start talking about stuff like that."

She appeared at the end of the hallway, the blue and champagne board in hand. "Alexander means a great deal to me, Alix. I count him as one of my dearest friends, and I don't want to see him hurt. All I ask is that you tell him how you feel about him. Perhaps it would be easier for you if you admitted your feelings to a neutral and trusted friend."

Neutral? Isabella? I snorted. "Oh for heaven's sake— you're not going to let go of this until I tell you what you want to hear, are you?"

She made a suggestive little moue. I gave in. If I didn't, she'd probably follow me down to my flat, nagging me all the way. I put both hands on my hips and glared down the corridor at her.

"Fine, you want to know everything? I'll tell you everything. Yes, I'm madly in love with him. I love him so much it hurts. I can't stop thinking about him. I'm breathless with wonder when I remember our time together." Isabella clapped her hand over her mouth, but I ignored her attempt to contain her laughter and continued. She wanted to hear it, she was going to get it all. "He fills me with happiness and warmth and hope and all the other things that have been missing my whole, entire miserable life. He is irritating and aggravating and is without a doubt the perfect man for me, and it's going to kill me when he dumps me. Happy now? Good. I'll be on my way."

I spun around, slamming the door behind me, and ran smack into a big, blocky, suit-wearing shape.

"Oh, Lord, this is all I need," I said, hanging my head and banging it gently on the suit's chest.

"Good morning," the suit said to me. "Having a little chat with Isabella?"

I must have turned twelve shades of red. He heard everything, *everything*. I'd just admitted everything I had intended to keep locked away. There was nothing left now. I took a deep breath.

"Why, Alex, how nice to see you again. Home so early? Yes, indeed, Isabella and I were just having a chat about our favorite movie actors. I was telling her how much I admired Alan Rickman, the actor." I peeked up at him through my eyelashes. "I have a little crush on him, you see."

His eyes glittered back wickedly at me. He wasn't fooled. "I do see."

I sighed. It was hopeless. "Yeah, I thought somehow you would. Are you busy?"

He shook his head and opened the door to his flat. I walked in ahead of him, determined to smooth over the mess I had just made of our tenuous relationship, but the words froze on my tongue when I glanced over at the wall that ran at a right angle to his couch. When I had been in his living room before, there were floor-to-ceiling shuttered doors closed across the wall, sheltering what I had assumed was a closet. I was wrong. The entire wall was devoted to electronics.

"Good Lord, the guys on Tottenham Court Road must love you! The one with the most toys wins, eh?"

Alex glanced over at his wall o' computers. "Something like that."

I pulled out a comfy leather computer chair and sat down before one of the two monitors. "Let's see, you have a Mac, a PC, a scanner, a camcorder, something I don't recognize, something else I don't recognize . . ."

Alex tossed a stack of papers on top of a small black box with lots of knobs and wires poking out of it. "The small round one is a webcam. The black box on the right is a device you have no need to see. I think you'll be more comfortable on the couch, Alix."

I ignored his attempt to oust me from his computer chair and unblanked his screen saver to see what it was he did to nail those nasty child-porn guys. "Alexander!"

"Christ, I thought I'd—Alix, go sit on the couch."

I slapped his hand away from the mouse and clung to the chair, refusing to be hustled out of the way. "Those have got to be fake, you know that, don't you? No woman could grow boobs like that naturally. Jeezumcrow, what's she's got in her hand? Is that what I think it is?"

Alex wrestled the mouse away from me and closed the browser screen. I cocked an eyebrow at him. "You know, that dull red flush gives you a healthy outdoorsy glow, the kind of glow a man who spends his days sitting in front of a monitor staring at a naked woman with jugs the size of watermelons who is holding a cucumber in a suggestive manner and leering at the camera just doesn't naturally come by. What's on this computer—holy cow! Now, that's my kinda man! Geez, what is he, half horse or something?"

Alex swore under his breath as he flipped the power switch somewhere on the wall. Both of the computers went black. "Son of a . . . that is part of a case we've recently undertaken on a suspected online pornography studio."

"Huh. I thought you only worked with pedophiles? I can see that you want to get kiddy porn shut down, that's important, but why would you guys be spending time and money going after a woman and her trained cucumber? She doesn't seem to me to be hurting anyone."

He pinned me back with a glittering emerald-eyed glare. "Pornography in any form is degrading, reprehensible, and an abomination to anyone who has made love to someone they have strong feelings for."

Oops. Guess he had strong feelings on the subject. I suppose, given the fact that he dedicated his life to eradicating perverts who liked little kids, that wasn't surprising. Still, I'd yet to meet a man who didn't enjoy looking at pictures of naked women. I waved my hand at the now black monitors. "So you don't get even a tiny bit turned on by some of the stuff you see?"

He looked at me as if I were the spawn of Satan. "No, no," I hastened to correct, "not the kiddy stuff, the adult pictures. I thought men got their jollies from looking at women with big boobs and guys who were . . . well . . . getting it on with them."

"I don't find it the least bit exciting, no." It's a wonder he could speak, his jaw was so tight. He pulled me out of the chair and up to his chest.

I tickled his Adam's apple. "You say that like you're a prude, but you, Detective Inspector Manly Thighs, are anything but chaste."

His lips feathered across mine, sending little sparks of heat out to all corners of my body. Oh, what he could do with just a pair of lips!

"What we have together is not obscene or degrading, sweetheart. What we have is an honest expression of something more than mere lust."

"Mmm," I teased, allowing desire to ripple through me, building stronger and stronger with each warm touch of those delicious lips. "Seems to me something doesn't quite add up right. You spend your day looking at porn . . ."

He narrowed those gorgeous eyes at me. I smiled against his mouth.

"And then you and I . . . well, you know what we do."

"Is there a point to this?" he asked as he grabbed my hips and pulled me tight against him. Those sparks of heat he generated turned into a roaring blaze.

"Yup. My point is that you can have your cake and"—I fluttered my lashes at him—"eat it, too."

"It's my job, Alix, nothing more," he growled as he gave me one last feather-light kiss, then waved me toward the couch, pulling his suit jacket off and tugging on his tie as he headed toward the other end of the flat.

"Tough job, eh, sport?" I followed him into his bedroom, plopping myself on his bed and giving it a test bounce or two. It didn't squeak. I held up a hand when he started to argue. "You don't have to say it, Alex, I understand. It is your job to close those people down. I saw the police reports sitting on your scanner; I'm just teasing you a little. It's good for you. It'll loosen you up a bit."

He peeled off his shirt. My jaw dropped at the sight of that glorious chest.

"Is that so?" He kicked off his shoes. My eyes followed his hand inch by slow inch as he unzipped his zipper. "I had something else in mind that would loosen me up."

I swallowed a couple of times so I wouldn't drool. "Hooo, baby, *do* you!"

"I'm hot." *That* was the understatement of the year! I was feeling a bit parched myself. "I'm going to take a shower. Perhaps you would care to continue the discussion in there?"

He inclined his head toward the bathroom. I almost ripped my dress trying to get it off while removing my shoes, bra, and underwear, all the while moving toward the bathroom.

"Well, you could help," I snapped as I stood tangled up in my dress, the hook from my bra caught in my hair, hopping on one foot and trying to shake my underwear off from where it had snagged on my sandal buckle. "You don't just have to stand there laughing at me."

Alex doubled over and whooped as I shuffled toward him. I had adopted a hunched-over, Quasimodo sort of gait due to my hasty attempts to extricate myself from my garments.

"You're just getting back at me over that little raincoat episode, aren't you?" I tried to kick my feet free of underwear and dress as I manipulated my bra hook one-handed, finally releasing it, but pulling a clump of hair out in the process. "Ow! Damn! See what you did? Are you happy now? Now I've got a bald spot."

Alex straightened up and gestured toward his groin. "It matches mine."

"Hrmph. No one but me will see yours. At least," I glared at him as he unbuckled my sandal and slid his hand up my calf, "no one but me had better see your bald spot!"

His hands continued to trace a path up my legs, his lips following, kissing higher and higher until both hands were on my head, rubbing the tender spot, while his lips were fluttering across mine, teasing me, igniting me, making me burn for him. I sent my own hands out on an exploratory mission, enjoying his groan of pleasure when I dug my fingers into his wonderful behind, pulling him closer to me, rubbing myself across the hardness of his arousal.

Somehow, without my being aware of moving, I was in the bathroom and he was turning on the water.

"Um . . . Alex . . . shouldn't we be in the bedroom? Your bed has to be more comfortable than the floor."

"Later," he mumbled against the ticklish spot at the nape of my neck, his hands stroking down my back, over my behind, and up my sides to make my breasts ache with desire. His head dipped as he tasted first one, then the other nipple. I dug one hand into his shoulder as I arched my back so he could have better access, and cupped his balls with the other hand, squeezing and tugging with the gentle pressure I had found drove him wild.

"Alex, I really think the bedroom is a better choice than a cold bathroom floor."

"We're not going to be on the floor," he said, his breath hot against my breastbone as he pushed me into the shower. "Haven't you ever made love in a shower?"

The water was lukewarm, body temperature, not hot but not cold. He backed me up against the wall of the shower, covering me with his wonderful heat, the hairs on his chest tickling my breasts until we were both wet.

"Um . . . not really. I guess the closest I came to sex in a shower was when a boyfriend made a banana split out of me."

Alex paused in the act of soaping up a washcloth and raised one adorable eyebrow.

"You know, with whipped cream and chocolate sauce and cherries. It was really messy, but this . . . are you sure about this? It's kinda different, isn't it? You're not going to suddenly turn all kinky on me, are you? Because if you are, I think you should know I'm a white bread kind of girl when it comes to sex."

He leered and rubbed his soapy hands up my belly to my breasts, soaping my entire front. "You've told me to loosen my control, sweetheart. This is as loose as I'm going to get."

His hands slid down my back, moving like hot silk over my skin as he made sure every bit of me was lathered up. The feeling of his hands running up my legs almost made my knees buckle, especially since I knew where those hands were headed. Inside me, deep inside me, the fire he started spread its heat, warming me, readying me to receive his most intimate touch. His fingers spread and swirled an intricate serpentine path up my thighs, pausing once to re-soap before continuing their dance up to my center.

"Open your legs for me, love," he whispered, his voice hoarse with desire. I moved enough to give him better access, and gasped when his fingers slid along me, teasing me, parting me and dipping inside to feel the heat he was generating.

"Christ, you're hot," he moaned against my neck, his breathing almost as ragged as my own. I wanted to touch him as well, to do the things he was doing to me, to make him wild and uninhibited, but I could do nothing more than cling to his arms, unable to speak when his fingers danced their magic dance, building my desire and pleasure until I thought I was going to scream from the sheer joy of it.

"Alex, please," I whimpered, unsure of what it was I begged for, but knowing that whatever it was, only he could give it to me.

"I can't wait, love," he groaned, nibbling on my neck, his hands gliding around behind me, grasping my behind and pulling me upwards. "I've thought about you all morning, thought about the taste of you, how your skin feels, and how you feel when you tighten around me. I want you now, Alix. Wrap your legs around me."

He hoisted me higher up his chest as I locked my legs around his waist, pressing my back against the wall as he held onto my hips. Gently, with a slowness I thought would kill me, he entered me, parting me easily, filling me and making me complete. I nibbled and kissed at his lips until he gave me what I wanted, then suckled his tongue as he rumbled his pleasure deep in his chest. I flexed my legs around his waist, crying out my discontent when he slid out of me, then repeating my cry, this time of joy, when he filled me again.

"Christ, I'm not going to be able to take my time," he gasped as I dug my fingernails into his shoulders and lightly scored his back. "I've tried, but I'm not—ah, God, I'm sorry, Alix. This is going to be fast."

He groaned loudly into my mouth as he slammed deep into me, his control snapped, his body taking over from his mind. My body responded likewise, matching his frenzied rhythm, my heart racing with his as we struggled against each other, trying to push each other higher, closer to that one moment of bliss, the moment when we would be joined by a means far more profound than just the physical. He rocked into me as I thrust back at him, his dark, heated words of praise heavy in my ears, stirring my soul until he possessed all of it, all of me, merging with me so when we climbed to that last peak, that moment of profound pleasure, there weren't two people making love in a shower, there was just one glorious creation that was the best part of both of us.

Alex's roar of pleasure reverberated through me, crescendoing above the sound of the shower, echoing in my heart as I gave him the only gift I had to offer.

"I love you, Alex," I gasped against his neck, kissing the wet skin of his collarbone. "I love you."

His head turned until his lips were almost touching mine. Spiky dark brown eyelashes framed eyes so green they would make a leprechaun weep. I know he heard my whispered confession, I could see the mingled passion and doubt in his eyes, but he said nothing.

The warm water continued to pour around and over us as he kissed me and held me tight against him until my trembling legs could stand on their own again, the words of love I'd spoken hanging portentously in the humid air.

Until I looked down.

"Aw, hell! We forgot your raincoat!"

Chapter Ten

"Fool!" Rowena railed to herself as she paced the length of her damp prison. "I am a thousand times a fool!"

"Oh, say that not, my lady!" cried Babette, Rowena's little maid as she clung to the latch on the iron-banded door that kept them prisoners in the Mysterious Spaniard's subterranean crypt. In between pounding on the door for help, she spoke. " 'Twas not your fault that the Mysterious Spaniard overheard your declaration of love to Lord Raoul! 'Twas fate that brought us this low, not love, my lady. Never love. Above all, do not deny your love for Lord Raoul! Why, love is a wonderful and grand emotion—"

"Be quiet," Rowena snapped, dismissing the maid's unwelcome words. "Love is foolishness. Love is folly. I do not love anyone, least of all Lord Raoul. I was temporarily insane when I told him that, swayed by his overwhelming and extremely pleasing manly attributes and

*suchlike. Love? Ha ha! I laugh at the very thought of it!
I've never heard of anything so foolish in all . . . my . . .
days!"*

As I read the last few words my voice took on a piercing,
strident tone that made me flinch, but I gritted my teeth
against the need to apologize for it, and instead sat quiet,
waiting for the prognosis. When none was forthcoming,
I felt it behooved me to prod my audience into speaking.

"That's as far as I am now. It's almost to the end—
Lord Raoul will save Lady Rowena from Lord Thomas—
he's the Mysterious Spaniard in disguise—and that's it.
My agent thinks she has a publisher who will like it."

I sent my gaze from the familiar planes of Alex's face
across the heavy oak table where a man sat in a shimmering pool of shadows cast by the candles that were
the only lighting in the room. Daniel, Alex's writer
friend, was a recluse who seldom ventured out of his
house. At first I had thought access might have something to do with his hermit-like state, since he was confined to a wheelchair, but as it turned out, he just
preferred to remain alone, visiting with friends around
the world via the Internet, and watching the several
thousand movies in his personal movie collection.

That didn't let him off the hook as far as giving me his
opinion about my book, however. "Um . . . Daniel? I realize that I only read a chapter to you, but what do you
think so far? Does it have promise? I know it's not perfect, and it's a bit rough in parts, but everyone I've asked
seems to like it."

I leaned forward as I spoke, hoping to get a glimpse
into his eyes so as to better judge whether his response
was merely polite, or if he really meant what he said. It

helped that he had lovely velvety brown eyes that seemed to hold eons of wisdom in them. Alex had told me on the way over to Daniel's flat that he was originally from Rhodesia, his family having fled to England during one of the more violent political coups. Considered an ignorant native by prejudicial school systems, Daniel had triumphed over adversity to emerge as one of Britain's strongest voices in fiction, his books selling as popularly in the U.S. as they did in England.

Daniel sat still as a rock. I leaned over to the other end of the table to ask, "Is he breathing?"

A bark of laughter from the dark corner confirmed that Daniel was still with us, but Alex wasn't about to be distracted by a minor thing like a sense of humor. His long fingers turned a glass of wine around and around in his hands. He wasn't drinking it, just periodically frowning into the golden depths as if seeking some insight. "Alix, I warned you earlier it wasn't fair to ask Daniel's advice about a type of book he doesn't write, and, I assume, doesn't read as well. It's like comparing apples and oranges."

"No, it's not," I interrupted, smiling apologetically on Alex's behalf at the shadowed figure of Daniel. "Good writing is good writing—you can recognize it no matter what the genre. Right, Daniel?"

"That may be so, but you're still putting him in an untenable position."

I turned back to Alex, narrowing my eyes at his innuendo. Blast the man, couldn't he see I was trying to establish a writerly rapport with his friend? That's why he had brought me to meet Daniel, wasn't it? Didn't he know how important this was to me? And just *what* was he hinting at? "Are you saying that I'm putting him on the spot because my writing sucks?"

"No, of course not, but you must admit that it's not very . . . erm . . ."

I gasped as the full intent of his words hit me. "You are, too, that's exactly what you're saying, you think my story is awful, don't you, you pompous . . . jaded . . . *non-reader!*"

His lips thinned. "You're putting words in my mouth again, Alix, but this time I'm not going to let you blame me. If you want to work yourself up over something so trivial—"

"Trivial? *Trivial?* My writing career is not trivial!"

"I never said it was," Alex snarled at me, slamming down his glass of wine. I expected to see the stem shatter, but it was well made and just vibrated a warning.

"That's what it sounded like to me! You said my writing was trivial—"

"Christ!" Alex shoved a hand through his hair, leaving it standing on end. "Will you stop attributing your insecurities and self-doubts to me? All I said was that you were working yourself up over something trivial— namely my opinion of your story."

"Your opinion isn't trivial, dammit! And what insecurities and self-doubts? That's insulting in the extreme! I don't have insecurities and self-doubts! I'm the most secure person I know!"

He took a deep breath, letting it out slowly. A muscle in his jaw jumped as he unclenched his teeth long enough to say, "Alix, you're taking this far too personally. All I said was that Daniel might not care to comment on something he's unfamiliar with. Literary criticism is difficult enough—"

"Ha!" I snorted, hurt by his cruel words. I wasn't insecure. I simply faced up to my flaws, admitting them rather than hiding them. "That's rich coming from a man who probably couldn't critique his way out of a paper bag. Go ahead, tell us all about it, Alex. I'm sure you've picked up lots of critiquing skills staring at pictures of naked women pleasuring themselves with garden produce!"

"You insist on taking this personally." Alex shook his head in mock sadness. I spat out an invective as I got to my feet, marching over to where he sat so I could poke a finger into his chest.

"Why not, you just told me my writing stinks!"

"I didn't," he growled, his eyes glittering in the half-light as he pushed back his chair and rose, towering over me. "But if you insist on pressing the issue, I will tell you exactly what I think of it."

"Well, you'll notice no one is asking your opinion, Detective Bloody Inspector Blackheart!" I poked him in the chest again, just to annoy him. It worked.

"That's a damn good thing, too!" he said.

"Oh, yeah? And just what is *that* supposed to mean?"

"Exactly what you think it means!"

"Ahem."

We both turned to look at the head of the table where our host sat.

I turned back to Alex, my hands on my hips. "Well, hell. Now see what you've done? You've made me lose my temper in front of your friend. I hope you're happy, Mr. Never Make a Scene!"

I marched back to my chair and mustered a ragged smile for Daniel. "You'll have to forgive Alex. He is, as I'm sure you know, the most aggravating of men, and could drive the Pope into swearing a blue streak."

"Alix—" came a warning growl from the other end of the table. I ignored it and kept my smile firmly aimed at Daniel.

"It was your opinion I was seeking, Daniel. I'm all alone in London, you see, and I have no one else upon whom I can call for assistance—"

"For Christ's sake, I should have brought my violin."

It took immense effort, but I didn't react to Alex's goading. Why he was in such an unreasonable mood, I didn't know, but I suspected it had something to do with my admission of love the previous night. Men, I had found, always got touchy when the subject of love entered the picture. "As I was saying, I don't have anyone else I can turn to for assistance with my book, so I would greatly appreciate it if you could give me a word or two of advice, and perhaps let me know what you perceive to be problem areas in the story."

"I think . . ." The words rolled out of the corner almost as smoothly as the wheelchair glided forward into the light. I was relieved to see a smile on Daniel's face. Thank God he hadn't been offended by Alex making such a scene.

"Yes? You think . . . ? What is it you think?" He was smiling—that had to be good!

"I know what *I* think . . ." came a mutter from the other person in the room.

Daniel pursed his lips. "I believe . . ."

I held my breath. Surely it couldn't be criticism he had on his mind, not with that twinkle in his eye as he steepled his fingers under his chin and considered me.

". . . and it has to do with certain people's ability to twist every word I say into meaning something else . . ."

I frowned quickly at Alex's unwelcome interruption, then sent a rapt gaze back toward the man to my left. "You believe . . . ?"

"I'd wager . . ."

Oh, God, the suspense was killing me! I clung to the edge of the table, leaning forward and willing him to say it.

". . . in her attempt to justify a self-fulfilling prophesy of doom . . ."

I whirled to the right for a nanosecond. "Alex, will you be quiet!" Daniel was grinning when I turned back to him. "What? What would you wager? For God's sake, *WHAT?"*

". . . simply because she has commitment issues and doesn't want to face that fact."

"Oh!" I leaped out of my chair and slapped the flat of my hand down on the table as I leaned over Alex. "I do not have issues, commitment or otherwise, you horribly annoying man! You're the one with all the issues! You're anal and controlled and you wouldn't know spontaneity if it danced on your thickheaded . . . er . . . head! Just because I'm willing to face reality while you live in your sheltered little world where nothing and no one ever touches you, don't you dare tell me I have issues! You want to talk issues? I'll talk issues—you're so bloody rigid it's a wonder you can sit!" I straightened up and glared at Daniel, who was shaking his head and laughing softly to himself. Men! They were universally aggravating. I took a deep breath and tried to keep the bellow from my voice. I wasn't completely successful. *"Now what the hell were you going to say about my story?"*

Daniel laughed even harder, wiping his eyes with the corner of his napkin, waving me back into my seat. "I'm sorry, Alix, I didn't mean to make matters worse, it's just that you're so very . . ."

He erupted into another bout of laughter. I picked up the tiny shrimp fork that lay across the top of my plate, weighing it in my hand, wondering how much damage it could do. "I'll take you down with this cocktail fork if I have to, Daniel! Don't think I won't!"

He wiped his eyes again as he gave in to a big old belly laugh, sputtering and wheezing as he tried to speak around the laughter. ". . . you're so very *perfect* for Alex!"

I stared at him for a moment, then looked at Alex. "I'm sorry to be the one to tell you this, but your friend is a choice candidate for the booby hatch."

Alex was still scowling over being called thickheaded. He ignored me and shot Daniel a surly look.

"No, truly, you two are perfect for each other. I can't remember the last time I saw Alex lose his temper, really lose his temper, and over something so asinine, too."

I bristled anew over the slanderous comment. "Well, thank you very much!"

He was quick to smooth over his mistake. He took my hand in his and kissed my fingers. "No, no, that was no insult, sweet Alix, it was a compliment I'm paying you."

There was something sounding suspiciously like a low growl from the opposite side of the table.

Daniel covered my hand with his and squeezed gently. I smiled, a bit unsure about his method of doling out compliments, but unable to withstand the effect of his lovely dark eyes at close quarters. If our genders were reversed, I'd swear he was fluttering his eyelashes at me.

"I'm not surprised, however, that it took a woman as beautiful as you to get under his skin."

Ah, flattery. It worked on me every time. I increased the wattage in my smile, deciding to remove Daniel from my mental list of pigheaded males even as I relegated to the top of the list the man rumbling ominously from the other side of the table.

"It would take a stronger man than he to withstand the seductive promise in your provocative, deeply mysterious eyes."

"Oh," I said, a bit flustered when he lifted my hand to kiss my fingers again. Seductive? Provocative? Mysterious? Me? His lips lingered over my knuckles, his dark moustache tickling as he did a little eye-flirting with me. "Oh."

"Stop mauling her," Alex growled.

Daniel smiled and winked at me as he released my hand. "He sounds jealous. Are you jealous because I was enjoying your pretty lady's hand, Alex?"

"I'm not jealous."

We both looked at Alex. He *looked* jealous. It made my heart flutter around and sing a happy little song about how wonderful it was when handsome green-eyed men ground their teeth and sounded like they were talking through gravel because they were positively seething with jealousy.

"Are you sure?" I asked, tipping my head to one side as I noted the muscle twitching in his jaw. "Maybe we should try it again, just to be sure."

I held out my hand and wiggled my fingers at Daniel.

"Alexandra!" Alex bellowed, slamming a fist down on the table. I looked at Daniel and withdrew my hand.

"He's jealous."

"Yes, he certainly is," Daniel agreed with a pleased nod. "That bodes well. Now, to get back to the—Alex, calm down, we're through experimenting with your new-found jealousy, tuck it away and rejoin civilized man-kind—to get back to the question you asked me, Alix, I would be happy to give you my opinion, advice, and help with your manuscript, but I must read the whole thing. I couldn't begin to offer any help based on just one chapter."

The little voice in my head pointed out it was unrea-sonable to feel let down because Daniel hadn't declared it the best novel since *Gone With the Wind*. Despite such sage advice, I had a hard time keeping my voice from sounding as disappointed as I felt. "Oh. I suppose that makes sense. I'll drop the entire manuscript by tomor-row, shall I?"

"As you like." Daniel nodded, and made a dashing turn in his wheelchair, leading us out of his dining room toward an elegantly appointed sitting room. "And now, my friends, I have a treat for you both—a special movie in Alix's honor."

"A special movie? How lovely!" I grabbed Alex's hand as we followed after Daniel. Alex, still miffed, tried to pull his hand away, but I wasn't having any of it. "Stop acting so jealous," I whispered.

"I . . . am . . . not . . . jealous," he hissed in return.

"Fine," I whispered, and dropped his hand. "I'll just go hold Daniel's hand. I like him—he's got bedroom eyes. I'm sure he'd be happy to hold my hand. He does the cutest little tickling thing with his forefinger—"

Alex grabbed my wrist. I smirked to myself. He was jealous.

"Don't be so bloody obvious, Alix. I can see right through your little ploys."

"Ploys? What ploys are those? I have no ploys. I don't

know what you're talking about," I lied, wondering which ploy it was he had noted—the ploy to make him insanely jealous, the ploy to make him confess his undying love for me, or the ploy to drive him into the shower with me again. It could have been any number of other ploys I had entertained, but those were the first three that came to mind.

"I know you're flirting with Daniel just to get a response out of me, but it won't succeed. I am indifferent to such petty wiles."

Daniel was busy selecting a video to play on the huge, wall-mounted television.

"You're right," I told Alex, shaking his hand from my wrist. "That is petty of me. Shall I flirt with you instead?"

"No," he snapped, plopping down onto a lovely chocolate brown leather couch. "Yes. Oh, hell, I don't care, do whatever you bloody well want to do. It's not as if I have a say in my life anymore."

"My friend," Daniel said, wheeling over to clap a hand on Alex's shoulder, "you have learned the first truth of any relationship: Your life is no longer your own." He glanced curiously at me as I stood before Alex. "If you sit in this chair next to me, sweet lady, I will be happy to hold your hand and do the cute little tickling thing with my finger."

"That's very considerate of you, but I suppose I'd better humor the 'tec here. He does some pretty cute things with his fingers as well."

As I curled up next to him, Alex looked a little less starchy, actually unbending so far as to wrap an arm around me and tug me closer to him. I rested my head against his shoulder, breathing in that wonderful scent that always surrounded him, and wondered if Daniel would see if I slid my hand up Alex's thigh.

"Yes," Alex breathed into my hair.

I tipped my head back to look at him. "Hmm?"

"He'll see. Don't do it."

"How did you know what I was thinking?"

Daniel flipped off the lights in the room, but not before I could see Alex's lips curl up into a grin. "Because I was thinking of doing the same thing to you," he said just before his lips descended upon mine.

I went limp against him, unable to withstand the delicious onslaught of his mouth. If I had been a spy, I would have told him anything when he kissed me like that. "Your tongue ought to be registered as a dangerous weapon," I murmured when our lips parted.

"If you two are finished snogging over there, I'll show you my special movie. Alix, when the man here told me he was bringing an American with him to dinner, I knew I had to locate a special little something for you. It took Paula—she's my research assistant—all day to find me a copy, but find it she did, and now we can all enjoy the fruits of her labors. Alex, you'll like this one, too. The Yard plays a role in it."

"O-o-oh, I love mysteries," I cooed, snuggling against Alex, prepared to be entertained by a special movie in my honor. "Is it the history of the Black Museum? I'm dying to go there, but Mr. Never Breaks the Rules won't take me."

"It's better than that," Daniel said, brandishing his remote control with a flourish. He hit a button, and the big TV screen in front of us was filled with the image of the moon. "It's *American Werewolf in London*!"

"So it is." I glanced at Alex.

"Werewolves?" he asked Daniel.

"Werewolves. Just wait, you'll love it."

Alex didn't look convinced.

The movie wasn't as long as I remember it being, and it did have the benefit of being partially shot in London, so I got to snicker at scenes like the one of a man running through the seemingly endless, labyrinthine, yellow-tiled tunnels in the tube station. I'd been in tube stations like that—in fact, that evening Alex and I had come through the very one shown in the movie—which added to the fun of seeing it being gently mocked onscreen.

I would pay later for my enjoyment of that mocking.

The rest of our evening at Daniel's went well, with only minor complaining on Alex's part. It was quite late when we left, and I was feeling no pain, having allowed Daniel to ply me with several glasses of a particularly succulent white wine that packed more of a wallop than I imagined. By the time we took our leave, I was mellow and happy and a bit light-headed. Alex was all for ringing up for a cab, but I told him he was being a sissy.

"Come on, here's our chance to walk through the Leicester Square tube station late at night, just like in the movie. You wouldn't want to miss seeing a werewolf, would you?"

Alex glanced up at the night sky and allowed me to tug him along the sidewalk. "It's not a full moon."

"Good, it'll be a wussy werewolf then, one weakened by the lack of a full moon. You ought to be able to take him on handily!"

"Are you implying I couldn't handle a burly werewolf?" Alex asked, pulling me toward him so he could nibble on my neck, growling a growl that sent shivers of delight up and down my arms.

"You're snockered," I giggled, happy with him, happy with London, happy with the world.

"I am not," he said with great dignity as we rounded a corner and headed across the street to the tube entrance. "I've just loosened my vaunted control for you."

I giggled again. "Snockered."

On some days, Sundays especially, certain tube stations close down late at night. Such was the case with the Leicester Square tube. We just managed to squeak in before the guard closed the entrance gates.

"You'd best hurry, then," he nodded toward us as Alex dug out a few coins for the ticket machine. "Last train's due here in four minutes."

We hurried down the stairs and started to wind our way through the eerily empty corridors, our footsteps echoing off the tiled walls.

"Crikey, this is creepy," I muttered as I clung to Alex's hand and jogged alongside him, my nose wrinkling at the smell of stale urine kissed with just a hint of disinfectant. The air pulsed around us through the long, dimly lit, yellow-tiled tunnels connecting the platforms, making me think it was just like someone breathing down our backs. I looked behind us nervously, but there was nothing but blackness as the guard shut down the outer station lights. I swallowed hard and tried to fight down a rising sense of foreboding. There was no reason to worry about being alone in a tube station, was there? "Alex, there's no one else here! That always weirds me out, like when I'm alone in a building. It's just like in the movie, eh?"

"Crikey is another word that sounds odd when Americans say it," he replied, then swore when we turned the corner. A metal gate had been drawn across the passage,

217

locking off the easy approach to the platform. The hair on the back of my neck stood on end when the ceiling lights in the tunnel behind us blinked off one by one. It was almost as if some unseen person was walking toward us, turning off the lights as he approached. I watched horrified as the dense, inky blackness swept toward us, my mouth suddenly as dry as the Sahara. Alex tugged me in the opposite direction. "Come along, we'll take the other passage, but hurry! We've only two minutes left."

He pulled me to the opposite tunnel, grumbling to himself about me wanting to take the tube rather than a taxi. I slid on the slippery floor as we hurtled around a corner, and I would have gone down if Alex hadn't been holding on to me.

"All right?" he inquired as he hauled me along. "Damn! I can hear the train."

I could hear it, too, the peculiar rushing sound that echoed down the underground tunnels. The combination of the absence of people, the lights shutting down behind us, and the eerie echoing of our footsteps raised goose bumps along my arms. The very last thing I wanted was to be stuck in the creepy tube station—not even to be alone with Alex would I suffer that! My heart in my throat, I dropped his hand, hiked my skirt up above my knees, and raced ahead of him down the corridor. The rushing sound got louder as I dashed to the right, bursting out onto the empty train platform. The lights down at the far end flickered, then started going out in succession. I could hear Alex calling for me back in the passage, but that wasn't what held my attention—*that* was consumed by the shaggy gray thing that lurked at the other end of the platform, curled up next to a candy machine. I thought at first it was a pile of trash, but when it suddenly moved, I was horribly aware that I was all alone. By myself. With the lights going out. In a tube station I had just seen on film, a tube station that had been the scene of a grisly murder by a—

"WEREWOLF!" I screamed as the light above my head buzzed, then went dark. My evening bag slipped from my fingers as my heart stopped dead in my chest. *"WEREWOLF!* Aaaaaaaaaaah!" I spun around as the hideous gray thing got to its paws and lunged after me.

"Werewolf! Werewolf! Jesus effing Christ, it's a werewolf!" Alex was a dark shadow in the dimly lit passage I had just come down. "Run!" I shrieked, grabbing his arm as I pounded past him. "For the love of God, run! Werewolf!"

"What the hell are you yelling about?" Alex jerked his arm back, bringing me with it. I peered over his shoulder, tugging on him, frantic to get him out of the corridor where the horrible thing could get us and rip us to shreds.

"Run, Alex! It was right behind me! Please oh please oh please oh please, run!" I pulled him along with me a few feet, toward the platform on the opposite side where the rushing sound was getting louder. "Train! Werewolf! Come on, Alex, I don't want to die!"

The infuriating man just shook his head and put both hands on my shoulders. "In the future there will be no more horror movies when you're drinking wine, sweetheart."

"Aaaaaaack!" I screamed, seeing the horribly mutated Undead emerging from the blackness beyond, heading straight for us. It had risen up onto its hind legs and was waving its razor-like claws at Alex's back. *"WEREWOLF!"*

Alex started to turn to see what it was I was shouting at, but I had a grip on both his arms, and with a strength I doubt I'll ever again possess, dragged him with me to the platform. I looked around, desperate for a weapon, but there was nothing, no one to help us, no one to act as a sacrifice while I saved Alex and myself.

A blast of air from the train tunnel presaged the arrival of the train, filling me with hope that we might yet escape an early grave. I prayed like I've never prayed before that it would get there before the Monster of Leicester Square feasted upon our tender throats. Alex was trying to talk to me, no doubt to calm me, foolish man, but the sound of the approaching train and my own terrified thoughts—along with my chant of "Please God, please God, please God"—made me deaf to his words.

Just as I was sure the dread beast was going to burst upon us, the train pulled up, empty of all but one tired old man asleep on a bench. I lunged into the train, pulling Alex with me, and tried to force the doors closed behind us.

"Now what are you doing? Alix, you haven't been smoking your spiky plant, have you?"

From the corner of my eye I saw a movement from the corridor we'd just escaped from. I almost wet my pants when I saw what it was. A horrible gargled scream rose from my throat as I threw myself in Alex's arms, cowardly hiding my head in his shirt. "It has us! Oh, God, Alex, I'm so sorry for everything I've ever said that annoyed you. If I'm going to die, I want to die with a clean conscience. I love you! I love you more than anything in the world, and you're not rigid, and you don't have issues—well, you do, but they're pretty minor ones—but I love you and I don't want to die! Oh, God, I can hear it slathering behind me. Is it on us? Do you see it yet? Do you see the Hellhound of Satan?"

"All I see is an elderly transient in a gray coat who is holding your bag. Here, madam, I'll take that. Thank you. This is for your trouble."

Alex had to drag me with him because I wasn't about to let go of him, not when he was delusional and seeing bag ladies when there were werewolves about. I forced my eyes open enough to peek over my shoulder, and almost died of shame.

"Well, she *looked* like a werewolf," I said defensively a few minutes later as the train was racketing and swaying its way toward home. "She was all gray and hairy and filthy. How was I to know she was a person and not a werewolf? People shouldn't be allowed to have unkempt dreadlocks if they're going to spring out on unsuspecting victims late at night in empty tube stations! They need to make that a law."

"Look on the bright side," Alex said, a faint smile playing around his handsome, manly lips. "At least you're sober now."

Chapter Eleven

Lady Rowena slipped her hand down the long, hard length of Raoul's thing.

"Oops, typo. That should be *thigh,* not *thing.*"

Lady Rowena slipped her hand down the long, hard length of Raoul's thigh, curling her fingers through the dense forest of hair covering his leg

"Ew!"

I looked up from the page and frowned at the interruption. "What? I told you *thing* was a typo."

The young woman standing at the table next to me shook her head as she reached for another item of clothing from her basket. She folded it carefully and stuffed it into a long green duffel bag. "I understand about the thing, but the way you describe his leg hair—it's too

222

grotty! It makes him sound like an ape man or something."

I looked at the page. "Well, he is kind of hairy—is that a turn-off? I've always had a bit of a thing for a hairy chest."

"Chest hair is fine, but hairy legs!" She gave a mock shiver as she stuffed a handful of underwear in her bag and cinched closed the opening. "It's too barb!"

I blinked. "Barb?"

"Barbarian!"

"Oh. Sorry it's barb. I'll watch that. Um . . . I'm afraid the rest of this scene has references to body hair, but I can skip that part and go straight to—"

"I'm sorry, but I have to go now." She gave me a rueful smile and shrugged. "I thought that the part you read me was really good, although Rowena was a little too subjugated, don't you think?"

The buzzer went off on the washing machine behind me. "Hold that thought," I said, and hurried to add my cup of fabric softener. "Subjugated? You mean, like she was browbeaten?"

The young woman waved at someone outside the window and edged away. "Subjugated as in all of her freedom and choices were stripped from her by the male-dominated society. She had to do whatever the duke told her to do. *He* told her to touch him, it wasn't her choice."

"And that's bad? It *is* a historical fact. Dukes were like that back then, always demanding their women to touch them."

She curled a lip at me. "Who wants to read a story about a spiritless, wimpy woman who can't even stand up for herself?"

I gnawed on my lower lip. Who, indeed? "I guess I see your point. You think she should be more proactive or something? The story is finished, but I suppose I could go back and change a few things."

She shouldered her bag and gave me another half-smile. "Sorry, but my friends are waiting. I have to go."

"Thanks anyway." I gnawed a bit more on my lip, wondering how I could make Rowena more independent and still keep the flavor of the time. The woman weaved her way through all the people in the laundromat, stopping at the door to turn and wave for my attention. "Have her refuse her lover. That'll teach what's-his-name to walk all over her."

"Raoul," I said sadly, and pushed the manuscript back into my bag as I contemplated Steph's bath towels spinning in the dryer in front of me. Somehow an independent, forceful Rowena just didn't mesh with my idea of her. The old self-doubts came back with a vengeance as I watched the towels spin. What if the story didn't hold together? What if my mother was right and I wasn't cut out to be a writer? What if Maureen couldn't sell the story and I had to go home after all?

My mind ground to a halt as it suddenly hit me what I had been doing: assuming I would stay in England. In London. Specifically, at 35 Beale Square. With Alex.

"Oh, man, am I in over my head," I moaned.

"You what?" asked a guy with pink hair and head-phones who was sitting next to me.

"Nothing," I said with a feeble smile. "Just a complication in my love life."

"Ah," he nodded, then, looking me up and down, leaned close and put a hand on my knee. "You lookin' to have it away?"

"Have what away?" I looked down at his hand, then pushed it off my knee. "Oh, have *that* away. No, sorry, I have a perfectly good man, I'm not looking for another."

He leered and replaced his hand on my knee. "How will you know unless you give it a go?"

I plastered a thoughtful look on my face. "Well, that's true. I suppose I could ask Alex what he thinks. That's my sweetie. Alex Black. *Detective Inspector* Alex Black of Scotland Yard."

My pink-haired Romeo snatched his hand off my knee and moved a few seats down the wall. A warm glow grew within me as I thought about Alex, thought about being with Alex, spending my days and nights with Alex. He was unlike any man I'd ever known—he was loving and thoughtful and the tiniest bit jealous, which did wonderful things for my ego. He was supportive, too. True, he had made some comments at Daniel's that were awfully critical, but I knew that was because he expected a lot from me. No one had ever expected the best from me before. It was a heady feeling, knowing he believed I wouldn't fail. Best of all, as the last seven blissful nights together had shown, he was constant. His attention to me never wavered, his desire never faded, not once. Each evening I fell asleep lying in his arms, each day he called me during a break just to talk. If this wasn't love, it was a convincing approximation. I basked in the warmth of his affection, feeling secure and truly wanted for the first time in my life.

The timer went off on my dryer, interrupting my happy musing. I collected my towels, and smiled at the young man with pink hair as I was leaving. He avoided my eye. I made a mental note to tell Alex later about the newfound perk of dating a detective, but alas, the opportunity never arrived.

"What do you mean, it lacks coherence? The characters are exactly the same all the way through the story. That's coherence, isn't it?"

Daniel bent upon me a gaze so filled with anguish that I squirmed uncomfortably in the chair he had waved me into. It was late morning, an hour after his assistant had called to tell me he wanted to talk over my story with me, but my discomfort had nothing to do with the fact that I was sitting in a pool of sunlight streaming in through an open window. It was that look of pained pity in his deep brown eyes that left me twitchy and restless.

"In this case, no, that's not what is meant by coherence. Your story is . . . it's . . ."

My heart stopped, solidified into something resembling lead, and dropped into my stomach. Whatever it was, the verdict wasn't going to be good. I fought back the urge to run and steeled myself. As long as the problem was something easily fixed, I'd be OK.

"Go ahead," I rasped. "I can take the truth. I *want* the truth. I know it needs work, so if you tell me what's wrong with it, I'll fix it."

A grimace flickered across his face. "It's not as easy as pointing out the flaws and telling you to fix them."

My stomach dropped to my shoes. "It's awful, isn't it? You're saying it's terrible?"

"No, not that, I wouldn't say it was terrible—"

"Then what's wrong? Daniel, I'm not stupid, and I don't have a fragile little ego that's going to crack if you point out the areas that need a bit of polishing, so go ahead—be honest. Tell me what you think and what I can do to make it better."

His shoulders slumped. I waited silently, gnawing on my lower lip while he gathered his thoughts.

"It's not a matter of simply polishing a few rough spots, Alix. You need to reexamine the storyline as a whole. You have no explanation for the characters' underlying motivations, you haven't explored the causality of their actions, there's no balance in the ebb and flow between plot and story, your pacing . . . well, your pacing never gives the reader a chance to catch their breath. I'm sorry, but you wanted me to be honest, and my honest opinion is that your story needs significant rethinking, replotting, and rewriting."

Oh, God, it was worse than I had imagined! I couldn't decide whether to be angry or hurt at his comments. I decided anger was the safer route. "Well, I'm sorry you think that, Daniel, but I do have an agent, and she thinks the story has great potential. Maybe you've just missed the point of it."

He frowned and rubbed his knuckles. "You didn't tell me you had an agent. That's wonderful news. Has she . . . erm . . . read the whole story?"

A wave of nausea bit deep in my stomach as the anger faded under the pity clearly visible in his eyes. Daniel was being polite, but no politeness in the world could disguise what he thought: I didn't cut it as a writer. He was too nice to come right out and say I wasn't good enough, but I was very adept at reading between the lines. Failure was no stranger to me.

"Well, not all of it. Just the first three chapters. But she has the whole manuscript now. I dropped it off when I left you your copy."

He didn't say anything, just looked at me. The pain grew within me as I struggled to think of something to say, something that wasn't pleading or begging with him to take back his words.

"Do you think . . ." I swallowed back the lump of tears aching in my throat. "Do you think it's so bad that when she sees the whole thing she'll want me to rewrite it?"

He didn't answer, just looked at me with those big brown eyes swimming with pain.

"I see," I said after a few moments of profound silence. I licked my lips, surprised to find them numb. I looked down at the bag in my hand. My hand was numb, too. Nerveless. It was odd how the bone-deep bite of pain sometimes had that effect of deadening everything in its path—skin, muscles, a soul. The mixture of concern, regret, and pity on Daniel's handsome face forced me into speaking when my bloodless lips wished to remain drawn into a tightened grimace. I had to say something. It wasn't his fault that I sucked as a writer. Swamped with anger, pain, and guilt that I had put him in this position, I did my best to pretend nothing was wrong. "Hey, Daniel, don't worry about it! I'll be OK. You haven't said anything that hasn't been said to me before."

"Alix, your story has a great deal of potential . . ."

"But it fails in execution. I get the idea, and honestly, I'm OK with it." His words, the truth, had cut my insides to ribbons, but I wasn't about to tell him how I was bleeding to death. I have always found that when there's nothing else left, dignity means everything. I lifted the strange, heavy hand that I recognized as mine and told the fingers to squeeze his shoulder gently. "I told you I wanted your honest opinion. It means a lot to me, so stop beating yourself up because you had to be brutal with me."

"Oh, God, Alix, I didn't mean to come across as brutal."

I bent down and pressed my cold lips against his cheek. "It's OK," I repeated, the words spinning in my mind. My brain must have been numb as well. I couldn't seem to hold on to my thoughts, but I knew I had to get out of there, get away from Daniel's sympathetic misery before the feeling came back into my body and I snapped. I slipped away, heedless to his entreaties to stay and talk the book over.

I walked away from the noise and bustle of Leicester Square, aware of nothing but the simple pleasure of the rhythm of my feet beating against the ground as I walked the streets of London. I wanted to cry, but despite the heat of the mid-summer day, my body was too cold to manufacture tears. I wanted to scream, but the words were voiceless howls caught deep inside me. I suddenly stopped, shivering despite the sweat soaking my back. More than anything else, I wanted to be wrapped in the comfort of Alex's warm arms, but he was at work. Rubbing my arms to eliminate some of my inner chill, I spotted a phone box and hurried to it. Alex was the answer to my problem. I knew he wasn't expecting to be at his office that morning, but he had given me his cell phone number to be used in emergencies. I looked down at my bloodless, trembling hand. This was an emergency.

"Alix! Are you all right? Daniel called an hour ago to say you left his house very upset. I called your flat, but you weren't home. Where are you?"

I looked around. Did I know this area? It didn't look familiar, but a glance behind me gave me some information. "Apparently I'm at the Tower of London. You aren't at your office?"

"No, we're on the road. What do you mean *apparently*? Don't you know where you are? I know you're upset about Daniel's comments, but that's no reason to run off half-cocked."

Alex's voice dropped and took on the slightly muffled sound that results when a hand lightly covers the mouthpiece. Even diluted as it was, even though he was speaking to someone else, the rich, warm timbre of his voice rolled over me and left me filled with yearning. Need built up inside me, deep inside me, welling out from the shredded bits of my soul that lay bleeding and inert in the cage of my heart. I needed Alex. I needed him so much I could feel the dark, yawning void of need within me, I needed his comfort and warmth and tenderness. I needed him as I'd never needed anything before.

"Alex, when are you coming home? I—" My voice cracked with the strain of keeping from shrieking out all of the pain and hopelessness that consumed my soul. "I really need to be with you. Could you maybe meet me for lunch or something?"

A staccato burst of radio noise was audible even through his cell phone. "Alix, I'm sorry, but I can't talk now. We're conducting a raid and I must turn off my mobile phone."

A sob escaped, burning its way up my throat. I clutched the black plastic housing of the phone with a grip that left my nerveless fingers tingling.

"Please, Alex, I really do need to talk to you. I wouldn't ask if it wasn't important, but—"

"I'm sorry, but I'm going to have to ring off now. I'll call you as soon as I'm free."

"Alex . . ." The word was a whisper, a plea torn from my heart.

"I'm sorry, sweetheart," he repeated in a low voice. "I can't get away. We've been planning this raid for six weeks."

"But I need you!" I'd never said those words to any person before. I clutched them now as if they were a lifeline to salvation. "I need *you.*"

"There's nothing I can do now, Alix." His voice was thick with frustration, but it was nothing compared to the pain he was heaping upon me. "This raid is important."

The realization that Alex was no different from any of the other men in my past settled like a lead weight on my shoulders. My body bowed under the agony. I leaned my head into the phone, ignoring the curious looks of people walking by. "More important than me?" I asked softly, so softly I was sure he hadn't heard.

But he did. His voice, that lovely voice that was all rounded vowels and richness that never failed to send shivers of delight down my spine, that voice that evoked a sense of intimacy ripe with promise, now scraped against me as if it were etching into stone. "Sweetheart, you know I . . . oh, Christ, what now? Terry, are you monitoring the radio? Isn't that our suspect in the blue mini leaving the premises? Alix, I really must—"

Someone tapped on the door to the phone box. I turned around to stare, uncaring that the stranger would see the tears rolling down my cheeks. A harassed-looking woman with two kids hanging off her shopping bags made an impatient gesture. I nodded, but when I turned back to the phone, it was dead. Alex had hung up on me. Without even saying goodbye, he'd just hung up on me. On the worst day of my life. I meant that little to him.

My forehead fell forward to rest on top of the phone again as I hung up the receiver. Standing up straight seemed like too much effort. "Goodbye," I whispered, sure that this time I would die of my broken heart.

I didn't die, of course—people don't really die of such a thing. Although I know from experience that the pain of rejection is often so great it does seem possible. But I wasn't pathetic enough to simply crumple up at a phone box outside the Tower of London. Instead, I fell back on a trusted standby, a tried and true safety net. I made a mental list as I plodded home.

Topping the list in the position of supreme importance was having a good long cry, at least a two-tissue-box sob-fest. Following that, I was going to have a nice wallow in self-pity, and then a lengthy sulk. Only after I had worked the sulk out of my system would I turn my attention to making voodoo dolls of Alex and inflicting horrible tortures upon them. After that, of course, I would eat three pounds of chocolate, be sick for a week, and slowly return to the land of the living with yet another layer of scars on my poor embittered heart.

Only this time I wasn't sure I was going to recover from the wounds.

"Bawling, pity party, sulking, horrible tortures, chocolate," I ran over the list as I made my way home. Lists are important things to have in your life. Lists are good. They keep you organized even when you don't want to be organized. Focusing on the list kept my mind busy, occupied in a nice, orderly fashion without allowing it to dwell on the horrible, gut-wrenching pain Alex's betrayal had caused . . . no! I wouldn't think of that. The list! The list was important! I must remember the list! "Crying for hours and hours, huge wallow in self-pity, major sulking session, cruel, inhuman tortures that would render a mere mortal into a twisted, pain-riddled ball of flesh with absolutely no future but that involving endless torment, to be followed by a lifetime membership in Godiva's Chockie of the Day club."

Someone had propped the front door open to catch a draft in the house. I stumbled up the stairs, a fervent thanks trembling on my lips. I wasn't up to struggling with the stroppy lock.

Ray thumped down the stairs toward me with a bag of garbage in her arms as I slowly made my way up to my floor.

"You look like hell," she said, pausing as I lumbered upwards. "Freemar?"

"Crying jag, pity-a-thon, sulk city, tortures that would make the Spanish Inquisition look like a love-fest, enough chocolate to drop a horse," I told her.

"A few of your favorite things?" she called up after me as I continued onward. I shook my head at the concern rife in her voice. I appreciated it, but couldn't face it at that moment. Even one remotely nice word and I would break down, dissolve into a big old puddle of misery. While I knew that was inevitable, I wanted to do it in private, not on the stairs where everyone would witness the pitiful remains of my life.

"Freemar?"

I ignored her and kept walking.

"Alix, are you all right? Something the matter?" Ray stomped back up the stairs after me and grabbed my arm. "You look like you're going to be sick."

I frowned. "No, that comes after I eat enough chocolate to fill a bathtub. I can't be sick now. I have a list and I have to stick to it."

"A list?" Her forehead wrinkled in concern.

I nodded. The list took on all-encompassing importance in my poor heated brain. I had a list of tasks, therefore I must accomplish them. It was as simple as that.

"The order is of extreme importance," I told her. "First things first, Ray. First I cry for eighteen hours straight, then I fall into self-pity and don't emerge for a year or two, then I wreak vengeance upon Alex's hideous mortal form via voodoo dolls, then I consume such quantities of chocolate as to cause diabetes in anyone who comes within a five-mile radius of me, *then* I get sick. You see the importance of the order of the list, don't you?"

"Erm . . ."

I nodded at her again and started up the next flight of stairs. "First I cry . . ."

"Bert!" Ray bellowed.

". . . then I descend into pity hell . . ."

"Bert, come out here!"

I rounded the landing nodding to myself as Ray stood with her hands on her hips, yelling through the open door of her flat. "Aren't you out of the bath yet?"

I was sorry she was worried about me, but concern for others wasn't on the list, so I couldn't devote any energy to that now.

"It's an emergency! Freemar is having man troubles!"

Later, after I had worked through everything on the list, then I would reassure her that I was OK.

"You're better at this than I am. She's blathering something about torturing Black!"

I ignored the voice drifting up from the floor below and let myself into my flat, then started rounding up items I would need for my first task. I plumped up the pillows on the daybed, looked in vain for tissue, and ended up corralling all the available rolls of toilet paper instead, lining them up on the table next to the bed. I looked around the room.

"Pillows for sobbing into, bed to fling myself upon, toilet paper for nose-blowing and eye-mopping . . . I think it's all there. Excellent. The weeping and wailing can commence. Oh, hell, now what?" The phone rang just as someone pounded on the door. I put my hands on my hips and glared at both before grabbing the phone with one hand and opening the door with the other. Ray stood in the doorway, a box of tissues in hand. She held them out to me.

"I'm sorry, I can't talk now. I have a list, and it's important I stay on schedule," I told whoever was on the phone. "If I slack off on the crying time, I'll have to short-shift the self-pity and sulking."

"I thought you might want to talk," Ray said hesitantly, still offering the box of tissues.

"Alix Freemar? This is Maureen Tully. I'd like to talk to you about *Ravening Raptures*."

"My book?" A dim ray of hope shot through the black storm clouds of misery. She wanted to talk about my manuscript? That was good, wasn't it? That meant Daniel's assessment of my writing talent was wrong! I put my mental list on hold, waved Ray into the flat, closed the door, and used my foot to snag the ladderback chair next to the table. "Oh, hello, Ms. Tully. Sure, I'd be happy to talk to you about my story. I take it you've had a chance to read—"

"I'm sending you a check for half of my editing fee."

I blinked at Ray perched uncomfortably on the edge of the chaise. Was the story so good she didn't do any editing on it? No, even I didn't believe that! "You're sending me a check? I don't understand, why are you—"

"I'm invoking the refusal clause in the contract. I don't feel the entire manuscript has held up to the promise of the initial chapters. As I've done some work on it, I'm only refunding you half of my editing fee."

My knees weakened and gave way under me. I plopped down onto the ground with a hollow, "What?"

Ray jumped up to offer me the box of tissues. For lack of anything else to do, I took them.

"I'm sorry, Miss Freemar, but your story does not fit my needs at this time. I wish you the best of luck with it, however. I will return your manuscript with the check. Good day."

She didn't want my story? She thought it was lacking in promise? My stomach roiled as the putrid stench of yet more rejection hit me.

"Alix?"

I blinked to clear my eyes and stared wordlessly at a worried Ray, then handed her the phone receiver. She hung it up gently, frowned at it for a few seconds, then squatted next to me. She prodded me with the tissue box.

"Erm . . . I brought them for you to use. Bert's better at this than I am, but she's in the bath. She should be along presently, so it would be best if you could hold off the histrionics until she's here."

I stared at the box, then realized that my mouth was hanging open. I closed it, swallowed back a big lump, and handed the tissues back to her. "Thank you, but I don't need these. I have my toilet paper rolls all lined up and ready for use."

She shot me a look of disbelief. I gave in and took one of her tissues and blew my nose.

"I take it that was not good news?"

I shook my head and mopped at my damp eyes. "No, it wasn't good news. It was bad news. Exceptionally bad news. My agent has dumped me."

"Dumped you?"

"Dumped me. As in, she doesn't want me. As in, she thinks my story isn't good."

Ray grimaced as she patted my hand. I patted her arm in return. "It's OK, I'm no stranger to rejection, especially not today, not on the single worst day of my whole, entire life. Daniel rejected me today, too."

Ray glanced nervously at the door. "Daniel? Who's Daniel?"

"Alex's friend. He's a writer. He looked over my story and told me it was crap, utter crap."

She patted me again.

"Utter and complete crap without any redeeming value whatsoever."

"I'm sure it isn't *that* bad. Bert was quite taken with it. I thought it sounded very colorful."

I shook my head. "No, he's right, it is crap. I see that now." Another painful lump arose in my throat. I swallowed it back and plucked two more tissues from Ray's box. "But that's not the worst of this hideous day."

Ray nodded sympathetically. "Black."

"Exactly. He dumped me, too."

Her eyes widened. "Doesn't sound like Black to me."

"Well, it is. He's an insensitive, selfish, self-consumed, workaholic boob who doesn't care about anyone unless they happen to fulfill a purpose for him. He's so caught up in himself, he can't bother with anyone else." Tears welled up at the thought of what a selfish beast he was, and how much his lack of concern about me hurt. How could I have been so wrong about him? How could I have been so blind to the fact that he was no different from any other man? Why couldn't he be perfect?

She frowned. "You're upset with him. Emotional. You're not thinking rationally. Black isn't like that."

"He can't even take the time to support me when I'm having an emotional crisis!" I grabbed more tissues and mopped at my streaming eyes. "I called and told him what happened with Daniel, and all he did was tell me he was in some stupid car going on some stupid job and that I should just go home and he would call me later."

She watched me blow my nose again, her eyes warm with concern. "His job is important. You know that."

"I know it's important, but I want to be *more* important to him than catching some dirty old man! If the shoes were on the other feet, I would drop everything to comfort him! The truth is . . ." My voice caught on a breathy sob. I pushed my way up the wall and locked my knees until they stopped shaking. "The truth is, he just doesn't care enough about me. Not really. I was wrong when I thought he might love . . ." My throat closed on the word. I snatched the box of tissues and opened the door. "I'm sorry, Ray, but I can't talk to you now. I am determined to see to the items on my list, and I can't indulge in sobbing and wailing and rending my clothing in front of you."

I closed the door on her protest and started toward the bed, drying my tears en route. If I was going to do this, I was going to do it properly, and that meant a full-fledged hissy fit rather than the silent, hot tears that had been etching their way down my face. I threw myself down on the bed and waited for the bawling to commence. It didn't happen. Instead I lay on my back and stared up at the interesting network of cracks in the plaster ceiling, my eyes hot but suddenly dry. I found that if I squinted, the cracks morphed themselves into the shape of a heart with a dagger plunged into its depths.

A knock at the door disturbed my contemplation of the murdered heart.

"Alix, Ray said you're having a bit of a blue day." Bert's look of sympathy wrapped around me like a warm coat. "How are you?"

"I'm fine. I'm just here sobbing my eyes out. It's the first item on my list."

"Is it?" She hesitated, sneaking little glances around the flat. She sniffed delicately. "You're not . . . er . . . doing anything rash, are you?"

"Rash?" I leaned one hip against the door and considered the question. I wasn't being rash, I was being orderly and productive. I had been dealt three horrendous blows, each blow capable of crumpling me singly; together they had enough destructive power to level a midsized city. And yet, despite all that, I had gathered my wits and come up with a list of productive tasks that would push me well into the recovery zone.

Or so I hoped.

"No, I'm not doing anything rash. I'm just taking care of item number one of my list. Crying."

"I see." Bert pursed her lips and glanced over her shoulder. Ray was hovering in the shadow of the stairs. I waved a hand at her. She waved back. "May I come in?" Bert asked.

I shook my head and propped my arm out against the door frame at an obstructive angle. "Thanks, but not right now, Bert. I've got all this crying to do, you see, and it's always embarrassing to be swollen-eyed and snarfy-nosed around people."

"But . . ." Bert shifted to the side and cast another glance over my shoulder. I swore I heard her sniff again. "But you're not crying now."

I blinked at her. "Yes, I am."

She bit her lip, then laid a gentle hand on my arm. "No, Alix, you're not. Your eyes are dry. Bloodshot, but dry."

I blinked again. Trust my body to turn against me along with everyone else. Now that I wanted to sport a few tears, where were they? "I'm . . . uh . . . I'm crying on the inside."

Her sympathy almost undid me. "Oh, Alix, I'm so sorry. I'm sorry your agent has turned out to be unreliable, and I'm sorry that Alex's friend didn't care for your book, but I'm especially sorry that you've had an argument with Alex."

I debated going into the situation with her, and decided I didn't have time. If item one was completed, and it appeared from my dry-eyed state that it was, item two loomed up large on the horizon.

"I'm sorry, Bert, you're a dear to be so concerned, but since I'm evidently finished with the crying, I have to go wallow in self-pity, and it's not a pretty sight. Perhaps we can get together a few days from now for dinner? Oh—" I stopped myself, remembering the extent of my plans. "Silly me. I'm planning on being depressed and sick and busy with voodoo dolls for the next few days, but perhaps next weekend? Yes? Good. Thank you for stopping by."

I closed the door gently and turned to consider the flat. What would be the best spot for a wallow in self-pity? The chaise? The three-legged stool? The tiny two-person dining table?

Someone knocked on the door.

"Go away," I yelled, not unkindly. I perched on the stool. It wasn't comfortable.

"Alix? It's Isabella."

I should have known. Ray and Bert probably called her in as reinforcement. I made a second mental list and added to it a notation to thank them all for their support and friendship.

"Hello, Isabella. How are you?" I bellowed at the door as I hauled the ladderback chair over to the table and sat. It wasn't as uncomfortable as the bucking stool, but I wasn't sure I could get a good wallow going with the table sitting bleak and barren in front of me. On the other hand, what was my life if not bleak and barren? The table seemed fitting.

"Alexandra? Won't you open the door?"

I rose and plopped down on the chaise. The pillow was an uncomfortable lump in my back. I moved it and lay down. My nose, still stuffy from the tears, filled up and prohibited breathing. I sat up and straddled the end of the chaise. My hip joint made an ugly popping noise as I stood up.

"No, I don't think I will, but thank you for asking. I'm a wee bit busy now with my pity party. It's the second item on my list, you see. I kind of hurried the first one, so it's important I do the second one properly. Why don't you come to dinner with Bert and Ray and me next weekend? You can be nice to me then."

"I must insist that you open this door, Alix. Bertrice says you are in a desperate mood, and I'm very worried over this disagreement you've had with Alexander."

I kicked aside a floor pillow and sank down into a pool of sunlight beneath the open window, leaning back against the wall and stretching my legs out before me. My legs needed shaving, I noticed. My toenail polish was starting to chip. The scab on my knee from the rug burn looked like it was ready to come off.

"Alix? Please open the door."

"I'd rather not, Isabella. I'm fine, honest. I won't do anything rash. I won't try to kill myself or anyone else, I won't nail unlucky omens on Alex's door, I won't even send him a tersely worded e-mail. I just want to be alone for a bit to think things through."

Silence. I brushed a hand down my linen shorts, picking off a few bits of carpet fuzz. Amazing how that stuff procreated. I bet a thousand years from now this orange shag carpet will look the same as it does now.

"As you wish. If you need to talk, I'll be home all afternoon."

"Thank you. And thank Bert and Ray, too."

Faintly I heard the sounds of her shoes tapping their way upstairs. The usual Beale Square noises drifted in from the open window, along with the scent of the mimosas from Ray and Bert's window box. I closed my eyes and let the sounds and scents and air waft over me as I leaned against the wall, the upper part of my body sizzling in the sun while the lower half enjoyed the shade. It was restful there in that corner of the flat, conducive to calming thoughts, peaceful and relatively quiet. I clutched the floor pillow to my chest. Oddly enough, even the heartbreaking sounds of sobbing didn't disturb my newfound peace.

Chapter Twelve

In the end, the list failed to keep me from thinking too much.

"This sucks," I told my spiky little plant later that evening when I was fretfully picking balls of orange carpet fuzz and making a pyramid of them. "I don't like wallowing in self-pity like this. I'm tired of crying. I don't even want to torture Alex. Well, I do, but not as badly as I did earlier. I'm going to scrap my list and just deal with my horrible life. After all, it's not like I haven't done it before. God knows I have, all too often for my sanity, which, I must admit, is extremely questionable right now given the fact that I'm talking to a pot plant."

The plant's cute little spiky leaves trembled in the breeze from the window.

"Sorry. *Alleged* pot plant. I really don't believe Alex's unfounded slurs against you.

I grunted a little grunt as I hoisted myself off the floor

and padded barefoot over to where my novel lay. "I have to decide what to do." I waved a hand at the stack of manuscript papers. "About this, that is. And everything else. Alex. My life. My heart—or at least the shattered remains thereof. That stuff. Oh, hell, now I'm crying again. That's it! I give up! I'm taking a shower. Maybe I'll drown in there and end my suffering."

Twenty minutes later I emerged with my skin wrinkled and pruney, red as a geranium, accompanied by a billowing cloud of lemon-scented steam. I was just reaching for the Mickey Mouse oversized T-shirt that I sleep in when movement from the kitchen almost scared the crap out of me.

"Jeezumcrow, Isabella," I snapped, clutching with both hands the part of my chest housing my heart. "Just give me a heart attack, will you? What are you doing here?"

"I'm sorry, Alix, but Alexander and I were worried about you. Is that a tattoo?" She peered with interest at my pubic bone.

I slapped a hand over it and the accompanying terrain. "No, it's . . . uh . . . just a little love bite."

"But it's indigo. Almost purple."

"It was a very *involved* love bite."

She raised both brows, made a little moue of understanding, then glided back into the kitchen. "I brought wine. Or would you prefer tea?"

I hustled over to my T-shirt and pulled it on. "What I'd like is for you to go home, Isabella."

She paused in the act of uncorking a bottle of wine.

"Damn. I didn't mean to make it sound that way. I'm always happy to see you, you know that, but right now I'm a bit emotional and I really would rather be alone so

I can deal with things in my own way and in my own time."

She finished uncorking the bottle. One eyebrow rose in question as she held up a glass.

"You're not going to leave me alone until you've had your say, are you?"

"No."

I sighed and held out my hand. "OK, but just one glass. I got ripped with Bert and Ray last week and made a fool of myself with Mr. Emotionally Stunted. I don't care to repeat the experience."

Isabella took the bottle and her glass to the chaise. I followed and plopped not very gracefully down onto the floor pillow, tugging my T-shirt over my knees.

"Alexander is very concerned about you. He said you're not answering your phone."

"Alexander doesn't give a damn about me, and you know it," I corrected her. "No, I'm not answering my phone. I have no desire to speak with him. I have no desire to listen to his excuses. He has been put to the test and he failed. What more is there to say?"

She sipped her wine with a steady, unreadable expression. I shrugged off the cool look and took a healthy swig of my wine. It burned nicely going down.

"Why are you doing this?"

I took another swig. "Because I like wine."

A faint frown creased her brow. "No, why are you being so unreasonable with Alexander? You know the nature of his job, and you know how important it is to him. Why are you making him feel guilty for having commitments he is unwilling to break just to satisfy your vanity? Why are you being so selfish?"

I reeled backwards as if I'd been struck. "Selfish? My

vanity? Well, thank you very much, Miss Holier Than Thou! Maybe you and Alex had a such a perfect relationship that you know the answers to everything, but I don't recall asking you for your advice!"

"Now I've hurt your feelings—"

"Of course you hurt my feelings!" I bit back the desire to shout and tempered the volume of my voice. "If I told you that you were selfish and vain, wouldn't you be hurt?"

"Not if it was the truth," she said, her gaze holding firm to mine. "Alix, I consider you more than just an amiable tenant, I consider you a friend. Alexander is very dear to me, and I dislike seeing anger and pain between you, especially when there is no purpose to it."

Probably due to the fact that I hadn't eaten all day—and my notoriously low tolerance of alcohol—the wine hit me with a wallop. I struggled to my feet with as much dignity as possible when clad only in a thigh-length T-shirt. "I'm sorry to distress you over your precious Alexander. I'm sure he'd welcome as much comfort as you would care to give—and yes, that means exactly what you think it means."

I stalked to the door and threw it open dramatically, standing with a stony face that I hoped would inspire her to take her damn pity and understanding and kindness and leave. I didn't want them. I didn't need them. I didn't need *her*. Life had pounded into me over and over and over again the fact that no one needed me and I needed no one. It was about time I stopped fighting fate and admitted that truth. I was a rock! I was an island! I could get by well and fine without anyone!

I burst into tears.

Ten minutes later I was sitting beside Isabella on the

chaise. She looked curiously at the toilet paper before tearing off pieces and handing them to me while I wept.

"I'm sorry," I apologized as soon as I was able to speak. "I ran out of tissues. All I have is toilet paper."

She raised her silver-blond brows. "I have a handkerchief, if you would prefer."

I waved away the offer. "No, I'd just get it all blubbery. I'm very sorry about what I said. I didn't mean any of those terrible things."

She handed me a fresh piece of toilet paper. I blew my nose.

"You are having a trying time right now. I understand what you were doing."

I let that go. I had no desire to psychoanalyze my latent feelings of jealousy whenever I thought of her and Alex. Sniffling wetly, I mopped up and gave her a watery smile. "What do you say we start the evening over again?"

She returned my smile with one that was bright enough to light up Beale Square. "That sounds like an excellent idea. But before we do"—she glanced at the watch on her slim wrist—"I think I should warn you that . . . ah, there he is."

I glanced from her to where my phone had started ringing. "There who is? Alex? I don't want to talk to him."

"Alix, please, he's worried about you."

"Ha! Fat chance. He's probably only worried that he's ticked me off enough so that I won't want to play squishy-squishy with him anymore!"

She slid a sidelong look at me as one graceful hand fluttered about in a gesture of distress. "I'm quite sure his feelings for you are deeper than those for a casual sexual partner. He is very worried. Please answer the phone."

"No."

"Alix, please!"

"I don't want to."

"You must!"

"Like hell I must! I won't sit here and be coerced in my own flat! I can't believe my mother is paying good money so you can bully me about!"

A mulish expression settled on her perfect face. I snarled an oath, but she just raised one platinum eyebrow at me. She must have had some sort of secret mindray powers that I'd never suspected, because I suddenly found myself with the phone in my hand.

I took a deep breath and peeked at Isabella out of the corner of my eye. She raised her eyebrows even higher. I turned my back on her. Maybe if I made a little Juliet cap out of tinfoil I could withstand her powers, but until then . . . "If this is Detective Inspector Blackheart, I don't wish to speak with you. If this is anyone else, I will happily talk to you tomorrow. Thank you for calling. Live long and prosper."

Before I could hang up, his voice caressed my ear, sending waves of pleasure rippling through my body, the same body that warred with my mind, one wanting nothing more than to fling itself in his arms, the other proclaiming I never wanted to see him again. "Alix? Wait, don't ring off. Where have you been? Why haven't you answered the phone? Isabella says you're upset—"

I snorted. *That* was the understatement of the year.

"—and in hiding. If this is because I'm on a case and can't be home, I'm sorry, but you know how important this raid is. We ran into a hostage situation, and it's taking longer than I anticipated to arrest the suspect. Alix? Are you there?"

An unsure, hesitant note in his voice plucked at my heartstrings, but I tried to ignore it. I wanted to tell him to go do something anatomically impossible to himself. I wanted to tell him I didn't want to see him again. I wanted to hurt him like he'd hurt me. I wanted to, but Isabella's words kept rattling around my head. *Selfish. Vain. Unreasonable.* Was there validity to her accusations, or was she just being overly defensive of Alex? In my muddled mental state I didn't know for certain, and suddenly I was too tired to care.

"I'm here. I'm tired. I want to go to sleep. I hope your raid goes OK."

"Sweetheart—"

My eyes closed in pain at that word. *Once* it had meant something.

"—I have to go now. If I ring you up in the morning, will you answer?"

I considered my bare toes. They had no answers for me. "Yes."

"Good." Relief was evident in his voice. "Get some rest. Things will look better in the morning."

I murmured something noncommittal. It was my experience that things always looked worse in the stark light of morning, but I had noticed that Alex had a tendency to a hideously cheerful morning mood no matter how early it was.

"Alix?" His voice dropped until it was a whisper of velvet against my ear. The hairs on the back of my neck stood on end. "You know that I . . . Christ, I have to go! Take care of yourself. I'll be there as soon as I can."

I nodded at the phone and hung it up, rubbing my ear,

still feeling the brush of his voice against my skin, leaving the entire right side of my body bathed in warmth. Isabella corked the half-empty bottle of wine and took it out to the kitchen.

"Good night," she said as she passed me, pausing to tip her head to the side in that adorably cute manner that would be affected on anyone else, then pressed a kiss to my cheek.

"Truly good things are worth working for," she said with a tiny smile. I blinked back a bit of moisture, swallowed, and nodded. "Sleep well."

"Fat chance of that happening," I muttered as the door closed behind her. I flipped off the overhead lights and curled up in bed. I wouldn't sleep, that I knew. I was too emotionally strung out. Whenever I'm extremely fatigued, I don't sleep, and at that moment I felt as if my nerves had been used on a cheese grater. I wasn't just tired, I was exhausted. I pulled out a book and prepared to read my way through the night.

Seven hours later I dragged myself out of bed, blinking the sleep out of my eyes. I doubt if I had managed to read even a complete sentence of my book before slipping off to nighty-night land. I was a little surprised by that, but decided while I took a shower that it didn't matter. What *did* matter was that I get my life back on track. I had some serious decisions making to do, and it was best done soon, before I lost my nerve.

Two pots of Starbuck's Espresso Blend later, I figured my brain was strong enough to tackle the horrible tangle I'd made of my life. I looked down at the list I had written.

1. Scrap *Ravening Raptures*. Burn to exorcise evil spirit that lives within it.

2. Cancel death contract on Agent Tully (hit man=great expense).
3. Destroy paper voodoo dolls of Alex. Vacuum up all evidences of paper emasculations.
4. Purchase three pounds of orange truffles. For medicinal purposes.
5. Write new book. Medieval? Need something catchy and clever. Blind heroine? Blind hero? Blind horse?
6. Answer phone when Alex calls. Be polite. Be sure not to address him as Detective Inspector Poopy-Pants. Even though he deserves it.

Appreciation of such a comprehensive list was interrupted by knocking on my door.

"I'm fine, Isabella, just fine," I called as I gave the list one last admiring glance and went over to the door. "Honestly, the way you're worrying, you'd think I was going to jump off a bridge or someth—"

It wasn't Isabella at the door.

"From the various calls I fielded yesterday from Isabella, Ray, and Bert, you sounded as if you *were* ready to jump," Alex said. His eyes glittered darkly, almost black with fatigue, the skin beneath them bruised and shadowed. Dark brown whiskers caressed his jaw and cheeks, making him look tired, careworn, and utterly sexy. I fought a little skirmish with my body to keep from pouncing on him.

"Detective Inspector Black," I said, hoping he wouldn't notice the little quaver in my voice.

"Miss Freemar," he replied, not even a hint of a smile quirking his lovely lips. I held his gaze for a few seconds, then stepped back and waved him into the flat.

"You look like hell." I closed the door, crossed my arms, and leaned against it.

He made a courtly little bow. "Thank you, I feel like hell. Is that coffee I smell?"

"It is."

He waited.

I heaved an exaggerated sigh and indicated the table. "Sit. You want cream in it?"

"Please."

I brushed past him into the tiny kitchen, fighting with myself every step of the way. He looked so wounded! So needy! So *little boy lost!* I wanted nothing more than to peel those layers of sorrow and exhaustion from him and ply his manly body with every part of my womanly body, but I couldn't. There was item number seven on my list to consider.

> 7. Tell Alex it was good while it lasted, but now it's over. Buy superglue. Patch together remains of heart and get on with life. *Again.*

The ladderback chair creaked as Alex slumped back. I plugged in my coffee grinder and started grinding up a fresh batch of espresso bean coffee, trying not to be obvious in my quick glances at him. There were deep lines around his mouth that hadn't been there the day before. Guilt rippled through me at the sight of them. Even if yesterday's betrayal meant the destruction of our relationship, I couldn't make myself believe he'd been on a day's frolic out in the countryside; his air of subdued despair belied that. It made me want to comfort him all the more, to wrap my arms around him, to press his

adorable head to my chest and kiss his troubles away.
. . . I shook the image from my mind. What was I doing?
I wanted to comfort *him*? He was the man who'd re-
jected *me* most cruelly when I needed him!

Alex leaned forward and moved my list aside. He
pulled a tiny bit of blue paper out of a pile, holding it
carefully in his hand. "You've been cutting out paper
dolls?"

I glanced at what he held in his hand and blushed.
"Maybe."

He looked at the blue object. "This looks like a . . .
erm . . ."

I poured boiling water into the French press and fixed
the plunger. "It is."

"Why are you cutting out minuscule blue paper pe-
nises?"

I shrugged. "It just seemed like the thing to do."

Alex didn't say anything to that. He poked in the pile
of paper again, then lifted up one of the paper Alex voodoo dolls.

"This one has my name on it."

I busied myself pouring cream into a black and white
cow-shaped creamer. "Does it? How very interesting."

"Someone has drawn a great hairy wart on the chin of
this paper Alex. And heavy glasses. And it would appear
there are horns sprouting from his head."

I pursed my lips and whistled a little innocent whistle.

"If the angle at which the legs have been severed and
taped back on is any indication, I would also say it has
suffered compound fractures." He looked closer at the
doll. "It has also been, for lack of a better word, *cas-
trated.*"

"What do you know about that?" I asked, placing the
coffee, cream, and a mug on the table.

He leveled a look at me that was impossible to read, and accepted the mug of coffee.

"So," I said conversationally as I refreshed my cup. "How's tricks?"

He put his mug down. "What did you ask?"

"Tricks. How are they?"

"Tricks? How are my tricks—is that what you're asking?"

I nodded. If he weren't so tired, if I weren't so heart sore, I would have found the look of disbelief that crossed his face comical. As it was, I hardened my heart and remembered my many grievances, but even that didn't do me much good.

"Alix, I've been up twenty-eight hours straight. I have spent the night crouching in a patch of blackberry bushes in case my suspect released the woman—his wife of fourteen years—whom he was holding hostage, only to have him kill himself five hours ago by drinking a common household cleaner. I spent the next three hours explaining to my superior at the Yard what went wrong with what should have been a simple raid. In addition to which, I have seen the results of a case I've been working on for the last four months end not in an arrest of a child pornographer, but in a messy, unnecessary death that will generate at least a five-meter-high stack of paperwork. During the past twenty-four hours I have fielded innumerable calls from individuals residing in this house who were concerned that you and I had some sort of falling out, leaving you in a desperate state of mind. I have been worried out of my head because you were reported to be home and yet refused to answer my numerous calls to you. I am tired. I am covered in scratches. I itch. I suspect several insects have taken refuge on various locations of my body. How are tricks? Tricks are bloody awful, thank you for asking!"

I bristled at his tone. "Don't you take that tone of voice with me! I asked a civil question, I expect a civil answer. If you're so frigging unhappy with me, you can just take your bugs and leave!"

He rubbed a hand over his weary eyes. "Christ, Alix, I don't want to argue with you."

But *I* wanted to argue with him. Anger was the only thing that was going to keep me from throwing myself on him, becoming a doormat with an invitation to walk all over me stamped on my forehead.

"Fine." I said. "Don't argue with me, then. Drink your coffee and go to bed."

A wistful look passed over his face, but he set his jaw and shook his head. "You said you needed to talk to me. Here I am. I assume this is regarding what Daniel said about your story?"

Oh, the inner struggle! Part of me wanted to pour it all out to him, to sob out how Daniel's evaluation had destroyed my creative spirit, to cry over the pain of my agent divorcing me; but another part of me, the survivor part, said no. I had thought Alex was different from the other men in my past, but he had proven he wasn't, and I knew from hard experience that if I gave in now, I would be lost for good. He would never respect me, never treat me like I mattered to him. There was no future with Alex, I knew that now, but I could still end things with dignity.

"No, that doesn't matter anymore." I pointed to where my manuscript was currently residing in the wastebasket before I hauled it down to the trash bin. "I've scrapped that story. I'm going to write a new one, a medieval this time, about a knight and his blind horse. It's going to be very poignant. I see Rupert Everett in the role."

"As the blind horse?"

I thinned my lips at him, but he was too busy frowning at the wastebasket to appreciate my gimlet-eyed glare.

"Why are you throwing away your story? Daniel said it needed work, but it had promise."

"He said it needed a complete rewrite. Forget about it, Alex, it's trash. I'm starting over, starting fresh with a bigger and better story. I may only have a month to get it written before my time runs out on the flat, but I can write a book in a month. And if I have to punch up a bit of it once I return home, that's no problem." I hoped he noticed my reference to returning home at the end of the month. I wanted it clear to him that our relationship was over, and that we had no future together other than perhaps the occasional tumble into bed. Anything else, anything of a more permanent nature, anything involving emotions and feelings outside of the genital region, were off. Impossible. Wasn't going to happen. Not again, anyway.

He ignored my hint and clamped down like a terrier on a bone to the subject of my failure. "Daniel said he offered to help you restructure your story. Why are you giving up on it so easily?"

I gritted my teeth and rose. "Have you had breakfast?"

He shook his head and took another sip of coffee, his lovely bruised eyes watching me closely. I went into the kitchen and pulled out a bag of almond croissants I had purchased earlier.

"Knock yourself out," I said as I placed the croissants before him, then turned my back on him to water my cute little spiky plant.

"Alix—"

I whirled around. "God! You're just as bad as Isabella! Nag, nag, nag—is that all you people do around here? Find visiting Americans and nag them to death?"

He looked startled by my outburst. "I was just going to ask if I could have more coffee."

Oh. Coffee. He wanted more coffee. Poor man, he looked so tired, so wounded-hero . . . I gave myself a mental shake and fetched the French press for him.

He thanked me. I mumbled a response. We stared at each other, Alex peering at me over the rim of his mug, me standing next to the window with my arms crossed over my boobs in what I knew was a "hands off" body stance. The silence was profound and pregnant with unspoken queries.

"All right, all right, I'll answer your bloody questions! I can't stand this constant badgering! What do they do, give you detectives a class in administering the third degree?" I stomped over to the table, ignoring the surprised look on his handsome, tired face, and sat down. "I'm starting a new story because the first one would take too much work to finish. Even"—I raised my hand to forestall his objection—"with Daniel's help, it would still mean I have to rewrite the story, and I don't want to do that. I'm sick to death of Rowena and Raoul. So instead I'm going to start a new story, a better one, one that won't be so much trouble to write. I'm going to plot it all out in advance, so I know exactly where it's going and who's going to do what and say what and just how the blind horse is going to regain his sight at the end of the book."

Alex set down his mug and leaned back in the chair, the thumb of one hand rubbing along his whiskery jawline. "Let me make sure I understand this—you're going to give up on the project you've put so much time and work into in order to start a new story, just because you're tired of the first one?"

I nodded, pleased he understood the importance of cutting your losses and starting over. Lord knows that had been one of the first life lessons I had learned. "You got it in one. *Ravening Raptures* isn't worth the trouble it would take to fix it."

He stilled. "And what about us?"

I froze as well, my eyes caught in his dark emerald gaze.

His words were as quiet as they were soft. "Is our relationship worth the trouble to fix it?"

Yes! Yes, it is! a voice shrieked in my head. The joy of being with him was worth any amount of trouble, any sacrifice! I loved the man; wasn't love all about martyring yourself for the happiness of your loved one? To hell with my ego. To hell with my broken soul, my crushed feelings, the pain and suffering he had dealt me, would *continue* to give me because I wasn't first in his heart as he was in mine. All that mattered was that he was happy, right? I took a deep breath.

"No, it's not worth the trouble."

The voice inside my head keeled over in a dead faint. I knew just how she felt. I would have given good money to be able to faint just then. I would have given my soul—shattered as it was—not to have seen the flicker of pain in Alex's eyes. The pain *I* had caused. I swallowed hard and plunged onward. It would be a cleaner cut to get the worst over with quickly.

"I'm sorry Alex, there's just no nice way to say this." I knew the words, knew them well, but I had never been the one to say them. Odd how with each word spoken, a bit of me died inside. "What we had was nice, but . . ." I shrugged. "Well, these things happen."

He wasn't breathing. He didn't move. He was a statue, sculpted from some incredibly lifelike substance, fashioned in the image of the better parts of several Greek gods. Beautiful to look at, but without the breath of life.

"What things?"

I swear his lips didn't even move. I had the worst urge to hold a mirror to his mouth to see if he was breathing, but figured that I'd better stay out of grabbing range just in case he was alive and was going to take it harder than I anticipated he would.

"Oh, you know . . ." I shrugged again. "Just things. Us. Our relationship. Our future, or rather, the lack thereof. *Things.*"

His shoulders slumped in defeat, and I bled a little more inside at the sight of his head bowing with anguish. How could I do this to him? How could I willingly hurt the man whose existence lit up my life? How could I? *Survival,* the little voice in my head whispered. *It's him or you.*

"I'm sorry, Alex, but it's clear that although you're a raging stallion in bed, outside of sex we don't have a whole lot going for us. You are a workaholic, and I'm—"

"—an insecure woman riddled with self-doubt who has no concept of her own worth." Alex's head snapped up with his words, his eyes glittering with heat and fury and something I had never seen before. "And I'm too tired to play your games right now, so if you'll excuse me, I'm going to bed. You're welcome to join me, although I make no promises as to how good a ride my stallion will be this morning."

I shook my head, swallowing back misery. "Thank you, but no. Take your stallion for a ride by yourself."

One lovely glossy chestnut eyebrow rose. I blushed a blush of pure idiocy.

"I didn't mean that the way it came out. I just meant that you can go to bed by yourself."

He pinned me back with that fiery green gaze for a few seconds, then released me and tiredly rose from the table. "We're not finished talking about this."

"Yes, we are. It's over, Alex. It's better this way, honest. I'll be going home in a month and will be out of your life. You can find yourself some other woman." I closed my eyes at the pain that thought brought with it. "Someone who has all the qualities you like, someone who fits in with your life, someone you really want and need."

The doorknob rattled as he opened the door. I kept my eyes closed and leaned against the kitchen wall, hoping my knees would hold out until after he left.

"I have the woman I want and need."

Delivered by a velvet-soft voice, his words cut through my flesh and made unerringly for my shattered heart. The door clicked shut just as my knees gave way and I slid down to the floor, my arms wrapped around myself to keep the shaking to a minimum.

Twenty minutes later a note was slipped under my door. I crawled over to it and held it for a few minutes before I blinked away enough tears to read it. It was a printout of an e-mail, sent to me at an e-mail account Alex had opened for me so I could correspond with my mother. On the back of it Alex had written *We can talk about it over dinner. 6 p.m. Stella's.* I shook my head at the note and turned it over to read the message from my mother.

It was a threat to turn my novel—sent to her a few days before—over to the attorney general as indecent literature. I had no idea my mother knew so many words for "smut." She must have found a thesaurus somewhere, because I just couldn't imagine her using words like *prurient* and *salacious* in everyday conversation. The tirade about my novel transitioned seamlessly into an evaluation of my writing style, my character, and my life in general, ending with a demand that I return home immediately and stop wasting her money. *If you insist on writing pornography,* she wrote, *you can do so from Grandma's trailer. That's where this sort of trash belongs!*

I wadded up the letter and looked around my flat. Sometimes you just couldn't win. Sometimes you didn't even come close.

Chapter Thirteen

*"Fare thee well, Sir Christopher! May God speed you on
your way to the Holy Land."*

With a curt nod of his manly head, Sir Christopher
donned his conical helmet and wheeled his mighty destrier about, putting his spurs to the great horse's belly.
So the Lady Fenella wished him Godspeed, did she? Ha!
He'd not soon forget her cutting remarks about the wisdom of riding Black Demon. As if he'd give up his favorite destrier just because of a little problem with the
horse's vision. Why, just look at what a fine mettle The
Demon was in as they galloped through the bailey toward the drawbridge. His head was up, his nostrils
flared, his ebony mane streaming back over Sir Christopher's hands, the very picture of a noble steed at his
most glorious.

*   *   *

"Blast!" I glared over to where the phone was ringing, interrupting me just as I was really getting into the rhythm of my story. I knew who it was. Oh, yes, I knew who was calling me, who had been finding excuses to call me all morning, and I was on to her game. I wasn't going to be browbeaten into hearing yet another lecture on the shambles of my life. The phone continued to ring, finally driving me to snatching it up and snarling, "Isabella, I'm busy right now!"

"Oh . . . Alix? Good morning. This is Bert. I just wanted to call and see how you were feeling this morning. I know it's none of my business, but Ray and I were concerned."

I stopped glaring at the phone, touched by the genuine kindness in Bert's voice. "Thank you, I'm feeling much better. In fact, I was just working on my new story when you called. I had no idea you were home. Why don't you pop up for lunch? I make a mean grilled turkey, Swiss, and bacon sandwich."

A smile warmed her voice. "I'm glad to hear you're writing again. I know how such a setback can affect creativity. I'd love to have lunch with you, but I'm at work, not at home. I spoke with Isabella, and she mentioned that you were still a bit blue, so I thought I would telephone."

I snorted a particularly disbelieving snort. "Bert! I'm surprised at you!"

"I . . . why?"

"Allowing yourself to be used as Isabella's tool of vengeance! Or rather, in this case, curiosity."

"Oh, but I—"

"Isabella's miffed at me because in the space of the last two hours she's invited me to lunch, tea, and dinner, as well as made offers to indulge in a cozy chat or a walk in Hyde Park. I've turned her down because I have no desire to hear her lecture me on *What I'm Doing Wrong with Alexander the Great.*"

Bert apologized, which made me feel guilty for snapping at her, so after I apologized and we spent a few minutes in mutual reassurances that we were both doing well, I hung up.

"Right," I told my laptop. "Where was I?"

"My pardon, Sir Rennick," Sir Christopher called as Black Demon suddenly swerved and slammed against his knight's gray gelding. He pressed hard with his right knee, muttering as he did so, "To the left, Demon, the left! No, no, back to the . . . God's teeth, my apologies, Sir Henry. The sun must have been in Demon's eyes. You were not injured? Excellent. Onward, my knights! Onward to the glory of God!"

I swore an appropriately medievalish oath when the phone rang again. It would be Isabella, I was sure, calling to apologize for setting Bert on me. "Hello?"

"Freemar. Ray Binder here. Heard you're not feeling the thing. Not still crying over Black, are you?"

"Hi, Ray. No, I'm not wasting any more tears on him. In fact, I'm in the middle of writing a scene now, so if you don't mind, I'd like to get back to it while the story is still fresh in my mind."

"Ah. Good. Remount when you've been thrown. We'll see you on Friday."

Ray rang off as I fought to eliminate the picture of taking Alex's stallion for a ride. It was touch-and-go there for a moment, but at last I wrestled my mind from the contemplation of his nether parts and onto my story, where it belonged.

Lady Fenella rolled her eyes as her obstinate, pigheaded, "always right, never wrong" betrothed led his men off in a decidedly zigzag path. At least she wouldn't have to put up with his self-righteous insistence that she yield all decisions to him. She was the chatelaine of Rosehill, after all! He was merely a lowly knight. True, she would miss his secret visits to her bedchamber in the dark of the night, but surely his wasn't the only stallion in the stable.

"Now I have stallions on the brain," I muttered, and hit the backspace key, then made an annoyed noise as the phone rang yet again. "What am I, the operator or something? Hello, yes, it's Alix."

"Alix, how very nice to hear your voice!"

I sighed. "Good morning, Karl. How are things in the wild, wacky world of dentistry?"

"As expected, Alix, as expected. How are you holding up? Isabella tells me you've had a falling out with Alex and are a bit under the weather."

"Isn't that just so sweet of Isabella notifying everyone I know in London to call and check up on me," I ground out between clenched teeth. "I'm fine, Karl, just fine. Not suicidal, not crying over my broken heart, just trying to get on with my life by writing a new story. So if you'll excuse me—"

"Ah. Yes. Certainly. Just as you say. Perhaps you'd like to go to the theater with me some night?"

"That would be lovely. Thank you for calling. Good-bye!"

I set the receiver down in the cradle with all the care of a mongoose with a ripe egg. After ten seconds, when it didn't ring I returned to my story. Who else was left to call but Isabella herself and Alex? Alex was probably working his long, sensitive fingers to the bone and couldn't be bothered to call me even if he wanted to, which he certainly wouldn't after I'd told him we were finished, while Isabella was no doubt busy dreaming up new ways to torment me until I gave in and allowed her to lecture me.

Edythe, the willowy, flaxen-haired maid, burst into Lady Fenella's solar, her naturally slender hands dancing madly as she choked out an unintelligible word. "My lady! Oh, my lady! You must come quick! It's Sir Christopher!"

Lady Fenella glanced at the angle of sunlight streaming through the opened shutters. Surely it had only been a few moments since she had seen her betrothed off? "What about Sir Christopher, Edythe?"

The maid's hands fluttered helplessly. "His horse has fallen into the moat, my lady! With Sir Christopher on his back! And now . . . oh, now, my lady . . ." Edythe's hands stopped fluttering long enough to cover her eyes as she sobbed and wailed.

"What? Don't tell me—now the horse can see?"

The phone rang. "Yes?" I snarled into it, ready to blister the ear of Isabella or Alex, whichever one had the nerve to disturb me. I'd never get the story written at this rate!

"Hello, Alix," a soft, almost breathy voice said.

"Uh . . . hello." I didn't recognize the voice or the accent, but assumed that since the man knew my name, it must be someone I'd had contact with. Perhaps it was one of Daniel's friends? Someone from Maureen Tully's office?

"This is Philippe. Philippe from downstairs."

Philippe? Philippe was calling me? Whatever for? "Hi, Philippe. How nice to hear from you. I take it you must have received some of my mail by mistake?"

"Yes. No, I mean, yes it is nice to hear from you as well, no I do not have any of your post. Isabella—"

"Aha!" I knew it! I knew she had to be behind Philippe's call. Why else would he call me with that distracted, worried-sounding voice? Well, I'd nip this in the bud! "Thank you for calling me, Philippe. Isabella was wrong, I'm not depressed or sad or blue or anything, I'm just fine, fine and dandy, peachy damn keen in fact, so you can go about your day secure in the knowledge that you've done what you could to save me from destruction."

"Ah," he responded breathily. "Ah. I see. Yes. Then I will ring off."

"Thank you," I said even as I plotted my revenge on a certain slinky landlady. "Have a nice day."

"Ah," he said again before I hung up. I looked at the phone. It looked back at me. I waited. I waited some more. I got tired of waiting after five minutes and went back to my story.

Edythe peeked through her fingers, her mouth an O of astonishment. "How did you guess, my lady? Yes, 'tis said that now the great black brute can see again, but oh, my lady, at what price? At what price?"

"I don't know at what price, Edythe," Fenella

snapped, tired of all the fuss about a mere horse. And an ugly one at that! "You must tell me."

"Oh, my lady, the horse can see, but . . . but . . . Sir Christopher hit his head on the tapstone as he was pulled out and now . . . now he is blind!"

I pounced on the phone before it completed the first ring. "Isabella?"

There was a momentary pause. "Why, yes, it is me, Alix. How prescient of you to know that. I was doing a little dusting and found I have a box of Belgian chocolates that I will never eat, and thought perhaps you might like—"

It was useless, and I knew it. Isabella knew it, too. I could hear amusement in her voice. "I'll be up at four for tea. Earl Grey. Curried chicken sandwiches. The chocolates. OK?"

"What an excellent idea! I'm so glad you want to come to tea. You can tell me all about your new book. I'll see you then."

"I don't understand how you can write a novel if one of the characters is blind."

"The characters aren't blind," I snorted. *"That's* been done before. In my story, it's not the hero who's blind, it's his horse. Well, actually, the hero is blind for a bit, but not for very long, just long enough for the heroine to save him from the dreaded Indigo Knight."

"Ah." Isabella adjusted a lovely Creamware vase of salmon-pink roses and glided over to tweak the colorful table runner on her dining room table straight. "Why is the horse blind?"

I opened my mouth once or twice while I struggled for

an answer. "It's . . . uh . . . unique. A unique story angle."

"And unique is good?"

"In the world of fiction, sometimes. Well, OK, not often unless you're Stephen King or someone famous like that, but I decided that the only thing I have going for me is my dedication to writing the story of my heart, so that's what I'm doing."

She paused in adjusting a cluster of knickknacks residing on the top of an elegant rosewood sideboard and slid a glance my way. "Indeed? And that story of your heart concerns a man and his blind horse?"

I nodded, waiting for her to spit out what she really wanted to say.

"Indeed," she said again, and moved off to the sitting room to fuss with the tea tray. I plodded after her, feeling about as graceless as a moose in a closet. It must be her mind ray working overtime on me. I sat where she directed me and accepted a cup of steaming tea despite the fact that it was another hot August day.

"Tell me more about this story of your heart."

I plucked two tiny curried chicken sandwiches from the plate and sat back. "You want to know more about the storyline?"

"No, I want to understand just what it is that makes a story the story of your heart."

"Oh, that just means the story is very near and dear to me."

One rose-tipped finger traced the gilt rim on her teacup. "So the story is one that has meaning for you? It has a connection with you beyond merely a plot you think the public will enjoy?"

"That's right." I watched her finger continue to stroke

lazy circles around the rim of her cup. A faint feeling of guilt was manifesting itself, and I had no idea what caused it, but I didn't like it. I tamped down on it and continued. "I read about this in a writing magazine. A story of the heart is something more than just an ordinary story, it's one that has its source in the heart and soul of the writer. It's personal, oftentimes based on real emotions and events in the writer's life."

"Yes, I can understand that. So this story you've decided to write, the one with a stubborn knight who refuses to acknowledge the importance of his lady love because it is more important that he go on a Crusade than save her from marauding rogue knights—that story has a deeper meaning to you?"

I narrowed my eyes. Suddenly I knew what she was about—she was trying to trap me into admitting that my latest book featured a thinly disguised representation of Alex and me. Ha! Other than some cosmetic likenesses, nothing could be further from the truth!

"That's not quite true. This new novel, *A Harlot's Love*, is a story of my heart simply because I . . . er . . . well, I know what Lady Fenella . . . that is, I can relate to the . . . uh . . . *stresses* she's under . . . uh . . . trying to . . . well, you'll just have to take my word that it's not what you said. It's just a story of my heart, and that's all there is to it."

Isabella raised an eyebrow at the tone of belligerence that had somehow crept into my voice. I jumped ahead before she could dissect my writing any further. "So you can just forget about trying to draw parallels between Sir Christopher the Obstinate and Sir Alex the Boob. And speaking of Alex, why don't you go ahead and do it?"

Both eyebrows rose now. "Do what?"

I chewed my tiny triangle of a sandwich and licked a bit of curried chicken off my finger. "Lecture me. Go ahead. You know you're dying to tell me exactly what I'm doing wrong with Alex. Oh, come on, don't even *try* to look surprised! You know that's the whole reason you've been trying like mad to get me up here, so you can tell me to back off of Alex and be a nice little doormat to keep His Puissance happy while he walks all over me. Well, sister, I'm here to tell you, that is not going to happen in this or any other lifetime!"

"Alix, honestly, I wasn't trying to meet with you to lecture you about your problems with Alexander, and I certainly would never advise you to be a doormat."

I made suspicious squinty eyes at her. She batted her lashes in a damned good imitation of innocence.

"If you didn't want to tell me what I should be doing with Alex, then why were you trying so hard to get me up here?"

A warm smile spread across her lips. The sight of it made my eyes go even more squinty.

"Because you are my friend and you are troubled! I simply thought you might like to have some time away from your problems, and perhaps to take advantage of a shoulder to cry on."

"Huh," I said, my voice oozing disbelief. "Well, I'm sorry that I accused you of trying to get me up here to yell at me, and I do appreciate you offering your shoulder. That's very selfless of you."

"Alix, you're my friend," she said simply, and lifted the teapot. I shook my head and sipped my now luke-warm tea.

Silence wrapped around us. Only the faint whir of a fan disturbed us as we both sat and contemplated the view across the square to the tiny green. An old lady with an elderly corgi wandered the perimeter, while in the center of the lawn a group of teens lay in various states of undress looking like so many slabs of beef at a butcher.

"But as you've mentioned the subject . . ."

I groaned and closed my eyes. I knew she wouldn't be able to resist!

". . . I believe you have a mistaken impression about Alexander's intentions toward you."

It was no use, there was just no fighting her. I put my cup down, stifled the sigh I wanted to heave, and sat back against the gold and rose settee, resigned to hearing her out. I made a mental note to not visit Isabella again without a protective tinfoil Juliet cap, and slapped a smile on my face. "Go on, I'm listening."

She shot me a questioning look, then leaned forward to select a chocolate from a footed crystal dish. "Would you prefer to hear the polite version of my thoughts or the honest one?"

"Polite," I said quickly. A flicker of disappointment flashed in her eyes, but was quickly gone. She opened her mouth to speak, but I interrupted her before she could. "No, no, I didn't mean that. Go ahead, give me the full poop."

"Very well. Alix, you know I think you are a very smart woman."

I released the death grip I had on the settee's arm. Perhaps the truth wouldn't be as bad as I expected.

"You're witty, clever, and have a generous heart. I know your joking manner with Alexander hides some rather deep feelings for him, and I know he returns them."

273

I snorted and reached for the teapot.

"You don't believe me, but I am in a position to know. I knew how he was with his ex-wife, you see—and of course, how he acted with me."

I paused in the act of stuffing an orange liqueur chocolate in my mouth. "His *what?*"

She looked surprised by my shriek. "His ex-wife. Jill. Hasn't he mentioned her? She was a friend of mine in university. You might wish to eat that, dear. You're dribbling liqueur down your blouse."

I looked down at the chocolate squashed between my fingers. He had been married and he never told me? I'd told him about my ex-husband, why hadn't he told me about his ex? Tears pricked behind my eyes as I answered my own question. He hadn't told me because I didn't matter that much to him. I was merely a comfy body to dally with, but no one he wanted to become emotionally involved with. No one he wanted to truly share his life with, no one he wanted to gift with his heart.

The bastard.

"I'm sorry, Alix, I appear to have put a foot wrong here. I assumed he had told you about Jill."

I swallowed back a lump of unshed tears and popped the sticky, squashed chocolate in my mouth. "No," I said indistinctly around the now-tasteless chocolate, wincing as the tiny shards that were all that remained of my heart ground into powder at yet more proof that Alex didn't think I was worthy of his love. How could he love me when he didn't even trust me? If I didn't believe it before, I did now—I just wasn't an important part of his life. "No, he didn't tell me."

Isabella looked uncomfortable for a moment; then her

usual poise returned. "I'm sure he had a reason why he didn't, and after all, he has been divorced for almost ten years, so it's not as if it is recent news. The only reason *I* mentioned it is because I wanted to reassure you that I know Alexander very well, and I can see the difference in the manner he has treated every other woman he's dated, and the way he is when he's with you."

I was nothing to him. I was less than nothing, I didn't even exist. Expendable, unimportant, trivial. An ache started deep inside me, deep within my womb, deep in all those secret, dark inner places that only he had touched, really touched. "Oh, great! Not only did he break my heart, utterly destroying it so it will never be whole again, now he's broken my womanly bits as well!"

Isabella's mouth hung open in surprise for a nanosecond before she said, "I don't believe I've ever heard of the end of a romantic relationship resulting in a broken uterus."

I rubbed my hand on my abdomen. "You underestimate Alex's power of destruction. No"—I raised my hand when she started to object. "I take it back. He doesn't have the power to give me cramps, and I'm sure that's all this is. Would you mind wrapping up your lecture? I think I'm going to want to go lie down with the heating pad."

She hesitated for a minute, then set down her plate and folded her hands nicely upon her lap. "All right, I'll say what I need to say and leave you alone. You're an exceptional woman, Alix, with many good qualities, but you are probably the most selfish and self-centered person I've ever met."

I stared at her with my mouth hanging open, and not

just a little bit. My jaw rested on my knees. Selfish? Self-centered? *Me?*

"All you seem to be concerned about is what Alexander can do for you, how he can make you feel better, how he can fulfill your needs. Have you ever once considered what *he* needs? Have you ever tried to put yourself in his shoes to understand the decisions he makes? Has it never struck you that you entered into the relationship with the idea of taking what you could from it while you could, because you had no intention of staying with Alexander after the summer was over? Don't you understand the power you have to destroy him? Don't you see how you are destroying him *now* with your unthinking, selfish actions?"

Tears bullied their way forward in my eyes, but I blinked them back, too stunned by Isabella's words to muster a coherent response.

"Alix." She put a hand on mine and squeezed. "I know the truth can be cruel and hurtful, but you and Alexander are my friends. I see the love you both have for each other, and I see the pain that the obstacles you've created are causing. If you could just see them as clearly, I believe you would be a very happy woman, very much in love and loved. Won't you try to open your eyes and see what I see?"

I swallowed down my grief and stood up, wiping at my eyes with the linen napkin I still held crushed in my hand. "Thank you for a lovely tea, Isabella. I'm afraid I'm not feeling terribly well, but perhaps we can do this again one day."

Maybe when hell froze over.

She reached out to grab me before I could slip away. "Alix, please don't do this. I only want to help you—"

Help me? Did she really? Maybe she was right, maybe I was wrong . . . but no, I couldn't be. Every event of the last couple of days stood as a familiar signpost along the road to rejection. I knew them well, I couldn't mistake them for something more benign. "I know you want to help, and I appreciate your good intentions, but this is something I have to work out by myself."

She shook her head, her platinum hair swinging as she rose in one graceful movement. "You see? You're thinking only of your own problems, as if the problems are yours alone and not affecting both you and Alexander. As long as you continue to isolate yourself from him, as long as you guard your heart against the pain that comes from loving, you'll never be able to truly love him in return. And, oh, Alix, he deserves to be loved by all your heart, not just the tiny bit you're willing to let him see."

I spun around at her hall door, furious at her soft entreaty. "I *beg* your pardon? Guard my heart against the pain of loving Alex? Have you heard nothing I've said? My heart is broken! Crushed! Completely destroyed, by Alex, because of Alex, due solely to Alex! If I didn't love him so much, he wouldn't have that sort of power over me!"

She shook her head again. "You *think* your heart is broken. You're re-creating what you know from your prior experiences with men. You're evoking the feelings that followed when you were rejected in the past, the feelings of being small and unworthy. But that's not love, Alix. You may love Alexander—in fact, I believe you do—but you're guarding your heart by thrusting him away before he has a chance to betray that love. Oh, Alix, if only you could see his eyes when he looks at you, you would realize you have no reason to fear him."

I stared at her, aghast by what she said, tears filling my eyes as fast as I could blink them away. "Fear him? Now I fear him?" I raised my hands and dropped them helplessly. "Well, thank you for that insightful analysis, Doctor Isabella! Just send me a bill for your time, would you?"

I started to leave, then thought better of it. I couldn't let her hurl those accusations at me without answering them. I marched down her hallway and stood before her, my hands fisted at my hips. "Just so you know, just so you have it clear in your mind, I am *not* guarding myself against Alex. From the very first moment I met him, he got to me, really got to me, got under my skin so that I had no choice in the matter—I had to have him. And I knew, *I knew* what would happen! I knew there wasn't going to be any happy ending for me, because there never is! Tell me how going into a relationship knowing it's doomed to end in heartbreak is guarding my heart, Isabella! Tell me, please, because I'd really like to know!"

"Alix—"

"No!" I spun on my heel and stomped off a few steps, then whirled back around on her. "I love him. I always will. He is everything to me, do you understand? *EVERYTHING!* Leaving him is going to kill me!"

She was silent for a few seconds, watching me angrily swipe at my eyes with her damned napkin. "I see I was wrong."

"Damned straight you were wrong!" I sniffed and turned back to the door, but stopped when she called after me.

"Alix? Would you answer one question, please?"

I ground my teeth as I stood before the door, my hand on the knob. I didn't want to answer any more of her charges. I didn't want to look any closer at my motives than I already had. I just wanted to escape and be left alone to nurse my shattered heart in peace.

"What is it?" I growled.

The faint scent of her perfume, light and flowery and completely Isabella, wafted by as she glided up behind me.

"If you love Alexander, truly love him with all your heart, isn't he worth any sacrifice to be with?"

My stomach dropped down to my feet. I ground my fingernails into my palms to keep from screaming out that I couldn't give him what he wanted, that it would all end in disaster if I pretended to be something I wasn't. No matter how much I loved him, I would never be the woman he needed. So I said nothing. I bit my lip until I tasted blood; then I turned the doorknob and left Isabella without a word.

Chapter Fourteen

"If ye'd stand yersel' a wee bit closer to the laird, m'lady, ye'd be able to reach his puir fevered haid wi'out dribblin' water all over him."

"He's not a laird, McReady, he's a knight. A simple knight. A very simple knight," Lady Fenella replied with smug satisfaction. She swished the cloth around the bowl of water, and reached across Sir Christopher's broad chest to slap the soggy piece of linen on his forehead. Storm off in a pique, would he? Ride off on a horse that couldn't see its hoof before its face, hmm? Wouldn't listen to her advice, eh? Well, he'd be eating his words once he regained his senses, and she'd be there watching him swallow every mouthful!

I set my laptop aside with a muttered, "Crap. It's all crap. I'm doomed." Then I decided it wasn't really the story that was at fault, it was me. I hate Mr. Monthly Visitor.

Oh, I know, who enjoys it? But I *really* hate cramps. I can live with all sorts of other pain—headaches and backaches and various assorted and sundry aches—but I can't function with cramps. In fact, while reading and writing historical romances I've always wondered just how women dealt with cramps. Willow-bark draughts and possets would never have been enough for me.

No, my way was much more effective: I swallowed painkillers, fired up the heating pad, and retired to my bed with a collection of comfort-read books, a tall glass of the fizzy lemon drink the Brits call lemonade, and a chocolate orange I had hidden for emergencies.

If a broken heart and throbbing reproductive organs isn't an emergency, I just don't know what is.

An hour later I was feeling much more human and less likely to kill innocent passersby. A quick glance at the clock left me pondering fate, however. It was seven minutes to six o'clock. Six was the hour Alex had designated for my attendance at the restaurant on the corner. I wasn't going, of course. I had made that decision long before Isabella's unjustified attack on my character, an attack that left me so infuriated I still couldn't think about it. No, I wasn't going to have dinner with Alex. It would serve him right to sit there all by himself, waiting for me. Everyone in the restaurant would be smiling to themselves over the poor man who was left to dine alone, pitying him because he was clearly waiting for someone, someone who didn't care enough about him to keep a date with him. I pictured their smug smiles as they talked behind their hands about him, no doubt speculating as to just what he had done to drive his dinner date away. I wondered how long he would sit there before he realized I was standing him up. An hour? A half hour? Ten minutes?

"Selfish and self-centered! The nerve of her!" I complained as I pushed the heating pad off my stomach and padded over to the wardrobe. "I'm the least self-centered person I know. And selfish? Ha! That's a laugh."

I pulled out a lightweight blue and green batik print dress made of cotton so soft it felt like silk next to my skin. I loved the way the dress made me feel when I wore it, sexy and seductive and attractive, not in the least bit bloated and cranky. I swore the dress must have had pheromones woven into the fabric.

It was a lovely dress, the very dress I might wear were I going out to dinner, but I wasn't. And Alex, sensitive, intelligent Alex, would sit in the restaurant by himself and feel the weight of all those stares and snickers. He would be embarrassed, shamed that he was the focus of so much speculation, uncomfortable because I had made him an object of pity by standing him up.

I slipped on my midnight-blue sandals with the cute jeweled ankle straps.

It served him right. Who did he think he was, crushing my heart, then ordering me out to dinner without so much as asking me if I wanted to go?

I yanked a comb through my hair and spritzed it with some hair spray so it would stay kicky and out of my face.

What would he do once he realized I wasn't showing up? Would he eat his dinner alone, a sad, pathetic, solitary figure in a room of happy, chatting groups? Would he leave in a huff?

I stared at myself in the mirror as I applied a quick slash of crimson to my lips. Would he call someone to have dinner with him? Someone close by? Someone he knew well—very well? Someone he knew on an intimate level? Someone blond and cool and elegant who probably never, ever raised her voice to him?

I couldn't decide which was worse, the picture of a humiliated Alex sitting in lonely splendor at the restaurant, or the image of him dining cozily with Isabella, their heads together as they had a good laugh about the stupid American who thought she was entitled to love.

"Hell!" I told my reflection, then snatched up my purse and turned off the fan. "Fine, I'll go to the restaurant, but I *won't* have dinner with him. I'll just go there to tell him I'm standing him up. That way he can leave if he wants to, or he can stay and have his dinner by himself."

I nodded to myself as I glanced again at the clock, then dashed out the door. After all, I didn't want to hurt him, I just wanted to make him understand that we weren't together anymore. I could do that without cruelty. It certainly wouldn't cost me anything in pride to simply go to the restaurant and tell him I would not be dining with him. In fact, it might serve very well as a good demonstration of how *not* together we were. I could tell him I wouldn't be eating with him, then move to another table and have dinner by myself. That should certainly drive home the point! Yes, yes, it was a good idea!

Five minutes later I stood in the entrance of the restaurant and glanced around. The place was almost full, but I spotted Alex immediately. He was sitting in a corner table perusing a menu as if he had no other concern in life but to decide between the Galletto alla di Avola and the Petto di Pollo al Pepe Verde.

The rotter.

I marched over to where he sat and stood with my hands on my hips until he looked up.

"I half expected you to stand me up," he said with a self-deprecating smile.

His devilishly sexy voice raised goose bumps on my arms. I ignored both them and his smile. "Why didn't you tell me you'd been married?"

He looked surprised for a moment, then stood and pulled out a chair for me. "I didn't think it mattered."

I pushed the chair back in and glared at him. "I'm not having dinner with you, Alex."

One delectable eyebrow went up. God, how I loved those eyebrows! I loved how he cocked them just so, making my fingers tingle with the desire to trace along their smooth arch. Worse yet, they never failed to make me want to kiss that look of disbelief/surprise/questioning right off his face.

"You're not having dinner? Then why are you here?"

"I came to tell you I was standing you up so you wouldn't sit here and be the object of everyone's pity because you're such a terrible man that no one wants to have dinner with you. That's all. I am, however, having dinner. Just not with you."

He tapped one long finger on the table top for a few seconds while he considered my statement. "Does this have anything to do with the fact that I didn't mention my previous marriage to you, or are you still in a snit because I was on duty yesterday?"

I picked up the menu lying in the place that would have been mine and took it to the table next to Alex's. I waved the waiter over as I appropriated a chair. "Giorgio, I will be dining by myself tonight. And I don't want to share my table with anyone."

Giorgio, a small man with a neat beard and the most beautiful black wavy hair I've ever seen, looked puzzled for a moment, glanced over at Alex, then back at me. He shrugged and asked if I was ready to give my order. "Not yet. Give me a few more minutes," I said nonchalantly, casting my eyes over the menu as if it were the most fascinating object I'd ever seen.

To my left Alex heaved a martyred sigh, then picked up his drink and menu and sat down at my table. I glared at him over the top of my menu. "I am *not* having dinner with you!"

"Fine. I'll have dinner with you. Does that salvage your pride?"

I stood up. "No." I took my glass of water and my menu and sat down in Alex's recently vacated spot. I would be damned if I'd have dinner with him! He had to understand we were through. Over. Finished. Finito.

He gave me an annoyed look, tossed back his drink, then stood up like he was going to join me. I stood up as well, prepared to move to whichever table he wasn't at. His jaw tightened. His eyes narrowed. His fingers clenched around the edge of the table in front of him. With a grim smile, he heaved it to the side, pushing it up against the one I was occupying.

I glanced around the room. The rest of the tables were filled, all but a large one in the center with a reserved card on it. Damn! "May I ask just what you think you're doing, confiscating my former table like that and having the nerve to push your unwanted self up against my new stronghold?"

Alex's grim smile lost a little of its grimness and warmed up just enough to kindle several small but intense fires in my innards. I sent out a call for the internal-organ fire brigade and sat back down.

"You seem to be unable to make up your mind as to which table you wish to sit at. I'm just trying to make it easier for you."

"Whatever. Just so long as you realize I've stood you up and am now *not* having dinner with you."

He sat down at my ex-table. "Yes, I am aware of that fact. Might I say that I appreciate your telling me in person that you are standing me up?"

I gave him a quick little nod and picked up the menu. "I thought it was the polite thing to do."

He waved for the waiter's attention, pointed at me, and did that weird mental-telepathy drink-ordering thing that men can do. I frowned at him. "I don't like whiskey."

"I'm not drinking whiskey."

"I don't like vodka, either."

"I'm not drinking vodka."

I transferred the frown to his glass. There was no color in the little pool of liquid at the bottom, which eliminated any of the rye or bourbon type drinks. What else was clear?

"I don't like ouzo, either."

"Neither do I."

I switched my frown from his glass to the waiter as he approached with two drinks on a tray. Gin? Rats. I liked gin. The waiter pursed his lips and shot us both a look that spoke volumes, but he placed the drinks down at each of our tables with nothing more than a noncommittal murmur.

I poked at the wedge of lime in the drink, then sucked

my finger. "Gin and tonic? How did you know I like G&Ts?"

Alex looked up from where he was reading his menu. "I beg your pardon, madam? Were you speaking to me, a stranger dining here quite alone at my own table?"

"Oh, very funny." I pulled my menu out and stared at it, wondering what the hell I was doing sitting there trying not to throw myself on him. Maybe showing him just how not together we were wasn't the best of ideas. He didn't seem to be overly offended by my refusal to have dinner with him. In fact, he wasn't even sitting at the same table as I was. Pushed together or separated by distance, they were still two different tables. Well, fine, if our breakup wasn't going to give him any grief, that was great! That was fabulous! It made my life so much easier! I would just sit here and ignore him and have my dinner by myself, and by the end of the meal he would go his way and I would go mine, and that was all there was to it.

Except of course I would never recover from the loss of him in my life, but that was my issue, not his, no matter what Isabella thought. *Selfish? Self-centered?* Certainly Alex didn't think I was selfish and self-centered. Or did he?

I glanced over at him. He was studying the back of the menu, but he looked up when he felt my gaze on him. "Isabella said you've started work on a new story."

Oh, so he wanted to do the polite-conversation thing? I debated ignoring him completely, but decided I was bigger than that. I lowered my menu and plucked the wedge of lime out to suck on it. Alex watched with an indescribable look of horror on his face. I chewed the lovely pulpy bits out of the lime, then waved it about nonchalantly. "Why, yes, as it is, Isabella is quite correct." I narrowed my lips at him. "About *that* she is correct. She's very, very wrong about other things."

"Is she? I have no doubt of that. Despite what you seem to think, Isabella isn't perfect."

"Big words, coming from her former partner in Hide the Salami."

Alex blinked twice. "Christ, don't tell me you're jealous of Isabella, too?"

What? Jealous? Me? He had to be kidding. "You're kidding, right? You think I'm jealous? Of Isabella? And what the hell do you mean, *too*? As in, I'm jealous of more than one person? Is that what you think? You think I'm jealous? Of Isabella and someone else? Some mystery person? Who? Bert? Ray? *Philippe?*"

He leveled an emerald gaze at me, one that sizzled its way down to my scarlet-painted toenails. I loved those looks, I just hated the way they left me wanting to slither across him and lick every square inch of his skin. "Actually, I think you're jealous of my ex-wife."

I goggled at him. There was just no other word for it, I goggled. At him, at his ridiculous ideas, at his suggestion that I could be jealous of anyone, but most of all, I goggled at the expression of pity on his face. He was serious! He thought I was jealous!

"You're out of your friggin' mind!" I finally de-goggled enough to say. "Totally and completely out of your mind! Jealous of your ex-wife? Oh, I grant you, I might be the teensiest bit envious of Isabella's perfect face and perfect hair and perfect clothes and perfect life and perfect relationship with you, but you think I'm jealous of your ex-wife? A woman I don't even know? Why would I be jealous of her?"

That rattled him enough to wipe the look of pity off his face. He frowned instead. "Alix, my relationship with Isabella—"

I held up a hand and interrupted him. "No! Don't tell me! I don't want to know! I don't care at all! I don't want to know anything about how you and Isabella were, not how much you loved/liked/worshiped her, not how long you were together, not how she lay in your arms at night and talked to you about all sorts of interesting, intelligent things, the sort of things that I never talked to you about because we never stopped doing it long enough to have time for talking—none of it! I don't want to hear anything about you and Isabella!"

"My relationship with Isabella—"

"Alex, no!" I said loudly, ignoring the surprised looks from people dining around us. Damn it, didn't he see I couldn't take any details about him and the Ice Maiden? Not in the frail mood I was in, thank you very much.

"—was never—"

He was a stubborn, stubborn man. I knew he was going to insist on telling me things about himself and Isabella, and I didn't want to hear them. I couldn't hear them. One more shot to the heart like the last one he gave me and I'd be through. Finished. Dead as a doornail right there in Stella's. There was only one thing that I could think of to say that would keep him from finishing that sentence. I took a deep breath.

"Did I tell you I'm not pregnant?" I bellowed across the sound of his knee-melting voice.

Well, I was right, it worked, it shut him right up. Unfortunately, it also shut up everyone in the restaurant. I know because they were, at that moment, all staring with great interest and no little speculation at us. Alex, on the other hand, just looked like he wanted to throttle me.

I raised my hand and waved it at Giorgio. "Check, please!"

Alex caught up with me at the stroppy front door.

"When I ask someone to go to dinner with me, I usually expect to eat at some point," he commented as he took my key from where I was trying to gut the lock, and gave it a gentle twist. The door opened. I didn't know who I hated more at that moment, the door or him. I didn't have a chance to decide, however, because he took a firm grip on my elbow and hauled me upstairs.

"Hey!" I protested as we passed my landing and continued up. "What do you think you are doing? I'm not going to your flat with you!"

"Why not?" he asked, sounding suspiciously like he was speaking through grinding teeth. I peered at him in the darkness of the stairwell but couldn't see anything other than the determined set of his jaw.

"Because once I get there you'll just want to get naked and have me kiss you all over and maybe even bring out that bottle of lemon-flavored massage oil that I love and will want me to oil you up and clean you off again, or worse yet, you'll want to oil me up and then you'll slide your—"

"Alix," he growled, hauling me to his side while he pulled out his key.

"What?" I asked a bit snappishly, annoyed he had interrupted the lovely scene that was building in my mind.

"I brought you up here to talk, not to make love to you, although I'm not excluding that from the list of things I wish to accomplish tonight."

"Well exclude it, buster," I snarled, pushing away from

him and stalking through the door to his flat. "Because Mr. Monthly Visitor is here, and I'm crampy and bloated and I don't want you touching me anywhere south of my chin, OK?"

"Ah. I should have guessed from your petulant mood you were indisposed."

I whirled around from where I had been looking out his window. "Oh, you do *not* want to go there! Just leave my hormones and moods out of it!"

He dropped his keys on a small table and held his hands up in a gesture of surrender. "My apologies. Would you care to sit down?"

I sat, suddenly tired of fighting the endless battle within myself to deny the love I felt for him. He sat in a chair next to the couch, turning it so he faced me. "Now, perhaps we could discuss matters calmly, without bellowing intimate details across crowded public places."

A little blush crawled up my neck and heated my cheeks. "I'm sorry about that. I didn't realize everyone would hear."

He nodded gravely and leaned back, his lovely long fingers steepled under his chin. Oh, how I loved that chin!

"I feel as if we've been speaking at cross purposes, and I would like to clear up a few points. First of all, your distress yesterday was not solely due to my being unable to talk to you, was it?"

I was so tired. Tired of feeling horrible, tired of wanting him and knowing he was never to be mine again, tired of trying to figure out a way to change so I would be what he wanted. My body felt as if it were encased in cement, pressed down onto Alex's couch cushions with-

Katie MacAlister

out a hope of ever again moving. "Why would you think your rejection wasn't what bothered me?"

He shifted in his chair. "Alix, I didn't reject you, I just couldn't deal with your problems at the time. You're the only one who sees duty to my job as a rejection."

I stared at my fingers lying limp on my legs and said nothing. There was nothing to say. His job came first.

"I want to know why you are so determined to destroy what we have between us."

I looked up at him in surprise. He leaned forward and took one of my hands in his. My fingers curled around his.

"Why have you chosen to leave me? What have I done to make you think that this relationship is anything like the ones in your past?"

A familiar pricking sensation behind my eyes heralded trouble. I swallowed back the lump forming in my throat. "What are you trying to do, make me cry by being so nice to me? I warn you, it's not pretty when I cry. My eyes get all puffy and red, and my nose runs, and sometimes I get the hiccups. So I'd think twice about making me cry if I were you."

He slid to his knees and pulled me down until I was resting against him. I was as boneless as rubber, not wanting to be so close to him, close enough to smell that wonderful spicy scent that was exclusively Alex, but I lacked the strength and will to push him away. It was just so much easier to give in than to struggle to maintain my indignation.

"Ah, sweetheart, I don't want to make you cry. I just want to understand what I've done wrong. I want to know why you're hurting so much, and how I can make it stop. I want to know what it will take to prove to you that I won't ever leave you, no matter how terrible you think your life has become."

The tears were building again, filling my eyes as I leaned into his chest and felt my hair ruffle as his voice slid softly, so softly over me.

"I want to love you, Alix, but you won't let me." His lips, warm and soft and indescribably delicious, were nuzzling around the nape of my neck. My breath caught in a half sob as I closed my eyes on the tears. It was wrong letting him melt me like that, but I couldn't stop him, not even if I wanted to. Still, I should at least make a token effort.

"Alex, please . . ." The words dried upon my tongue when I opened my mouth to speak.

"Please what, sweetheart? Please stop, or . . ." He tipped my head back and steamed my lips. All those little pieces of my shattered heart started glowing with a burning white heat as his sensitive lips swept across mine, caressing, teasing, seducing my mouth. My eyes opened briefly when he persuaded my mouth to part for his seeking tongue, but his emerald gaze was too hot to look into for any length of time. It scorched my eyes just as his mouth scorched mine. ". . . or please make love to you? Which is it, love?"

"You've got something magical in your saliva, don't you?" I mumbled as I pulled away long enough to draw some air into my needy lungs. "You're not human— you're some sort of god with magical, seductive spit who brings women to their knees with just one touch of your tongue."

Amusement and desire and warmth danced through his eyes as he grinned, then dipped his head to my jaw and began nibbling a line that made me melt into a big puddle of desire. Warning sirens went off in my head, but I was powerless to do anything about them. Despite our ruined relationship, despite the fact that what existed between Alex and me wouldn't last, I couldn't fight the feeling of rightness with him. I slid my hands over the wonderful terrain of his back and buried my face in his hair, that wonderful soft, silky, chestnut hair that smelled so Alexish. He nibbled a trail down my neck to the bodice of my dress, sliding both of his hands up my sides, pausing to span my waist while he nibbled on the spot on my collarbone that never failed to make me tremble.

"Alex," I whispered into his ear, then bit gently on the outer edge. "Alex, you have to stop."

His hands teased the underside of my breasts for a moment before sliding around behind me, his fingers hot on the skin exposed as he pulled the zipper down.

"Why? You're not still angry with me?" The words were spoken against my lips as his tongue dipped inside again while he peeled off both the top of my dress and my bra. Flames followed his fingers as they stroked my spine, tracing along my ribs, his mouth never once releasing me from the terrible, ceaseless, mind-meltingly wondrous havoc he was creating.

"What?" I couldn't breathe, I couldn't catch my breath, let alone my thoughts. I suckled on that delicious spot where his jaw met his ear and heard him groan.

He pulled two cushions down from the couch and laid me back on them, his mouth claiming mine once more before answering me. "Why do I have to stop?"

I tugged on his shirt until he stopped kissing me long enough to pull it off. A sigh of satisfaction escaped me as I curled my fingers into the lovely hair on his chest, teasing little circles around his adorable nipples. He slid down my body, pulling my dress with him until I was wearing nothing but my underwear and sandals. He lifted one foot and looked at the sandal with the sparkly ankle strap, lifted an eyebrow at me, then kissed the sandal. "Shall we be naughty and leave them on?"

I shivered at the look in his eyes, but remembered my objection when his hands moved up my thighs towards my undies.

"I can't Alex. Mr. Monthly Visitor, remember?"

He laid down a line of kisses on my belly. "I don't mind, if you don't."

I couldn't keep from making a face at that offer.

"Are you in pain?" he asked, his fingers pausing in the act of caressing beneath the waistband of my underwear.

"No, but I think I'd rather not."

He sucked on one of my hip bones, the silk of his hair and heat of his mouth against my bare skin setting me ablaze. "There's more than one way to make love," he murmured as he nibbled his way over to the other hip bone, then headed northwards.

"No fair," I complained, rubbing my leg against his and fumbling with his belt. My life as I knew it might be over, my heart destroyed with no chance of repair, and I wasn't feeling fit enough to indulge in our usual between-the-sheets fare, but that didn't mean I didn't want to do wicked things to his body. All of it. Every sweet inch of it.

He rose up off from where he was just about to torment my breasts and quickly stripped.

"Better?" he asked as he knelt beside me.

"Much better," I cooed, tracing the long line of muscles in his thighs. I put a hand on his chest to stop him when he leaned forward over me. "Alex, you realize that this is just a temporary cease-fire brought on because I have no immunity to your magic saliva, and that it in no way implies that we're getting back together. You understand that, don't you?"

"No," he said, then ignored my restraining hand and leaned over to take one of my nipples in his mouth.

Words stopped in my throat as heat coursed out from my center to the farthest points on my body, then slammed back, centering in the deep, hidden core of me. I opened my mouth to object, to make sure he understood that this meant nothing, but gasps of pleasure came out instead of words, gasps that soon turned to moans when one of his hands teased its way down my chest, over my belly, and down farther, nudging aside my underwear to stroke gently at that one tiny little spot of utter bliss.

"Alex!" I protested, bucking under the effect of his fingers. "You . . . can't!"

"Let me love you, sweetheart," he murmured against my nipple before tugging on it gently with his teeth. I gasped again and arched up beneath him. "I won't hurt you, I promise."

I wanted to cry out that the ache he had created deep inside me was too much, but the hot, dark words he whispered against my breast wiped all thoughts from my mind but of the wonderful magic his hands and mouth were creating. The pleasure inside me coiled tighter and tighter until I couldn't distinguish it from the ache of want he had generated; then suddenly his lips were on mine and I was shouting my joy into his mouth. I trembled with the power of the pleasure he gave me, tears slipping from my eyes as he held me tight and kissed my cheeks, my eyes, my mouth.

An eon later I had collected the shreds of my being that had come apart under his seductive spell, and had recovered enough to speak. Alex was lying facing me, one muscled thigh pressed between mine, his lips teasing my temple as his hands stroked my back.

I gathered my wits together enough to make my mouth work. "Why?"

"Hmmm?"

I swallowed to ease the ache in my throat. "Why did you do that after everything I've said to you? After I stood you up? Why did you want to . . ." I choked back a moan as he bit my neck, then licked a path up to my ear.

"Because I wanted to."

I pushed him until he rolled onto his back, propping myself up on an elbow to frown at him. "But why did you want to after I explained to you that we were through? After I told you how I feel?"

His lovely lips curved upwards as his wicked green eyes mirrored amusement, patience, and something warm and fuzzy that I didn't want to put a name to. "Alix, sweetheart, it's about time you realize that I don't back down from a challenge. I never have, and even if I did, I certainly wouldn't let you slip through my fingers over something so ridiculous as—"

Oh, how I loved this man! I put my hand over his mouth. "Don't say it."

"Mmmarf?"

"Because," I told him, my hand lifting enough to trail my fingers along his wonderfully warm lips, "if you do, you'll make me angry, and that would be a shame. Say uncle instead."

"Uncle?" His brows came together in a puzzled frown as I let my fingers drift down over the muscled plane of his chest. I tickled a finger in his belly button. His stomach contracted in response. "Why would I want to say uncle?"

"You need to say it now because you won't be coherent later."

His frown deepened as I slid away from him and avoided his grasping hand. I nudged aside his legs and knelt between them, my hands on either side of his hips. Comprehension flooded his lovely eyes, desire turning them almost black when I leaned forward and rubbed my cheek against the full glory of his dangly parts.

Only he wasn't dangling.

"Oh, Christ," he breathed, his voice hoarse and rusty. I smiled the smile of supreme power and licked my lower lip while leaning into him. His body twitched once; then he let his head fall back as he groaned and grabbed at the carpet beneath him. I turned my head and ran my tongue up the long length of him.

"Christ, Alix, you're going to kill me if you . . ." I swirled my tongue around the sensitive underside, and his hips arched up beneath me as he sucked in probably half the air in the room. "Ah, sweet Jesus. Uncle! *Uncle!*"

"Mmm, not good enough. You can still speak." I closed my hand around the base of him and stroked upwards. A tremor shook him as I found a rhythm he liked.

"Let's see if this does the job." I flicked my tongue across the very tip of him, then took his heated length into my mouth and let my tongue go wild. Alex came unglued and began to babble.

I smiled to myself. I *told* him he was going to be incoherent! It's always nice to be proved right.

Chapter Fifteen

Sir Christopher rushed forward, his eyes blazing and his hair standing on end as he threw himself at the dastardly coward who had struck Black Demon a blow to the side of the head.

"You spleeny, fen-sucked varlet!"

Steel clashed with steel as the brave warrior lunged at the Indigo Knight.

"You pox-hearted maltworm!"

How dare the bastard attack an innocent horse? Sir Christopher could have sobbed with agony when he saw that horrible blank look return to brave Demon's eyes. So short a time! So short a time had the noble steed regained his sight, and now that foul, dog-hearted younker had returned Demon to his sightless state.

"You churlish base-court ratsbane! I shall gut you like the beslubbering milk-livered stinkweed you are and feed your entrails to the toads! Prepare to die!"

* * *

"What do you think of it so far?"

Alex remained quiet, lying on his side, our legs twined together just as his fingers were twined through my hair, idly twisting strands as he listened to me read to him. I looked up from where I was sprawled halfway across his chest and met his frown.

"What? Why are you frowning at me like that?"

His emerald gaze skittered away from mine as he disentangled his hand and flipped back the curtain. "It's getting late. I'd best be going."

I pushed my manuscript pages aside and tightened my grip on his bare chest. "No. Not until you tell me why you frowned when I asked you what you thought of my new story."

Alex tried to slither out from underneath me, but I clung like a determined limpet. After our passionate, if intercourse-free, episode the previous night, we had continued the détente by returning to my flat so I could whip up a little dinner. With my willpower and good intentions flown out the window in the face of my desire for him, I asked Alex to stay the night even if we couldn't indulge in our usual pastimes. He agreed, and I used the remaining hours before bedtime planning all of the things I would say to him, and a goodly number of the ones he would say to me. I spent a lovely fifteen minutes lying in his arms, savoring the feeling of just being with him, of being able to touch and stroke and feel him, but best of all, I savored the anticipation of our chance to talk, truly talk, to explain exactly why we weren't going to work things out, and make him see reason . . . but then I fell asleep. By the time I woke up the following morning, there was only time for me to read him a couple of pages of my new story before he had to get ready for work.

"So?" I prodded him. "What do you think?"

He sighed one of his patented Saint Alex the Martyr sighs and let me push him back onto the pillows. "Let me ask you a question instead."

I narrowed my eyes at him. What was this? "OK, I guess. Shoot."

He put both hands on my shoulders and kissed the tip of my nose. "Why does it matter what I think of your story?"

"Well . . ." Dammit, he had me there! I couldn't tell him that his opinion mattered greatly, because that would be tantamount to admitting that he was still vital to me, and thus we were still a couple and still had a future. We weren't and we didn't. And yet I had to tell him something. "Uh . . . I'm just curious as to whether you think it's better than the first story."

He smoothed back a strand of my hair that was caught on my lip. "And if I told you I thought your story lacked insight into the heroine's reasons for her actions, what would you do?"

I kissed his fingers and slid off his chest. "I'd probably go back and make sure I added insight to the story."

"Will you show the story to your friends? To Isabella?"

Isabella was still a bit of a sore point with me, but I supposed I would if she expressed any interest. I thought it best I keep those thoughts to myself, however, lest I give Alex more grounds to fling charges of jealousy at me. "Sure, if she wants to hear it, I'll read some of it to her."

"And if she says she thinks the dialogue is weak?"

I shrugged and pulled on my fuzzy bathrobe. "I'd probably punch it up a bit. Why are you asking me these questions?"

Alex continued to lie on the bed, his hands behind his head as he watched me toddle to the kitchen for the coffee grinder. "I was just curious why you cling to destructive patterns."

I dropped the bag of coffee. "I what?"

He sat up and pushed the sheets off his long, long legs. I dragged my eyes off the good parts of him and kept them firmly on his face. I wasn't about to be distracted by his gorgeous body, not when I sensed an argument coming on.

"Alix, if you have one failing in life, it's that you lack courage."

I threw down the hand towel I was holding and stomped over to where he was heading for the bathroom. I blocked the door, hands on my hips, scowl on my brow. "In the last few days I have been called selfish, self-centered, and jealous. Now I'm a coward as well?"

He pushed my hands off my hips, grasped me firmly, and tried to hoist me out of his way. I dug my toes into the orange shag carpet and stayed put.

"I didn't say you were a coward, I said you lacked courage. And you do."

I slapped the flat of my hand against his chest. He didn't budge. "Explain that if you will, Detective Inspector Judgmental!"

He tried to shift me again. I grabbed on to the door frame with both hands and refused to be moved.

"Alix, I need to use the toilet." He looked down pointedly at that part of his anatomy that was often a barometer of such things. I looked down as well, pursing my lips, then reached out and wrapped my hand around him.

He growled a warning. I smirked and stepped aside. "Oh, OK, go ahead. But you have to explain yourself as soon as you're finished in there!"

It took him twenty minutes, but only because he made use of my shower, my spare toothbrush, and even the razor I use to shave my armpits. He voiced loud opinions about the state of the blade, none of which I paid any attention to as I poked him in the chest.

"OK, you've used the facilities. Now explain that nasty little crack you made."

He started to steer me over to the ladderback chair, then swerved and pushed me down onto the chaise, squatting next to me with my hands in his.

"Sweetheart, I didn't mean what I said as an insult."

I snorted and tugged on my hands. His fingers tightened around them.

"No, I'm not going to let go of your hands, not until I've said what I want to say, and I'd like you to promise that you'll hear me out without interruption."

"Why? Is it going to be so bad you don't think I can listen without objecting to what you want to say?"

"Just promise me you'll give me a fair hearing." His eyes, those lovely eyes, watched me warily. I gnawed a bit on my lower lip until I noticed he was watching my mouth with an avidity that started familiar fires inside me. I didn't have time for those fires anymore. I clamped down on my lips and nodded, crossing my arms and lifting my chin in preparation for what I was sure was going to be yet another detailed examination of my shortcomings.

I wasn't disappointed.

"Alix, when I said you lacked courage, I didn't mean you were a coward. During the last month that we've known each other, I've come to recognize that you have a significant problem with your self-image." I opened my mouth to dispute that dastardly opinion, but he squeezed my hands in warning. I gave him a good glare instead. "I suspect your feelings of inadequacy stem from your early home life and your relationship with your mother, reinforced later by the negative experiences you've had with the men who've shared your life."

I ground my teeth at him. He might have a degree in psychology, but did that give him any right to dissect my psyche? His thumbs stroked feathery little circles on the tops of my hands, but it wasn't enough to distract me from the horrible, hurtful things he was saying.

"When I first met you, I assumed you must be aware of how you perpetuated failure by repeating the same patterns of destructive behavior. It seemed to me that you had taken the necessary steps to break that pattern—first by leaving your family circle and coming halfway around the world by yourself, then by setting yourself a goal that was well within your ability to achieve. But it soon became apparent that you were unaware of the source of your past unhappiness. I had hoped that our relationship and your success at finishing a project would break the cycle of failure that you've used as an excuse for surrendering whenever life becomes difficult, but your determination to see rejection around every corner has eliminated that hope."

Fury like no fury I've ever experienced filled me at his words. I snatched my hands from him and shoved him. Hard. He fell backwards onto his butt. I jumped off the chaise and ran to the door, throwing it open.

"Out. Get out of here." My voice was low and ugly, laden with all of the hatred I felt for him at that moment.

"Alix, you promised you'd hear me out." He slowly got to his feet, holding out his hands, palms up.

"Get out of my flat." I never once took my eyes from his, wanting him to see the pain and anger and every other emotion that roiled around inside me.

He shook his head and walked up to me, placing his hands on my arms. I shook them off. He took a hold of me again, his fingers hard on my arms. "No, Alix. You're not going to run from this again. You can throw me out if you want, but you're going to have to face the truth first."

"I am not going to listen to you anymore!" I ground out, my voice starting to rise with the panic that swamped me.

He shook me, but without any real force. "You repeat the same pattern when any chance at happiness presents itself, Alix, whether it's a relationship with a man or a job. You set yourself up for failure, then use that as an excuse to quit when things become difficult. Life doesn't work that way. You have to fight for what you want."

"*GET . . . OUT . . . OF . . . MY . . . FLAT!*" I bellowed, mindless of the open door, mindless of the tears streaming down my face, mindless of the look of sorrow and anger that mingled in Alex's eyes.

"You said you loved me. Aren't I worth fighting for? Aren't *we* worth the effort to stay together? Or is your love for me nothing but cheap lust, nothing but a shallow, meaningless little fling? I see the results of that every day, Alix. I thought we had something more than just sex."

I wanted to hit him. I've never wanted to strike another person before in my life, not even my mother when she made me angry enough to spit, but, God help me, my hand itched to slap Alex, to hurt him, to make him go away and leave me alone and, above all, to make him stop looking at me with those emerald eyes that saw right through to my soul.

"No, it's not just lust. I did love you. I still do, but that doesn't mean I have to like you. I want you to leave, Alex. I don't want to see you again. It's over between us. You can believe whatever you want about me, but believe this—we are finished."

"Ah, sweetheart, you may be willing to give up on us so easily, but I'm not." He stepped forward to touch me, but I stumbled away.

I went to the phone. I had a grip on my turbulent emotions once again, and even managed to speak without shrieking. If my voice was raw and made up of sharp, cutting tones, I couldn't help it. "If you don't leave now, I'll call the police."

He blinked at me in disbelief.

I picked up the phone and dialed 999, the emergency number that would connect me with the police, my eyes never flickering from his.

He raised his hands in defeat and let them fall as I put the receiver back on the cradle. "You win. I'll leave. But I want you to know this: No one can take happiness away from you, they can only put obstacles in your path. How you overcome those obstacles determines how happy your life will be." He took two steps toward me but stopped when I backed up, still clutching the phone to my chest. "Alix, you're a smart, witty, attractive woman. You don't need me or any other man to make you a success, you can do that on your own. You have everything you need within you to be whatever you want—a famous novelist, a world traveler, or even a brain surgeon if that's what you want. All you have to do is let yourself have that success."

He raised a hand as if he was going to touch me, then curled his fingers up into a fist and without another word turned and left. I shuffled forward to close the door in case he tried to come back.

I don't remember much about the next few hours. They seemed to stream by while I was in a fugue, but after a few hours had passed, basic bodily urges began to poke through my abstraction, and I discovered myself sitting at a chair at my tiny table with an untouched cup of coffee in front of me. My stomach was rumbling loudly, I had to go to the bathroom, and my hands were stiff and painful from gripping the table. I massaged my fingers while I took care of necessary business, but was conscious the whole time of an extraordinary sense of fragility about myself. I felt as if I were made of a delicate, eggshell-thin porcelain. At the slightest touch I would shatter, my body crumbling into a fine, chalky dust.

Slowly, as if it traveled from a great distance, awareness returned to me, and with it pain so deep I did not at first think I would survive it. I curled up into a little ball on the bed, but the sheets still held Alex's spicy scent, so I ended up in a corner of the room clutching a floor pillow.

Lying in a fetal position soon lost its charm, so as the pain began to ebb back to a level of acceptability, I uncurled myself and sat up to consider the wreckage of my life. Out of the disorganized chaos of my thoughts, recognizable patterns began to form. I hugged the pillow to my chest to deaden the pain and thought about what Isabella had said. I thought about the things Alex had said as well, although the memory of his words almost sent me back into a fetal ball. I thought about the warmth and concern that Bert and Ray—even Philippe—had shown me. I thought about my mother and my ex-husband and every horrible job I'd ever had. I even thought about the Cheeto-rubbers. I looked at my life from every possible angle, but there was no escaping the conclusion:

I had failed in everything I'd attempted. Failed jobs, failed relationships, failed bids for attention and love—they all swirled together into one dense lump of soul-eating blackness that resided within me.

The recognition of my true self brought with it immediate turmoil. Ideas and thoughts bounced wildly around in my head, disjointed and confusing, but soon even they settled into some sort of order, and from that order one bright, shining desire was born. I couldn't do anything about the past, but I could start over again, start fresh, and this time make sure I did things right. Like the phoenix, I would rise from the ashes of my failures and would be reborn new and clean again.

I drew up a list of steps I would take to make that desire a reality, then sat at the table with my list in front of me until shadows lengthened and stretched their inky hands across the flat, changing it from a sanctuary to a prison.

I glanced at my list, then went to the phone and dialed Daniel's phone number.

"Alix! I'm delighted you've forgiven me my trespasses and have allowed me to apologize again for my comments."

"Don't be ridiculous, Daniel," I said with a faint smile. I was surprised a bit by that. I hadn't expected that the new, serious, driven Alix would smile a whole lot. Not until she worked her way through the list. "Everything you said had merit. No, don't try to apologize, I don't want to hear it. I do want to take you up on your offer of help, though. I'd like to ask you a question."

"I would be delighted, my dear. You want the name of a good freelance editor? I know one who—"

"No, thank you, that's sweet, but I don't want an editor. I want to ask you a question about my manuscript."

A note of caution crept into his voice. Poor man, he probably thought I was going to pin him down and ask him to help me rewrite it. A warm sense of purpose filled me as I smiled at my list.

"Ask your question, dear lady, and I will answer it to the best of my abilities."

"When you mentioned that the story lacked consistency, were you referring to the storyline or to the writing style?"

Daniel cleared his throat. I listened to him fidget on the other end of the phone before he finally spoke up. "I would have to say the latter was the more grievous flaw, although I hasten to point out that both could be overcome with serious revision."

The warm glow inside me spread to the far reaches of my body, filling me with hope. Still, I needed clarification. "Would I be wrong to say that the bulk of the coherence problem lies in the fact that each chapter changed the tone of the story?"

"No." Daniel's voice warmed with relief. "You wouldn't be wrong to say that. You've pinpointed the problem exactly. With regard to coherence and clarity, each chapter on its own would have been fine, but when they were placed together, the seams were evident."

I nodded my head even though I knew he couldn't see me. So about that, at least, Alex had been right. What he had hinted at earlier, what he had tried to make me understand, was true. By seeking advice on the story as it was being written and applying that advice without thought as to how it was affecting the writing as a whole, I had done more damage than good. "A painful lesson, but an important one," I mused to myself.

"Writing is never easy," Daniel agreed. I thanked him for his time, reassured him I was suffering no undue effects from the opinions he had offered, and hung up the phone with a firm sense of accomplishment.

I crossed off the first item on my list, then dug the manuscript for *Ravening Raptures* out of my wicker wastebasket. I tossed away the printout of the chapters I'd finished for *A Harlot's Love,* and scratched two more items off my list.

Armed with a bouquet of flowers I picked up at Kamil's grocery, I knocked on Isabella's door the following morning. I held them out to her when she opened the door, healthy and glowing in a peach gauze blouse and matching trousers. Her face, however, was guarded. I noticed tiny lines around her eyes that I was sure hadn't been there before.

"I've come to apologize." Her mouth relaxed into a smile as she accepted the flowers. "I'm very sorry for jumping all over you the other day when you were just trying to help me. If you can see your way clear to forgiving me, I'd like to ask for your assistance."

Her smile widened as she stepped back and waved me into her flat. "Alix, of course I will help you, but there's no need to apologize for your behavior. If anything, it is I who should apologize for stepping in where I wasn't wanted. I do hope you understand that I was only motivated by my affection for both you and Alexander, and that I wasn't trying to tell you what to do or how to live your life."

I nodded and followed her into the sunny sitting room. "I know, and I appreciate it, although it's a moot point now."

Isabella slowly sat in an antique rocker with hand-embroidered cushions. I had admired the rocker ever since I had first spotted it, but had thought it was too fragile for use. Certainly it was too fragile for my Amazonian bones, but Isabella curled one foot under her and looked perfectly at home in the chair. I pushed aside the little pinprick of envy at her seeming perfectness. The new Alix wasn't going to be distracted by petty jealousies and unworthy emotions. The new Alix had a job to do, and do it she would!

"What is a moot point?"

I waved a hand and tried to steer her away from rocky shoals. "Alex and me. We're moot. But that's not what I needed your help with. I'd like some advice, and a big favor."

Isabella rocked in silence for a few minutes, then clasped her hands on her knee and tipped her head to one side. "I should tell you that I had a long talk with Alexander last evening. No, you needn't worry, I'm not about to lecture you or offer unwanted advice, I just want you to know that I spent the evening with him. We went to dinner, as a matter of fact."

There are some benefits to being reborn. The old Alix would have seethed with jealousy at that fact, her teeth gnashing and her eyes shooting sparks. The old Alix would have been hurt and felt betrayed by this news, but the new Alix, the phoenix Alix, took it all in stride.

I unlocked my jaw. "Really?" The word came out a little rasping and grating. I cleared my throat, refocused my thoughts, and tried again. "How lovely for you both. I hope you enjoyed yourself. Now, as to my problem, I'd like two things from you, if you are willing to help me."

She blinked in confusion, but nodded her head and indicated for me to continue.

I took a deep breath. This new path wasn't easy, but then, as some wise man once told me, anything worth having is worth fighting for. "I'd like you to release me from the lease you arranged with my mother, and refund me the balance of the money."

She stopped rocking, her face smooth, showing no expression.

My heart was beating like a jackhammer, but I had to get the worst of it said. "I'd also like your help in finding a new place, somewhere cheap where I could live for a few months on the remaining rent money."

That made her raise her brows. I smoothed my damp palms over the skirt of my summer dress and tried not to gnaw on my lip.

"You want to leave here?" Isabella finally asked.

I nodded. "I need to leave. I can't stay here anymore, not with . . ." I gestured in the direction of Alex's flat. "I need distance from the situation. From Alex. I have a new life to make, and I just can't get started on it if I stay here. I realize I'm asking a lot of you to release me from the lease and hand back the money for this month's rent, but I'm desperate. I've only got a couple of hundred pounds left, even if my ex-agent sends me back my editing fee, and I've maxed out my credit card."

Isabella's face remained smooth, although I thought I saw a flash of dismay in those bright blue eyes before they returned to their normal calm, collected appearance. "I'm not sure I understand your intent, Alix. I will, of course, allow you out of the lease, and will return the money for this month's rent, but I don't understand your need to move. It's not necessary for you to leave the house just to avoid seeing Alexander." She hesitated for a moment, her fingers fretting a bit of material covering her knee. "From what he said last evening, I assume you are quite serious in not maintaining your relationship with him?"

"Yes. That's in the past. I can't go back to that. It was doomed from the start. But I'm moving on, Isabella. Like the phoenix, I'm rising from adversity and starting fresh, and I need your help to make sure I don't plummet and fall to earth before I've even had a chance to try my wings."

A gentle smile curved her lips. "That was beautifully spoken, Alix. I can see why you want to write novels. I still don't understand the necessity of leaving the house, but I will do everything I can to help you fly away from your nest."

I answered her smile with one of my own. "Thank you. For both the warm fuzzies and the willingness to help. Most of all, what I need is advice on how to find a cheap flat."

She pursed her lips in a little moue of consideration. "I believe you'd have better luck finding a bedsitter than a flat. That's a room with a bed but without a private bath," she explained to my look of confusion. "They're much less expensive—although really, Alix, anything you look at in town is going to be much more expensive than if you went to one of the smaller cities. Are you determined to stay in London?"

I nodded. I didn't want to go too far from the object of all my goals.

"Very well. If you are looking for cheap digs, I would suggest you look at student housing."

"Student housing?" I mulled the thought over. "But you have students living here, and—no offense intended, Isabella, but your flats aren't even remotely in the cheap range."

Her madonna-smooth face took on the faintest of smug expressions. "It's true that Miss Goolies and Mr. Skive are students, but Miss Goolies is also the only child of the British Ambassador to China."

"Ah. Big money, eh?"

"Quite."

"Well, OK, I understand that most students live pretty cheaply, but there's one problem—I'm not a student."

"I believe you'll find that most student houses aren't too strict on attendance at university."

"Ah," I said again, thinking about it. I could live without my own bathroom and kitchen if it meant I could stay in London and write. "OK, so where's the best place to look?"

She mentioned a few areas that were likely to have economical housing, and even offered to help me move my things.

"Thanks, Isabella, you're a gem. I appreciate your doing all this after I was so nasty to you."

She waved away my thanks and walked me to the door. "Think nothing more about it. I understand how hurt you felt." One rose-tipped finger tapped on her chin for a moment as we stood before her front door. "If you have truly broken with Alexander, what will you do about Friday?"

"Friday?"

"Alexander's birthday."

Oh, God, I'd forgotten all about his birthday! In a rush, it all came back to me—the plans Isabella and I had made the week before, the money I had squeezed out of my budget to buy tickets for six to an opera I was sure Alex would like, the dinner out at a swanky restaurant that Isabella had arranged as her present to him, and . . . my eyes closed in horror as I remembered the little surprise I had arranged for afterwards. What was I going to do about that? Heedless of my audience, I gnawed on my lower lip. "I don't suppose I could get my money back, do you?"

"For the tickets to *Madame Butterfly*? I'm sure you could. They are very much in demand now, as you know from the trouble it took you to get them."

"It wasn't trouble that was taken, just a sizeable bribe to the scalper. I wasn't talking about the show, though. You and Karl and Bert and Ray and Daniel and his date can have the tickets and take Alex. No, I was talking about whether or not I'd be able to get my money back for . . . you know. The *entertainment.*"

Enlightenment dawned. "The dancers, you mean? Hmmm. I rather doubt that you would be able to have your payment refunded. Those sorts of businesses tend to frown on cancellations of that nature."

"Rats, that's kind of what I figured." I sucked on my lip while I considered and discarded several ideas.

"I have a suggestion," Isabella offered in a mild tone that immediately made me suspicious.

I gave her a quelling glare. It had no effect on her. I made a mental note to hone my quell before I trotted it out again, and gave in to the inevitable. "You think I should just leave things as I planned?"

She smiled and patted my shoulder. "I did say you were an intelligent woman."

I frowned at the door as I thought about the one option I had been avoiding. "It would mean I have to spend the whole evening with Alex."

"But with six other people who will effectively act as a buffer. If you wanted us to, that is. Perhaps . . ." She let the sentence trail off suggestively.

"None of that, missy," I chastised, waving my finger in front of her before reaching for the door. "Next thing I know, you'll turn into a matchmaker."

Her smile deepened until it burst out of her on the breath of silvery laughter. "Oh, Alix, you're closer to the truth than you know."

I stiffened. "I am?"

She laughed again, then reached around and gave me a hug. "Do you remember when you first moved in and I told you I had the perfect man for you?"

How could I forget? Karl was anything but perfect, but he still had turned out to be a nice guy who I enjoyed spending time with, even if I didn't want to get into his pants like I did . . . the blood drained from my face. She didn't mean . . . "You don't . . . not . . . Alex?"

She laughed even harder at the look of horror on my face.

"But of course Alexander! You two are perfect for

317

each other." Her smile dimmed a little. "Perhaps I was wrong, but I thought you were."

"But . . . Karl . . ."

"I decided to bring Karl in as a—what do they call it?—red herring to keep you from realizing that Alexander was the man I had intended for you. You didn't have too many kind things to say about him then, if you recall, and you weren't interested in a serious relationship, while I knew Alexander wouldn't be happy with anything less. . . ."

Once again her voice trailed off, but this time there was no coyness or pleasure in her face. I opened my mouth to say things I had no business saying—not anymore, that is, not since the New Alix had buried the old. Instead I closed my mouth and gave her hand a little squeeze before slipping out the door. I couldn't help but sliding a quick glance to Alex's door. It was as dark and emotionless as the huge, empty hole that lived inside my heart. I dragged my eyes from the sight of it and remembered my list. Today was Monday. Would I be able to gird my loins, harden my heart, and tighten my belt enough to survive an evening in Alex's presence in four days? My chin went up. Of course I would. It was just an evening. The new Alix could do anything she wanted. Alex himself had pointed that out.

"About Friday . . . we'll leave things as they are. I don't know how I'm going to get through the evening, but that's my problem." I turned back to give my now ex-landlady a tepid smile. "Thanks again, Isabella. I appreciate your help." My eyes wandered back to Alex's door. "With everything."

Chapter Sixteen

Lady Rowena gasped as Lord Raoul slowly undid the buttons to his waistcoat. The soft woolen fabric slid down the long length of his muscled arms. Her eyes widened as the duke's son, with a heated look that promised untold delights, unbuttoned his shirt and pulled it over his head slowly, giving her time to accustom herself to his bared flesh.

Her breath caught in her throat, Rowena thought she might swoon as he slowly moved forward. She fought the rising sense of panic that accompanied the sight of his muscled strength.

"Mercy!" she all but begged. "Please, my lord, it is too much. It is impossible. I cannot—"

"Nothing is impossible, beloved," Raoul growled, cradling the softness of her slender body to the hard planes of his. She expected roughness, for how could such a strong man have a touch that was anything but heavy, *but his fingers were the merest whispers upon her skin as he teased the hair at her nape.*

"If you are not ready for this, beloved wife, we shall wait until you are. You have nothing to fear from me. Ever. Of that I swear." His breath was hot against her mouth.

She sighed with the pleasure of his touch and the promise in his eyes, and leaned into the hardened steel of his chest, offering up her lips. At last she had found a man she could trust with her life.

"Where do you want this, Freemar?"

I looked up from the manuscript to see what Ray was holding. The box said "stuff" on the side. Helpful, that. I peered into the carton.

"Oh, that's my souvenirs from the tourist sites. Just stick it over there next to the bed if you please, Ray."

She grunted an acknowledgment and skirted her way around a three-foot-high stuffed Beefeater I had somehow mysteriously acquired.

I frowned, setting the manuscript on top of the box of books at my feet, wondering where I was going to put the books. There wasn't much choice, since my new digs were a little on the small side. The minuscule side of small, that is. There was enough room for a spartan single bed, a battered wardrobe, an even more battered desk with backless chair, and a window seat beneath a window that looked out over the busy street below. I designated a corner as a holding area and dumped my box of books there just as Bert came into the room brushing her hands off on a kerchief, which she folded and tucked in her trouser pocket.

"I left your box of food in the kitchen, Alix. I would

suggest you go down and claim it fairly quickly. There were several hungry-looking young men hanging about."

I made a face. "They're welcome to everything but the chocolate, and that I packed with my clothes. And speaking of my clothes . . ." I did a complete 360-degree turn. "Has anyone seen a box labeled 'clothing'?"

"I have it," a muffled reply came from behind Bert.

"Thanks, Isabella. You can set it there on the chair. Well!" Not nearly so dainty as Bert, I wiped my grubby hands on my jeans. "I guess that's everything, then. I can't believe I've bought so much stuff in just a month's time!"

"You're in London, dear; shopping is inevitable," Isabella chided gently as she surveyed my new domain. I looked around with her, grimaced, and warmed up a smile. The new Alix didn't whine or complain.

"I can't thank you all enough for helping me get settled here. I appreciate your support more than you know."

Ray pounded on the frame of the window in order to get it to open more than six inches. "Painted," she tossed over her shoulder, then turned back to the street. She waved Bert forward while I turned to Isabella.

"And I especially want to thank you for"—I shot a quick glance at Bert and Ray and dropped my voice— "for being so sweet about the lease. That money will let me live here for three more months."

Isabella tried on her bright smile, but it didn't seem to have the wattage it normally wore. Maybe it was just the dingy surroundings. She looked around worriedly.

"It's OK, Isabella, really it is. I know it's not any great shakes as a bedsit, but it'll be just fine. All I want to do is have some peace and quiet so I can write, and there'll be nothing here that will . . ." My gaze met hers. I ignored the sympathy in them and clung to the admiration. The new Alix didn't indulge in pity parties. ". . . *distract* me."

She squeezed my arm in sympathy or reassurance, I wasn't sure which.

"Alix?"

"Hmm?" I turned to where Ray and Bert were standing at the window. Ray looked angry. Bert looked worried as she sent some sort of eyebrow semaphore to Isabella.

"Have you . . . erm . . . met your neighbors?" Ray asked.

Why was she so worried about a bunch of students? They seemed all right to me, if a bit young.

"Just the two women next door. There's another room on this floor, and the shower, so I figure it'll probably be pretty quiet."

Some sort of secret unspoken communication passed between Isabella and Bert. Ray's frown turned into a scowl. What on earth was wrong with them? I caught the merest shake of Isabella's head before Bert spoke again.

"Actually, I was referring to the people who live on either side of the student house."

I went over to peer out the window. I didn't see anything worrisome, just a busy London street with a fish-and-chips shop across the street (handy!), an earring piercing place next to it, and a pinball arcade.

"Well, the pinball place is bound to be a bit noisy at night, but Alex fixed my CD player and I have headphones, so I'll be fine."

Ray cleared her throat. "Man next door. Big, burly fellow. Bald, too. Shaves his head, probably. Has tattoos of snakes on his neck. You stay clear of him."

My mouth dropped open. "Really?" I peered down at an angle to see if I could spot him. "Snakes? On his neck? Cool!"

"Alix."

I smooshed my cheek against the not-terribly-clean windowpane and tried to see who stood in the doorway next to the one for the student house. I hadn't particularly noticed the building next to the student house, so I had no idea if it was a business or another student house, but I could see the tips of a pair of dirty-looking tennis shoes poking out from the doorway.

"Alix."

"What?"

Isabella tugged on my elbow. "Alix, I don't wish to alarm you, but King's Cross isn't a terribly safe neighborhood."

I peeled my cheek off the window and turned to look between her, Bert, and Ray.

"What? Not safe? This is London—of course it's safe! I mean, look, the train station is right there, you can see it from the window. Of course it's safe!"

Ray rolled her eyes.

I forestalled the inevitable objections. "Oh, I know, you guys have crime, but nothing like back home, trust me! I've been around student areas before, I'm not stupid."

The three women exchanged dubious glances with each other.

"You're all mother hens, you know that?" I herded them to the door, thanking them again for their help, and after promising them faithfully that I wouldn't wander the streets at night and would take care not to speak to Mr. Snakes, I sent them on their way.

I went down to the kitchen on the ground floor, put my meager foodstuffs away on the shelf marked with my room number, chatted for a moment with the resident kitchen loungers, then hurried back up four flights of twisty, uneven stairs to my new room.

An hour later I had everything tucked away, my newly purchased clean sheets and blanket on the bed, and was ready to begin work. I pulled out the list I had created two days before, and crossed off another item. My list was getting shorter, although adding in all the steps necessary to get through Friday evening had lengthened it considerably, but still I took pride in the fact that I was moving forward rather than standing still as I had for so many years.

I pulled out *Ravening Raptures*, made a mental note that I needed to find it a new title, and examined the first chapter, which I had finished revising the night before. As I read the words, Alex's image was superimposed upon Lord Raoul's, filling me with desire and anguish and all the many emotions I had fought back the day before. I closed my eyes against the sting of tears, and reminded myself that I couldn't go back. I had been reborn, and I would not go back to that prior existence. I opened my eyes and propped up my list.

I was strong. I could do this. I had my plan, and I would stick to it, no matter how much my heart ached.

That night I met Beryl. I had toddled over to the fish-and-chips shop for dinner, splurging despite my new, extremely strict budget, and after dodging my way around all the people wandering the sidewalks, I crossed the street and headed back to my student house. As I passed the dark blue and purple painted exterior of the building next to mine, a man stepped out of the doorway. He was at least six and a half feet tall, and probably a good yard across, but what immediately caught the eye was not his huge body, but the blue and red snakes coiled around his neck, writhing and twisting their way up the sides of his bald head.

Surprisingly handsome gray eyes peered out of a face that would have given the Gestapo nightmares. Unfortunately, those eyes were narrowed in suspicion and focused on me as I stared back at him. Two massive arms the size of my thighs crossed in front of his chest when he leaned forward, menace rolling off him like dust off a wheat field.

"What're ye about, then?"

Who, me? I had to swallow twice before I could make my tongue work. "Uh . . . hi. I live . . . um . . . just there." I pointed a hesitant finger over his shoulder at the pink door to the student house.

His eyes narrowed even more as he raked me over from head to heels. I suddenly became aware that there was no one else on this side of the street, and the people on the other side, the side with the busy shops, had all stopped and were gathered into small, silent groups.

Oh, great, my first day out in my new neighborhood and I run smack dab into the neighborhood murderer.

"I've never seen ye before."

"I just moved here. Today. This morning." I tried to edge my way around him, but a parked car blocked one direction, and he easily blocked me from the other. I clutched my fish and chips to my chest as one would a crucifix when faced with a vampire. "Look, I'd love to stand here chatting with you, but I've . . . uh . . . I've got to call my boyfriend. He gets worried about me, you know." I hoped the snakeman wouldn't notice my crossed fingers as I tried to sidle by him. "Scotland Yard detectives are awfully funny about that sometimes. Ha ha ha ha!"

He didn't join me in laughter. Instead, two bushy black eyebrows met in the middle of his face and formed one long, continuous entity. Somehow the sight didn't inspire hilarity.

"Wot's that ye say? Scotland Yard?"

My head bobbled up and down like one of those dogs people put in the rear window of their cars. "Yes. Scotland Yard. My boyfriend—we're going to be married soon, he's very fond of me, *very fond*—he works for Scotland Yard. He's a detective inspector. That's an important guy," I added just in case Snakes didn't know that little fact. It appeared from the alacrity with which he stepped back that he did know that, or at least decided to consider it before killing me. I made an odd sort of bobbing motion that felt suspiciously like a curtsey as I scurried around the behemoth toward the safety of the student house. The weight of my snakey friend's eyes on me had my palms sweating while I scrabbled for my key, but even so I managed a weak smile at him as I squeezed in through the opening.

"Holy cow," I panted once I had the door closed safely behind me. I leaned against it, my legs trembling, and decided that although the New Alix was many things, she was not a fool.

A slight blonde with bad skin and a cheery smile poked her head around the door to the TV room. "Looks like you've just met Genghis."

I stiffened my knees and tightened my grip on my dinner. "Genghis?"

The blonde grinned and nodded in the direction I had last seen the monster of King's Cross.

"Bloke with the tattoos. His name is really Beryl, but we call him Genghis. He's barb, isn't he?"

"Oh, barb, yes. Totally barb. The barbiest man I've ever seen, and God help me, I hope I don't ever see him again."

She laughed a lighthearted little laugh and introduced herself as Jasmin. "Old Genghis won't bother you once he's shaken you down."

"Uh . . ." Shaken me down? Good Lord, what sort of place had I moved into? "What do you mean, shaken me down?"

Her gaze razed me in a calculating sort of manner. "Blunt. Money. Didn't you pay him anything?"

"To walk down the sidewalk? No."

Her eyes widened until they were almost perfectly round, and she backed slowly away from me as if I were a rabid dog about to attack.

"Oh. I'm sure . . . that is, you probably . . . well, it was a pleasure to meet you."

I watched her disappear slowly back into the TV room, never taking her eyes from me until the door closed softly behind her. I pondered whether I wanted to eat my dinner in the kitchen with what were sure to be the same three skinny guys slouching around a sticky Formica table, or if I wanted to dine in the comfort of my room, or if I wanted to drop everything and run screaming into Alex's arms.

That pesky little inner voice who insists on giving me the benefit of her advice chose the last option, but New

Alix shoved her aside and gave me the strength to make my way up four flights of stairs, past the toilet on the third floor, the tiny, claustrophobic shower on the fourth floor, to the safe haven of my room. I pulled down the blinds, pushed the rickety desk in front of the door, and sank bonelessly down onto the bed. I knew that if I turned my head I could see my list lying on my laptop on the desk, but it somehow seemed to lack the comfort it usually gave me. Despite the heat of the day, I wrapped the blanket around me and curled up into a ball on the bed.

My decision to leave Beale Square suddenly seemed hasty and not terribly well thought out. I prayed it would all come out right.

"The new Alix," I told Bert and Ray as I spun around obligingly for them, "may not be perfect, but she no longer allows herself doubts as to the correctness of the path before her."

"Sounds foolish," Ray grumbled as she twitched the blinds back to peer down onto the street.

"Not foolish, dear, just ambitious," Bert corrected her as I came to a halt. "Remaking yourself is never easy. I wish you all happiness with your new life."

I pushed aside the thought of the tears I had been unable to hold back in the warm darkness of the previous three nights, and struck a fashionable pose. "So what do you think?"

She smiled. "I think you will dazzle the eye of every man you meet, and one man in particular."

I let my smile slip just a little. "Well, that doesn't matter, it's not on the list for tonight. I'm going to have enough on my plate without tackling off-list items."

"Alix, about this list of yours—"

"They're gone. Wonder what happened to them."

We both turned to where Ray was peering through the window at the street opposite.

"Who's gone?" I asked, moving over to look out the window with her. I didn't see anything out of place, just the usual people coming and going at the shops, generally acting just as they had every other of the three days I had been in residence. "What happened to who?"

"Whom," Bert corrected softly as she followed me to the window.

"Tarts," Ray said succinctly.

"What?" I nudged her aside so I could see better. "Where's a tart?"

Ray shot me a disbelieving look. "They *were* right in front of your nose. Gone now."

I glanced down at the people on the street. None of them *looked* like tarts. "You're kidding! There were tarts on the street? How'd I miss them? I don't see anyone now but two bobbies and some kids in the video arcade place."

"Exactly." Ray gave me an expectant look that I had no idea how to meet. I turned to Bert for help.

"Surely you noticed the unusual amount of activity on the street when you moved here?" Bert asked gently.

"Well, yeah, but I figured it was just the video arcade. Lots of people seemed to hang around there . . ." My mouth dropped open as it struck me that the people hanging around outside were mostly women, women dressed in a flashy manner that would have instantly screamed *hooker* to me if I had seen them back home. Somehow, though, the idea of prostitutes in London just seemed alien. "Oh. They were tarts?"

Both women nodded.

I frowned out the window. "But I only saw them the first day I was here. I remember thinking the next day how nice it was that the street had quieted down." I gnawed on my lip a wee tad bit. "There've been lots of bobbies on the street, though . . . oh, good Lord! Genghis!"

"Genghis?" Bert asked, scooping up her bag and a silk scarf that complemented the soft green sleeveless silk sheath dress she wore.

"Yeah, Genghis. The guy next door with the snakes on his neck. One of the students told me yesterday he had disappeared, that no one had seen him since Tuesday night! That was three days ago, the day I moved in. You don't suppose there's some sort of Jack the Ripper type murderer running amok in King's Cross, do you? I mean, the hookers are gone, the head pimp who extorts money from innocent students disappears, bobbies are crawling all over the place—good Lord, that's probably it! There's some vigilante madman running around cleaning up the streets! And I'm right in the middle of it!"

Ray gave a short bark of laughter and exchanged glances with Bert. "Simpler explanation than that. Black's had his hand in this."

Really, I was getting quite good at that goggling look. I practiced it now on Ray, staring at her as if she had completely lost her mind. "Black? Alex? You think he is the vigilante?"

"Could be," she said with a wicked grin.

"Ray, don't tease Alix, she's had a difficult week. We really should be going now." Bert slid her arm through mine and tugged me toward the door. I resisted. I wasn't going to leave the room until Ray was straightened out.

"Alex is a lot of things, but he wouldn't subscribe to vigilante justice," I argued. "He's very law-abiding. If it came right down to it, he'd get a bunch of his police buddies and have them crack down on—"

Ray's smirk stopped me cold. A little thrill of excitement rippled through me—excitement and a warm glow of pleasure. "Oh. You think Alex is protecting me? But why? And how does he know where I'm living?"

Both women just looked at me. I nodded at their silent answer. "Isabella. Isabella would have told him that I had moved here."

Ray shrugged. "Might not be him. Could be a coincidence."

It could, but if it wasn't . . . the warm glow of pleasure burned a little hotter. Despite everything, he was trying to protect me. No one had ever protected me before! It was a very heady feeling to know that Alex cared.

Heady, but not allowed on my list. I pushed down the warm glow and paid heed when Bert nodded at my alarm clock. "If we don't wish to be late, we'd best be on our way."

Half an hour later we piled out of a taxi and stood in front of the glass doors of The Ivy, one of London's most popular restaurants, certainly the most popular in the area around Leicester Square, the heart of the theater district. Normally it took up to six weeks to book a table at The Ivy, but the prior week when I was explaining my plans for making Alex's thirty-sixth birthday something he'd never forget, Isabella mentioned being a friend of one of the owners. Three phone calls later, a miracle had been granted us.

"Miracle or plague, I wonder," I muttered as I stood outside the shaded glass doors and tugged unobtrusively

331

at the hem of my little black dress. It was a twin of the red one hanging in my wardrobe, both having been purchased at a consignment shop back in Seattle, the brand label and fit too good to pass up. Whereas I hadn't felt anything but pleasantly sexy when I wore the red version to the dinner at Isabella's to meet Karl, at the moment I felt sick to my stomach with apprehension.

I clutched at the tassels of the silk scarf Bert had thrown over her sheath dress. "Bert, I don't feel very well. I don't think I'm going to be able to get through this."

"Alix, you'll be fine. Just try to relax."

I clutched the tassels even harder. "What if he's not here? What if he's so ticked off at me that he decided not to come? What if he wants to humiliate me in front of everyone? *What if he brought a date?*"

She smiled and gave my arm a reassuring squeeze. "You're being silly. Isabella said she and Karl would be sure to bring him with them, and he wouldn't be so tactless as to bring a date. Now stop worrying and try to look like you're not going to be sick all over the floor."

I released my stranglehold on her tassels for a moment, then lunged after her as she started for the door.

"Wait! Maybe you should go in first, just to see if he's there, and to see where he's sitting and if Isabella is sitting next to him, and if he's laughing and looking like he's having a good time, or if he's looking sulky or angry or hurt or something—"

Bert turned back to say something to me, but I'll never know what, because Ray, previously engaged in paying off the taxi, grabbed my elbow and marched me toward the white and black door. "The new Alix wouldn't whinge," she said firmly, and pushed me inside. I cursed her for her insight. She grinned in return.

The inside of the restaurant was everything it was rumored to be, all wood-paneled and stained glass and old-world ambience, but I didn't consciously notice any of it as we approached the large round table in the back.

Alex was there, sitting with his back to the room, leaning across the table to say something to Karl. Isabella sat between them, while next to Karl sat a cheerful-looking red-haired woman and Daniel. Three empty chairs loomed up to the right of Alex. I stared at the empty chair next to him and felt my stomach contract into a dense ball approximately the size of a neutron.

"Please," I whimpered to Ray as she heartlessly dragged me forward. "Please, Ray, if you have any mercy in your soul, take the chair next to Alex."

She made an inelegant snorting sound and hustled me forward.

"No, I'm serious," I whispered as we approached, my hands sweaty and my stomach rolling over with every step. Alex started to turn around to see whom Karl and Isabella were smiling at. "I have money! I'll pay you! Just take that chair and you can name your price! Any price!"

Twin shafts of emerald pierced through the armor the new Alix had erected. My knees buckled under that look, and only Ray's grip on my elbow kept me from collapsing on the spot. Or turning tail and running. I wasn't sure which I wanted more at that point, but Ray grunted an encouragement in my ear, and I managed to stiffen my knees and meet Alex's gaze when he and Karl stood. I slapped a smile on my face and did the pleasantries. "Good evening, everyone. How nice you look, Isabella. Karl, it's a pleasure to see you again. You must be Paula.

I'm delighted to meet you. Daniel, you look to be in a devilish mood."

There, that took care of everyone but the man standing next to me waiting while Bert and Ray greeted everyone. I took my new sense of purpose in a firm grip, and turned to face him. The shock of standing so close to him, of having those green eyes glitter into mine so intimately, stunned me for a moment, but at last I dragged my brain from the contemplation of all the things I wanted to do to him and mustered a smile. "Happy birthday, Alex. How does it feel to be thirty-six?"

"You look lovely tonight, Alix." I stopped breathing at his words, teetering on the brink of falling into the deep well of emerald of his eyes, but he saved me from going over the edge. With a wry twist of his lips, he added, "Thirty-six feels much the same as thirty-five—ancient." Everyone laughed at his sally. Everyone but me. I was too busy trying to keep my heart from slamming its way out of my chest at the sight of those lips, so close, so tantalizingly, teasingly close that for the chance to give myself up to them, I was almost willing to sell my soul.

The new Alix shouldered her way forward and reminded me I had almost done just that, and it had ended in disaster. The plan, the new Alix reminded me; we had a plan, and we had to stick to it, and damn it all, kissing Alex wasn't on the list. I tore my gaze from his lips and sank wordlessly into the chair he held out for me, praying for the strength needed to get through an evening spent sitting next to the man I loved with every atom of my being.

Champagne was brought while menus were distributed. I managed to maintain a flow of chat with everyone, although I felt light-headed and dizzy even without the champagne. As the waiter collected the menus, Alex shifted in his chair, causing his leg to brush mine. I shot up out of my chair. Heads swiveled to stare at me, but I saw only the question in one pair of eyes.

"I . . . uh . . . have to use the little girls' room," I stammered, and edged backward. "I'll be right back."

"Would you like me to come with you?" Isabella asked.

"No, thanks, I've been going to the bathroom by myself for a long time now," I assured her, and with one last glance at Alex, made my escape.

If I had hoped to find sanctuary in the loo, I was mistaken. The Ivy was one of those high-class places that had an attendant in the bathroom, a little white-haired Indian woman with a polite smile and lovely dark eyes. She nodded to me as I burst into the bathroom. I nodded back and claimed a stall, wondering what she would think if I spent the whole evening in there.

I was being ridiculous, and I knew it. Just because I wanted Alex and couldn't have him didn't mean I couldn't be polite to him, sit next to him and converse in an adult, mature manner. To run away just because his leg had inadvertently touched mine, sending flames of desire skimming along the surface of my skin, was neither here nor there. I was a grown woman. I had a plan. Alex may have thought I lacked courage, but I was no coward. Chin held high, I emerged from the stall and washed my hands with the assistance of the loo lady, dropping a pound coin into her tip basket before striding back into the restaurant, self-assurance and poise dripping from every pore.

Alex rose and held out my chair. Karl did that little

half-rise-from-the-chair crouch that men make whose mothers have taught them to stand when a woman enters the room but who are now too enlightened to give in to such sexual stereotyping. I smiled at both and sat, determined not only to survive the evening, but to triumph over my traitorous heart and body. I inquired of Alex how work was going. He replied in the same polite, emotionally bare tone I used. I began to relax as everyone at the table laughed and joked over trivialities, confident that at last I had got myself under control.

I turned to say something to Alex and found him watching me with a look of longing on his face that almost undid me. The words dried up on my lips as he leaned close and stroked one finger down a path on the inside of my bare arm. Flames followed his touch, igniting the rest of me into a blaze of love and lust and desire and need. I jumped back, almost knocking the chair down as I leaped out of it.

"Bathroom," I told the astonished look on Alex's face. "I have to . . . uh . . . excuse me, please."

Bert called out something after me, but I didn't wait to hear it. I dashed into the ladies' room, smiling wildly at the surprised attendant, and flung myself into an empty stall, rubbing my arm to extinguish the flames.

"This is intolerable," I mumbled to myself as I stood in the marble stall, my arms gripped hard around myself to keep the trembling under control. "It was just a finger, just one finger, not even a whole hand, just one little finger on an unerogenous part of the body. Stop acting like a bowl of jelly and get back out there!"

I couldn't just leave the bathroom without washing my hands—the attendant would think I had poor personal hygiene habits—so I washed, gave her another pound for standing next to me and offering me a clean towel, straightened my shoulders, and returned to the table.

Seven pairs of eyes turned on me with concern as I tried to slip inconspicuously into my chair. Isabella leaned across Alex and whispered, "Is there any trouble?"

Heat flowed up my neck into my cheeks. "No, thank you, everything's fine," I whispered back and gave Alex a toothy smile. "Everything's fine," I repeated to him before turning my attention back to the table. Knowing I'd be sloshed out of my gourd if I drank the champagne, I asked for a glass of water to relieve the dry mouth my nerves had wrought. The waiter refilled my glass when he brought a second bottle of champagne with the appetizers. I meant to sip my water as everyone toasted Alex, but when I get nervous I get thirsty. I downed the second glass of water, and signaled the waiter for more.

"Not still feeling sick, are you?" Ray asked quietly, watching me as I started in on the third glass of water.

"No, just a little parched."

"Ah." The look she bent upon me spoke volumes, but I didn't have time to decipher it, I was too busy trying to inch my knee away from Alex's without him noticing. It was a lost cause. They don't make people detective inspectors if they aren't observant.

"What's wrong with you?" Alex hissed as I tried to edge away from the pressure of his knee against my leg. "Why are you acting like this?"

I gave up on my leg and just let it go up in flames. "Acting like what?"

"Why are you squirming in your chair? Is it so bloody difficult to sit next to me?"

My temper rose at that. Of course it was so bloody

difficult! My hands were shaking with the attempt to keep myself from wrestling him to the ground and stripping him naked in front of everyone. The least he could do was help me!

"Yes, as a matter of fact, it is," I snapped back. "Why can't you keep your limbs to yourself? Every time you touch me I—"

He leaned closer to me until I could see the lovely black edges of the emerald facets in his eyes. "Every time I touch you, you what?"

"Nothing," I ground out between my teeth. I had a plan. My plan was good. Nowhere on my list was there an item which included the seduction of Alex in a restaurant.

I turned my head away from him, intending to ask Daniel a question, when Alex turned my insides to pudding by leaning close to my ear, his breath ruffling my hair as he spoke. "You're a terrible liar, sweetheart."

I pushed him back with one hand and shoved myself away from the table with the other. Once again every eye at the table was on me as I stood with one hand on Alex's chest.

"Bathroom!" I squawked, and ran for my life.

Five minutes later I returned, another pound poorer, but with my hands soft and perfumed from the scented lotion the attendant had offered.

"Sorry," I apologized as I sat down again, reaching for my glass of water. I drank half of it before realizing everyone was watching me.

"What?" I asked them, looking from one face to another. "Why are you guys looking at me like that?"

"Alix." Isabella reached across Alex and took my hand in hers, giving it a comforting little squeeze. "You are among friends here. You can tell us if something is amiss with you."—she waved a vague hand toward her torso—"inside."

I blinked at her. "What?"

She frowned at Alex until he sat back in his chair; then she leaned across him. "Dear, we're concerned about you. These frequent trips to the WC could be indicative of a serious problem. Are you experiencing any burning when you . . . ?"

Lord, yes, every time Alex glanced at me I went up in flames, but I didn't suppose that was what she was talking about. My cheeks burned anew under the sympathetic expressions everyone at the table was sending me.

I glared at my plate and avoided meeting anyone's eyes. "I'm fine, Isabella. There's no need for anyone to worry."

"Bladder infections can be quite serious, you know," Paula said from across the table, her red curls bobbing earnestly as she spoke. The ladies at the table all nodded sagely. "A girl I worked with had one, and she ended up going into hospital with kidney damage because she didn't take care of herself."

My blush hitched up a level as speculative looks were focused on me. I cleared my throat and tried to think of something, anything else to talk about but bladder infections. "Thank you, Paula, but I can assure you that I don't have a bladder infection. So, is everyone looking forward to the opera tonight? Do we have any opera virgins here?"

"If you don't have a bladder infection, then why are you running to the WC every two minutes?" Isabella asked. "Do you have food poisoning? Have you had—"

"No!" I shrieked, wondering if it was possible to fall down dead with embarrassment.

"Well, if it's not food poisoning or a bladder infection that's making you use the WC so frequently, then what is the matter?"

"Venereal disease," Ray offered.

I prayed for the ground to open up and swallow me whole.

Everyone looked at me for a moment, then at Alex. He withstood their gazes well by simply cocking an eyebrow. "Don't look at me, I didn't give her anything."

"Oh, dear God in heaven," I moaned, my head sinking to my hands.

"If she had an STD, she would have some sort of sign, a rash or discharge, surely," Karl said, frowning. "Alex, have you noticed if she has had any—"

"That's it!" I stood up, clutching my evening bag to my chest and glared at everyone at the table. "I'm leaving, but before I go I would just like to tell you all that I do not have a bladder infection, food poisoning, or a sexually transmittable disease, thank you all for asking. Good night!"

"Alix, sit down."

I glared down at Alex. "No. If I sit they'll start discussing my last pap smear or something."

He grabbed my wrist and tugged me down to the chair. "No one is going to discuss anything you don't want discussed. Sit."

I allowed myself to be reseated, but resolved to leave at the first mention of anything else to do with my reproductive organs.

"What's a pap smear?" Karl asked Isabella in a whisper that could be heard across a crowded room. Daniel winked and gave me one of his sultry smiles. Ray muttered to Bert that they would need to make sure I went to see a doctor. Alex smiled encouragingly at me as he placed his hand over mine.

I sighed, resigned to hell. It was going to be a long, long dinner.

We survived the opera without any further speculation as to the causes of my frequent dashes to the ladies' room. Alex finally seemed to catch on to my subtle hints that I wasn't open to his advances toward a reconciliation. I think that point was finally driven home to him when, before the opera began, we had a bit of a squabble over who had the right to our shared armrest. It wasn't pretty, it wasn't quiet, and I'm not proud of calling him a tottyhead in public ("What did you call me?" "Tottyhead. You, sir, are a tottyhead. Tottyhead, tottyhead, tottyhead!"), but the argument served its purpose. He claimed the armrest by dint of it being his birthday, and ignored me for the whole of the opera.

"What has angered Alexander?" Isabella asked during intermission. I glanced over at where he was weaving his way through the crowd at the bar.

"He's just being a big baby because he doesn't like opera."

A tiny smile graced her lips as she sipped at a vodka on the rocks. "I have to admit I wondered at your choice of entertainment, but thought perhaps you knew something about him that I did not."

I shrugged. "I thought it would be good for him to be exposed to a little culture. He's so hidebound and straightlaced, new experiences are bound to broaden his horizons. And besides, this isn't the entertainment." I glanced at her out of the corner of my eye. "That comes later."

Her smiled increased in brightness. "Are you going to do it?"

I scooted aside so Daniel and Paula could pass us on their way back to our seats. "I don't know. I can't make up my mind. Every time I think I will . . . well, let's just say I change my mind."

"I'm sure it would mean a lot to him if you did."

That was what worried me. "I'll think about it. I still have the rest of the opera to decide. You're going to, regardless, aren't you?"

She gave me an unfathomable look. "Perhaps."

"Isabella, it was because of you that I suggested the whole thing! You can't back out now!"

"That's what *you're* talking about doing."

"Yeah, but Alex and I aren't . . . together anymore. And besides, your costume is better than mine. And you've had lots of practice. I just look lumpy."

She laughed her silvery laugh and deposited her drink on a table before hooking her hand through my arm. "Come, they're about to ring the bell, let's return." As we squeezed through the door, she leaned her head close to mine and added, "Alix, I don't know what it is you are doing with this list and plan of yours, but I suspect you will very much regret it if you do not take part in the festivities you have planned for later."

I thought of what was coming up and blanched.

Chapter Seventeen

She was right. Isabella often is, which is one of the things that most irritates me about her. But I knew she was right, I'd regret not having the balls to stand up and do what I had planned, which is why two and a half hours later I found myself with Isabella and eight other women as we huddled together in the dank, cold, dimly lit backstage area of a very exclusive club (arranged with Daniel's assistance—never let it be said that I looked a gift horse in the mouth), shivering as I shimmied my way into a skimpy belly dancer's outfit.

"I look lumpy," I snarled as I hooked together the top part of the outfit. "Look, my boobs are bulging over the top of this vest thingy. I'll probably pop out during one of the dances and expose myself to everyone. I just hope you'll be happy then! I just hope you'll be able to live with yourself knowing I exposed my breasts to your friends because you refuse to allow me to do my part in a comfy caftan."

She gave a laugh that would be a giggle on a lesser person, but as Isabella was too elegant to giggle, the result was light and sparkling rather than silly. "You can't possibly belly dance in a caftan. Stop being so difficult, Alix! You'll have a wonderful time."

I cast an envious glance over at her slender silver-and-blue-clad body, then grumbled as I tugged the low bodice up a bit higher. It did no good; the weight of my substantial bosomage pulled it back down. I glared at my reflection. "Fleshy. There's just no other word for it, I look fleshy."

"You look lovely and you know it, so you can stop fishing for compliments. I don't understand why you're being so coy; Alexander has seen you without your clothing."

"Yeah, Alex has, but no one else here has except you and all of the other dancers. I didn't mind him seeing me naked in the heat of passion, but in the cold light of reason, I'd rather not have all the acres of my skin exposed to view." I turned around to look at the back view. "Dear God, you can see all of my butt through the skirt! Isabella, look! You can see my butt! I'm not going to go out there and have everyone and his brother get a gander at my bare butt!"

She looked. "Why aren't you wearing the panties?"

"You told me to take them off."

"Not the panties you came in with, the ones specially made to go with the outfit. You should be wearing those."

I looked in the box that held the outfit I had bought the prior week. There was nothing else in it.

"Well, hell, they gypped me!" I held up the empty box. "I'm not going out there with my butt visible through this flimsy material!" A horrible thought struck me. If my behind was visible, then . . .

I looked in the mirror.

"Pubic hair! You can see my pubic hair! Dear God, it's right there where anyone can see it! I refuse to do this! I refuse to parade around baring all my assets to everyone, and you can't expect me to! It's illegal! It's cruel and unusual punishment!"

"Alix, calm down."

"Alex is a policeman! He'll probably arrest me for indecent exposure!"

"We'll find you another pair of panties."

"And if he doesn't, someone else will. They'll probably raid the place, and then my picture will be plastered all over the paper with the headline YANK WANNA-BE WRITER IN SEX CLUB SCANDAL. My mother will hear about this, and then she'll disown me, not that that means much, because she doesn't really like me now, but this will be the straw that broke her back, but what's worse, what's much worse is that no publisher will consider me after I've had all my fleshy bits spread across the tabloids! I'll end up broke and destitute and living in a car because I can't afford an apartment, so desperate for employment that I'll have to resort to posing for men's smut magazines just before I die of malnutrition, friendless, alone, and probably an alcoholic to boot." I paused long enough to take a deep breath. "I hope you'll be happy with that end for me, Isabella, because that's what's waiting for me if you force me to go out there with everything I own on display!"

345

"Alix, will you listen to me? I'm not going to make you do anything you don't wish to do!"

The sight of my scantily covered pubic mound haunted me. I closed my eyes and hugged my filled-to-the-brim bodice. "It's not fair of you to ask me to go out there like this. It's not fair of you to make me feel guilty for not wanting to go out and have everyone see my pubic hair and bare butt."

She grabbed my hand and shoved a piece of cloth in it. I opened my eyes and looked. "What's this?"

"Panties. Put them on."

They weren't the same color as the flame red and orange of my outfit. These were pink. "Where'd you get them?" I asked suspiciously, holding them up to see if they looked like they'd fit.

"They're Susan's."

"Susan?"

I looked down to where she was pointing. One of the entertainers I had hired—a troupe of women who specialized in dancing various themed dances for mostly male parties—was clad in a hot pink and turquoise belly dancer outfit. She smiled and gave me a thumbs-up sign. I gaped at her for a moment, then shoved the panties back at Isabella.

"I'm not going to wear some other woman's underwear! That's just gross!"

"Alix, they're clean—"

"No!" I dug through the bag holding the garments I'd been wearing before changing into the gauzy peepshow costume. "If I can't wear the panties that were meant for this outfit, I'll wear my own." I pulled out a pair of black lace undies and stepped into them.

Isabella eyed my groin critically. "It doesn't match the

rest of the ensemble. In fact, it's quite noticeable."

I glared at her. "I *told* you I should wear a caftan!"

I hoped the hat and veil would be enough to keep my identity secret, but the three belly dancing lessons Isabella had given me weren't sufficient to allow me to keep up with the other professional dancers. They might not be any great shakes as belly dancers, but they were willing to come forward and dance a sinuous, bumping and grinding circle around the birthday boy, whereas I kept to the rear and tried to hide behind everyone else.

There was one moment when I claimed the limelight. Isabella, the only one among us who really knew how to belly dance, wiggled her way in front of Alex and started shaking her groove thing at him. He looked pleased by the show—very pleased, much more pleased than a man who had had his hand on my knee earlier in the evening should have looked. I gnashed my teeth and clanged the little bells strapped to my fingers with much fervor, slowly but surely pushing my way forward until I was just to the left of Alex, in front of Daniel. The latter was trying to not too obviously enjoy the antics of a long-legged blonde grinding away in front of him. I nudged her aside, bared my teeth at Daniel, and accidentally bumped into Isabella, sending her spinning toward Karl.

I looked down at Alex and met his emerald-eyed gaze. "Laugh and you die," I warned him. His lips twitched as he looked me over from head to feet. I clanged my bells at him when he stopped his perusal and peered closer at my black undies. "Eyes up, buster. And stop drooling over Isabella. It isn't seemly in a man of your elderly years."

He laughed at that, and after a few more warning bells

chimed perilously near his nose, coupled with the three sinuous hip shakes that were the only elements I could remember how to do, I moved on. Bert wanted to know how hard it was to belly dance, so she got up with Isabella and had an impromptu session, joined soon thereafter by Paula. I glared as the other dancers continued to surround Alex, and plumped myself down next to Ray.

"This was a rotten idea."

"I think it's a grand one," she replied, her toes tapping in time to the blare of belly dancing music that filled the private room. "Took courage."

I glanced at her in surprise, then sat back to think about that. I supposed it did take courage to arrange to make a fool of myself in front of the man I loved. I slid a glance to the left toward Alex. He was laughing at something Daniel was saying, watching as Isabella encouraged Bert and Paula to join the other dancers.

"Well, I will say that Alex seems to be having fun. He looks happy and relaxed and isn't exhibiting the least bit of resistance to being exposed to something out of the norm like he did at the opera."

Ray nodded, clapping her hands in time to the music and calling out encouragement as Bert and Paula danced by in the line of dancers.

"I wasn't sure how he would like this, but I guess . . . *Hey!* No touching! I specifically told you there was to be *no touching!*"

I stood up and started toward Susan of the underwear as she gyrated before Alex, doing some sort of pelvic thrust movement at him while curling her fingers through his lovely hair.

"Back off, sister," I snarled. Ray caught my arm as I

stalked past her, pulling me back to my chair.

"Don't."

I pushed her hand away. "Don't what?"

"Don't degrade yourself. Black's not the sort of bloke to play while the cat's away."

I glared at the hussy. She had shot me a smug glance when Ray hauled me back, then continued to dance her crotch toward Alex in a manner that would shame a nymphomaniac. I toyed with the idea of ripping the hair right off her head, but decided Ray was probably right. When I had set up the belly dance, Alex and I were still firmly a couple, and I had imagined how pleased (and aroused) he would be by my participation. I hadn't for one moment worried that he would be equally turned on by the other women, even Isabella. Now, however, all bets were off, even if Alex was looking a bit embarrassed about Crotch Woman thrusting herself in his face.

"Oh, yeah," I growled to myself watching the she-wolf undulate in front of the man whose children I had once hoped to bear. "Brilliant bloody idea, Alix. Just brilliant."

Alex saw me home. I didn't want him to see me home, and told him so in no uncertain terms, but short of shackling him to a chair in the club—something I might have considered had I possessed shackles—there was nothing I could do to stop him from following me into the tube station or a taxi, so I gave in.

"OK, but you get to pay for it," I warned him, and climbed into one of the wonderfully roomy black taxis that dart about town. He gave the driver my address on Pentonville Road, and sat down next to me.

I let him have my best glare. "How'd you know my address, smart boy?"

He didn't even glance at me. "Isabella told me where you had moved. Was it a secret?"

No, drat it, I hadn't told her it was a secret, and he knew it.

"No, it wasn't. Alex, why are you doing this?"

"Seeing you home? I was raised to always see a woman to her home after a date."

"We weren't on a date. Tonight was a party, not a date. We are not dating. *Comprende?*"

He shot me a quick look out of the corner of his eye, then leaned back against the seat, crossed his arms over his chest, and closed his eyes. "Why did you jump up every time I touched you?"

"Maybe I don't like being touched." I rolled my eyes as soon as the words left my mouth. Lord, I was stupid sometimes!

"Mmm. Do you know, I've found that when witnesses swear to a statement I suspect is false, often it is quite easy to prove or disprove their claim."

Uh oh, did he mean what I thought he meant? He didn't mean . . . "Ack! Alex, unhand me!"

"In a minute. I'm investigating your statement."

"You are not, you're groping me." I tried to push back from where he was holding me to his chest, but I couldn't do anything but run my hands over him. Helplessly. The new Alix could sometimes be a weak, weak woman, I discovered to my delight.

He nuzzled the side of my neck and zeroed in unerringly on the one spot guaranteed to turn me to blancmange in his arms. I alternately burned and shivered with desire, with need, but each time I was about to melt into his arms, I remembered my plan. It was too important to mess up.

"Alex . . . we're not . . . you shouldn't . . . oh, just a hair to the left . . . no, no, you must stop . . . *ALEX!* The driver can see you! Remove your mouth this instant!"

He lifted his head just enough to speak. "No, he can't." His mouth returned to my left breast.

"Actually, I can, but you're not doing anything I haven't seen before, so carry on, mate. No, I tell a lie— I haven't seen that done in a cab before. I didn't think there was enough room. Is your lady's hand where I think it is?"

I rolled my eyes forward to the front of my head and peered over the top of Alex's hair at the grinning face of the driver in the mirror, simultaneously snatching back my hand from where it had drifted. Of its own accord, I hasten to point out.

"Alex, stop," I begged, trying to tug him from where his face was buried in the bodice of my dress. "We can't do this in a cab. It's wrong, it's morally wrong, ethically wrong, and probably legally wrong as well."

"You'd be surprised what people get up to in a cab," the driver chimed in. "All sorts of things, and not a one cared whether it was legally, morally, or ethically wrong."

I glared at his smiling reflection and dragged my free hand from where it had slipped under Alex's shirt, threading my fingers through his silky hair, tugging on it until he came up for air. "Alex, you have to stop! You're making a scene!"

He grinned and wrapped one hand around my neck, holding my head still as he prepared to plunder. "I know. Makes a nice change, doesn't it?"

I didn't reply, being too busy entertaining his tongue as it dropped by for a visit. By the time he counted all of my teeth—twice—my objections had evaporated and the only thing I could say when he lifted his mouth from mine was that I needed to buy him an eye patch.

"Why?"

I tried to ignore his fingers dancing a fiery finger dance up and down my spine. "You'd make a hell of a pirate." I hiked up the bodice of my dress and managed to push myself a reasonable distance away from him. The new Alix took several shaky breaths and reminded me that such behavior was unauthorized and would lead to complications I didn't think I could cope with at that moment. I licked my lips, trying to catch one last taste of him, and told myself to be stalwart. One of us had to be strong, one of us had to be reasonable, and it looked like it was going to have to be me, dammit. "OK, you've had your birthday fun. Now it has to stop."

He looked disgruntled sitting there in the darkness of the cab, lights from the street flashing over the strong planes of his face, his eyes glittering like a cat's in the night. I knew that if I didn't stop him now, if I didn't steer him from his present path of seduction, I would end up compromising everything I had worked so hard for in the last five days. And the memory of the Old Alix was enough to ensure that that didn't happen. I looked into Alex's heated emerald eyes and knew I was doomed unless I stopped him dead. My heart fractured a little more with the realization of what I had to do. I didn't want to be cruel, but it was clear by his actions and the look of desire in his so beautiful eyes that I was left with no other choice. I summoned a shaky little laugh and tried to pass it off as insouciant.

"Really, Alex, I would have thought snogging in a cab was beneath your dignity. How the mighty have fallen."

Two lines of frown appeared between his brows. Guilt stabbed at me, but I knew I had to do it or I'd lose everything, and I wasn't prepared to go back to my old life. Not now. Not when I was so close to success. Not for anything would I go back to that.

I smiled a smile I didn't feel, and traced a finger along the strength of his jaw. "You know, I owe you an apology."

"You owe me several," he growled, trying to capture my finger, but I pushed him back with one hand on his chest. His strong chest. His manly chest. His chest that was so hot it was scorching my fingers. I wanted to cuddle up to that chest. I wanted to stroke that chest. I wanted to rub myself all over that chest. I snatched my hand back instead.

"Think so, huh? Well, the one I think I owe you is for scoffing when you told me I could do anything I wanted to do, be anyone I wanted to be. I thought at the time you were just being overly gushy, but now that I've had time to make my plans, I see you were right. I *can* do whatever I want. So thank you, Detective Inspector Alex Black, for being the person who set me onto the path of success. When I get all the fame and glory due me, I will remember it was you who opened my eyes."

Alex's frown was steadily increasing at my bloated, egotistical statement. I didn't blame him for the unhappy look he cast me. If I had a pin, I would have tried to pop my own ego.

He took my hand and rubbed his thumb over my knuckles, his eyes wary as he watched me. I never thought knuckles could be sexy before, but mine were suddenly located smack dab in an erogenous zone. I hardened my heart for one last attack.

"I'm glad you've realized your potential, Alix. I have always thought you would be a success at whatever goal you set out to achieve. I assume your excitement means the book is going well?"

"Oh, it's not just the book," I assured him with a Judas smile. "I have this plan, you see, and each step of my plan is detailed on a list. So far, my new strategy has been very successful. I'm almost through my list, and the brass ring is waiting for me."

His frown melted into a look of bleakness that had me weeping inside. "Am I to take it that my name does not appear on your list?"

I thought I'd try for another light little laugh, but I couldn't summon anything up, not even with all of the new Alix's weight behind me. I couldn't lie to him, not to my Alex, but to explain myself would mean my plan had failed before it had a chance, and that would be the end of everything for me. So I told the truth, hoping against hope that he wouldn't hate me for the rest of his life because of it.

"I'm sorry, Alex, but I'm not sharing my list with anyone."

The love in his eyes had me dying a thousand deaths. "Not even me?"

I had to swallow twice before I could get the words out. "Not even you. I have to walk my path alone."

"You don't have to do anything on your own," he said softly, his voice a warm brush of the softest velvet against my skin. I shivered at the contact, the ache inside me building to a level of pain I hadn't known was possible. "You have me. Come back with me, Alix. Be with me. Live with me. Marry me."

He was everything I wanted. He was the perfect man

for me, a perfect fit, every facet of our beings a complement to the other. He was my life, my heart, my soul. I would never be complete without him, but to join my life to his now would end up in disaster. It was better to hurt him here and now than to destroy him later. Wasn't it?

The cab came to a halt in front of the gaudy pink door of the student house. I glanced from the door to the mirror where the driver was watching us silently, then to the man sitting beside me, offering me his heart. I hoped he would see the love shining in my eyes as I spoke the words that might well spell my doom.

"I'm sorry, Alex. I truly am sorry. I *have* to do this. It's important to me."

"Whereas I am not worth the trouble."

I flinched as he tossed my own words back in my face, and reached out to touch him, to comfort him, to cling to him as I told him he had been right, that I had finally seen what a mess my life had been before and how I had taken steps to change it, but he slipped away and held the door open for me. I scooted out of the taxi, my heart dead and cold as he tossed some money at the driver, then turned and walked off toward the train station without a glance back at me.

"Hoo." The driver blew out a long breath, looking me up and down. "I knew you Yanks were an aggressive lot, but I never thought you were cruel."

I watched as Alex's dark figure disappeared down the stairs to the tube station. I was beyond tears, beyond something so simple as a mere fatal blow. I had nothing left but myself. So be it.

I lifted my chin and regarded the driver steadily. "Sometimes you have to be cruel to be kind."

Chapter Eighteen

The three weeks following Alex's birthday passed quickly. I posted my list on the wall and used a big red marker to cross off each item as I completed it. I wrote all day long, and spent most of my evenings at Daniel's flat, talking, writing, learning. He hadn't been sworn to secrecy about my work, and one night he mentioned that he had met Alex for lunch.

I couldn't bear to ask, but I couldn't bear not to. My misery must have shown in my face, because he covered my fingers with a warm hand. "He's fine, Alix. A little heartsore, I think, but otherwise well."

I nodded, unable to speak for the tears pooling in my eyes, but I wasn't going to let myself give in, not then, not when I was so close to achieving my goal. That night I finished revising my story. I stared at the laptop blindly, not seeing the words as I felt the familiar sense of emptiness that accompanied me everywhere these days, wondering if it was worth it, wondering if I had made the right choice after all. The memory came to me of Alex lying in bed, his body relaxed and sated, the spicy scent of him sending curls of desire licking my body. I saved my file, hit *print,* and crossed off another item on my list.

Three weeks to the day after Alex walked out of my life I met with Maureen Tully, agent. She was my only connection to the publishing world, and after discussing with Daniel the possibility that she might be one of the unscrupulous agents who prey on newbie writers, I decided to give her another chance. After all, she *did* originally like my story, and she *had* returned part of my money, and it certainly was true that the story in its original version didn't stand up under anyone's scrutiny. So, after pleading with her secretary Jacquie for an appointment, I spent four hours with Maureen in her smoky office while she read my revised manuscript from start to finish. By the time she was through, I had an agent again.

"I didn't think you could do it," she said as she turned the last page, reaching for another tissue. I smiled a gracious smile as she mopped at her eyes and blew her nose, and predicted great things for my literary future. Later that day I drew another red line through an item on my list.

One task remained. I scooped up a handful of coins and headed out for the nearest red phone box, the kind that could handle international calls.

"Hi, Mom, it's me."

"Alix? Where have you been? Why haven't you answered your e-mail? Where are you? You're not still in England, are you? I told you to stop wasting time and come home!"

"Yes, I am still in London. Sorry about not answering the e-mails, but I've left Stephanie's flat and I don't have access to e-mail anymore."

"You've left the flat? What on earth are you talking about? You're not drunk, are you? What happened to that man you were seeing?"

I looked out of the phone booth to where a couple was sitting kissing on a bench in Russell Square. "He's still there. Mom, I don't have a lot of time to talk, so if you'd let me just say what I have to say, I'd—"

She made a snorting sound. "I knew that wouldn't last. No man would want a woman who writes pornography!"

"It's not pornography, and you don't have to worry about that version I sent you, I've revised it. Mom, I've got about forty seconds left to talk, so I'm just going to say this right out: I'm not coming home."

"What? What? What are you saying? You *are* drunk!"

"I'm not drunk, but I'm not leaving, not unless I get thrown out of the country. I love this place, I love everything about it, especially"—I glanced back at the couple on the bench—"especially Alex. If he'll have me, I'm going to stay."

"If that isn't the stupidest, most idiotic thing I've ever heard you say, throwing yourself away on a man who will probably kick you out as soon as he's tired of you. Well, don't come crying to me when you find yourself pregnant and stuck in some foreign country!"

"I have to go. I have only ten seconds left, but I wanted to say one more thing."

She was silent on the other end, probably trying to think up a string of invectives to heap on my head. But this was my money, my plan, my hopes for success.

"I love you, Mom, and I forgive you for not believing in me."

"What? What? Alix, what are you talk—"

The phone clicked twice and went silent.

A great weight lifted off my heart as I stared at the receiver in my hand. I was free. I was whole. And best of all, for the first time in my life I had done something right. I had fought for what mattered most to me, struggled on my own, and I hadn't once given in and taken the easy way out. The unknown face of success stared at me, and I welcomed it with open arms. I hung up the phone and danced a little victory dance right there in the phone booth as I crossed the last item off my list, laughing with a joy I hadn't felt in a month.

I had done it. I had done everything I planned to do, and I had succeeded. Now all that remained was for me to reap the rewards of my success.

I headed off to my flat to gather the necessary items that I'd need to capture my prize. It wasn't going to be easy, but as a very wise, very sexy man once said, the things that are worth having are worth working for.

And he was *very* worth working for.

I was more than a little nervous when I knocked on Alex's door. I knew he was home; I had taken the precaution of calling Isabella and asking her if he had returned from work yet. She called me back ten minutes later and told me he had, then wished me luck in regaining Alex's heart.

I laughed at the knowing tone in her voice. "Isabella, you are a witch, aren't you?"

"Certainly not. I simply value my friends and want to see them happy."

"Keep your fingers crossed for me, then. I'm going to need a lot of good wishes in order to get him back."

"If anyone can do it, you can," she replied.

I smiled at a man outside the phone box. "Yup. That I can."

I wasn't quite so confident when I was actually standing outside Alex's door, but I was excited. Excited and scared, and tossed between love for him and the fear that he'd slam the door in my face.

I reached out to knock again when the door opened.

"Hi, Alex," I said breathlessly, and bit my lip. He looked hot and tired, just as he had that first day I saw him. "Would it be possible for me to come in and talk with you a bit?"

No expression filled his eyes; no sign of any emotion passed over his face. He just stared at me for a moment with eyes that were flat and empty.

"Um . . . Alex, you're scaring me some with that look. Can I come in? Please?"

He stared at me in that chilling manner for another few seconds, then stepped back and let me enter his flat.

I knew that explaining my plan wasn't going to be easy, but I had hoped he'd at least be happy to see me. The way he was standing leaning against the door, his arms crossed over his chest and his eyes about as warm as those of a really pissed-off serial killer, did not bode well for the happy reunion I had been mentally planning, lo, these last three weeks.

I chewed on my lip for a few moments, then held out my package. He didn't even glance at it. I took a step forward and shoved it at his chest. "I brought you something."

He took it and allowed his uninterested eyes to examine it.

"It's my manuscript," I pointed out helpfully. "I finished revising it."

I waited for recognition to strike him. I waited in vain.

"It's the original story, Alex. The one that Daniel thought was so bad. I didn't give up on it after all, you see. I took your words to heart and went back and revised it until it was a much better story. More consistent. And I didn't ask anyone's advice about it. . . . well, almost no one. Daniel helped a bit with some plotting advice and he talked to me a lot about writing, but I never once asked what he thought of the story. So you see, I owe this whole manuscript to you."

Nothing. He just stared at me, his eyes cold enough to trigger a second ice age.

I licked my lips, leaned forward, and flipped the first page back. "There's something I want you to read, there."

His gaze never left mine. I gritted my teeth and poked at the manuscript page. "Alex, I know you're pissed—I mean, angry—but you could at least look at where I'm pointing!"

His eyes narrowed.

"Fine!" I snapped, and stood next to him, my head at an angle so I could read the page. "I'll read it to you, since you're so busy being all pride bound and prickly and everything. It's the dedication. It says, *'To Alex, the only person who saw my true worth, my friend, my lover, my everything, the man who is worth any amount of trouble just so long as he's by my side. I will love you forever.'* "

I looked up hopefully, tears blurring my vision. "I

know you're hurt and angry with me, Alex, and you have every right to be, but if anyone can understand, you will. I love you. I have from that first day when you took my pot plant, and that scared me more than anything I've experienced. I've never felt about anyone the way I feel about you, and I figured it would all just end up in the toilet the way all my other relationships have, and so . . . well, Isabella was right about that, too. I was protecting myself from being hurt when you dumped me by not giving all of myself to you, and then when you didn't dump me, I got all panicky and scared and worried, and are you going to let me blather on like this without saying *anything?*"

"You don't love me."

I sniffed and wiped my tears on the sleeve of my blouse. "I knew you'd say that. I do love you, Alex. I love you with every teensy tiny bit of my being. I love you so much I knew I had to do something to change, so you'd love me, too."

"You don't love me," he repeated stubbornly. "You left me. You told me I had no place in your life."

"Oh, Alex." I turned to face him and slid my hands up his taut arms to his neck. He was stiff and unmoving under my hands, but there wasn't a snowball's chance in hell that I was going to give up on him now. "I never said that, not once! It was all my plan, you see—my plan to turn myself into the woman you wanted."

"I wanted you as you were."

I shook my head and brushed my lips against his. He didn't kiss me back, but he didn't run screaming from me, either. Point one for Team Alix. "You didn't want me, you wanted a woman who wasn't riddled with insecurities and flaws. You wanted a woman who valued what she had, who fought for what she wanted, who knew the good things in life don't come easy. I had to leave you to find that woman, Alex."

"Why? Christ, Alix, I offered to help you—"

"I know, love—oh, don't think I didn't know and wasn't tempted by the thought of just caving in and letting you fix everything for me, but I couldn't do that, don't you see? If I didn't stand on my own two feet and do it alone, I'd never be able to respect myself, and worse than that, you'd never respect me. I had to get away so I could rewrite my manuscript. I had to get away so I could work by myself, without the support of my friends. I had to leave you in order to prove I could be the woman you deserve. Don't you see? I had to leave you so I could find my way back into your arms."

I stood pressed against him, my body warm against his, my hands on his tight shoulders. He hadn't budged one inch; his arms were still crossed over his chest, his jaw was still tight. But his eyes had life in them again, even if it was only the hot glare of anger.

I didn't blame him. If the shoe were on the other foot, I'd want to put his lights out. With a wry smile, I lifted my chin and stepped back. "Go ahead, punch me. Right on the chin."

He did a damned good impression of my goggle. "What?"

I tapped my chin and turned my head slightly. "Punch me on the chin. I deserve it. You'll feel better afterward."

"I'm not going to strike you, Alix."

I kept my chin firmly turned away from him. "I know violence isn't the answer to any problem, but sometimes you just really need to deck someone. I figure you're pretty angry with me, and you'll feel much better if you vent your spleen with a little physical contact."

"You're right," Alex said after a moment's consideration. He started toward me. I opened my eyes wide at the look of emotion on his face, then slammed them shut hard as I braced myself for pain. He didn't touch my face, but grabbed me around my waist and pushed me backwards toward his computer table. My butt bumped up against the table as he leaned forward and swept off the stacks of papers, notebooks, and books that littered the surface.

The look in his eyes left me in no doubt that he was in the grip of a strong emotion, but which emotion was it? He hadn't decked me when I invited him to, but he certainly didn't look like he had forgiven me, either. My newfound courage suddenly deserted me when he turned those hot, burning eyes on me.

"Uh . . . Alex, maybe I ought to come back a little later when you're not so—"

The words were cut off as his mouth descended upon mine. It was a kiss, but like no kiss he'd ever given me before. This one was demanding, unyielding, a dominating kiss that said better than words that I had no choice but to surrender. The thought didn't even cross my mind to dispute that fact.

"You left me," he growled as he put both hands on my waist and hoisted me up onto the table. His hands were all over me, in my hair, holding me for another one of those ravaging kisses, tracing along the curves of my breasts, on my bare legs, sliding up my thighs, pushing my dress up as he headed for the promised land. My heart soared at his touch, at the look of pure, unadulterated desire burning in his eyes. He might not forgive me for what I had done, but he sure wanted me.

"I had to leave you," I whispered, offering the sacrificial lips up a third time without the slightest murmur. I started to fumble for his shirt buttons, but he snarled and forced my hands lower. "I had to leave you so I could take charge of myself, of my life. I had to know I could do it on my own."

"You told me I wasn't worth your trouble."

"I was hurt and wanted to hurt you, too. I was an idiot! I was stupid! I was crazed with grief and didn't know what I was saying!"

My eyes widened again as his hands slid up either side of my hips, hooking his thumbs around the thin waistband of my slinky underwear, underwear I was wearing especially for the occasion. He didn't miss that fact.

"You ran from me when I touched you," he said as his lips curled into a hot, tight smile just before he literally ripped the undies right off me.

"Good Lord, Alex!" I stared down at the torn bits of satin in his hands. "I had to run from you—you have no idea how badly I wanted to give up and just throw myself in your arms, but you were worth any amount of pain. Don't you see, I had to run, or else I'd never be able to leave you, and if I didn't leave you, I'd never have been able to stand on my own."

My gaze jumped from his hands to his face. The look there made me shiver with need and wanting and excitement and love and a whole slew of other emotions I couldn't begin to untangle. "You're not going to . . . you don't mean . . . Alex, I'm on a desk!"

"Physical contact," he rumbled as his hands pushed mine away from where they had been trying to get a purchase on his belt. He ripped his belt off and yanked down the zipper. "I offered you my heart that night in the cab and you turned it down."

With one hand he spread my legs and stepped between them, going straight to the heart of my desire by slipping a finger inside me. I trembled with the joy that filled me at his touch.

"I was so close, my sweet Alex. I had to stick to my plan in order to succeed, or you'd never want me, never be able to love me as I love you."

I felt the tip of him nudging against the spot where his finger had been just a second before, and suddenly needed to be sure he understood. I spread my fingers and slid my hands into his hair, tugging him closer. "I couldn't have lived with myself if you ended up pitying me because I was too weak and stubborn to realize my full potential."

His arms went around me, grabbing my behind and yanking me forward just as he moved into me. I screamed his name with the pleasure of it.

"You left me." His voice was as rough as granite as he pulled back until he had almost left my body.

"No!" I howled, both at his accusation and at the sense of loss.

"You abused me." His fingers tightened on my behind as he thrust his full length back into me.

"I didn't mean to." The words caught in my throat as the familiar tension began to build within me. I kissed his lips, his cheek, his hair, trying to pull him closer, deeper inside me, trying to merge the two of us together.

"You rejected me." He grabbed my legs and hoisted them up around his hips until I locked my ankles behind him.

"Never," I vowed, flexing my legs to pull him tighter.

He was so deep inside me I could feel him touch my heart, but that still wasn't deep enough. I needed all of him, his heart and soul and mind as well as his body.

"You love me." His thrusts were increasing in speed, his breath rasping in my ear.

I kissed his neck and bit gently on the tendon that stood out there. "Always."

"You love me." His body slammed against mine, desperate now to finish the race. I arched upwards and welcomed him.

"Forever."

He heard my gasp and bent me backwards until I was splayed across the desk, pinned back as much by the emotion in his eyes as by his body invading mine. "You love me."

I framed his face with my hands and drew his head down until my lips could whisper along his. "I love you."

He roared a wordless victory as he lunged forward against me, his body joining so fully with mine that there were no distinctions between him and me. He filled me with his love, sending us both spiraling off together into a blinding moment of understanding that left me sobbing with joy.

"Tears," he said softly a little later, his voice as warm in my ear as his body lying next to mine on his couch. His fingers swept gently across my wet cheeks. "You cry again, Alix? Did I hurt you?"

I turned my faced into his shoulder and nipped the bare flesh. "No."

"Good." He smiled smugly as he said it, and closed his eyes as he pulled me against his naked chest. I slid a knee up his leg and decided I'd groveled enough. I nipped his shoulder again.

He grunted in response. "I'm not as young as I used to be, sweetheart. Give me a chance to catch my breath and I'll be happy to oblige."

"You haven't said it, Alex."

Two pure green eyes opened to meet mine, and I wondered how his beautiful eyes could ever have appeared cold and lifeless. "I haven't said what? That I always knew you could succeed at whatever you set your mind to, that I'm proud of you, that I understand why you didn't take the easy path? That I think you are a woman of strength and intelligence and I thank God for you every day, despite the fact that you're a troublesome vixen who drives my blood pressure up each time I get near you?"

"Vixen!" I pushed myself up and glared down at him, warm and secure in the glow of his love. "Vixen! That's the sort of word a romance writer would use, not an important Scotland Yard detective. You know bloody well what you haven't said, so just get on with it."

"Ah." He pursed his lips in a silent whistle for a moment while he let his eyes wander over my bared upper parts; then he put both hands behind his head and cocked an insolent eyebrow at me. "So you want me to say it, do you?"

I tapped my fingers on his chest. "Yes. Then you can apologize for calling me a vixen."

A slow, sensual smile started at the corners of his lips and soon spread. I leaned down, caught in the web of his smile, unable and unwilling to resist the lure he posed.

"Very well," he breathed just as my lips were about to touch his. "I will say what you want to hear."

I paused, flicking my tongue out to tease the corners

of his mouth until his eyes went dark and his hands came around to hold me.

"I forgive you for not having enough trust in me to tell me your plan."

Huh? I tried to jerk back so I could glare at him properly, but his arms were hard as bands behind me. He sucked my lower lip into his mouth and chewed gently on it for a moment.

"And I forgive you for not having faith in me, or in our relationship, doubting that either could withstand imperfection."

I curled my fingers into the hair on his chest and tugged. Not gently, either. He grimaced, and tightened his arms until my mouth was fitted against his.

"And I forgive you for making me suffer untold hell by making me think you had stopped loving me."

The best defense is an offense, I always say. I untangled my hands squashed between us and grabbed him by his ears, licking and nipping at his adorable manly lips until he gave me what I wanted. It was my turn to surge forward and plunder, and surge and plunder I did, reveling in the fiery taste of him, my soul singing with the knowledge that he was mine, and that nothing would keep me from him again.

"Say it." I did my best impression of his angry growl into his mouth.

"I love you, Alix."

I smiled down at him as he pulled me over his waiting stallion, fitting himself to me, joining our bodies and hearts and souls as if we had been made for each other.

"Perfection," I sighed.

AUTHOR'S NOTE

The Obscene Publications and Internet Unit is a very real department in New Scotland Yard. The purpose of the unit is similar to what I have depicted in this story, although the details and specific examples used are completely fictional, and any errors are mine. For the purposes of this book, Alex worked only in the Internet division of the Unit, which does indeed focus its attention on closing down UK-based pornography sites, as well as occasionally dealing with private individuals who are suspected of having pedophilic material on their computers.

My thanks for background details and information about the Internet Unit are profusely offered to Sean Robbie, a PC with the Unit who took the time to explain exactly how Internet pornography is dealt with at New Scotland Yard.

"Craig's latest will DELIGHT . . . fans of
JANET EVANOVICH and HARLEY JANE KOZAK."
—*Booklist* on *Gotcha!*

Award-winning Author

Christie Craig

"Christie Craig will crack you up!"
—*New York Times* Bestselling Author Kerrelyn Sparks

Of the Divorced, Desperate and Delicious club, Kathy Callahan is
the last surviving member. Oh, her two friends haven't died or anything. They just gave up their vows of chastity. They went for hot sex
with hot cops and got happy second marriages—something Kathy
can never consider, given her past. Yet there's always her plumber,
Stan Bradley. He seems honest, hardworking, and skilled with a tool.

But Kathy's best-laid plans have hit a clog. The guy snaking her drain
isn't what he seems. He's handier with a pistol than a pipe wrench, and
she's about to see more action than Jason Statham. The next
forty-eight hours promise hot pursuit, hotter passion and a super
perky pug, and at the end of this wild escapade, Kathy and her very
own undercover lawman will be flush with happiness—assuming they
both survive.

Divorced, Desperate and Deceived

ISBN 13: 978-0-505-52798-1

✂

☐ **YES!**

Sign me up for the Historical Romance Book Club and send my FREE BOOKS! If I choose to stay in the club, I will pay only $8.50* each month, a savings of $6.48!

NAME: _____

ADDRESS: _____

TELEPHONE: _____

EMAIL: _____

☐ I want to pay by credit card.

☐ VISA   ☐ MasterCard   ☐ DISCOVER

ACCOUNT #: _____

EXPIRATION DATE: _____

SIGNATURE: _____

Mail this page along with $2.00 shipping and handling to:
Historical Romance Book Club
PO Box 6640
Wayne, PA 19087
Or fax (must include credit card information) to:
610-995-9274
You can also sign up online at **www.dorchesterpub.com**.
*Plus $2.00 for shipping. Offer open to residents of the U.S. and Canada only.
Canadian residents please call 1-800-481-9191 for pricing information.
If under 18, a parent or guardian must sign. Terms, prices and conditions subject to change. Subscription subject to acceptance. Dorchester Publishing reserves the right to reject any order or cancel any subscription.